MURMI

MURMURING THE JUDGES

MURMURING
THE JUDGES

Quintin Jardine

HEADLINE

First published in Great Britain in 1998
by HEADLINE BOOK PUBLISHING

10 9 8 7 6 5 4 3 2 1

British Library Cataloguing in Publication Data

Jardine, Quintin
Murmuring the judges
1. Detective and mystery stories
I. Title
823.9'14[F]

ISBN 0 7472 1945 1

Typeset by Avon Dataset Ltd, Bidford-on-Avon, Warks

Printed and bound in Great Britain by
Mackays of Chatham PLC, Chatham, Kent

HEADLINE BOOK PUBLISHING
A division of Hodder Headline PLC
338 Euston Road
London NW1 3BH

This is for Jack and Brenda

1

Brian Mackie's attention wandered as the advocate sorted through his papers, looking for a misplaced note. Court Eleven, in Edinburgh's old Parliament House, was a small, unprepossessing room, with drab brown-panelled walls and varnished wooden benches which had not been designed with spectator comfort in mind. Austerity, rather than grandeur, was a Scottish characteristic, and it echoed through the buildings in which the nation's justice was dispensed.

The policeman felt no sense of history as he looked around from the witness box, nor any sympathy for all the evil which, across the decades, had come face to face with retribution in its dock. He wondered how many men had stood there, where Nathan Bennett sat now, listening to a black-capped, red-coated judge make the pronouncement which would lead to sudden, brutal death at the end of a rope.

A cough from across the room snapped him back to the present as abruptly as the noose had snapped the necks of the condemned.

'Are you seriously asking this Court to believe, Superintendent,' said Her Majesty's Counsel, 'that the accused is so stupid that he would carry identifying material to the scene of a violent crime, far less leave it there?'

The man's tone carried a sneer, for which Brian Mackie did not care at all: but fifteen years in the police service, and experience of far greater cross examination skills than those of the Honourable Richard Kilmarnock, QC, had taught him that there was nothing to be gained by rising to such bait.

Instead, he looked across at Lord Archergait, perched on the elevated Bench in his wig and his white-trimmed red robe; he looked at the jury; and finally, he looked back at the Senior Counsel for the defence. All the while he wore his most serious and honest expression. This was easy for him, since the tall, thin, dome-headed detective was always serious and honest.

'I am not an expert witness in the field of intelligence, sir,' he responded. 'All I have told the Court is that a credit card belonging to Nathan Bennett was found on the floor of the crime scene, that Mr Bennett was found to answer the description given by all of the witnesses to the robbery, and that subsequently he was identified by every one of those witnesses.'

'Even though he was wearing a mask?'

'A hockey face mask, sir, that is correct.'

'Well?'

1

'Mr Bennett has vivid red hair, sir, and he has two fingers missing from his left hand. In addition he has a strong Aberdonian accent.'

Richard Kilmarnock's eyes lit up. 'Ah, and I suppose the witnesses were shown a line of men with red hair and two missing fingers.' The sarcasm in his voice was even more pronounced, so much so that Lord Archergait threw him a quick warning look from the Bench.

'They were shown a line of red-haired men, wearing white hockey face masks, each with his left hand in his pocket.'

Mackie was surprised when the advocate persisted. 'Yes, but there's red hair, and there's red hair, is there not, Superintendent? Mr Bennett's is particularly vivid. Surely he must have stood out. Let me be blunt. Wasn't this line-up more of a set-up?'

'Every man in the line-up had his hair dyed to match Mr Bennett's colouring, sir,' replied the detective, his expression unchanged. 'They were all dressed identically, in jeans and grey sweatshirts. Yet every witness picked out the accused first time.'

'My point exactly.'

A half-cough, half-growl came from the Bench. 'I'm not sure what that point is, Mr Kilmarnock,' said the judge. 'However, if you are implying that the police identification procedures were in any way dishonest, then you'd better not do it in my Court, not without damn strong evidence. Now get on with it, please. The afternoon is not endless.' With a final frown, Lord Archergait reached for his carafe and poured himself a glass of water.

'Very good, My Lord,' the defence counsel acknowledged, in a tone which implied that it was anything but. He turned back to Mackie.

'Superintendent, how do you know that my client didn't drop his credit card in the bank much earlier in the day? After all, he does have an account there.'

'I have no idea when he dropped the card, sir. All I know is that it was found immediately after the robbery, in an area where Mr Bennett had been standing.'

'Doesn't it strike you as odd that someone should rob his own bank? Have you ever known this to happen before?'

'No, sir.'

'Mmm,' said Kilmarnock, with a meaningful glance at the jury.

'Now let's turn to the money, Superintendent,' he went on. 'You said that you haven't recovered it, didn't you?'

Mackie shook his head. 'Not at all, sir.' He too risked a quick look at the jury. 'I said that we recovered, from Mr Bennett's attic, twenty-two thousand six hundred and seventy pounds, exactly one sixth of the total stolen. My evidence was that the rest of the money has not been traced. Neither have the other two participants in the robbery.'

'These weren't new notes, were they?'

'No, sir.'

'But my client will say that the money in his attic was his winnings from gambling. What do you say to . . .'

2

An outraged, spluttering sound came from the Bench. Kilmarnock turned to face the judge, resignedly. 'Yes, My Lord.'

Mackie looked round also. For a few seconds he thought simply that Lord Archergait was apoplectic with rage at the futility of the defence examination. The Senator's face was vivid red, with white patches, matching the colour of his robe, as he began to rise to his feet. His mouth worked as if trying to find appropriate words of condemnation. Then the first white flecks appeared on his lips.

'Oh Christ,' whispered the policeman to himself as the truth hit him. He stepped out of the witness box and jumped up on to the Bench.

But even as he did, Lord Archergait clutched at his throat and pitched forward, falling across his notes on his sloping desktop, his grey wig slipping from his head and into the well of the Court, the glass beside him falling on its side and rolling along the Bench.

Mackie reached him just as he began to slide to the floor. He held him by the arms, in a surprisingly strong grip for one so lightly built, then lifted him back into his chair, feeling the violent shuddering which swept through the old man's body, and hearing the choking sounds in the back of his throat.

The judge was barely back in his seat before his body stiffened, and his legs shot out straight in front of him. There was a drumming of heels on the floor beneath the desk, until without warning, Lord Archergait went completely limp once more, seeming to collapse into his enveloping robe, eyes half-closed and glazed, red face suddenly gone completely grey, jaw hanging open.

Having been its instrument during his career, Brian Mackie knew death when he saw it. Yet still he turned towards the onlookers below him. He fixed his gaze on the Honourable Richard Kilmarnock, QC. 'Find a doctor, man, and call an ambulance as well,' he ordered. The advocate stood rooted to the spot, staring back at him.

'Now,' barked the policeman. Kilmarnock, unfrozen by the unexpected shout, nodded and turned towards the door, only to see it swing behind his junior as she rushed off to look for medical help.

The Superintendent looked towards the dock, where Nathan Bennett still sat between two white-gloved policemen, a bewildered look on his broad face. 'Take him back to the cells,' he told the escorts, quietly and calmly. They nodded and rose to their feet, drawing the accused with them, then slid awkwardly out of the dock. The few spectators parted before them as they moved towards the side exit. As he left the Court, the prisoner looked over his shoulder, smiling at an attractive young woman in the second back row, with hair as red as his.

'Is he . . .' The whisper came from over Mackie's shoulder. He looked round to see the black-uniformed macer, the judge's attendant, who had emerged from the door to his chambers, behind the courtroom. His face was white and shocked.

'Aye, Colin, I'm afraid he is. It looks like some sort of a seizure.'

3

The little man shook his sleekly groomed head sadly, and stood, for almost a minute, looking down at the body. 'What a damn shame,' he whispered at last, recovering his composure. 'I liked old Billy. A bloody good judge he was, and a bloody good advocate before that.'

He nodded, almost imperceptibly, but grimly, towards the well of the Court, where Richard Kilmarnock, QC, sat, sorting through his papers. 'That one'll think it's good news though,' he growled. 'He's next on the seniority list for a red jacket.'

Mackie's eyebrows rose. 'They won't make him a judge, will they?' he muttered quietly.

The Court officer grunted. 'Not a hope in hell. Fortunately, it goes on more than seniority.' He paused. 'It's a bugger for you though. They'll have to start the trial all over again, with a new judge and a new jury. Damn quick too, if the boy Bennett's getting near the hundred-and-ten-day limit, so they don't have to release him. I hope you don't have any holidays planned.'

Mackie shook his head. Like many policemen, he believed secretly that the strict Scottish limitation on the time for which a person could be held in custody before trial lent too far towards the accused. 'Not till November.' As he spoke, he realized that his mouth had gone absolutely dry, something he had experienced before in moments of tension. Without thinking, he picked up the water carafe from the bench, and raised it to his lips. He was about to take a sip, when his companion put a hand on his sleeve.

'I wouldn't, if I were you.'

The policeman looked at him, with a puzzled frown.

'You'll get more than you bargain for there,' said Colin. 'The Senators of the College of Justice have their own wee ways, you might say. Old Billy there, I doubt if he ever drank straight water in his life. He always liked a measure of gin and a wee bit of lime mixed into his jug.

'Just to give him a taste, like.'

Mackie looked down at the crumpled figure in the chair. 'He wasn't rat-arsed on the Bench, was he?'

'Christ no! It'd take more than one wee gin to put Lord Archergait away. Still,' the little man added sadly, 'it seems that something has. Where is the bloody doctor anyway? There's always a doctor about here somewhere, when the Court's in session.'

He shuffled his feet, and looked up at Detective Superintendent Mackie. 'By the way, I meant to ask you,' he began, 'how's Big Bob getting on?'

'DCC Skinner?' said the policeman, surprised. 'You know him?'

'Everyone about here knows Bob,' his companion replied. 'Some man him. I've seen him give evidence here a right few times. That one down there –' he nodded towards Kilmarnock once more – 'I saw him try to come the smart-arse wi' Bob one day. The big man left him in ribbons, so he did.

'I heard that he and his wife had patched it up. That right?'

Mackie nodded. 'Yes, Sarah's back.' He smiled. 'I suppose you know her too?'

'Aye, of course. I've seen her in the witness box too. Lovely lass she is, and right clever with it. I don't know what the big fella was thinking of, getting involved with yon other woman. Pictures in the papers and everything.'

The officer looked towards the door. 'Speaking of doctors, where is the bugger?'

His question was answered almost at once, as the courtroom door swung open.

2

The tall man stretched his lean, tanned body along the length of the white plastic lounger beside the family-sized swimming pool which took up much of the garden of his Spanish villa. His grey hair was wet and slicked back against his head, as the sun glistened on it, and on the droplets of water which still clung to him.

'Have I told you lately, honey,' he said, in his rugged Lanarkshire accent, 'that the day I met you was the best day of my life?'

The woman, on another sun-bed a couple of feet away from his, propped herself up on her elbows and looked him in the eye. She was as tanned as he was. Her auburn hair hung down over her shoulders, and her long naked back shone with a mixture of lotion and perspiration.

She smiled. 'Yeah,' she drawled. 'You've told me. Like every day of the twelve we've been here in L'Escala.'

His face grew serious. 'Och, Sarah love, it's just that I can't tell you often enough. Just like I can't say sorry often enough for being a complete arse, and for driving you away, like I did last year.'

The sturdy child who sat between them looked up at him and smiled from beneath his wide-brimmed sun hat. His features, as they developed, promised to take on the characteristics of both parents; his father's dominant nose and chin, his mother's wide hazel eyes, and her open grin. 'Arse,' he said, beaming.

'Jazz! No!' his mother called out, turning the boy's face towards her and shaking her head in disapproval. 'Don't copy everything Daddy says.

'And you,' she said, grinning at her husband, 'how often do I have to tell you? His ears are like blotting paper, soaking up everything we say, so that he can perfect the sounds he likes best.'

Bob Skinner looked suitably reproved. 'Okay,' he acknowledged. 'I'll swear in Spanish in future.'

'Not even in Spanish.'

Beside Sarah, James Andrew Skinner pushed himself to his feet. 'Mark,' he called out loudly, half walking, half running, carefully and deliberately, on his solid toddler's legs between the sun-beds, towards the pool where another child swam.

As his mother sat up and caught his arm, reaching for two flotation bands, he eyed her full breasts, hunger stirring a memory of infancy. Meanwhile Bob rose once more and dived into the pool, making only a small splash. He surfaced beside the blond-haired boy, who wore armbands also, and who was swimming laborious breadths.

'Hey, Mark,' he said, putting a hand under the child's chest and lifting him to the side of the pool, where he clung to the tiled edge, 'your swimming's come on a power in the time we've been here. But don't overdo it. You don't want to fall asleep over your pizza tonight, do you?'

'Pizza!' the boy yelled. 'In the pink place by the beach?'

Bob Skinner nodded, pleased hugely by his foster-son's juvenile delight. Although he was only seven, young Mark's life had been so scarred by tragedy, with the separate violent deaths of both his parents, that the policeman had feared that he would never be a child again.

His offer to adopt the boy after his mother's murder had been welcomed by all three of his surviving grandparents, each of whom recognised their inability to raise a child to manhood. Even more vitally, it had been welcomed by Mark, who had come to know the Deputy Chief Constable well through his adventures.

Skinner grinned as he remembered their earnest conversation, on the beach, back at their other home in Gullane.

'*So, wee man, you'll come to live with Sarah and me, as our adopted son, and as James Andrew's big brother?*'

'*Yes please. My daddy promised me a wee brother. But then he died.*'

'*Well you'll have one now, ready made, and he'll be a handful, I'll tell you. Now, is there anything you want to ask me?*'

'*Will I call you Daddy and Mummy?*'

'*No, I don't think so. You should always honour your natural daddy and mummy. Uncle Bob and Auntie Sarah would be better, don't you think?*'

'*Yes, I think so. Will I be called Mark Skinner?*'

'*What would be right, do you think? When we adopt you, legally you'll be our son, Auntie Sarah's and mine. But that doesn't mean that you have to change your name. Your mummy and your daddy were both very special people, and you can still carry their name if you want to. Do you?*'

'*Yes, I think I do.*'

'*That's good, because although I'll give you my name if you want it, I think it's right for you to go on being Mark McGrath.*'

It had been virtually plain sailing after that, although there had been one minor concern when Mark's grandfather had questioned Bob's decision to send the child to the local primary school in Gullane, and later to high school in North Berwick.

'*Look, Bob, if it's a matter of money, Mark will inherit a fair bit from his parents. I can arrange for school and university expenses to be met from his trust fund.*'

'*Mr McGrath, I'm not going to adopt the boy and expect him to pay for his upbringing. This has nothing to do with money. I believe that it's better for him to be educated in his own community, especially if the facilities are excellent. My daughter went to those schools and left Glasgow University with a First in Law.*'

'*Okay. I concede that. The truth is, I'm ambitious that Mark should go to Oxford or Cambridge. He's very bright, you know. It might be difficult getting in there from an East Lothian school, but sometimes the private sector can pull strings for its pupils.'*

'Hah! The way things are heading in this country, all that privilege crap will be swept away by the time Mark's eighteen. Even if it isn't, and there are strings that have to be pulled, I think you'll find that there are few people better at that than Chief Police Officers. Anyway, as you say, Mark is very bright, and when that time comes, he may well have his own views about his education, which should be respected. Right now, he really does want to go to the local primary.'

Bob grinned once more, this time at the sight of Jazz, buoyant in the blue water and paddling away furiously with his legs. Unlike his adoptive brother, who pushed himself off the poolside and thrashed off to meet him, he was a natural born swimmer.

Sarah eased over beside her husband at the deep end of the pool, and linked her arm through his. She kissed him lightly on the cheek. 'It's been a success, hasn't it, this family-building holiday in L'Escala. D'you think we could stretch it to a third week?'

'Seven more days of Spanish sun?' he replied. 'I'd love to, but for one reason and another my Chief Constable hasn't seen enough of me this year. I owe it to Proud Jimmy to get back. Anyway, you and I have a new house to sort out, *and* our older boy has to start his new school.'

He chuckled. 'No holidays in term-time from now on, lady. Get used to the idea.'

Sarah wrinkled her nose, and pulled herself up against the wall of the pool, her breasts breaking the surface of the blue water. 'Ugh. For how long, d'you reckon?'

Bob's chuckle turned to a frown. 'Christ, given our wish for at least one more child, probably until I'm about seventy.'

'All the more reason to take another week, then.'

He slipped his free arm around her waist, as Jazz and Mark swam towards them. 'I'll give you two extra days, assuming we can change the ferry booking to Saturday night, but that's as far as I can stretch it.'

He paused. 'I really need to get back for Andy as well.'

Sarah's eyebrows rose as she reached out to take Mark's hand. 'Detective Chief Superintendent Martin? What's bothering our future son-in-law? Nothing to do with him and Alex, I hope.'

Bob grinned. 'Not this time, I'm glad to say.

'No, he's got himself worked into a lather about a spate of armed robberies on the patch. When we put Jackie Charles out of business we thought that we'd see a reduction in that type of thing, and a virtual end to organised crime in general. But it hasn't happened. Now Andy's thinking is that we may have a new Mr Big on our hands.'

His smile had faded. 'If he's right, and he usually is, then I agree with him. Whoever it is needs to be squashed, and damn quick. I don't like criminals in general, but the sort who carry guns . . .

8

'I tell you, Doctor Sarah, if there is someone back home who thinks he can turn my Edinburgh into Dodge City, then for sure the bugger is going to wish that you'd persuaded me to stay on here . . . even if it was only for another week!'

3

Detective Chief Inspector Maggie Rose looked up in surprise as Brian Mackie walked into her tiny office in the Haddington Police Station. She ran her hand over her red hair . . . less vivid than that of Nathan Bennett, Mackie noted idly . . . as she stared at the Divisional CID commander.

'What are you doing back?' she asked him. 'I thought you'd be tied up in the High Court all day, and maybe into tomorrow. What happened? Did the defence case fold up?'

The tall, bald detective shook his head. 'No,' he replied, without the trace of a smile. 'The judge did.'

'Eh?'

'Lord Archergait. He dropped dead on the Bench; right in the middle of my cross examination.'

Rose's hand went to her mouth. 'Oh no,' she said, frowning. 'Not old Archergait. That's too bad.' She hesitated. 'What was it? Heart attack?'

Mackie nodded. 'Yeah. A sudden massive coronary, the doctor said. He also said that he was surprised that it didn't happen more often in the High Court, given the age of a few of the judges.'

He smiled suddenly. 'Here, you'll never guess who the doctor was. That guy Banks.'

'What,' his deputy responded, surprised, 'the bloke that Andy Martin fell out with? The guy he had thrown off the list of force MEs?'

'Aye, that's right. He was giving evidence in a civil case on one of the other Courts. He was puffed up like a wee bantam cock at being called in to help.'

'I'll bet.'

She looked up at Mackie once more as he leaned against the window of the small room gazing out on to the main street of the little market town. 'So what happens about the trial?' she asked.

'We begin all over again . . . unless Kilmarnock recognises that he's flogging a dead horse and offers a plea.'

'Is that likely?'

'Shouldn't think so. He'll fancy another go at me.'

'What if he did offer a plea to a lesser charge? D'you think the Crown would accept it?'

'Not if Andy Martin got wind of it. He'd raise hell with Mr Skinner, and he'd have a word with his pal the Lord Advocate. With one thing and another the Crown Office owes the Big Man a few favours.'

'No, Mags, Mr Nathan Bennett is going to be convicted of armed robbery, nothing less, and he's going to get the ten- or twelve-year stretch that he bloody well deserves. Remember the old lady customer who fainted right at the start of the raid. Those bastards just left her lying there, while they got on with it, and she died of her stroke a week later.

'Bennett's on a reduced charge already as far as I'm concerned. If it was down to me, they'd be trying him for murder.'

Rose raised an eyebrow. 'But what if he decides to co-operate with us?' she asked. 'What if he suddenly remembers the names of the other two guys who did the bank with him?'

'What if he wakens up tomorrow with the power to heal the sick,' said Mackie, ironically. 'There's about as much chance, I tell you. I've interviewed Bennett umpteen times. There's no way he's going to give those two guys up.' Unexpectedly, he chuckled. 'It's nothing to do with honour among thieves, you understand. Bennett's scared stiff of someone.

'Whether it's those two, or someone else: that's the question.'

'Hmm,' Maggie grunted. 'I know that's what's worrying DCS Martin.'

'Speaking of our Head of CID,' said the Superintendent, 'I had a call from him in the car on the way back here. He's called a briefing of Divisional CID commanders and deputies at Fettes, first thing tomorrow morning.

'After today's débâcle, there are no prizes for guessing what'll be on the agenda.'

4

Andy Martin and Alexis Skinner, his fiancée, had an understanding.

Early in their domestic life together, each had recognised and accepted that the other was constitutionally incapable of leaving the day's work behind in the office. Therefore they had agreed that the evening meal was for the discussion of professional problems and worries. The watershed was marked by the placing of the last dirty plate in the dishwasher.

She stepped up behind him as he tossed beansprouts, sliced peppers, mushrooms, and fish, in the hot oil, stirring the wok intensely all the while. He jumped, involuntarily, as she squeezed his buttocks.

'Careful,' he warned her. 'This is delicate work.'

'So is this,' she chuckled. 'But I'm glad you can still speak. I was beginning to think that you'd been struck dumb. Come on, out with it, my man. What's bothering you?'

He shrugged his shoulders as she slipped her arms, carefully, around his waist. 'Nothing new,' he muttered, still watching his stir-fry intently. 'The same thing that's been bugging me for a while.'

'Ahh,' said Alex, knowingly. 'Your hold-up men! The Hole in the Wall Gang.'

He shook his head as he lifted the wok from the hob and began to spoon the contents into two white bowls. 'Not the Hole in the Wall Gang,' he grunted, 'in any way. Everybody knew who *they* were. Old Butch and Sundance were famous in their own time, long before the movie.

'I haven't a bloody clue who these guys are . . . save the one we nicked through his own stupidity. That's failure, in my book, and it's down to me.'

Alex frowned as she picked up her dish and an uncorked bottle of white wine in a cooler, and carried them through to the dinner table. 'Andy,' she retorted, at last. 'You're getting to be as bad as my dad, for taking everything on yourself.

'You're the head of a team, not a one-man army.'

Andy laughed, ironically, as he poured the wine. 'Hah! You say that. Yet who gets it in the neck every time Rangers are blown out of Europe? The manager, that's who. Not the players. When he gets back from Spain, your old man isn't going to fire the awkward questions at Brian, or big Neil or anyone else. He's going to come straight to me.'

She looked at him as she despatched a forkful of supper. 'Are you sure that you're not seeing a conspiracy when there is none? Couldn't these

12

robberies just be a hat-trick of one-off crimes? You're not getting a bit paranoid, old chap, are you?'

'Of course I am . . .' he retorted, sharply. 'I'm a copper. But you know what they say, my love. Just because you're paranoid, it doesn't mean that the bastards aren't out to get you. These raids are connected, all right, but we don't have a clue who's making the connections.'

'So what are you going to do about it?'

'Turn the screw, sweetheart. Just as hard as I can. I've called the troops in tomorrow for some motivation.'

'Just like a good manager.'

'Sure,' he acknowledged. 'And I might just prove it by chucking a few teacups!'

He sipped his wine, and turned his attention to dinner. 'That's enough of my day. What about yours?'

She shrugged, tossing her mass of dark curls. 'I spent most of it up in the Court of Session with Mitch Laidlaw.'

'Still the senior partner's pet trainee lawyer, eh. D'you take him in an apple every day?'

Alex snorted, her big, round eyes flashing him a meaningful look. 'Don't push your luck, or your apples'll be in jeopardy,' she responded evenly. 'In fact I was assisting Mr Laidlaw in a very important civil case. We're acting for a law firm that's been accused of negligence by a disgruntled client. To be absolutely accurate, we've been instructed by the professional indemnity insurers, but it's almost the same thing.'

'What's it about?'

She looked at him, pleased by his genuine interest. 'It's quite interesting really,' she began. 'The pursuer was a hotelier. He owned a place called Merryston House, just outside Lauder, but he's bust now. That's why the action began. It centres around an extension he wanted to build, to allow him to open a new supper bar. He was given firm advice by his solicitor, a bloke called Adrian Jones, that there were no grounds for objection. The client's interpretation of that was that there was no need for planning permission.'

Andy looked at her in surprise. 'That's a bit of an assumption, isn't it?'

She hesitated. 'Yes . . . but Jones' letter was pretty poorly drafted, and it did say that full planning permission might not be required in cases where an extension was less than a certain percentage of the total area of the property. Also, the hotel was a big baronial place, in its own grounds, with no near neighbours.

'On the strength of the solicitor's letter, the hotelier . . . his name's Bernard Grimley, by the way . . . went ahead and got a builder pal of his to knock the thing up for him, cheap and cheerful. He'd been open for two days when the local authority came along to see him. It turned out that one of his first customers had written to them complaining.

'Not to put too fine a point on it, the faeces hit the fan for poor Mr Grimley, and consequently, for Green Symonds, of South Queensferry,

Adrian Jones' firm. As well as giving him dodgy planning advice, it turned out that they had neglected to point out that the hotel was a listed building, noteworthy for a particular type of architecture.

'Enter Historic Scotland, the Secretary of State's guardians of our heritage, raising objections. Grimley tried for planning consent retrospectively, but he was stuffed. The Secretary of State called in the application, and ruled almost at once. He was ordered to take down the extension and restore the building to its original condition . . .'

Alex paused, for breath and for wine. 'That was it for the man. His business was pretty marginal, at best, and the abortive costs finished him. He couldn't even afford the reconstruction work. In the end, the hotel was sold and turned into a nursing home, and he went back to his original trade as a metal finisher.

'To cap it all, his wife left him last year and went to live with one of the council planning officers. He's on his own now, in a rented house near Humbie.'

Andy shrugged. 'So how come the case wound up in the Court of Session? Sounds to me that your insurer's solicitor client is on pretty shaky ground.'

'Very,' she agreed immediately. 'In fact we admitted negligence ages ago. The problem is the quantum, the amount of damages. The insurance company started off with an offer of seven hundred thousand. Bernard Grimley wants five million.'

'Eh? Why are they so far apart?'

'It's a matter of wishful thinking. Grimley never made more than twenty-five grand in profits in the three years he owned the place. He's forty-three, so the insurers did their sums based on likely income till his retiral, plus the costs of the work, plus loss of potential profit on the sale.

'But the basis of Grimley's argument is that the new bar was the missing link that would have helped him turn Merryston House into a five-star country house hotel. He's projected vastly increased income, and a sale value of millions.'

The meal at an end, Andy rose from his seat and picked up the bowls. 'But the planners wouldn't have let him build the extension anyway. Doesn't that flatten his case?'

Alex followed him into the kitchen and watched as he reached down to open the dishwasher door. 'We think that it damages it,' she agreed. 'But Grimley's argument is that if he'd been given proper advice, he'd have found another, unspecified, solution. From what we can tell, the judge seems to be impressed by it.

'He's had all sorts of witnesses. Architects, hoteliers, even a doctor to give evidence about the damage to his health resulting from the negligence. He's an old acquaintance of yours, in fact. Doctor Banks.'

She frowned. 'There was quite a commotion during his evidence. He was excused from the witness box to go and attend to one of the judges who'd collapsed on the Bench.' She paused. 'I heard later that he had died.'

14

'That's no surprise with Banks in attendance!' said Andy, his vivid green eyes flashing. 'If I never meet that man again it'll be too soon. He must have loved being the centre of attention, the glory-seeking wee bastard.

'What was he like as a witness in your case?'

His partner wrinkled her nose, as she considered her answer. 'He was okay, I suppose. He just gave a straightforward opinion as the pursuer's GP that during the course of the dispute, he had suffered from stress, anxiety, depression and raised blood pressure, requiring continuous medication.

'He didn't say anything that we could argue with. I reckon he did Grimley's case quite a bit of good.'

Andy stood straight once more, still with dishes in hand, and looked at her. 'It sounds to me, from what you're saying, like you're going to lose.'

She frowned and nodded. 'The truth is that we expect to. We'd have gone to arbitration, but the other side wouldn't accept anything short of a full Supreme Court hearing. So now it's a matter of how much the judge decides the claim is really worth. Our guess is one and a half million, but you never know. Grimley could wind up getting the whole five.'

Her fiancé chuckled. 'Just like winning the lottery. What's he like, this Grimley bloke?'

'A bit rough-hewn, I'd say. And sort of fly with it; a bit of a chancer. He's got shifty little eyes, and he doesn't like looking at people directly. I don't like him much.'

'Are we likely to have known him?'

'Does he have a criminal record, d'you mean? Not as far as we know. He's certainly never declared any convictions. He made the money to buy Merryston House in the pub trade in Glasgow though, in a part of the South Side where you wouldn't go after dark, but we can't found any defence just on that.'

'No,' said Andy, 'but still . . .'

He slid the plates into the dishwasher and closed its door with a bang. 'Anyway, enough of Mr Grimley, and of the Hole in the Wall Gang. Shop talk's over for the evening.' He reached out and drew her to him, with a smile. 'Now let's do our best to rid ourselves of the tensions of a stressful day.'

5

'When DCS Martin says first thing in the morning, he really means it, doesn't he.' Maggie Rose glanced at the clock on the wall of the briefing room at Police Headquarters in Fettes Avenue. It showed fifteen minutes after eight a.m.

She and Detective Superintendent Mackie were seated at a long conference table with ten other officers, CID commanders and deputies from the other five Divisions of the force. All of the others had helped themselves to coffee from Thermos jugs on a tray by the long window, but Rose had taken a glass of water, her preference at that time of day. She glanced around, conscious of the fact, as she always was at such meetings, that she was the only woman in the room.

The officer seated on her right leaned over towards her. 'What's this about, Mags? Any idea?'

She looked round at him. Detective Superintendent Dan Pringle was bleary-eyed. There were nicks on his chin, as if he had shaved with a shaky hand, and even his heavy black moustache had a tired look about it. 'Can't say for sure,' she replied, 'but we reckon . . .'

She stopped in mid-sentence as the door swung open, and the blond figure of the Head of CID strode into the room, accompanied by the fresh-faced young Detective Constable Sammy Pye, of his personal staff, and by the familiar bulk of Detective Sergeant Neil McIlhenney, DCC Bob Skinner's executive assistant.

'Morning all,' called Andy Martin, his tight-cropped hair shining under the neon light as he stood at the head of the table, flanked by his two companions. 'Everyone got coffee? Good. I'd have laid on bacon rolls as well, but the canteen can't handle big numbers this early.'

He took off his navy blue blazer and hung it across the back of his chair, then lowered himself into it. 'Okay, if you're all sitting comfortably then I'll begin.' He nodded to his right, then to his left. 'Sammy's here to take a note of this meeting. Neil, as you all know, is Mr Skinner's Vicar on Earth.'

There was laughter round the table, as McIlhenney genuflected quickly. Martin stilled it by holding up a hand. 'How many of you are wondering what this gathering is about?' he asked.

Around the table, eight hands rose, some of them hesitantly.

'Is that right?' said the DCS, softly. 'Then I'm disappointed. I suggest to all of you guys that you pay more attention to what's going on outside

16

your own Divisions, if only by reading the *Evening News* every day.

'If you had done, then you'd know that over the last three months there have been three major armed robberies in this force's territory, two of them from banks and one from a building society. Total funds liberated, one million, two hundred and seventy-three thousand pounds. Oh yes, and thirty-four pence. Total funds recovered, twenty-two thousand six hundred and seventy pounds. Total number of arrests, one . . . Nathan Bennett, who was stupid enough to drop his credit card at the scene of the first raid.

'These robberies have been spread around our area, at random, and without any obvious time pattern. The first was in Dalkeith, three months ago, as I said, where the Bank of Scotland was held up. The second of the subsequent crimes took place last week in Edinburgh, and the third was in Colinton on Monday.

'In case you're wondering, there have been no similar robberies in other force areas during this period. I've checked. For the moment at least, these people are concentrating on the Edinburgh area.'

He paused. 'Questions or observations?'

'Need there be a connection?' asked Pringle.

'You've had two on your territory, Dan, one of them right in the middle of George Street,' Martin retorted as quick as a flash. 'You tell me whether they're connected.'

The gruff detective nodded. 'I'd say that those two were. The physical descriptions don't tally, but in each case there were three robbers, all of them armed with shotguns, and in each case they made the staff hand over the video tapes from the security system. However, I can't say that all three are linked.'

'I can,' said the Head of CID, with emphasis. 'I've been looking at the big picture . . . which is, after all, my job.

'Let's consider the common factors. There have been three men on the team at each robbery; enough to get the job done, but not so many that they're getting in each other's way. In each case they've worn different types of face masks.

'Witnesses have said that every man has been armed with a sawn-off shotgun. They have all said that they were left in no doubt that they would be used if necessary. Fortunately, they haven't been . . . so far, at least.

'In the first robbery the camera surveillance system was disabled with a paint-spray. In the other two the video tape was taken from the recorder.

'In each case, the strong-room has been open or available, never locked on a time-switch. Some banks have very helpful notices advising robbers that safes can only be opened by two members of staff. I'm not quite sure what that achieves, other than it puts two people in added danger, rather than one.

'In each case the means of escape has been efficient and appropriate to the surroundings. For example, in Dalkeith they simply used the public car park across from the bank, In George Street, they stole a taxi and left it parked outside the building society with its hazard lights flashing. In

Colinton, the target bank has its own car park. They drove into that just like ordinary customers.'

He looked at his colleagues. 'Am I convincing you?' From around the table came an assortment of grunts, and nodded heads.

'That's good. Now let's look a bit further. Each of these robberies has been very carefully planned, and every one has gone like clockwork. So who's been doing the planning? Is it one of the team? More than that, has it been the same team every time?'

Martin smiled. 'We know the answer to that one, since Nathan Bennett was nicked on the first raid, three months ago. The second and third raids have both taken place within the last seven days, still with three men in the team, so there's been someone on hand to take his place.

'Now let's take up Dan's point. He said that the physical descriptions from the two robberies on his patch didn't tally. That's true. To back that up, we do have a fragment of video footage from the first hold-up, taken before the system was disabled. I've had a good look at it, and I've compared the guys it shows with the witness statements from the other two crimes.

'In the first robbery, the tape shows a tall curly-haired man, who appears to be left-handed. That tallies with descriptions given after the third robbery, but not the second. The third man on the Dalkeith job was stocky and bald. That matches a witness statement from the second crime, but not the third.

'From that it seems that the teams were definitely different every time, and that no individual was involved in all three crimes. Going by the statements and the tape, that is. Counting Bennett, it looks as if we're dealing with a group of at least five gunmen.'

He paused and took a deep breath, allowing his colleagues to consider what he had said.

'This is what I think,' he went on, breaking, finally, the silence which hung over the table. 'These three robberies were all planned by the same man. However, I don't believe it likely that he took part in them himself.

'Remember the money that was recovered when Brian arrested Nathan Bennett? It was one sixth of the total stolen. Three men in each team, each playing an equal part, yet the split is half to them, and half going somewhere else. Even if the guys on the substitute's Bench are getting a share too, that still leaves someone else.'

'Could there be more than five in the team?' asked Pringle.

'Unlikely, or we'd have seen more than that by now, and I think, the second and third robberies would have followed more quickly. One possibility is that the ringleader took some time to find a replacement for Nathan Bennett, and maybe to train him as well. Another is that after the balls-up on the first raid, he had another look at his planning. A third is that he held off until he was sure that Bennett wasn't going to shop anyone.'

He looked at Maggie Rose. 'If you had that sort of set-up, if you were identifying and planning each job would you risk it all by taking part in the robbery?'

The Chief Inspector shook her head. 'I wouldn't see the need,' she replied. 'What you're saying then, sir, is that we're dealing with a logistics man who has a squad of robbers, interchangeable and well trained in what they do. Maybe there were only three at the time of the first raid. Maybe they learned from Bennett being nicked, and recruited two new men.

'Certainly it means now that if we do get lucky and lift one of the team, as we did with Bennett, the damage isn't fatal, and the operation can proceed. Even if we get super-lucky and catch the whole team, there's still one trained man left, and the Boss.'

'That's right, Mags,' Martin agreed. 'Does that remind you of anyone?'

'Jackie Charles,' she shot back at once, 'but he's in the jail, and his associates are either dead or doing time with him.'

'Exactly,' said the Head of CID. 'Jackie Charles *was* organised crime in Edinburgh. When we put him away, we were all dead chuffed with ourselves. I reckon we were a bit premature there. We created a vacuum, and it looks very much as if, in line with the laws of nature, someone's come along to fill it.'

He looked along the table once more. 'Anyone disagree with that? Come on, don't be afraid to say if you think I'm going over the top.' Detectives shuffled uneasily in their seats, and glanced from one to the other. Andy Martin knew that there were those among them who were jealous of his rapid promotion, and that he had given them a chance to undermine him.

Eventually, as was usually the case, Dan Pringle, the senior man among the Divisional heads, elected himself spokesman. 'I'd say that we've got no choice but to proceed on the basis that your reading is correct, sir. The problem is, how do we proceed?'

The Chief Superintendent nodded acknowledgement of the point. 'Remember what we did when the Boss was stabbed,' he fired back, 'and we were after the drug dealer whose people did it?' Without waiting for a response, he answered his own question. 'We crapped on this whole city from a great height until we got what we wanted. We raided the saunas, hassled the money-lenders, picked up even the meanest pill-pushers: we more or less pulled people in for farting in the street.

'Well, we're going to do the same thing again now. I want you all to crack down as hard as you can on every source of criminal intelligence in your areas. Lean on everybody, even your most private sources.

'Ask everyone what they know about these robberies. Ask them if they know of anyone in their circles who's been spending too much money lately. I want a name, any bloody name, as long as it leads to an arrest. Just one will be enough, for starters at least. I don't believe that we'll pick up this whole squad in one go.

'Of course it would be great if we were given a lead to a robbery that's still in the planning stage, but don't let's harbour too many hopes of that. These crimes have been too well put together for there to have been any leaks.'

Martin paused, and smiled. 'So go forth from here, all of you, pound your mean streets and see what news they yield.

'Those of you who haven't had robberies on your patch should identify likely targets. I'm having a meeting this morning with all the banks' security people, but I'd like your input on that too as quickly as possible. Let's never forget that the first job of the police is the protection of people and property.

'I want everyone fully committed to this. Even you, John.'

His bright eyes flashed along the line of detectives to Superintendent John McGrigor, CID Commander in the Borders Division. 'We can't afford to assume that these people will stick to urban areas. You might say that there's nothing on your patch worth stealing, but even so, I'd like you to have a word with all the bank managers in your area. Don't scare them shitless, but put them on alert, and make sure that they let you know whenever they're holding unusually large sums of money.'

McGrigor, a big, beefy, red-faced countryman, nodded. 'Will do, sir. This is the time of year when there tends to be more cash sloshin' aboot down there. The hotels are full, and the fruit farmers are selling off their produce. Can I ask one thing, though?'

'Sure.'

'Well,' the bulky detective began, 'you said we were needing a name. Surely we've already got one; this boy Bennett. Can we no' get anything out of him?'

Martin glanced at Superintendent Mackie, who leaned forward, looking down the table at his colleague. 'Bennett's pleading Not Guilty, John. His defence is that he dropped his credit card in the bank earlier, and that the money we found on him came from gambling. On-course bookies, he says, and of course he can't remember who they were.'

'That's a pile o' shite,' said McGrigor. 'Sorry Mags,' he added.

'Don't fucking mention it,' she said quietly. Even the studious Brian Mackie laughed at her reproof, knowing how much his deputy disliked being patronised in any way by male colleagues.

'I know that, John,' he went on, 'but that's his story. I've interrogated him for hours, so has Maggie, so have two of my most intimidating sergeants. Still he sticks to it. In my view, the man is scared.'

'Or he's expecting his family to be looked after when he's inside?' suggested Dan Pringle.

'He doesn't have a family. No, my impression is that Bennett believes that if he talks he'll be killed.'

'Maybe I'll have a chat with him,' said Martin from the head of the table. 'I can do that, now that his trial's been aborted.'

'When will it begin again?' asked McGrigor.

'As soon as they can dig up a judge,' the Head of CID replied.

'An unfortunate remark in the circumstances, sir.' Neil McIlhenney's growl took everyone by surprise, including Martin, who grinned at the big man on his left. He liked the sergeant, not least for his irreverence.

'Maybe so. Still, I'm pretty sure that's how old Archergait would have wanted to go. In harness, so to speak.'

20

'Oh aye?' muttered McIlhenney.

'Enough of the judge jokes!' cried the DCS. 'Okay, lady and gentlemen, let's get to it. The Boss is due back on Monday; that's four days from now. I'd like some sort of a result by then.'

He stood up, signalling that the meeting was over. Moving over towards Mackie, he took him by the elbow and drew him into a corner of the room. 'Can I have a word about an unrelated matter, Thin Man,' he said quietly. 'I know you haven't been on your patch for too long, but does the name Bernard Grimley mean anything to you? He used to own a hotel out Lauder way.'

The Superintendent knitted his brows. 'I can't recall having heard of him, Andy. Should I have?'

'Probably not. I'm just flying a kite. Alex's firm are appearing against him in a case in the Court of Session, and she thinks they're on a hiding. From what she said, Grimley's a bit shifty, and I just wondered . . .'

'I understand,' said Mackie. 'I'll ask the lads back at Haddington if they know of him.'

'Thanks. You might have a quick word with the criminal intelligence people in Strathclyde as well. He used to have a pub in the South Side of Glasgow.'

'Okay. I'll let you know.'

'Good man. Don't spend too much time on it though. Putting a stop to these robberies is absolute top priority. I'm certain that there's one ruthless, clever bastard behind all of them. What makes me really angry is that he thinks he's cleverer than us. I want to be there when he finds out that he was wrong!'

6

Martin looked around the low coffee table in the Deputy Chief Constable's office. The astute McIlhenney had suggested that they use Skinner's room for the meeting with the bank security chiefs, since two of their number were retired Assistant Chiefs, who would appreciate the courtesy of an invitation into the Command Corridor.

Six men and one woman faced him. On his instructions, Sammy Pye had invited heads of security from the four established clearing banks, from two recently converted former building societies, and from the two largest remaining mutuals. Five had accepted at once, two others, with no regional head of security in post, were represented by area managers, while the eighth, a building society, had declined the invitation.

The Head of CID looked seriously at each visitor as they settled into the low leather seats. Four of them, each well into his fifties and running to fat, fidgeted so uncomfortably that he wondered about the wisdom of McIlhenney's strategy.

But then Ronnie Manuel, the bulkiest of the quartet, and a former ACC in Tayside, smiled back at him. 'I guess we should be honoured that you've invited us in here, Mr Martin. Bob Skinner has become something of a legend, so to be in his office . . .'

The younger man grinned. 'The name's Andy. We thought you'd like it,' he said. 'On top of that, Bob's room has the most comfortable seats!

'If you're all settled into them,' he went on, 'let me tell you why you've been invited here.

'I believe that you've got a big problem.' As Martin blurted out his blunt message, he looked at Manuel, who was head of security of the Bank of Scotland, at David Sullivan, a trim ex-soldier from the TSB Bank, and at Moyra Lamb, regional manager of the Nationwide Building Society.

'You three have experience of it, having all been robbed recently. This rest of you are in the firing line.'

'You mean the hold-ups?' said Ms Lamb. 'The Bank's, the Clydesdale's, and ours?'

'That's just what I mean,' the Head of CID acknowledged. 'We're satisfied that they were all the work of the same people. We believe that we are faced with a highly organised, well-trained team which is targeting bank branches, in and around Edinburgh.

'I've invited you here to alert you to the continuing danger, and to advise you as strongly as I can to put all your branches on maximum alert.'

He paused, and looked around the table once more. 'May I ask whether any of you have increased security lately?'

Harry Durkin, who had been Head of Special Branch in Strathclyde until taking early retirement five years earlier to join the Clydesdale, shrugged his shoulders. 'I can't speak for the rest, Andy, but I'm always reviewing our security operation. And from what David was telling me on the way in, the branch that he had turned over the other day was kitted out with all of the standard stuff . . . video surveillance, bullet-proof glass screens for staff, a silent alarm system linked to the nearest police office.'

He shook his head, making his heavy jowls wobble. 'But when three guys walk in with shotguns and tell all the staff to get out front or they'll shoot one of the punters, they can't do anything but comply. Once the bank staff are under their control, the bank is busted; simple as that.'

'I know that,' agreed Martin. 'Like you said, though, Harry, you never stop trying to make them harder to bust. Look, in the last two robberies, the team has taken the tapes from the video surveillance equipment. That's easier and surer than disabling the camera.'

Eyebrows rose around the table. 'Have they, by God?' muttered George Hudson, a former Grampian ACC, now employed by the Royal Bank.

'Indeed they have,' his host emphasised. 'So let me suggest this to you. Either move the video units out of the branches into other buildings . . . your nearest police offices, for example . . . or install duplicate recording equipment. It wouldn't even need to be functional, just realistic enough for the robbers to be shown it and given a tape.'

'Would that fool them more than once, Andy?' asked Manuel.

'I reckon it would. These guys won't actually be bothering to run the tapes. They'd have trouble anyway, on a domestic player.'

The Bank of Scotland official looked at his colleagues. 'Okay, I'll look at the feasibility of those options.' Around the table the others nodded agreement. 'Got any other ideas, Andy?'

'How about security people outside the doors of the branches?' Moyra Lamb interrupted.

Martin shook his head. 'They'd need to be armed to have any deterrent value, and in this country that's not on. Unarmed, they wouldn't hold up an attack for a second. In fact, the team would have ready made hostages before they were even inside the bank.'

He hesitated for a second. 'Look, this is just a thought. I've seen banks in Europe where customers are only admitted when a teller unlocks the door remotely. I can even think of a couple of jewellers in Edinburgh who use that system. Have any of you ever looked at that possibility?'

Hudson glanced at Manuel and Durkin, then looked at the Chief Superintendent. 'Ronnie, Harry and I sometimes get together informally to swap ideas. We looked at that one a while back. We decided that it might be practical in country branches, or in smaller operations in the cities and towns. We ruled it out, though, on the basis that the annoyance to customers, on rainy days for example, would more than offset any security gains.

'In the big branches, it isn't a runner. They're just too busy, I'm afraid.'

'Fair enough,' Martin responded. 'You might like to have a rethink about the smaller ones though. Neither Dalkeith or Colinton seem like massive branches to me. I think if you polled your customers, you might find that they preferred a few seconds more in the rain to the possibility of looking down the barrel of a sawn-off.'

'All that's very fine,' broke in Paul Oxford, regional manager of one of the new banks, 'but what are the police going to do to protect us?' There was a hint of petulance in his voice, a sign, thought the policeman, that he was slightly out of his depth.

'The best way to protect you, Mr Oxford, is to catch these guys and bang them away for a long time. That's exactly what we will do. However in the meantime, we'll use our resources as best we can to make you feel more secure.

'I've asked ACC Elder, who's in charge of uniformed operations, if he can arrange panda and traffic-car patrols so that they pass by your branches frequently, and so that we can respond to an emergency in the shortest time possible. I'll also make the services of our crime prevention team available to all of you, to visit, if you wish, every branch in my area and to advise you on security improvements that might be made.

'But I can't emphasise enough that we need your co-operation too. For example, where you have a safe with a time-lock, make proper use of it, don't leave the bloody thing lying open all day.'

He paused once more and looked at the visitors. 'there's one thing more I have to say to you.

'Each of the three robberies has taken place at a time when the branch involved was full of cash. Please bear that in mind. Brief all your managers to vary their routines as much as they can. Tell them to try to ensure that cash is delivered as close as possible to the time when it's actually needed. And tell them also to be discreet.

'We'd be foolish to rule out the possibility that these criminals have had inside information. Therefore, please . . .' He leaned heavily on the word '. . . emphasise that staff should be told of big cash movements into branches only on a need-to-know basis.

'Careless talk costs money . . . yes, and possibly lives, too.'

7

With the rest of the legal teams on both sides of the Court, Alex Skinner stood and returned the bow of the judge, as he adjourned the Court for lunch.

As always, the corridor outside was crowded as she emerged with Mitchell Laidlaw, her boss. After a few minutes they were joined by their counsel, Jack McAlpine, QC, and Elizabeth Day, his junior, who had shed their black robes and grey wigs. Together, the quartet headed for the exit, only to find their way blocked as Andy Martin stepped through the double doors from the courtyard outside.

'What are you doing here?' asked Alex, surprised. 'You never said . . .'

He shrugged his broad shoulders. 'I didn't know this morning that I'd have free time. I've arranged to see a guy at Saughton, but that's not till two-thirty, so I thought I'd come up here to see if I could steal you for lunch.' He looked at Laidlaw. 'Is that okay, Mitch?'

'Of course,' said the rotund senior partner of Curle Anthony and Jarvis. 'But why don't you join us? We've got a table booked at Gordon's.'

'Fine by me,' agreed Martin. He nodded to the counsel, both of whom were known to him. 'Hello, Liz, Jack,' he said as the five stepped into the open air. 'How's it going in there?'

'Hard to tell,' McAlpine answered. The camp Queen's Counsel was one of the more colourful figures at the Scottish Bar. 'We lawyers always think we're right. The trouble is, invariably, fifty per cent of us are wrong.'

They crossed the High Street, ludicrously thronged as always with tourist buses, and reached Gordon's Trattoria after only a short walk down the hill towards Cockburn Street. Inside, they were greeted, immediately and effusively, by the head waiter, who was well used to dealing with lawyers in a hurry. 'Lady and gentlemen, welcome. You are now five, I see. Is no problem, it's a big table.'

'My God,' Laidlaw hissed to Martin as they moved through the narrow restaurant. 'There's the cause of it all.' Abruptly he advanced on a small table at the far end of the room. 'Hello, Adrian,' he boomed, hand outstretched. 'Been across the road, looking in on your former client?'

A tall man in his mid thirties, dark-haired and dark-suited, rose to accept his handshake. It struck Martin that he seemed to have trouble bending his right leg at the knee. 'No way,' he replied, with a half-smile. 'Having given my evidence the other day before that damned pernickety judge, if I never see Bernard bloody Grimley again, it'll be well too soon.

'No, I had a meeting down in George Street and my wife's been to Jenners.' He smiled down at a serious-faced young woman, with expensively groomed ash-blonde hair.

'You don't know Juliette, do you. Jules, this is Mitch Laidlaw, something of a legend around these parts. And . . . ' He hesitated, looking at Martin, whose path to his own table was blocked by Laidlaw's bulk.

'Oh, sorry. This is Chief Superintendent Andy Martin. He's Head of CID down at Fettes, but he's also engaged to my assistant.'

'Ah yes,' said Jones, extending his hand. 'I've heard of you, of course. Pleased to meet you.'

'Likewise.'

Suddenly, the man paused. His face froze and he stared over Martin's shoulder, towards the door. 'Oh Christ,' he whispered. 'Not here. It's bloody Grimley.'

The detective and Juliette Jones turned to look at the entrance, in which a tallish, dark-haired, middle-aged man stood, staring back at Jones. Sparks seemed to fly between them, until finally, Bernard Grimley turned on his heel and stalked out of the restaurant.

'Thank goodness for that,' said the solicitor, his expression softening. He looked down at his wife. 'After everything that man's put us through, I couldn't have stood eating lunch beside him.'

'Obviously he felt the same way,' she said, with a smile.

'Look, Adrian,' said Laidlaw. 'We must sit down. Tight schedule and all that. Give me a call if you'd like to be briefed on developments.' As Jones nodded and sat down, Laidlaw and Martin joined Alex and the two advocates.

'Just think,' muttered Laidlaw, 'all this is happening because that bugger over there couldn't draft a letter properly. If he'd only done a bit more research and added a few caveats to cover his arse, none of us need be here.'

'True,' McAlpine countered. 'But if he had, then some of us would be slightly less wealthy. We make a good living out of people like Jones; let's not grudge them their imperfections.'

The Queen's Counsel turned to Martin. 'Who are you seeing at Saughton, Andy? Anything in it for me?'

The detective shook his head as he looked at the business lunch menu. 'I'm afraid not, Jim,' he answered with a smile. 'This guy's already represented. By the Honourable Richard Kilmarnock, QC, no less.'

'Oh dear,' said the advocate, archly. 'Still, put a word in for me anyway, there's a good chap. Kilmarnock's clients always want someone else for the appeal.'

'If he listens to what I've got to say, there won't be an appeal. I'm going out there to try a bit of private plea-bargaining.'

'Mmm. Thought you chaps didn't believe in that sort of thing. Supping with the Devil, no?'

Martin smiled. 'It's the devil I'm after, Jack. Nathan Bennett's just a minor demon. I don't care about him.'

'Bennett?' said Mitch Laidlaw, suddenly interested in the conversation, rather than in the menu. 'Wasn't he in the dock when poor old Billy fell off his perch?'

'That's right. I'm not going to hold that against him, though.'

'Ha. No, I guess not. That was bound to happen some time. He was a hard old bastard, was Archergait. When he got worked up, the veins used to stand out on his forehead. I remember once . . .'

The solicitor's musing was interrupted by the trilling of Martin's mobile phone. He took it from his pocket and pressed a green button. 'Yes?' he said, tersely.

Watching her partner, Alex saw his expression grow thunderous. 'Okay, Sammy,' he said at last, a new, hard edge to his voice. 'I've got all that. Call Saughton for me and put Bennett off till tomorrow morning.' He pushed an orange button to end the call.

'What's up?' asked Alex, anxiously.

'Another bank robbery,' he answered. 'At the Royal Bank in Galashiels. And this time there are casualties. Sorry about lunch, but I have to get down there.'

8

John McGrigor's normally ruddy face was chalk-white as he greeted his Chief Superintendent in the doorway of the Galashiels branch of the Royal Bank of Scotland. In the street outside, around which traffic had been diverted, stood several police cars and an ambulance, its loading doors wide open.

On the pavement, about ten yards away from the doorway, there was a long trail of blood. It was being gradually washed away by the steady summer rain which had begun to fall half an hour before.

'Tell me about it,' Martin ordered. As they stepped into the banking hall, the Head of CID was faced by a wall, heavily streaked with still more blood. On the floor, in a a crimson pool, lay a huge man. His abdomen had been ripped open by the blast from a firearm, and entrails, unwound, mingled with his shredded clothing.

'This is just awful, Andy,' said the big Superintendent. 'Big Harry Riach, on the floor there, he and I were at the school together. I've locked him up a few times since then, too, when he's been out of order. I was the only fella that could ever arrest him wi'out a struggle.' McGrigor shook his head, and Martin saw a tear in the corner of his eye.

'He had a go, then?' he asked.

His colleague nodded. 'Most of the witnesses are still in hysterics,' he said, 'but we've interviewed those that can speak. It was the same as before. Three men, wearing Hallowe'en masks this time, and armed with sawn-offs, just walked in off the street.

'It was like clockwork. They had the customers up against the wall and all the staff out from behind the counter, lying on the floor. One held a' the folk at gunpoint, and the other two collected the money, and took the security video tape.' He paused.

'They were just about ready to go when the man who'd been keepin' everyone covered stepped a bit too close to Riach. "Fuck this for a game!" Big Harry says, and makes a grab for him. According to the witnesses, the guy just stuck the sawn-off in his belly and pulled the trigger. The doctor . . . he left just a minute before you arrived . . . said he'd have been dead before he hit the floor.

'None of the three said a word, or seemed to panic in any way. They just took the money in two big hold-alls and backed out. They took the bank keys as well, and locked everyone in as they left.'

'That's a new twist,' the Head of CID muttered. 'To make for an easier getaway, I suppose.

'What happened outside?' he went on.

'Sheer bad luck,' said McGrigor bitterly. 'A young police constable, Annie Brown . . . lovely wee girl . . . just happened to be there. I don't know why. She certainly hadn't been ordered to the scene. One of the boys found a birthday card in the street, though, addressed and sealed. She could have been on her way to post it.'

'No other officer was with her, then?'

'No.'

'So what happened?'

'According to one of the witnesses who was looking out the bank window, the robber who wasn't carrying a hold-all just took one look at her when he stepped into the street, and shot her.'

'Had she done anything, or called out?'

'Not according to the witness.'

'What's her condition?'

'Critical, according to the doctor. He came from the surgery round the corner; within two minutes, they say. They took her in an ambulance to Borders General. I've heard nothing since.'

Martin nodded, and silently held up crossed fingers.

'How did they make their escape?' he asked.

'In a grey Ford Escort,' McGrigor replied. 'It was parked right outside the bank. There were half a dozen people in the street, all on the other side. By the time any of them realised what was happening, the girl was down and the car was moving. No-one got the number, but I've ordered all cars to report every grey Escort seen in our area.'

'Careful, John. We don't want any more victims.'

'I know. I said report but don't approach, unless the vehicle is empty.'

'Fair enough,' Martin nodded. 'They'll have changed anyway. That's the usual pattern.' He looked at his colleague. 'Come on, and let's you and I go to the hospital. I want to be there when she comes round, and to speak to her relatives.'

He turned to the green-uniformed paramedics, a man and a woman, who stood waiting in a corner. 'You can take the body to the mortuary now. Hold for post-mortem.'

He let McGrigor out into the street, and together they climbed into the Head of CID's Mondeo. The Superintendent gave swift directions to Borders General Hospital, on the outskirts of the town. As he weaved his way though the narrow streets of the centre of Galashiels, Martin asked him, 'Have you advised the Chief's office that we have a wounded officer?'

'Aye. I spoke to Sir James himself, an hour ago. He said he'd be down right away.'

'Good. Not that I expected anything else from him.

'Tell me John,' continued the DCS, 'do you know whether the bank was flush with money?'

Beside him, McGrigor nodded. 'I spoke to the manager. He was well cashed up a'right. There's a big electronics factory outside the town still

29

pays most of its weekly wage staff in notes, and yon big DIY place up the road has a sale on.

'It'll take him a while to work out how much has gone, but he said it wouldna' be less than seven or eight hundred thousand.'

'Bloody hell,' whispered Martin, quietly. 'If we don't stop these people there'll be no fucking money left in our area!'

As he spoke, he reached the big, modern hospital. It was well sign-posted, and so the Accident and Emergency admissions unit was easy to find. The detective parked two hundred yards away, in the first available bay, jumped out and led McGrigor at a brisk walk towards its entrance.

As the two policemen strode through the double doors, Martin looked around for the admissions desk. Instead, he saw Chief Constable Sir James Proud, imposing in his heavily braided uniform. His face spoke the news for him.

'When?' the Head of CID asked, grim-faced.

'Half an hour ago,' replied the silver-headed Chief. 'The poor lass never regained consciousness. I've just left her parents and her boyfriend. It's his twenty-third birthday tomorrow: the same age as she was.'

There were a few people in the police force who believed that Sir James Proud took such pride in the wearing of his uniform because it helped him hide a soft centre. Anyone seeing the look in his eyes as he spoke to Martin would have been disabused of that notion. 'You make sure you catch these bastards, Andy,' he said, quietly, yet ferociously. 'Catch them quick.

'When you do, I'll interview them myself, just to see what sort of creatures they are. Because I surely don't detect any humanity.'

9

Bob Skinner, with Jazz dozing in a carrier strapped to his father's back, grinned at Mark as he fought with determination to master his in-line skates. The boy was highly gifted in terms of memory and intellect, but not in terms of athleticism.

Sarah's hand was in his as they walked back along the Passeig d'Empuries, from the beach where they had spent the hot August afternoon. She had a big beach umbrella, in a carrier, slung over her shoulder, while he carried their towels and the other debris of the day in a yellow bag.

As they passed from beneath a tree-shaded area of the walkway, Bob nodded to his right, towards a white-washed building which stood facing a small, sharply curved bay. 'Look at that,' he said with a smile. 'The Hostal Ampurias. I used to have a day-dream that one day I'd buy that place and make it one of the finest hotels on the Costa Brava.'

Sarah laughed, and slipped her arm around his waist. 'Why don't we?'

'Two reasons. One, the owners don't want to sell. Two, we can't afford it. No, three reasons, we've got two boys to bring up, and you're off the pill. Oh aye, and another. Four reasons, we've just bought a new family home back in Scotland.'

She smiled. 'Okay, but in a few years you'll be eligible for retirement on a pretty good pension. I could do consultancy and locum work during the school terms and we could spend all of the holidays out here.

'You could write your memoirs.'

His roar of laughter was so loud that it startled the walkers around them, and made Mark pause on his roller-blades to look over his shoulder. At his back, he felt Jazz stir.

'That will be right,' he retorted. 'The things that would make my memoirs a best-seller are the very things that I couldn't include in them. If I ever wrote about crime, it would have to be fiction, like that guy we know back in Gullane.

'Mind you, from what I hear there isn't too much money in that.'

She looked up at him as they walked. 'I'm half serious, you know,' she whispered, in her gentle New York drawl. 'I just want us to be as happy as we possibly can be.'

'I know that. And the way to that is for you to be what you are, and for me to be what I am, not for us to deny our natures. I promise you this, though, my darling. As soon as I know I'm past my sell-by date as a copper, I'll go. I'm not implying that Jimmy's past it . . . he's the best

Chief Constable in the land, by miles . . . but I've got no wish to hang on for the silver uniform and the knighthood.'

Sarah's arm tightened around his waist. 'You don't know how good a Chief Constable you'd be until you've tried it. I've no doubt that you'd be brilliant. The Strathclyde job's coming up soon, isn't it?'

'Christ,' he gasped. 'One minute you want me to retire, the next you want me to go after Jock Govan's job. I can tell you that is something I definitely will not do. If I become a Chief anywhere, it'll be in succession to Jimmy. My role with the Secretary of State, even though I've chucked it, gave me special eligibility.'

Sarah's face fell into shadow as they passed under another umbrella of trees on the wide red walkway. 'Do you regret not staying on in that job, even though you were asked?'

'Not for one second. I've had a bellyful of the duplicity of politicians.' Then suddenly and conspiratorially, Skinner smiled. 'But let me tell you a secret. I've been asked to keep my links with MI5 and the security service. That's where the real advantage lies.'

'You so-and-so! You never said.'

He nodded. 'That's true. Mind you, now I have told you, I'll have to kill you.'

For a split-second, she frowned at his joke. 'Hey, coming from you, that ain't so funny.'

'See what I mean about my memoirs then? Now, change of subject. Where do you want to eat tonight?'

They strolled on together, Bob, Sarah and their boys, along the last kilometre of the walkway, until they reached the headless statue which marked its limit. Directly across the street they climbed the one hundred steps which took them up to Puig Pedro, Mark counting every one out loud. Sarah's legs were still aching when finally they reached their villa.

Jazz was still asleep in the carrier as Bob eased it from his shoulders. 'I'll just put him in his cot,' he whispered.

'Yeah,' said his wife. 'While he still fits it. I may take a snooze too, if you and Mark want to play in the pool for a bit.'

She kicked off her shoes in the hallway and wandered into their big living area.

Sarah had always objected to mobile phones on holiday. However she had agreed to a fax being installed in the villa. 'For emergencies only, remember.'

When Bob came into the living room, bare-chested and barefoot, she was standing facing the door. Her hazel eyes were narrowed and the laugh-lines around them showed white against her tan. There was an expression of pain on her face.

Without a word she handed him a single sheet of fax paper, and watched his face grow first shocked, then dark with anger as he read. When he looked up at her, the question was asked and the answer given without a single word being exchanged.

'I'll begin packing,' she said. 'You explain to Mark.'

'Yes.' He nodded. 'We'll take the Channel Tunnel. That way we can be home in twenty-four hours.'

10

Like many policemen, even of the most senior rank, Sir James Proud was wary of the press.

Dislike was too strong a word to describe his attitude; he was shrewd enough to appreciate the role of newspapers and the electronic media in shaping public perceptions of his force and its effectiveness. For that reason he had always been assiduous in maintaining friendly working relationships with editors and proprietors.

However, facing a mass of hungry hacks across a table was another matter entirely. There was something about their collective attitude which made him feel as if he was in the centre of a pack of predators, every one with his scent in their nostrils, every one waiting to fire questions with teeth in them.

Proud Jimmy could not be described as shy, nor nervous. He feared no man, except, privately, Bob Skinner, when aroused to a rage. But it was in his nature to measure his words, and to weigh his reply to every question put to him. He envied his deputy and his Head of CID their calm assurance in media briefings, knowing that while they always seemed confident and assured, invariably he presented an image of hesitancy and stiffness.

He had once heard himself referred to as Pinnochio in a whispered aside by a journalist after a briefing, and he had never forgotten it.

Nevertheless, there were some situations in which he could not delegate the responsibility of facing the press, and the early evening gathering in Galashiels which he faced now was surely one of them.

The Chief Constable sat alone at the black-covered table, set up in the canteen of the small, country police office, having declined Andy Martin's offer to accompany him in the briefing. 'No, son,' he had said, 'it wouldn't be right for me to be seen to be leaning on anyone at a time like this.'

The wall behind him was bare and shabby, but he had refused to allow Alan Royston, the force media relations manager, to erect the portable backdrop which he had brought with him from Edinburgh. 'No slogans, Alan. Not this time.'

He picked up the statement which he had written half an hour earlier, glanced at his audience, and at the array of microphones on the table before him and began to read.

'At twelve-thirty-five this afternoon three men entered the Royal Bank of Scotland in Galashiels. They were armed with shotguns and threatened customers and staff, holding them at gunpoint and forcing bank employees to hand over a large sum of money.

'In the course of the robbery, a bank customer, Mr Harry Riach, grappled with one of the gunmen and was shot. Mr Riach died instantly. As the three men left the bank they encountered an officer of my force, PC Anne Brown. Miss Brown was shot also, and died shortly afterwards in Borders General Hospital.

'The three men made good their escape, in a car believed to be a grey Ford Escort. The most strenuous efforts to trace them are being made. On behalf of all my officers and staff, I extend sincere condolences to the families of Mr Riach and PC Brown, and promise them that none of us will rest until their killers have been brought to account.'

He sighed, squared the silver-encrusted shoulders of his heavy tunic and laid his statement on the tables. 'I will take questions, ladies and gentlemen.'

Every one of the eighteen journalists in the room raised a hand simultaneously. The Chief settled on the youngest face in the room, a girl in the front row. She looked barely out of her teens, and she was ghostly pale. 'Yes, miss,' he offered, kindly.

'Alice Collins, sir, from the local paper. Can you tell me how old PC Brown was?'

'She was twenty-three.'

'And Mr Riach?'

Sir James glanced at John McGrigor who stood, beside Andy Martin, at the side of the room. 'Harry was fifty-two, sir,' the Superintendent replied to the unspoken question.

'Was PC Brown married?' Alice Collins asked.

'No. She was engaged, to a young man from Galashiels, I believe. Mr Riach was married, though. He leaves a widow and three sons, aged between eighteen and twenty-seven.'

'Is this the same Harry Riach who played rugby for Scotland back in the early seventies?' Sir James looked across to the other side of the canteen, recognising the voice before he picked out the grizzled face of John Hunter, a veteran freelance from Edinburgh. 'From the youngest to the oldest,' he thought.

'That's right, John. He won nine caps, playing in the second row. He played club rugby for Gala. The other lock in the team was Detective Superintendent John McGrigor over there. He's known Mr Riach all his life.'

'It must have been terrible for the Superintendent, then,' said Hunter, 'when he got to the scene.'

'It was, John,' said Proud Jimmy, quietly. 'It always will be.'

'Where's Bob?' the old journalist asked, almost too casually.

'DCC Skinner is on holiday with his family, but he was informed by fax. He called me an hour ago, to say that he is returning at once. He's driving, so I expect him back tomorrow evening.'

If the Chief Constable had looked, he would have seen Andy Martin lean his head against the wall and close his eyes. He was imagining the next morning's headlines, given the spin which his commander had added unwittingly to an already hot story. *'Skinner rushes back to take charge of double murder hunt.'*

'Next question, please,' Sir James invited, ponderously. Once again the forest of hands shot up. 'Julian Finney, Scottish Television,' he said, pointing to a man who stood at the back of the room, beside a camera and its operator.

'Thank you,' the reporter acknowledged. 'Sir, do you know how much money was stolen?'

'The bank staff are still checking the exact amount, but we know it's more than seven hundred thousand pounds.'

A collective gasp sounded around the room.

'If that's the case,' Finney went on, his tone quiet and inoffensive, 'it can't have escaped your notice that it will bring the total stolen in armed robberies in your force's area over the last three months to around two million pounds, with over a million and a half taken in the last week.

'Are these robberies the work of the same gang, Sir James?'

As Proud shifted in his chair, a muscle clenched at the base of Andy Martin's jaw. He wanted to intervene, to give Finney a stalling answer, but he knew that he could not undermine his Chief. He closed his eyes once more and hoped. In vain.

Honesty is never a weakness, but an inability to prevaricate can be a fault. 'We're in no doubt that they are,' the Chief Constable responded solemnly.

Finney's eyes narrowed, very slightly. 'In that case, can you tell us something about your strategy to protect banks and public from future attacks . . . particularly now that these people have shown themselves capable of murder.'

Proud Jimmy stared back at him. 'I don't know if I can discuss operational matters,' he began, as the potential for disaster dawned on him.

'Surely, Chief, when lives and property are at stake, the public has a right to know?'

Looking at the little man, Sir James knew suddenly the torment and fears of a baited bull. 'Say nothing to start a public panic,' his inner voice told him. He gazed at Finney for several seconds, unaware of anyone else in the room.

'Well,' he said finally, 'we are in active consultation with the banks and building societies, and have offered them our advice on branch security. We are also scheduling our routine patrols so that as far as possible all bank premises will be under constant observation.'

'That's very reassuring, sir,' Finney agreed. 'But have you considered stationing armed police officers inside banks?'

Proud spluttered, in spite of himself. 'We don't have the resources, man.'

36

'Well have you considered allowing the banks to employ their own armed guards?'

For once the Chief did not measure his response. 'Not for a second,' he barked. 'That would just add to the public danger. Anyway, it would be against the law.'

As he looked at Finney, his mind's eye saw him moving in for the kill; and he knew that his own honesty made him defenceless. 'In that case, Sir James,' the television reporter went on relentlessly, 'what you're telling us is that if armed men succeed in entering any bank, it, its staff and its customers will be completely vulnerable. Is that true? Yes or no, please.'

For Andy Martin it was too much. 'I'm sorry, Julian,' he said firmly, from the side of the room. 'The Chief can't get into a discussion with you or anyone else about the security arrangements within banks. But you can take it that anyone who stages an armed robbery in the future is in for a few very nasty surprises.'

'Fair enough,' Finney nodded, looked across at Martin then back at Proud.

'May I ask one final question, Sir James?'

The Chief nodded his silver head.

'Other than the man currently awaiting trial for his alleged part in the first robbery, do you have any clue to the identity of these men?'

All that Proud Jimmy wanted to do now was to clear the room, to escape from the sharp-toothed questioning. 'No, Julian,' he said, weariness in his voice. 'As of now, we do not.'

'Thank you. Sir,' replied Finney, sincerely, his sound-bite secured.

Before another hand could be raised, the Chief Constable rose and swept from the canteen, Martin, McGrigor and Royston following behind.

Proud led the way into the Station Inspector's empty office. As the door closed, he turned to face the Head of CID, his eyes blazing. McGrigor and Royston each glanced at the exit.

'That fucking wee ferret Finney!' he exploded. Inwardly, each of his three colleagues breathed a sigh of relief. 'Mr Nice, but all the time he's at your throat.' His expression softened. 'Thanks, Andy, for jumping in when you did.'

'I'm sorry about that, Chief, but I just felt I had to.'

'I know. Christ, all the time I sat there looking at him with tomorrow's headlines, *Police powerless to stop killers*, swimming before my eyes.' He paused. 'Mind you, I felt I had to give him a straight answer to his last question.'

The Chief Superintendent nodded. 'I agree. If you had come out with something even as innocuous as *"Following several lines of inquiry"*, you'd just have dug a hole for us.'

'Yes, that's what I thought. Anyway, that'll be my last press briefing for a while. They'll be down to you from now on.'

'Or to Bob.'

'That's for you to decide, between you,' said Proud Jimmy. 'By the way,' he added, after a pause, 'what did you mean when you said the gang would be in for "*a few very nasty surprises*" if they tried again?'

'Ah,' said Martin. 'That was a device that I use very occasionally with the press in a tight spot, if I think it's in everyone's best interests.' He smiled, grimly. 'Even though Alan here cringes when I do.

'It's called a lie.'

11

'D'you ever wish sometimes, Andy, that you'd settled for being an engineer, after you graduated?'

'Or you a lawyer?'

'Yes, I suppose so. Anyway, does the thought ever cross your mind?'

'Yes, it does, and it goes straight out the other side.'

There was a sigh, audible on the clear line. 'Same here. With our sort of polisman, it's for life, or for as long as your head lets you stand it. How are you feeling?'

'Okay, I suppose.'

'That's good, but don't go suppressing anything, son. There's no worse experience in the job than looking at the bodies of innocent bystanders, be they colleagues or civilians.'

'So I've learned.' He heard the faint echo of his own words, feeding back from the satellite. 'Whereabouts are you just now?' he asked.

'Pulled up in a service area near Macon. Jazz is asleep in his car seat, and Sarah's taken Mark to the cafeteria to pick up sandwiches. We're making good time. It's ten-forty-five here, so I reckon to make the Tunnel by seven a.m. Look for me at Fettes between four and five.'

'If you insist, but go easy. See you whenever.'

Andy Martin put the phone back in its cradle, and looked at Alex, sat on the sofa. 'How did he sound?' she asked.

'Angry. As you'd expect.'

'That's him all right. He's a funny mixture, you know. As a dad he was the calmest, quietest man you'd ever meet. I don't remember him ever shouting at me, even when I was being a right wee tick. Yet at work, he can be so volatile. He hates sloppiness, and avoidable mistakes. He hates crime, especially crime against people.'

'Don't I know it.' He slumped down beside her. 'I envy him, you know, in the way he can just let it all out. You say he's volatile, and there isn't a man in the force who would cross him, yet no-one's afraid of him. He can be ruthless with inefficient people, yet no-one resents him. He has the ability to tear strips off folk, even bust them out of CID, yet have them thank him at the end of the conversation.

'Everyone describes Bob as a great detective, which he is, probably the greatest of his time, yet what they don't realise is that he's a great manager too, of people.' He smiled. 'A rotten delegator, but a great manager.

'And part of the reason for it is that he cares, and he shows it. I wish . . .'

39

Alex put her hand lightly across his mouth. 'Shh. Don't wish for anything. Be content to be different. You're everything my dad is, only you show it in different ways. Where he's explosive, you're calm. Where he can be impulsive, you're always logical.'

She kissed him lightly on the cheek. 'Think of this, my love. I've inherited my dad's volatility gene, and no mistake. If you were like that too, how long would we last as a couple?'

'Maybe so, but that's not what I'm worried about.' His forehead ridged into a deep frown. 'I know I can't change my nature, and I'm concerned that through it, I'm becoming brutalised. I have to stay controlled because that's my way. Now Bob, he's seen terrible things . . . he's done terrible things . . . yet through it all, because his emotional make-up allows him to let it out, he remains essentially a very gentle man.

'Yet look at me. Tonight for example. I get home late, you have dinner ready, you talk about your day, I tell you about my frustration in not having any real leads to these robbers, and about the Chief's stumbling performance with the press, we put away the plates and that's it.'

'That's fair enough,' she murmured, taking his hand.

'But, Alex! Harry Riach's guts were all over the floor. I saw young Annie Brown at the hospital. Those shotgun pellets tore her to pieces. What sort of a guy am I becoming if I can look at things like that and still be calm, unflappable Andy? Why don't I cry for the victims?'

'What do you think you're doing now?' she asked him, very gently. 'You have a very strong mind, my love. You should be grateful that it lets you deal with things like you saw today in that way. It helps you be good at your job and there's nothing wrong with that. If I can help you, by being your listening ear, and letting you unwind, that can only be good too. I'm not afraid of the details. I've seen things too, remember.' She paused, and shivered, momentarily.

'D'you know what Sarah told me about Pops?' she continued. 'Every time he goes to a murder scene these days, he has to make a conscious effort not to chuck his breakfast, and not to let the troops see any sign of weakness. He copes by being volatile, you cope by being controlled. You're different men, neither of you any the worse for it.'

He squeezed her hand. 'Thanks, love. You're a wise wee soul, aren't you. I'll let you be my sounding board from now on. But still, don't underestimate the effect of this bloody job. When you do it as your dad and I do, it can create a monster inside. We need Sarah and you, to help keep it at bay.'

40

12

Brian Mackie closed the door of his office and sat behind his desk, looking out on to the early-morning Haddington traffic. He took a small address book from his desk and opened it at the letter S, then picked up his telephone and dialled a number.

'DCI Afhtab speaking.' The voice at the other end had a strange mixture of accents; it was strongly Glaswegian, but with Asian lurking underneath.

'Morning Salim, Brian Mackie here, from Haddington.'

'Ah Brian,' said Afhtab cheerily. 'No' Edinburgh any more then?'

'Not any more. I've been promoted out of Special Branch just like you.'

'Superintendent it'll be, then. Congratulations. What can Ah do for you?'

'I want to consult the Criminal Intelligence Unit you're running now. Can you give me some assistance?'

'Of course I can. I'll deal wi' it myself; I need to practise using the technology. Who's the target?'

Mackie paused, as if to restrain Afhtab's eagerness. 'The name is Bernard Grimley. He used to own a pub on the South Side of the Clyde, before he sold up and bought a place through here. I've asked my lads, but he's not known to them.'

'I'll check. What's he lined up for?'

'I can't say, Salim. It's sort of unofficial, like in the old days. In fact I'd be grateful if you didn't keep a record.'

The Chief Inspector laughed. 'Ah don't know. Special Branch habits die hard, right enough. You got a secure fax there?'

'Yes. Right in this office.' Mackie turned and read the number from a machine on a small table behind him.'

'Okay. Leave it with me. I'll ask the Oracle and send you a report . . . one way or the other.'

'Thanks, mate. I'm due you one.'

'Guinness'll be fine.'

Mackie put down the phone and went back to the reports in his in-tray. He worked his way through them in half an hour, then made a call to confirm a lunch appointment with the Area Manager of the Bank of Scotland. Just as he agreed the time, the fax behind him rang and a connection was made.

He watched until the machine had finished excreting a single sheet of paper, picked it up, and read it through. He was smiling thinly to himself as he dialled the Head of CID's direct-line number.

'Martin.' The Chief Superintendent's voice sounded tired, Mackie thought.

'Andy, it's Brian. About that other matter you asked me to look into yesterday. There's nothing known locally, but I've had some feedback from Strathclyde. It's not going to help Alex, I'm afraid.'

There was a sigh. 'Ach well. Give me it anyway.'

'Grimley is known to our colleagues, right enough. He ran a pub called the Fireman's Lift, in Jeffrey Street. It was a right thieves' kitchen, and was known to be a contact place for Loyalist paramilitaries over from Northern Ireland on fund-raising trips.

'Both Special Branch and CID had the place under constant observation, and this resulted in a number of arrests. They also picked up several leads which led the security forces to Loyalist arms dumps in and around Belfast.

'The single link in all these successes was Bernard Grimley. For most of the time he owned that pub, he was a police informer, until he stopped co-operating around three years ago.

'Our colleagues reckoned that he'd lost his bottle. When he sold the place it was on their advice. They were scared that sooner or later someone in Ireland, or Glasgow for that matter, would put two and two together and come up with the right answer.'

'Ahh,' Martin growled. 'That cracks it for Alex's case, I fear. I have a feeling that Mr Grimley's going to end up quite a bit richer.'

'Unless you tip off the UVF,' said Mackie, dryly.

13

Most prisons in Scotland are grim-faced places, with a tendency to cast a blight on their surroundings. During his career, Andy Martin had visited Glasgow's massive, forbidding Barlinnie, the grey-walled institution which embarrasses Perth, and the top-security establishment at Peterhead.

Compared to those three Victorian citadels, he found Edinburgh's Saughton less intrusive upon the city, in its discreet location, tucked away on the outskirts. Yet it was a prison nonetheless, a place of incarceration, and the policeman experienced a feeling of despair every time he walked through its doors.

In his eyes, every man there marked a success for his force, but a failure for humanity.

He announced himself at the gate-house, showing his warrant card to the guards, and was escorted through a succession of corridors to the interview room set aside for his meeting.

It smelled of stale sweat and cigarettes. As he waited alone, shouts from the exercise yard outside drifted through the barred window. Eventually, after around five minutes, the door swung open and the tall red-haired figure of Nathan Bennett shuffled into the room, ahead of two prison officers, each one bigger than him.

'Thanks, lads,' said Martin. 'Would you stand guard outside, please. I want to talk to Mr Bennett in private.'

One of the warders eyed him doubtfully. 'Ah'm no sure about that, sir.'

'Don't you worry about me. Mr Bennett says he's an innocent man. In that case, he's hardly going to take a swing at me, is he?' He smiled evenly at the prisoner. 'Unless he fancies a transfer to the hospital wing, that is.

'On you go now. I'll give you a shout when we're finished.'

The two uniformed officers looked at each other. The doubter was unpersuaded. 'Ah'll still need to ask the Principal Officer about that, sir.'

Martin gave up. 'Okay,' he agreed. 'Stand over in the corner there, and chat to each other. Just don't be ear-holing me.'

As the men obeyed, Martin turned to Bennett, motioning to the red-haired man to sit at the small square table in the centre of the room, and taking a seat opposite. For a while, they gazed at each other, the policeman smiling lightly, the prisoner glowering, nervous and unsure.

The former broke the silence. 'We haven't met before. I won't say that it's a pleasure, but it's fascinating, all the same. It's not often that I'm privileged to be in the company of a genuine, fully-qualified idiot.'

43

For a second there was a spark of reaction in the dull lifeless eyes, before the head dropped. 'What d'you mean?'

'I've been reading the transcript of your trial. If you think that any jury's going to fall for that, you have to be daft as a brush. We both know that you're as guilty as sin, so let's cut the crap.'

'Ah never done it,' Bennett protested. 'It's mistaken identity. Ah wis at home in bed at the time. I'd been to the bank in the mornin'. That must have been when I dropped my card.'

The detective shook his head. 'Fuck me,' he sighed. 'This gets better. I'm dealing with the Invisible Man now. That must be a hell of an advantage for a bank robber. Nathan, we didn't get to that bit of the prosecution case before the judge popped his clogs, but we've looked at the tapes of the bank's customers that day, and the day before. You don't appear in any of them.'

'The camera must have been faulty, then.'

'Not till you sprayed paint on it. We've got a great shot of that, incidentally. You shouldn't have used your left hand, not with those fingers missing.' He nodded towards the table, where the man's hands rested, the third and fourth fingers of the left severed at the knuckle.

'How did you lose them?' he asked casually.

'In the Falklands. Fuckin' Argies shot them off.' Bennett was animated for the first time. 'We fuckin' sorted them though. Ah got five for each finger.' He held up his right hand with its full complement.

'How many had their hands up?'

As Bennett flushed and his gaze dropped once more, the detective wondered whether his aside had hit the mark.

'Got any fags?' the prisoner asked.

'That the tradition, is it? I chuck you twenty Bensons and you talk to me. Forget it, pal. I don't smoke, and I don't hand out presents to the likes of you. I'm here to give you life, Mr Bennett, that's all.' The red-haired man shot a look at him, suspicion in his dull eyes.

'There's two ways that can work,' Martin went on. 'One way I give you back your life. For that to happen, you turn Crown evidence, you name the other guys on the robbery, and you give us the man in charge, the guy who did the planning.

'We'll deal with you separately, let you enter a guilty plea, and advise the judge that you co-operated willingly. You'll do some time, of course. I guess you'll get five years, but I can fix it with the Parole Board so that you only do half of that.

'That's the best offer you're ever going to get. In fact, some of my team would be really pissed off if they knew I was making it. How does it strike you?'

Bennett gazed at him across the table, but said nothing.

'Okay,' said the Head of CID, 'this is the other way. Did you hear what happened in Galashiels yesterday?'

Slowly, hesitantly, the prisoner nodded.

'Right, so you know that your gang shot and killed two people. I was there, Bennett. I saw them both; the man with his insides on the carpet, the girl with the top half of her body in ribbons. You never came across worse than that in the Falklands, pal, I promise you.'

'Nothin' tae do with me,' the man said, hoarsely.

'Oh yes it has, Bennett. We know that your team did it. The method was just the same, and they used the same weapons; different masks, that's all. Two of the witness descriptions match the two guys who were with you in Dalkeith. You might be in here, but you're still part of it.

'This is how it's going to work. At your retrial, we both know that it will take the jury about ten minutes to convict. Even with the best brief in the world . . . whom you don't have, by the way . . . you haven't a fucking chance. You never had.

'But this time,' Martin continued, 'things will be different. I'm going to give evidence, and I'm going to tell the judge that you are part of a conspiracy which has led to a string of well-planned robberies, with murder involved. I'm going to tell him that your total haul is upwards of two million. Finally, I'm going to tell him that this is the most brutal and ruthless gang that I've ever seen in my police career, and that you were an active member.

'In short, I'm going to tell the judge that he should give you twenty years. And that's exactly what he'll do. You won't do it in this cushy nick, though. You'll be in Peterhead A Hall, freezing your balls off in the winter and roasting alive in the summer. You've got a sister, haven't you? How often d'you think she'll be bothered to travel all that way up there to see you? Oh yes, and if you're still thinking about parole, forget that. I can also fix it with the Board that you don't get any.'

He paused, to let his threat sink in. 'How old are you, Nathan? Thirty-seven, isn't it. Fifty-seven by the time you get out. Think of it! Boiled potatoes, cabbage and chewy beef for your next twenty Christmas dinners.

'That's your choice, my friend. Your life back, or your life taken away. No bullshit, that is it. Now . . .'

Bennett sat, head bowed, shaking slightly from side to side, hands clenching and unclenching on the table. His mouth worked as he gnawed his lip. When at last he looked up his eyes were glistening.

'You're wrong,' he muttered, plaintively. 'Ah dinna have a choice. I'm pleading Not Guilty.'

'You really are that afraid?' asked the detective, shocked beneath his calm exterior.

He nodded his red head. 'Its no' just me,' he said.

'Who is it then?' the detective shot back. But the prisoner fell silent once more.

'I won't be back with this deal,' he warned. Bennett looked back at him helplessly, his expression wavering.

'I'll tell you what,' sighed Martin. 'I'll give you the weekend to think it

45

over. I'll come back to see you on Monday morning.' He turned to the two officers in the corner. 'Guards, you can have him back.'

14

There was nothing grand about the office of the Head of CID. It was on the same level as the Command Corridor, but smaller and less well furnished than the Chief Officers' accommodation.

Nonetheless, DCS Andy Martin appreciated its location, beyond a general office where his assistants sat, allowing them to act as a barrier and to filter visitors, deflecting casual callers whenever their chief wished to be left alone.

No-one deflected Bob Skinner. He marched into the suite, just after four-thirty, and headed straight for Martin's door with a nod and a smile to Sammy Pye. He was dressed in light cotton jeans and a polo shirt, and a dark shadow showed on his chin.

'How are we doing, then, Andy?' he asked as he stepped into the room.

'No result, if that's what you mean,' the younger man answered tersely. 'These people are efficient as well as ruthless.

'We traced the grey Escort to a car park on the outskirts of Gala. The owner's a Mrs Mason. She works in a shop round the corner, and she says she leaves it there every day. As far as I can gather, they drove another vehicle into the park, stole the Escort to do the job, then just came back and swapped back to their own car.'

'Or cars,' said the DCC, 'unless you know for sure that they all travelled together. It would have been more secure to disperse separately.'

'That's true. I've no way of telling though. The car park is surfaced, and John McGrigor tells me there were no tyre marks.'

'How's big John holding up?'

'He's okay. He was very cut up yesterday, but he's a good professional. He's being very efficient, just as you'd expect.'

'How did we trace the car?'

'Mrs Mason was stopped on her way home. She didn't have a clue that her car had been used, and nor would we have, but one of the traffic lads who pulled her up noticed blood on one of the back seats. Harry Riach's blood as it turned out. He was the civilian victim.'

'I know, I had a look at the *Scotsman* before I came in.' Skinner paused. I didn't take to the headline much. '*Gang terrorises Scottish banks. No leads, police confess.*' Why the hell did you let Jimmy take the press conference?'

'He insisted. See that silver braid on his uniform? It means he's Chief Constable. He said it was down to him and him alone. Afterwards,

I think he'd like to have torn Julian Finney's heart out.'

'I've felt like that, too. Maybe I will some day.'

The tall, tanned DCC poured himself a mug of coffee from Martin's filter, adding a touch of milk. 'Have Arthur Dorward's team finished with the car?'

'Yes,' Martin replied. 'They found nothing, except Mrs Mason's fag-ends and Riach's blood. The witnesses said that the guy who shot him was drenched in it: as you'd expect after a contact wound with a sawn-off.'

Skinner shuddered.

'What do we have then?' he asked. 'Anything at all?'

'One very fine straw to clutch. I went to see Nathan Bennett today, the guy we've got banged up for the first robbery. I put the fear of God in him, to try to get him to turn Crown evidence. Somebody's beaten me to it though. As Brian Mackie thought, he's been told to plead guilty, or else.

'But something he said made me think that the threat might not be against him alone. He has an unmarried sister, name of Hannah, out in Bonnyrigg. I've checked with Saughton, and she's the only visitor he's had all the time he's been in custody. I reckon someone's been to see her, to give Nathan his orders, and I suspect that she's in the firing line should Bennett break ranks.'

'You going to see her?'

'First thing tomorrow, I thought. Maybe around eight o'clock. Catch her early, shake her up a bit.'

'Good idea. I think I'll come too.'

'Fine. I'll pick you up at seven-thirty.'

Skinner nodded. 'I'll be ready.' He hesitated. 'No, why don't you and Alex come to Gullane for supper tonight? We're having a Thai takeaway. You can stay over, and we'll leave from there.'

15

'Why have we never eaten at the Thai place before, Andy,' Alex burst out enthusiastically. 'If the takeaway's this good, it must be even better on the premises.'

'Probably because I've been too embarrassed about the ordering part of it. There isn't a single name on that menu . . . other than Pard and Prik . . . that I can get near pronouncing.'

'You are not alone, my friend,' said Bob. 'Every time we go there, we order by numbers.'

It was almost nine p.m., but the evening was warm and they were able to eat outside in comfort, on the terrace of Bob and Sarah's new bungalow in Gullane, into which they had moved two days before leaving for their Spanish holiday.

They had bought the house as part of their 'fresh start' agreement, and sold their Edinburgh home and Bob's old cottage on Goose Green, a quarter of a mile away, the latter for a price which had astonished them both. The bungalow was spacious, newly built on a plot which had once been part of the garden of a stone mansion on Gullane Hill. It had four bedrooms, a massive living and dining area and a conservatory. There was also a study for Sarah who had decided to fulfil a long-held ambition by becoming a consultant forensic pathologist, alongside freelance scene-of-incident work for the police.

The terrace and garden looked out across the Firth of Forth, to the Lomond Hills of Fife, and to the rosy sunset in the west which bathed the four as they finished their meal.

'This is really beautiful,' said Alex. 'When I was a kid, I had this private dream that one day my dad would buy a house looking on to the sea, so that I could just run on to the beach. You're going to have a great life out here, both of you. Especially now you'll be working from home, Sarah.'

Her step-mother grinned, running long fingers through her auburn hair. 'Yeah, that's a bonus. I have to take an examination here to top up my US qualifications, but I can start practice as an assistant now. I've had my first commission, in fact.'

Bob's eyebrows rose in surprise. 'You never told me.'

'I haven't had an opportunity,' his wife said. 'I checked my e-mail after you left. There was a message from Professor Hutchison, asking if I can assist tomorrow morning at an autopsy he's performing in Edinburgh.'

'It's as well you told me now. Andy and I are off on a visit tomorrow morning.'

Alex raised a hand. 'No problem,' she said. 'I'll baby-sit. It'll give Mark and me a chance to get acquainted.'

'How's Mark settling in?' asked Andy, as he forked up the last of his fish in red curry sauce.

'Very well,' Sarah replied. 'He's a remarkable little boy, and he thinks Jazz is just great. He loves having a baby brother.'

'It must be a very difficult job for you two, nonetheless, integrating him into a new family.'

'No, Andy, I'd describe it as a very responsible job. We have to make him feel as loved and secure as he's always been, and I like to believe that we're succeeding in that. At the same time we have to remember what he's been through. He still has times when he withdraws into his grief. The temptation is to throw treats at him to jolly him out of them, yet that's just what we mustn't do. He has to work all that out for himself, if he's to grow into a well-adjusted, happy young man.'

'But won't it be difficult,' Alex cut in, 'when he's old enough really to understand what happened to his father and mother? Couldn't he have big psychological problems when that happens?'

Sarah nodded. 'Yes, he could. So, as part of his upbringing, we'll make sure that he remembers them, that he's under no illusions about their death, but that he comes to see himself as their embodiment. We aim to encourage him to live his life positively, in their memory.'

'That's right,' said Bob, with a grin. 'No more negative thinking in this house. Don't you give up on that case you were moaning about earlier, daughter. You're not beaten till all the evidence has been weighed.'

'Hah! You haven't seen the judge, Pops. Grimley's evidence ended this afternoon, two days late. Yet Lord Coalville told us that he isn't going to extend the time he's allocated to the hearing. We have to complete by close of play on Wednesday. The dice are loaded, I tell you. Positive thinking for us is that the award might be under three million.'

'Come on, girl, that's no attitude to take into battle.'

'Oh no? Well, you ask your Head of CID just how confident he is about tracing this bank gang. His face has been tripping him all week.'

'In the circumstances,' Alex's father said gently, 'I think that's understandable. When did you ever see me smile about armed robbery and murder? It doesn't mean that we don't go after the bastards with complete determination, and the certainty that we're going to get them.'

'It took you long enough to get Jackie Charles,' she retorted, unsmiling.

'Aye, but we got him. What you should remember about Jackie, though, is that no-one was ever killed on any of the jobs he was suspected of bank-rolling. I'm not condoning him . . . God, you know how much I detest the little shit . . . but he wasn't a killer.

'The people we're up against now, they are. Ruthless, cold-blooded killers, as they showed yesterday. Whoever's running the operation . . . and

50

I agree with your thinking, Andy, that there's someone behind all this who hasn't been seen on any of the raids . . . he's the most ruthless of them all.

'But we know we'll get them, my friend, don't we?'

Martin looked at him, solemnly. 'Sure we do, Bob. No ifs or buts. I just wish to Christ I knew when. Every day they're at liberty, the public, and our people, are at risk.'

'Yeah, mate, I know. Still, we've got one lead at least. Let's hope that Miss Hannah Bennett has the guts to point us in the direction of whoever it is has her brother so scared that he's prepared to spend the next twenty years inside.'

16

'You know, Chief Superintendent,' said Skinner lazily, looking along the ordered street, 'the folk who believe that biggest is always best should be taken round places like Craigmillar and Pilton then brought here.

'For it seems to me that in housing terms, the opposite is always true. When I was a wee boy, I remember big council housing estates going up in my home town, that were half demolished before I was forty.

'Even back in the sixties, any copper could have told the planners about the link between monolithic housing, crime and social deprivation, yet they still went on building huge, unmanageable urban concentration camps.

'Not like this though.'

Behind the wheel of his Mondeo, Martin grunted agreement. 'Not a bit. These houses must be sixty years old, yet look at them.' Before them, the rows of semi-detached Snowcem-clad villas of Garston Avenue stretched in a gentle curve, each set in a garden, the size of which would have made a contemporary speculative builder salivate as he pictured the number of houses it could accommodate. They were uniform in design, yet no longer in finish, as the varied designs of replacement doors and windows showed which of the former municipal houses were now in occupier-ownership.

Cars stood in most of the driveways, and more were parked down one side of the narrow street.

'What's Hannah Bennett's number?' Skinner asked.

'Seventeen.'

'Let's walk up, then.'

They left the Mondeo parked at the entrance to the avenue and strolled casually along the pavement, counting off the numbers as they walked. The morning sun was risen and they felt its warmth on their faces, yet it was still only four minutes past eight a.m., and on a Saturday morning there was no-one else to be seen.

'This is it,' said Martin, pointing to the next house on their right. 'Seventeen.'

There were two cars in the driveway, one a Ford Sierra Cosworth, the other a Vauxhall Corsa which, from its registration number, was less than two years old. 'Decent motors,' the DCC commented. 'What do they do, Bennett and his sister?'

'She works for the council, on the admin. side of the social work department. Before he was nicked, Nathan was a civil servant.'

'Eh?'

'No kidding. He was an EO or something, in the new Scottish Office building down in Leith Docks. He was taken on after he left the army.' He was amused by Skinner's surprise. 'I agree; not the usual background for a bank robber. His job drives yet another nail in the coffin of his defence. He was on flexi-time; the silly bugger clocked out two hours before the robbery.'

The detectives stopped at the foot of the sloping driveway of number seventeen. The lawn in front of the house was immaculately groomed, and the flower-beds around it were neatly weeded, with a mixture of bedding plants in flower.

Skinner looked up at the house. 'No curtains pulled. She must be up, unless her bedroom's at the back. Let's go.'

They walked up the path, dressed in casual clothing, Skinner in slacks and open-necked shirt, Martin in his trademark jeans and leather bomber jacket. A single wide concrete step was set before the white, glass-panelled front door. The DCS stepped up and rang the brass-studded bell, hearing it sound clearly inside the house.

They waited on the step, looking for signs of movement behind the glass, listening for sounds. Eventually, impatiently, Skinner reached out and pressed the bell once more; but still they stood, with only birdsong to break the silence.

'Don't tell me she's gone out already,' the DCC growled.

'The two cars are still here,' Martin pointed out. 'Maybe she's got a bidey-in we didn't know about, and they're upstairs ignoring the bell.'

'Could be. It's only daft bastards like us that are up at this time on a Saturday. Come on, let's go round and give the back door a thump.'

He led the way past the black Sierra, past the garage, and through a tall latched gate, both of them wooden and brown-stained. The gate was warped and the policeman had to push hard to force it open. The garden to the rear was as neat as that to the front. Four green-painted clothes poles stood on the rear lawn, linked by a rope which formed a perfect square. Beyond, a cultivated area was planted with a mixture of vegetables, while behind the garage stood tall rows of raspberry bushes. On all three sides, the boundaries were marked by high fir trees, planted close together, thicker than any hedge, giving the area almost total seclusion.

'Must be the sister who's the gardener,' said the Head of CID, 'Nathan having been in the slammer for three months.'

'Looks like she's asleep on the job, then.' Skinner's voice was flat and cold. His companion felt a chill grip his stomach. 'There.'

Martin followed his pointing finger. In the dark shadows between two of the lines of raspberry bushes, he could see something white. For once his contact lenses failed him, and he had to step closer, on to the lawn, before he could see that it was a left foot, encased in a lady's white slip-on shoe. The right foot beside it was bare, and muddy.

'Oh no,' he whispered, as Skinner stepped alongside him.

'No wonder she didn't hear the bell, Andy.'

Together they approached, until they were looking down the alley between the rows of bushes.

The woman lay face-down in the earth. She was wearing black slacks, and a white sleeveless cotton top. It was difficult to be sure, but they guessed by her long legs that Hannah Bennett must have been tall, like her brother. Her hair was as vividly red as his, but it was red also with blood.

Martin stepped past the body, forcing the bushes aside as he did, and knelt down by her head. 'She's been stabbed,' he said, in an even voice. 'With great force; it looks like a broad-bladed kitchen knife. It's buried in the side of her head, almost up to the hilt.'

In spite of himself, the DCC felt his stomach heave. He fought it as always, by concentrating on what had to be done, and took his hand-phone from the pocket of his shirt. 'Better get Brian Mackie up here,' he muttered.

'Brian's away for the weekend, with his girl-friend,' his colleague told him. 'Try calling Rose instead.'

Skinner nodded and punched in the home number of his former personal assistant; it was filed in his memory.

'Hello.' The call was answered after four rings, by a gruff male voice.

'Morning, Mario, it's the DCC here. It's Maggie I need.'

'Ah, morning, Boss. Just when we were looking forward to a lie-in. Hold on.' There was a pause as Inspector Mario McGuire passed the handset to his wife.

'Yes, sir.' It occurred to Skinner that he could remember only one occasion on which he had known DCI Margaret Rose to look or sound remotely flustered.

'I'm sorry, Mags, but DCS Martin and I have come across a problem in your area. I need a team up here on the double, and everything needed to set up a murder inquiry. You call out your duty people, and I'll alert an ME and the scene-of-crime team. The address is Number Seventeen, Garston Avenue, Bonnyrigg. There's one victim, female, believed to be Miss Hannah Bennett.'

'Bennett?' Rose's voice was suddenly sharp.

'Yes. Nathan's sister. Let's not jump to conclusions, though. It may be completely unconnected with her brother, but then again . . . Just get up here as fast as you can. There's a street full of sleeping neighbours waiting to be knocked up and interviewed.'

He ended the call, then keyed in his own number. Sarah picked up the phone almost at once. 'You still in bed?' he asked.

'No. I'm just out of the shower. I'm standing here stark-naked, if you want to know.'

'That's very nice, but tell me; what time are you due at your autopsy?'

'Eleven-thirty.'

'That's good. In that case, I want you to chuck on some clothes and get here on the double. I've got a job for you before you see Prof. Hutchison.' He gave her the address, then called headquarters, and left orders to be passed on to Detective Inspector Arthur Dorward, head of the scene-of-crime team. By the time he replaced the phone in his pocket, Martin was standing beside him once more.

'That's Hannah Bennett all right,' he said. 'Facially, she looks very like her brother.'

'What?' growled Skinner. 'Does he have a big fucking knife sticking out of his head too?'

17

The interior of Hannah Bennett's home was as neatly ordered as her garden. Skinner, Martin, Sarah and Inspector Arthur Dorward sat in her tidy living room while a stream of uniformed police officers and detectives came and went from the mobile headquarters caravan which had been set up in the avenue, on the grass verge which ran between pavement and road.

It was nine-fifty: the avenue was wide-awake now. Small groups of residents stood together in the roadway, others alone in their gardens, staring in shocked wonder at the scene.

'What's happening in there?' Sarah asked, pointing at the vehicle.

'Maggie's co-ordinating the interviewing of all the neighbours,' her husband replied, 'now that you've given us a time of death to work on.'

'Estimated,' she cautioned. 'I won't be able to go firm on that until we can get the body back to the morgue.'

'I trust you. Between ten p.m. and midnight last night is good enough for me. Can you tell us anything else that might help us?'

She shrugged. 'I don't know how much help it'll be, but I think that the woman was hiding from her attacker, and that she was killed where he found her. There was mud on the palms of her hands, and her slacks were dirty from the knees down, as if she was kneeling in the bushes.

'I couldn't see any marks on her body, save one, a big bruise round the back of her neck. It looks as if it could have been made by a hand, a strong hand, grabbing her there and hauling her to her feet.

'There were no wounds at all, other than the one which killed her. My thought is that something happened in the house, that Miss Bennett evaded her attacker at first, and that she ran out into the back garden. He followed her . . . very definitely a man, from the size of the hand-print on her neck, and the force of the blow . . . found her hiding place, picked her up and hit her with the knife, just once.

'Death would have been instantaneous, given that size of cerebral shock.'

She looked at Skinner, then Martin. 'There's one thing I find strange, though.'

'What's that?' asked the Head of CID.

'Why did she hide in the garden? Why didn't she run out into the street, where it would have been safer?'

'Because the back gate was jammed. It would have taken her too long to force it open.'

'I see.'

Martin nodded. 'Poor woman had nowhere to run to. She was pretty well alone here too. Number Fifteen and his wife were in the pub till one o'clock, and Number Nineteen, through the wall, is on holiday.' He turned to Dorward, who was still wearing his white scene-of-crime tunic.

'Do you agree with Sarah?' he asked.

The Inspector nodded. 'Everything inside matches that theory. There were broken dishes in the kitchen when we went in, and there was a rolling pin lying on the floor. I wondered if she hit him with that before she ran outside. The back door was unlocked too, in support of Doctor Skinner's proposition.'

'Did you find any prints on the knife hilt?'

'No, although it wasn't easy to dust since the doctor wouldn't let us remove the weapon from the skull.'

'That must be done under autopsy conditions,' Sarah explained.

'Fair enough. Did you find any signs of forced entry, Arthur?'

'None at all, sir. I'd say that the victim let her attacker into the house.'

'Couldn't he have come through the back gate and in the back door?' asked Skinner.

Dorward frowned. 'Looking at the gate, I'd say it's only been opened once in quite some time, and that was when you came through it this morning.'

'Could he have come over the top?'

'That's possible, sir, but unlikely I'd say. The thing is two metres high. An agile bloke could scramble over it, but the wood is soft, and he'd be bound to leave a mark. You did, just shouldering it open, but other than that, it's clean.

'The way it looks to me, he rang the bell and she let him in.'

'Did she have a boy-friend?' asked Sarah.

'We don't know for sure,' Martin replied. 'But it was her birthday recently, and the cards are still on show. Apart from one from Nathan, none of them is from a single bloke. There are no give-aways in the bedroom either. No Y-fronts in her chest of drawers, no men's clothes in her wardrobes, no condoms or pill packets in the bedside cabinets.

'We're asking the neighbours, of course, but so far there's no indication that this could have been a lover's tiff. All of which takes us back to the possibility of a link to her brother, and the team that he was mixed up with.'

Skinner stood up. 'Right,' he boomed. 'And that's where we'd better go now . . . off to see him. When he finds out that his sister's dead, and we can persuade him that one of his associates killed her, maybe he'll be mad enough to give them up.

'If not,' he added, with a meaningful glance at Martin, 'then you and I will keep him sweating in an interview room until he does, however long that takes. You couldn't scare him enough, and neither could Mackie. If necessary, it'll be my shot next.'

He stood up. 'Sarah, love, you'd better be off to your post-mortem.' He jerked a thumb in the direction of the back garden. 'When you get there, see if you can persuade Joe Hutchison to hang on to do another.

'Arthur, you and your team take all the time you need to find any traces that this man may have left behind. DCS Martin and I are off to rattle Mr Bennett's cage.'

The two detectives and Sarah had reached the front door when Skinner's phone rang. He answered it, with an impatient frown. 'Yes?' he answered, pausing as the caller identified himself.

'What is it, Dan?' he asked. 'We're in a hurry to be somewhere.'

As Sarah watched, she imagined that she saw her husband's face go chalk-white beneath the tan. 'Jesus,' he whispered, as Detective Superintendent Pringle finished his urgent message.

'Do we know how?'

His companions looked at him as he listened to the reply, and saw the effect of the news, as the surprise left his eyes, to be replaced by cold fury.

'Okay,' he snapped at last. 'Tell the Governor that DCS Martin and I are on our way.'

He ended the call, and stared at the wall, the phone still held loosely in his hand.

'What is it, Bob?' Sarah asked him anxiously.

'A thoroughly bad day for the Bennett family: that's what it is.'

18

A garishly decorated traffic car stood at the entrance to Saughton Prison as Martin drove up the approach road. One of the two uniformed officers who stood beside it stepped forward, holding up a hand, but stopped as soon as he recognised the occupants, and waved them through the outer gates, which, unusually, lay open.

Skinner identified himself tersely to the prison officer who waited inside, showing the warrant card which hung on a chain round his neck.

'Very good, sir,' the man replied. Despite the growing heat of the day, he still wore his heavy blue tunic, rather than shirt-sleeves. 'You're expected. If you'll drive through the inner gate and park in the reserved space by the main office block, I'll let the Governor's secretary know you're here. The offices are round the first corner then first on the right. I'll send someone with you, if you'd like.'

Skinner shook his head. 'Thanks, but that's okay, I've been here before.'

The great steel inner gate slid open, and Martin drove through, taking the turns which the officer had described. The parking space which had been kept for them was beside the door of the administration block, in which Detective Superintendent Dan Pringle stood waiting. As always he wore his bleary-eyed look, the usual signal of a late night.

'Morning, sir,' he said, as Skinner stepped from the car.

'Hello, Dan. What was it last night then?'

'Masonic dinner dance, sir. We got home at two.'

'That sounds pretty quiet for the masons,' Skinner grunted. 'Where's the Governor, then?'

'In his office. Big Neil's with him, trying to keep him calm.'

'McIlhenney?'

'Yes. I called him out. I thought you might want him here, and he agreed.'

The DCC laughed out loud. 'Too fucking right he did. Big McIlhenney would go dookin' for turds at Seafield to get out of going to Sainsbury's with Olive.'

The grin left his face as quickly as it had appeared. 'The Governor's shaky, is he?'

Pringle nodded. 'And then some. He's taking it personally.'

Martin shrugged his shoulders as he locked the car. 'So he should, on the face of it. Let's go see him.'

Pringle led the way into the office, his business suit contrasting with the casual dress of the senior officers. The Governor's room was on the first floor, looking out on to the roadway. It was accessed through an outer office, through which Pringle marched, with the briefest of nods to the officer who was seated there.

Ian Whiterose, the Governor of Saughton Prison, was seated behind his desk as Skinner and Martin entered, his hands clenched together, twisted, wringing. He was in his mid forties, bespectacled, with dark, untidy hair, and wearing a creased grey suit. As he looked up at the policemen his jaw was clenched.

'Good morning, Governor,' said Skinner extending his hand as the man stood up. Whiterose shook it, limply.

'Good morning, Mr Skinner, Mr Martin. I can't tell you how sorry I am that you've had to be called here. It's appalling. I know that things like this aren't unprecedented in prisons, but it's never happened to me before.' The man's voice rose as he spoke, accentuating his tension and distress.

'Sit down, sit down,' the DCC insisted, putting a hand gently on the man's shoulder and pressing him back into his chair. He looked round at his assistant, who stood impassively beside the desk. 'Sergeant, if you've been here more than two minutes, you'll have sorted out the coffee. See if you can find some for Mr Whiterose and us.' McIlhenney threw him a dubious look, but said nothing as he withdrew to the outer office.

'Okay, Governor,' Skinner began as he took a seat facing the man across his desk. 'First things first. What's the state of the prison as of now? Where are the inmates?'

'Locked up,' answered Whiterose. 'Every one of them. My staff are conducting a detailed search of every cell.'

'Oh? Well, stop them at once, please.'

The Governor's eyes widened and his eyebrows rose. 'Why?'

'Because that search must be conducted by the police.'

'Why?'

'Do I have to spell it out? If this thing was planned, we can't rule out the possibility that one of your officers might have been involved. If that was the case, you could be helping them recover and conceal evidence.'

'You don't believe that, surely?'

'I don't believe anything yet, but I don't discount anything. Now issue the order, please. Get your men out of those cells.' Whiterose nodded, picked up the telephone, pressed a button and spoke to the man in the outer office, just as McIlhenney returned with a tray of coffee. Skinner took a mug, sipped from it, and knew at once why the sergeant had given him the doubtful look. It was the sort of brew that went straight to the heart. '*No wonder he's shaky, drinking that stuff,*' he thought as he looked across the desk.

'Tell us, then, Governor, what happened.'

'It's all very confused,' the man began, sounding apologetic. 'We exercised the remand prisoners at nine-thirty as usual, separately from the convicted men. We give them an hour.'

'How many do you have on remand?' asked Martin.

60

'Sixty-seven.' Whiterose paused, then continued.

'No-one seems actually to have seen what happened. Some of the men were circling the yard, some were standing smoking, others had a game of football going on. Bennett was with a group walking the yard, when all of a sudden he went down.'

'None of your officers saw him fall?' Skinner queried.

'No. I had eight of them on supervision, but most seem to have been watching the football.'

'Did any of them hear anything?'

'No, but it was very noisy in the yard, with the game going on.'

The detective nodded. 'I appreciate that. How did the men nearest to Bennett react, when he hit the ground?'

'As it was described to me, they backed off and stood in a circle, looking down at him.'

'And what did your officers do, once they'd torn themselves away from the football?'

Whiterose hesitated. 'Well, as it was told to me, when it became clear that Bennett wasn't going to get up, the senior officer in charge approached him. Carefully, you appreciate, just in case it was some sort of a ruse. The man was lying on his side, motionless, with his head bent and his face almost touching the ground. The officer spoke to him without response. Eventually, he bent over him and shook him. It was then that he noticed the blood running down his temple, and realised that he was badly hurt.'

Skinner nodded. 'That's clear up to now. What did he do next?'

'He cleared the exercise yard. All the men were escorted back to their cells. Then he sent for the MO.'

'Were any of the prisoners searched before they left the yard?'

'No.'

'When you said the MO, I take it you meant the prison doctor.'

'That's right. He was on site, so he was there in only a couple of minutes. He took one look at Bennett and said that he'd been shot.'

'Was any search made of the yard before my people arrived?'

'Yes, by the escorting officers when they returned. Nothing unusual was found.'

The DCC leaned back and stared at the dirty ceiling. 'How easy would it be to hide a gun in this prison?' he asked.

Whiterose sighed. 'Mr Skinner, in my experience, the inmates could hide almost anything in a prison.'

Piercing blue eyes swept down from the ceiling and fixed him suddenly across the desk. 'What a pity, in that case, that your officer cleared the yard. If he'd kept the men contained there until he'd found out what had happened to Bennett, they could all have been searched on the spot, with no possibility of concealing a weapon.'

The Governor nodded. 'I suppose you're right.'

'There's no fucking suppose about it. Still, it's happened, and it's your problem. What it means is that my people will have to tear your jail apart looking for a gun. However disruptive that might be, you're going to have to live with it.' He looked round at Pringle. 'Dan, how many men do you have on the scene?'

'Just the two uniforms so far, sir, and half a dozen CID. They're making a list of the men who were in the yard, and getting ready to interview them one by one.'

'That'll take forever. I want a hundred uniforms here, to begin the search and to help the CID people with the interviews.'

'On a Saturday, Boss?'

'I don't care what bloody day it is. A hundred, I said.' He paused, as Pringle nodded. 'What's happening about the press? Does anyone have wind of this yet?'

'The Prison Service has its own press office,' Whiterose interrupted.

Skinner shook his head. 'Not for this, you don't. Our Media Relations Manager will handle all enquiries about this.' He turned back to Pringle. 'Dan, Maggie Rose will have roused Alan Royston by now to deal with press about her investigation. Obviously you and she will need to co-ordinate, and take Royston's advice on statements and all of that.'

The Superintendent looked puzzled.

'Sorry, Dan,' the DCC burst out as he realised his oversight. 'There's no way you could have known this. When you called me on the mobile I was at another murder scene . . . Nathan Bennett's sister, Hannah. Someone killed her last night.'

On the other side of the desk, he heard Whiterose gasp. 'That's why your men can't undertake any searches, Governor. Clearly, this wasn't a prison feud. Bennett was killed to silence him, as, we believe, was Hannah. He was shot in the head, to make sure of the job. Maybe a prisoner pulled the trigger, but he surely didn't do it without help.

'Dan, when you speak to Alan Royston, tell him I want to know everything that's being said to the press.'

Abruptly, he stood up. 'Lead on, Governor, take me to visit the scene. I take it that the body's still there. Andy, you'd better speak to ACC Elder, to soothe his feathers over a hundred of his uniforms being called out. Neil, with me.'

'Sir.' McIlhenney rose from his chair in the corner, to follow Skinner and Whiterose from the room.

Outside the Governor broke into a brisk stride. 'Is the doctor still there?' Skinner asked him.

'Yes. I asked him to remain with the body, until you agreed that it could be taken to the prison mortuary.'

'It won't be going there,' muttered the DCC, grimly. 'We may as well stack it with the rest. It's going to be a busy day for Prof. Hutchison.'

As they walked on, towards the exercise yard, McIlhenney tugged gently at his commander's sleeve, and dropped a few paces behind their escort. 'Boss, I didn't like to interrupt in there, but when you get to the yard take a look outside the fence.'

'What d'you mean?'

'You'll see.'

They took another corner, and the fenced-in exercise yard was ahead of them. It was unpaved, rough earth, the grass that it had once boasted largely worn away by footsteps. The gate was open, with a prison officer standing just inside. Halfway across the open ground, close to the wall which served as its eastern boundary, the body of Nathan Bennett lay under a blanket. A man in a tweed jacket stood beside it.

'Doctor?'

The man nodded. 'Hoy, prison MO.'

'DCC Skinner. You sure this is a shooting?'

'Oh yes,' answered Dr Hoy, immediately and emphatically. 'Take a look at his face.' He drew back the blanket. For the second time that morning, the detective summoned up all his self-control. He bent over and looked closely at Nathan Bennett's head.

Dark blood was matted in his hair, at the back of his cranium, and dried on his temple. 'Has the photographer done his stuff?' he asked the sergeant.

'Aye, Boss. He's finished.'

Carefully, he rolled Bennett's corpse on to its back, and winced. There was a ragged black hole in the centre of the forehead. 'See what I mean?' said the MO. 'Exit wound.'

'And some.' Skinner straightened up, frowning. He looked around the yard, then remembering McIlhenney's muttered comment, turned and looked at the fence behind him. The top four storeys of a high-rise housing block rose above its highest point. 'Of course,' he whispered, then turned to McIlhenney.

'How far away are those flats, would you say, Neil?'

The big sergeant smiled. 'There's the width of a football field outside the yard, then a hundred yards to the road, then the car park of the block. Four hundred yards, I'd say; five hundred tops.'

'I see what you mean, Sergeant. It'd be an easy shot from that roof over there for someone with the right equipment. How tall was Bennett?'

'Looking at him, I'd guess he was about the same height as Mr Martin.'

'Okay, say five eleven. And with that red hair he'd stand out like a Belisha beacon, even in a crowd.'

Skinner drew the blanket back over Bennett's body, and stepped over to stand by its feet, with his back to the fence and the high-rise block. He put two fingers to the back of his head, plotting the entry wound, then looked at the ground a few yards ahead of where he stood.

'Before we start searching for a gun, Neil, let's look for a bullet . . . a high-velocity rifle bullet, bashed out of shape.' He pointed to a wide area in front of the entry to the yard. 'And let's look over there. When the first of the uniforms arrive, grab them and put them to work sifting through that patch of ground.

'While you're doing that, Mr Martin and I will go across and take a look at the roof of that block, to see if we can find any signs of a sniper.'

'Aye, and if you do, the hundred polis we've called out will spend the day interviewing every resident in those bloody flats!'

Skinner smiled. 'They chose the job, each one of them. Listen,' he added. 'That was a good spot, Neil. Just as well that you didn't mention it in there, otherwise Dan Pringle would have been well embarrassed. He should have seen that.'

The big sergeant shrugged his shoulders. 'The sun's over there, Boss,' he chuckled. 'I think the Superintendent's avoiding bright lights this morning. I was at that dance last night, too. I saw the state he was in when the taxi came for him.'

'You seem to have survived all right.'

McIlhenney looked at him disdainfully. 'Olive's mother was baby-sitting for us. Not even you would dare to come home rat-arsed to the Wicked Witch of the West!'

19

'I've never known your lot to do that before, Bob: to have Alan Royston
call us in for a briefing, give us a prepared statement then refuse to take
questions.'

John Hunter spoke quietly, almost into his pint, as he and Skinner faced
each other across their corner table, even though they were out of anyone's
earshot. Most of the other customers in the Stockbridge pub chose to drink
at the bar.

The policeman smiled at the elderly journalist. 'That's because I've
never faced a situation like this before, old friend. I believe in telling it all
and telling it straight when I've got something to say. But if we had declared
open house on questions, there would have been no knowing what the
press would have made of it. We were dealing with the Sunday papers
there, not with the daily people.'

Hunter shrugged, picking up the sheet of paper which lay on the table
and waving it at Skinner. 'Fine, but even the statement's crap. Two murders
it says, one in Bonnyrigg, the other in Saughton Prison, but no fucking
names. Just the usual shite about next of kin being informed.

'Did you know Royston was going to do this?'

'I told him to play it that way.

'Look, John, why do you think I asked you to come for a pint with me?
I mean, I like your company, but on a Saturday I should be at home playing
with my kids.' He looked at his watch. 'It's gone two-thirty. The best part
of the day's blown.'

He paused. 'If we had given the full story in there, all hell would have
broken loose. As it is, it won't take the hacks long to find out who the
Bonnyrigg victim is. They'll guess the rest from there. I want to put you in
the picture, so that I know it'll be written properly.'

The journalist smiled. 'Now that, I like. You'll piss off all the editors,
though. They'll have to pay me for the copy.'

'They'll be glad to, believe me.'

Skinner finished his Belhaven Best and went up to the bar for two more
pints. Returning, he placed one before Hunter, and saw that the man had
taken out his notebook and pen. 'There aren't many left like you, Auld Yin,
are there?'

'Naw. All these boys and girls with their wee tape recorders. The truth is
I envy them their new gadgets. They're a fucking sight easier than
shorthand, but that's the only way I know.' He took a bite out of his pint,

licking the foamy head from his grey moustache, then looked across at the policeman.

'So. What have you got for me?'

'Before we start,' said the DCC, 'I don't want to be quoted. This is non-attributable; senior police sources and all that.'

Hunter nodded.

'Right. Victim number one: Miss Hannah Bennett, age thirty-three, spinster, of 17 Garston Avenue, Bonnyrigg. Attacked last night in her home between ten and midnight, and killed with a knife in her back garden.'

'Sex attack?'

'I haven't got the PM report yet, but not unless he put her slacks and knickers back on afterwards.

'Victim number two: Nathan Bennett, age thirty-seven, currently of Saughton Prison, but normally of 17 Garston Avenue, Bonnyrigg. Shot dead just after nine this morning in the prison exercise yard.'

The old journalist's mouth dropped open. 'Bennett? The guy in the bank robbery trial, where Archergait . . .'

'That's right.'

'Coincidence?'

'We've got no evidence that it isn't, but be serious: of course the murders are linked. Andy Martin and I found the woman when we went to interview her this morning. You see, Bennett was pleading Not Guilty on instructions. We knew that he was in fear of his life from the ring-leader of this gang.

'We had reason to believe that Hannah was under threat, and that she may have known the man behind the robberies. So we were going to offer her a deal: total protection, and a lighter sentence for Nathan in return for the man's name.

'He beat us to it.'

Hunter's eyes were bright with excitement now. 'And he arranged to have Bennett killed in prison?'

Skinner shook his head. 'No. That would have put more people in the chain of knowledge, and exposed him in other directions. He shot him himself, with a sniper's rifle, from the roof of a multi-storey block overlooking the yard.'

'You certain of that?'

'Stone-cold certain. Andy and I found footprints in the dirt on the roof. It's closed off to the residents, but there's a stairway up to it. The lock had been picked, and the door was open. There was a metal pole lying there that we reckon he could have used to wedge it shut, just in case. On top of that, we've recovered the bullet.'

'Aye, but how can you say for sure that it was the killer up there?'

He paused and took a sip of Belhaven. 'From the angle of the wound, there's nowhere else he could have been.' He grinned, fleetingly. 'Anyway, one of the footprints matches one that our scene-of-crime team found in Hannah's garden.'

Hunter whistled. 'Jesus.'

66

The two men looked at each other across the table. 'Now do you understand why I'm anxious that all this should be reported properly?'

'You mean that it should be reported the way you want it?'

Skinner grinned. 'That's the same thing, isn't it? Look, John, after what happened in Gala on Thursday, we're especially vulnerable on this one. So are the public at large: they're vulnerable to scare stories and to panic.

'Off the record, the truth is that Nathan and Hannah Bennett were our only leads to these robbers. Now they're both out of the way, this guy will be feeling really pleased with himself. I want to get a message to him that we're on to him, that he's given us something new to go on.

'He has, too.'

'What d'you mean?'

'He's brought me into contact with him. He's let me stand where he's stood, and he's let me see how he thinks. He's cocky, this fellow, as well as ruthless, and I've never come across a cocky criminal who's been smiling at the end of the day.

'I want to knock him off balance if I can. That's why I'd like you to circulate a story saying that the police are closing in on the killer of the Bennetts, that he's left a number of important leads at both sites which will help us identify him.

'This guy, whoever he is, he's absolutely sure of himself. I want to undermine that certainty. I want him to know who he's dealing with, and I want him to be afraid of me.'

Hunter looked doubtful. 'I appreciate that, Bob, but I'm an ethical journalist. I never have filed a report that I knew to be untrue, and I never will.'

'I'm not asking you to lie, man. Those footprints are important. We're trying to identify the shoe, in the hope that the list of stockists won't be too big, and that the manufacturer might be able to help us. Some of Arthur Dorward's team are still going over Bonnyrigg picking up every hair, every piece of fabric, and the rest of them are climbing all over the roof of that high-rise.

'Hannah Bennett's neighbours were either watching telly, on holiday or in the pub, so there's not much joy from them, but we're hopeful that someone in the tower block will have seen the guy while he made his way to his firing position.'

Skinner looked at his friend again. 'So, are you up for it?'

'Aye, Bob, I'll write it that way. But can I say for certain that it's the same killer, and that it ties in with the bank robberies?'

'You can say that, John. You know that I can't, officially, in case I'm accused of prejudicing a future trial, but press speculation is another matter. I trust you to handle it right, and to protect me as your source.'

The old man finished his beer, draining most of the glass in a single swallow. 'Right then,' he said, pushing himself to his feet. 'I'd better be off and do it.'

He shook his head as he and Skinner reached the door. 'Christ, and I let you buy the beer too. Wrong of me, that: I'm going to make a fucking fortune. Every newspaper in Britain will take this copy.'

20

'Thank heaven you're back, Pops. Jazz has me run off my feet, and young Mark has me mentally exhausted. He's way too smart for me. I've spent half the day giving him a rundown on what lawyers actually do, and the other half trying to keep pace with him at his computer games.'

Alex gazed at her father and her fiancé as they stood in the doorway of the kitchen. 'Where the hell have you guys been anyway? It's ten past seven. If you were golfing, you might have mentioned it before you left this morning.'

Martin shook his head. 'I wish we had been, love. You say you're puggled? What a day we've had. Since you're asking what we've been doing, you obviously haven't been listening to the news bulletins.'

'No.'

'Take her away and explain what we've been up to,' said Bob. 'I'll make us all some coffee.'

'You can make supper for the boys too,' his daughter told him. 'I've done my big-sister bit.

'Where's Sarah anyway?' She shot over her shoulder from the doorway as Martin led her off to the living room. 'How long's a post-mortem supposed to take?'

'I reckon that Sarah's having a busy day too.' There was a weariness in Skinner's voice which made her look at him, suddenly concerned.

'What is this, Andy?' he heard her say, as she disappeared into the hall.

Forgetting about coffee for the moment, he prepared supper for the boys . . . pizza for Mark, mashed-down stew, peas, carrots and gravy for Jazz . . . then set it at the kitchen table. By the time he had helped his younger son spoon the last of his custard dessert into his hungry mouth, wiped his face, and seen both boys off to bed, the digital clock on the microwave showed four minutes past eight.

Deciding that coffee was by now completely inappropriate, he opened a bottle of Valdepenas, and took it through to the conservatory with three goblets, which he found with some difficulty in the new kitchen lay-out.

Alex looked up at him as he set the glasses on the table and poured the wine. 'Now I understand why you're tired.'

'We've just looked at the teletext,' said Andy. 'Old John's done the business. We're closing in on the killer, you'll be glad to hear.'

Skinner shot him a wry look. 'Aye, but closing in very slowly. It's a bugger about those footprints, turning out to be Clark's shoes; only one of the most popular brands in the country, that's all. Practically every independent shoe shop stocks them, not to mention the firm's own outlets.'

Alex frowned as she picked up her glass, and as her father sat in a chair beside her, the three of them looked out at the evening seascape. 'Pardon me for thinking like a lawyer, but since the shoes are so common, doesn't that reopen the possibility of there being two killers, and of their being unconnected?'

Bob laughed, harshly and without humour. 'That's the only break we've had all day. Arthur's lot found a wee piece of mud on the roof, which he's certain we'll match with Hannah's garden.'

'No, not the only break,' Andy cut in. 'We recovered the bullet.'

'Not the casing, though. No way this guy would have left that behind.'

'Still, we can learn things from the bullet. If the ballistics guys can give us a clue about the type of weapon which fires it, we can go round the rifle clubs looking for a match.'

'Even if they don't, I'll look for a match with every registered rifle in the country.' Bob sighed, a great tired sigh. 'And you know what? I won't find one. This man killed the Bennetts to cover his tracks, not to give himself away. He'll have used an unregistered weapon.'

'Hey,' Alex burst out, 'what happened to Mr Positive Thinking?'

'He's had a hard day!'

'But, Pops, are unlicensed guns so easy to come by?'

Her father snorted, disdainfully. 'Christ, lass, Ireland's still awash with guns. Apart from that, you should see what gets handed in every time we have a firearms amnesty.

'Still, you're right to throw my own words back at me. I've been tearing about for so long today, I haven't had time to sit down and think.'

'Why?' Martin asked softly.

'Eh?'

'No, not "Why have you been tearing about?" This is the "why?" we haven't asked. Why did he decide to close off the Bennetts, now, at this time?'

'I guess he decided that what happened in Galashiels might persuade them to talk after all.'

'That risk's always been there, to an extent. No, what if he learned that I'd been to see Nathan, and that he'd been a bit wobbly?'

'How would he learn that?'

'I can think of two possibilities: the prison escorts.'

Bob stiffened slightly in his chair. 'They were in the room when you interviewed him?'

'That's right. One of them was awkward about leaving, so I let them stay.'

For the first time that evening, Bob smiled. 'Looks like you're working again tomorrow, son.'

He reached forward and picked up his glass, but before he could put it to his lips, a slim tanned hand reached down and took it from him.

'My need is greater, believe me.'

He looked up. Sarah was standing there, in a sweatshirt and jeans. She looked as tired as he had ever seen her.

'Hello, love. How long have you been home? We never heard you.'

'About five minutes,' she answered. 'I looked in on the boys, then I just had to get out of the clothes I was wearing.'

He reached up and touched the back of her hand.

'Careful, honey,' she said. 'You wouldn't want to know where that's been today!'

He grinned and headed off to the kitchen to fetch another glass. 'You'd better bring another bottle,' she called after him. 'Dinner can wait for an hour.'

When he returned she had pulled a swivel chair between his and the settee on which Alex and Andy sat, and had collapsed into it, her legs stretching out before her. He poured himself a glass of wine and finished off the first bottle by topping up everyone else.

'Well,' Sarah chuckled, 'sounds as if we've all had hellish days, one way or another.' She glanced sideways at Bob. 'Sorry, husband, but you're going to have to wait until tomorrow for Nathan Bennett.

'We just didn't have time to start on him today. Our first job took a long time, so we didn't finish with Hannah until an hour ago. I'll be assisting again tomorrow.'

'Dammit,' Bob muttered. 'Still, I sent you the stiff, so I can't really moan. Did you turn up anything unexpected with Hannah?'

'Nothing at all. No skin under the nails or anything like that. No sexual interference, or recent sexual activity. Death caused, as you saw, by a single knife wound to the brain. Joe had a hell of a job getting the knife out, incidentally. It was very sharp, but still it must have been a massive blow for the blade to be embedded so firmly in her skull.

'The only marks on the body other than the one you saw was a bruise around her upper right arm, as if someone had grabbed her there too, with his left hand.' She smiled, with a degree of self-satisfaction showing on her face.

'Know what I think? I reckon the man was going to kill her in the kitchen.' She sat up, swung round in her chair and seized Bob's right arm in her left hand. 'I reckon he grabbed her like that, and took the knife from the set that was found on the work-surface. He made a mistake, though.

'From her muscular development, it was clear to us that Hannah Bennett was left-handed. Remember that rolling pin in the kitchen?' Bob and Andy both nodded. 'I'm sure Arthur Dorward was spot on. She picked it up with her strong hand and beaned him . . . maybe as he was reaching for the knife. That's what gave her time to get away . . . not far enough, though.'

'No, poor lass,' Bob agreed.

He leaned back in his chair and took a sip of his wine. 'How about your first job? What was that about?'

Sarah smiled; it was a deep smile and full of meaning. 'Honey,' she drawled. 'I thought you'd never ask. It was a real VIP: a judge, Lord Archergait, no less. He died on the Bench a few days ago, so I believe.'

Skinner and Alex stared at her simultaneously, in surprise. 'Who ordered a post-mortem on him?' asked her step-daughter. 'He was an old man who went on working too long and had a heart attack.'

'The Lord President asked Joe Hutchison to do an autopsy, as a formality. Apparently there are a couple of precedents, where a judge has died in a public place and a post-mortem was ordered, so he thought he should adhere. Joe and I aren't complaining; it's a nice fee for us.

'You guys may be though,' she added, grimly.

'About the waste of time,' said Bob, 'you're dead right. Why did it take you so long?'

'We had to wait for the lab work to be done,' Sarah answered.

'Bloody nonsense,' her husband muttered. 'From what I was told, Brian Mackie was right beside him when he keeled over. He died of heart failure.'

'Most of us do, love . . . but in this case it was cyanide that caused it.'

The two policemen looked at her in amazement, each with his mouth hanging open. 'You're joking, aren't you?' said Martin.

She looked at him, poker-faced. 'I would not joke about something like that after a day like today. Lord Archergait was poisoned.'

Bob looked at Andy, and shook his head. 'It never rains but it fucking well pours, mate. Just what we need on top of the robberies and the Bennetts . . . a Senator of the College of Justice bumped off on the Bench.'

'How are we going to play this one?' Martin asked.

'Quietly, for as long as we can. Look, as soon as Mackie gets back from his dirty weekend, call him in and take a statement. He seems to have been the closest witness, after all.

'Meantime, tomorrow morning in fact, while you're putting the screws on those screws, I'll pay a call on My Lord President. It's just as well he did order that autopsy. If we've got a poisoner on the loose, it's as well to know about it.'

72

21

In common with many of Scotland's judiciary and Bar, Lord Murray of Overstoun, Lord President of the Court of Session and Lord Justice General, Scotland's second Officer of State, lived in Edinburgh's New Town.

His home was a large apartment in Circus Place, an elegant residence on two levels, with a grand book-lined drawing room, dining room and principal bedrooms on the upper floor, and a veritable warren of bedrooms, stores and studies below.

Before his elevation to the Bench, the Lord President, then David Murray, QC, had been Dean of the Faculty of Advocates. He and Skinner had known each other well at that time, and had had frequent contact, but they had not met since Murray's first judicial appointment.

The diminutive, bespectacled judge greeted the policeman as he arrived, holding open the great grey-painted front door and ushering him into the tiled outer hall. 'Good morning, Bob,' he said, warmly. 'It's good to see you again. I was intrigued by your call last night. Let's go through to the drawing room and you can tell me all about it.'

He led the way through the inner hall and into a large room to the right, where two large, overfed spaniels lay in front of the unlit fire.

Skinner had a deep respect for the judiciary. 'Thank you for seeing me without proper explanation, My Lord.' he began.

'Forget the My Lord stuff, man. I'm not on the Bench now, and my name's still David. I knew you'd be prompt, so the coffee's ready.' He filled two cups from a jug on a tray on his desk, added milk to one and handed it to his guest. It was the first time the policeman had ever seen him casually dressed. His grey slacks and open-necked shirt made him seem even smaller. They contrasted with Skinner's relatively formal clothing, black trousers and navy blue blazer.

'Thanks then, David.'

'Sit over there, by the fireplace. Shift the dogs if they're in the way.'

The two men settled into comfortable leather armchairs, facing each other. Lord Murray's feet barely touched the ground, but there was something about his piercing blue eyes which made everyone who met him forget his lack of stature.

'How are the family?' he began. 'Last time we met you weren't long married.'

The detective smiled. 'They're great. Sarah and I have had our troubles since then, as you'll probably know, but, thank God, they're behind us.'

'Yes, I'd heard that too, and I'm glad. That's a fine thing you've done, adopting the McGrath boy.'

'To me it's a privilege. Wee Mark's what you might call a designer son.' He sipped his coffee, testing the temperature. Finding it tolerable, he took a deeper swallow.

'So,' said the judge. 'What's the problem?'

'Can I ask you something first?'

'Of course.'

'Was there any reason for ordering the post-mortem on Archergait, other than the one you gave Joe Hutchison?'

Murray's brow furrowed. 'No. There were precedents, and like a good judge I followed them. Why do you ask? Has Billy's family objected?'

'Not that I've heard. They'll be grateful to you, in fact. It turns out that the old boy was poisoned.'

'What!' The Lord President's mug slipped in his hand, spilling a little coffee on to his trousers. 'Poisoned, you said. Oh, that's awful. I take it you mean food poisoning. I've heard that some of these new bugs can be devastating to older people.'

'No, it wasn't food poisoning, certainly not in the sense you mean.'

'Then what possibilities are you looking at? You're not saying he committed suicide, are you?'

Skinner raised an eyebrow. 'Other than Nazi war criminals, I've never heard of anyone committing suicide by taking cyanide. I've also never heard of anyone taking an overdose in a public place.

'No, David. There's only one realistic proposition as far as I can see. Lord Archergait was murdered.'

'You're not serious.' The little man slumped even deeper into his chair, shock written on his face. He sat silent for a while, coming to terms with Skinner's news. 'Murmuring the Judges,' he whispered, at last.

'Pardon?'

'I said, "Murmuring the Judges". It's an old Scots legal term for public criticism of the Bench. A very serious offence, it was. But "Murdering the Judges"; that's more serious still.

'I can hardly credit it, Bob. You're telling me that someone actually killed old Billy, in his own Court, right up there on the Bench?'

'I see no other explanation.'

'How could poison have been administered, there in a public place?'

'My first priority is to find the answer to that question. I'm hopeful that more detailed analysis of the stomach contents will tell us.'

Lord Murray shuddered. 'When will that be complete?'

'Tomorrow morning, at the latest.'

'Does anyone else know about this?'

'Joe Hutchison, who did the post-mortem, my wife, who assisted, and my Head of CID. Oh, and my daughter, who was there when Sarah told us.'

74

'You haven't informed the Fiscal yet?' The Lord President laid his mug on the hearth. He pushed himself out of his chair, and walked to his desk, which was set by the window.

'Not yet,' Skinner replied. 'I wanted to speak to you first. I must tell the Crown Office soon though, or I'll be in default of my duty.'

'I'll come to see Pettigrew with you,' Lord Murray declared.

'Actually, in this case I intend to go over Pettigrew's head, and advise the Lord Advocate personally.'

'Yes, I agree with that. And since Archie lives just round the corner, he can come to see us. I'll give him a call now.' He picked up the telephone on his desk and pressed one of the instrument's bank of memorised numbers.

'Lord Archibald, please. It's the Lord President speaking.' In the brief silence which followed, Skinner glanced about the room. Bookshelves stretched from floor to ceiling along one wall, many of them filled with heavy leather-bound volumes in which much of Scotland's case law was enshrined. Facing them, above the ornate fireplace, which he guessed had been in the house since it was built almost two centuries before, hung the only picture in the room, a portrait of Lord Murray's great-grandfather, a predecessor in the office which he now held.

'Archie,' the judge resumed. 'Something rather serious has happened. Do you think you might look round to see me?

'Well, now, actually.'

Within five minutes, Skinner saw the stocky figure of the Lord Advocate as he bustled past the window and up the steps to the front door. Lord Murray greeted him at the door, and showed him in to the drawing room. Lord Archibald, casually dressed like his near-neighbour, started in surprise as Skinner rose to offer a handshake.

'Bob. What are you doing here? But then David did say that it was a serious matter. Don't tell me one of the judges has been misbehaving.'

'Actually,' said the Lord President, 'it's rather the opposite.' He pointed Archibald to the chair which he had vacated, taking a seat himself on the matching settee. 'Bob will explain.'

'I have a formal report to make, Archie, the detective began, of a serious crime which I believe has been committed.'

Scotland's senior Law Officer sat in amazement as Skinner repeated the findings of the post-mortem on Lord Archergait, and the inevitable conclusion which he had drawn.

'That's what I believe,' he said.

'In that case,' said Lord Archibald. 'I have no choice but to instruct you to begin an investigation.' The big policeman nodded.

'Now that formality is complete, Bob,' said Lord Murray, 'how do you intend to proceed?'

'As quietly as I can, David. Who else knows about the post-mortem?'

'Billy's two sons. His wife died three years ago. I didn't discuss it with anyone else.'

'That's good. Where can I find them?'

'Norman King, the older one, is a practising Member of Faculty. The younger brother is a big-firm accountant. He's at the Harvard Business School just now.'

'You don't happen to know where Norman was when his father died?'

'I do,' said the Lord Advocate. 'He was prosecuting in a High Court trial in Glasgow. He's an Advocate Depute.'

'I'll see Norman and tell him what's happened.'

'What about the funeral?' the Lord President asked. 'That is to say, can the body be released, in the circumstances?'

'For a burial, yes,' Lord Archibald agreed. 'I'd be reluctant if they planned a cremation, for fear of a claim by the defence in any future trial that the Crown had destroyed the evidence.'

'That's fine.' Skinner nodded. 'Let them have their funeral, as if nothing untoward has happened. I have an edge here, I think. I don't believe that Archergait's killer anticipated a post-mortem. A judge dies suddenly, up on the Bench; it looks like heart failure, so he thinks that's what everyone will assume. He couldn't have known that you're a stickler for precedent, David.'

He grinned. 'It's every detective's dream: to be investigating a crime which the perpetrator believes to be undetected.'

'Do you mean you're not going to issue a statement about the murder?' the Lord Advocate asked, surprised.

'I'll do whatever's in the public interest. In this case, I believe that I may have an advantage over a killer. In my judgement it's in the public interest for me to keep it secret for as long as I can.'

'How long will that be, though? I don't want any embarrassing questions in the House of Lords.'

'A few days, Archie, but that may be enough. We could wrap this up very quickly. But you're right, when we start interviewing people, the whispers are bound to start. I promise you; as soon as our confidentiality becomes compromised, I'll release the story.'

'Fair enough. Where are you going to start?'

'With the closest eye-witness I have, one of my own men.'

'Can I help in any way?' asked Lord Murray.

'I don't know yet, David: but if I don't get a quick result, my answer might well be yes.'

22

'You're here that bloody often, sir, ye'd be better just robbin' a bank and gettin' locked up.' The Saughton gate officer was in a surprisingly cheery mood for someone at work on a Sunday.

'In the circumstances,' said Andy Martin, 'you'll forgive me if I don't find that very funny.'

He drove on through the gate and parked once more outside the admin. block, then made his way inside, and upstairs to the Governor's suite. Sammy Pye, whom he had picked up en route, followed on his heels.

The outer office was empty, but the door to the Governor's room was ajar. Joyce Latham, Deputy to Ian Whiterose, was waiting for him inside. Privately, Martin was pleased that the unshakeable woman, whom he knew well, was on duty that day rather than her excitable boss.

They exchanged pleasantries, and Mrs Latham offered coffee. The Head of CID was about to decline, remembering the tar which McIlhenney had produced the day before, when she added, 'Gold Blend.'

She took her seat behind the Governor's desk as if it had been made for her. 'That was a terrible business yesterday. Between you and me, Andy, I've gone on and on at the Service about the height of that fence, and about the overview from those flats.

'They've always agreed with me, but there have always been other spending priorities. I bet I'll get attention now though.'

'I'll bet you will,' the policeman agreed. 'Was the problem common knowledge among the staff?'

'It was a joke. We used to have relatives going up on the roof of the flats and holding up banners saying "Happy Birthday, Jimmy" or Willie or whatever. Eventually we insisted that the access door should be locked.'

'You should have insisted on fitting the lock as well. The one the Council installed could have been picked by a kid with a piece of wet spaghetti.'

He leaned back in his chair and sipped his coffee. 'So, Joyce,' he said. 'Have you identified the two officers I asked about?'

'Yes, I have. Malcolm McDonnell and Tibor Albo.'

'Albo?'

'Yes. He says he should be in the Guinness Book of Records for the world's shortest Polish surname! He's on duty today; McDonnell was on the rota too, but he called in sick.'

'Call him back, then, if you wouldn't mind, and tell him to recover. Otherwise we'll go and get him.'

Mrs Latham looked at him in surprise, then nodded and looked up a telephone number from a list in the top right-hand drawer of the desk. She dialled and waited for thirty seconds and more, before cutting off the call and trying again. 'He must have recovered already,' she said. 'No reply.'

'Do you have an address there?'

She nodded, picked up a pen and, reading from the contact list, scribbled on a notepad. She tore off the page and handed it to Martin, who passed it in turn to Detective Constable Pye. 'Take my car, Sammy, find out where Mr McDonnell is, and bring him back here. While you're doing that, I'll see Albo.'

He handed his car keys to the young detective, who left without a word.

'What's this about, Andy?' asked Mrs Latham as the door closed behind him.

'Probably nothing,' said the detective. 'But after three months of keeping his mouth shut, and asserting his wide-eyed innocence, Nathan Bennett was taken out to make sure he stayed silent for good about the man behind the Dalkeith bank raid. His sister was killed for the same reason.

'When I saw Bennett on Friday, he let something slip which made me suspect that Hannah had been threatened. When she was murdered, that was confirmed.'

'And you're concerned that the killer had a source inside here, passing him information about Bennett?'

'Spot on, Joyce. Albo and McDonnell were in the room when I interviewed Nathan. No-one else could possibly have known what he said to me.'

'Why were they in the room? Didn't you make them wait outside?'

'I would have, but one of them was difficult about it, so rather than waste time finding you or Ian to order them outside, I let them stay in.'

'Which one raised the objections?'

Martin frowned as he pictured the two men in his mind. 'The older one.'

'That'll have been Malcolm McDonnell. He's at least ten years older than Tibor. Big man, moustache, dark hair?'

'That's him. How well do you know him?'

'Not that well. I've never had any complaints about him from senior staff. He does his job and he keeps order. The prisoners don't like him much, but he's not here to win popularity contests.'

'Can you remember how long he's been in the job?'

Mrs Latham picked up one of two buff-coloured folders which lay on the desk. 'Four years. He did his first year at Gateside in Greenock, and then transferred here.'

'What did he do before that?'

'According to this he was a delivery driver. Prior to that he was in the forces, for five years. Before that he had a number of jobs, and he was a professional boxer.'

'Is he married?'

'Divorced.'

'What about Tibor Albo? What's his background?'

She opened the other folder and glanced through it. 'Albo's been in the Service for six years. He left school at eighteen, did two years of a computing course at Jewel and Esk Valley College, then joined us. He's engaged, from what I can remember.

'He has a good record, and he's within six months of a promotion.'

'Let's have him in, then.'

Joyce Latham nodded, and picked up the phone once more, dialling an internal number. 'Mr McGroarty? DG here. Would you send Officer Albo up to the Governor's office, please, straight away.'

They waited for five minutes before there was a knock at the door. 'Come in,' called Joyce Latham, and a young fair-haired man in uniform stepped into the room. He was taller than Martin, and just as solidly built. His eyes gave a flicker of surprise as he saw the policeman, but it passed as he came to attention before the Deputy Governor.

'Stand easy, Albo,' she said. 'Take a seat.' She turned to Martin. 'I'll leave you alone, if you wish.'

He nodded. 'If you would, please.'

When they were alone, he stood up, and leaning against the desk, turned to face Officer Albo. He smiled, but not with his eyes. 'Tibor,' he began, 'someone in this prison has passed on information which set up Nathan Bennett and his sister to be murdered.

'She was a nice-looking woman, Hannah Bennett. Quiet, Christian, conscientious, kept a nice house, kept a roof over her brother's head, even though he was a difficult bugger. I only ever saw her once. She had a knife sticking out of the side of her head and she had shit herself.

'When I find the person who passed on that tip about Nathan, he can sit all fucking day and say, "I never knew", but it'll cut no ice with me, or with the Crown Office. We owe it to Hannah to see that he goes down as an accessory to murder. When he does, he'll be sent here.

'That's a nice thought, isn't it. A screw banged up in his own prison. A lot of guys are HIV-positive in here, aren't they?

'When I find that man, there'll be only one way out, and it'll be through the witness box, giving evidence against the man who paid for the information.' He paused and the smile left his face.

'Do you have anything to tell me, Tibor?'

The young man was white-faced in his chair, but his voice was even and controlled, with no trace of panic. 'No, sir.'

The detective stared at him, long and hard. 'Did you hear what Bennett said to me on Friday.'

'You told us not to listen, sir.'

'Aye, but did you hear?'

'Barely, but then I really wasn't listening. I could see Nathan was scared, though.'

'How well did you get to know Bennett?'

'Quite well. He was a strange bloke. I think the Falklands left a bigger mark on him than just his hand.'

'Did he ever talk to you?'

Albo nodded. 'I was the only one he did talk to.' He looked up at Martin. 'They all need it, sir. Even the really tough guys. Someone to talk to. Some of the staff don't want to know, but I see it as part of my job, to lend an ear to someone who really needs one. It's a hell of a thing, locking a man up in a place like this for half his life . . . maybe more.'

'What did he tell you? Did you ever ask him about the robbery?'

'You never ask them anything, sir, other than about their families. That's all Nathan talked about most of the time . . . his sister. He said that she was really good to him, and that he was afraid that he was ruining her life.'

'What did he mean?'

The young man shrugged. 'That he was getting in her way. That because he was there, living with her, it made it tough for her to have a proper relationship. He never said so outright, but I guessed that he took part in the robbery to raise the money for a place of his own.

'He did say to me one day though, that the worst thing he had ever done was to get her mixed up in his life. "It never had anything to do with her," he told me, "but now she's in it up to her neck." I guessed that she had been involved in the crime in some way, but I suppose now I know what he meant.'

'Did you never think to tell anyone this?' Martin asked. 'You're not a priest, man.'

'Some of these guys think we are. I think we have to respect that. Did you never keep a confidence in your job?'

The Head of CID nodded, in silent acknowledgement of the point. He knew that was how criminal intelligence gathering usually worked.

'Were you surprised on Friday, when Officer McDonnell insisted in staying in the room with Bennett and me?'

'A wee bit, sir. But Malky's like that. He can be a real book operator sometimes. He was right, of course; we're supposed to stay with the prisoners at all times.'

'How did McDonnell get on with Bennett?'

'Much the same as he gets on with everyone else. He treats all the prisoners as if they're just numbers. If they behave and don't bother him, generally he doesn't bother them. Very few guys give Malky trouble though. He used to be a boxer, and he can still handle himself.'

'Did you ever see the two of them speaking?'

'Not that I can recall,' he said, at last.

'So their relationship was normal in prison terms?'

Albo looked at the ceiling, as if for guidance. 'No,' he said at last. 'I can't honestly say that's true. They never crossed swords, and they never had a conversation that I saw. Yet I have to admit, there was something.

'Once or twice, when he didn't see me, I caught Malky looking at Nathan in an odd way.'

'Define "odd".'

'I can't. He was looking at him in a way he didn't look at anyone else, that's all I can tell you. It was as if he knew something about him.'

'Okay,' said Martin. 'Let's go back to you. Do you ever talk about your work, at home, or in the pub?'

'Only to my girl-friend.'

'Did you ever tell her about Bennett?'

'No. She wouldn't have been interested anyway. It's only the big names that excite her. Nathan was small-time.'

The Head of CID pushed himself up from his perch against the desk. 'All right, Officer, you can go. However, if anything occurs to you that might help us, I want you to contact me right away. You'll get me at Police Headquarters at Fettes.'

Tibor Albo stood up, saluted smartly, and left the room. A few moments later, Joyce Latham re-entered. 'Well?' she asked.

'I think he's okay,' Martin answered. 'When did his shift finish on Friday?'

'Six p.m.'

'McDonnell's too?'

'Yes.'

'If an officer wants to make a personal phone call during working hours, where does he go?'

'In theory,' said Mrs Latham, 'he uses the pay phone in the canteen. In practice, if they think no-one's looking, the lads use the prison phone in the senior officers' room.'

The detective's green eyes flashed. 'I don't suppose calls are logged?'

'Yes, they are. I'll check Thursday's count, from the time of your visit onwards.'

As she finished speaking, there was a soft knock on the door. Sammy Pye entered, without waiting for an invitation. He was alone.

'McDonnell?' asked Martin.

'Gone, sir. And I don't mean gone for the Sunday papers. When I got no answer to his door, I knocked up the neighbours. One of them said she saw him leave last night in a taxi, with a big suitcase and a hold-all. So I tried his back door.'

'It was open of course,' said the Chief Superintendent, with a smile.

'Well, I might have knocked a bit too hard, sir.' He paused, looking at Mrs Latham. 'I've sent for a joiner to make it secure.'

'There was nothing there. I looked in all the wardrobes, in the drawers, in the bathroom cabinet: they were all empty. There was nothing personal left in the place.

'No doubt about it, Officer McDonnell has done a runner. And at short notice too. I had a look in the fridge, and there was enough food there for a week at least: eggs, bacon, mince, cooked chicken, orange juice and three litres of milk, unopened. Oh aye, and three cans of McEwan's lager.

'Wherever it was he called in sick from, it wasn't his flat.'

Martin looked at Joyce Latham. 'We've got our answer, I think.

'Sammy, did you look for personal papers?'

'Yes, sir. I didn't find any, though. He's quite a methodical man is McDonnell. He had a big folder with all his household stuff in it, indexed. There was nothing in the slot marked "Bank", no account books or cheque books, and the slot marked "Passport" was empty too.'

'Did you look for an address book?'

'No, Boss. I thought I'd better report back.'

The Head of CID nodded. 'Fine, I'll come down there with you and together we'll strip the place. First, we'd better call Fettes, and get people started checking the airlines. If McDonnell caught a plane, maybe someone else bought the ticket for him.

'If he's sticking to overland and ferry travel, or better still if he's got a bolt-hole somewhere in Britain, I'm going to give him something to think about.

'Joyce, can you give me a photograph of McDonnell?' The Deputy Governor nodded.

'Good. In that case I'm going to raise Alan Royston, our press officer, and have it circulated nationally, with a statement saying that he's wanted for questioning in relation to the murders of Nathan Bennett and his sister. After that, I'll alert police forces throughout Europe.

'Officer McDonnell has the answer to our problems, and I want him.'

23

There was something about Bob Skinner's expression which sent a shiver running through Brian Mackie as he opened his front door. Following his promotion to Divisional Commander, he had moved to a new house in Musselburgh, in the heart of his territory.

'Hello, Boss,' he said, managing to show surprise rather than concern. 'What brings you here? Is it about Nathan Bennett and his sister? I heard about that on radio last night. Bloody awful, eh.'

The DCC nodded. 'In a way, it's about Nathan that we need to talk. I was on my way home, so I thought I might look in to see if you were in.'

'Only just. We got back twenty minutes ago.' He nodded towards the driveway of the villa, where two cars stood. 'Sheila's in the kitchen.'

'She's in the kitchen? This must be serious, then.' The Superintendent had always separated his private life very firmly from his career, but Skinner had been aware of his relationship with Sheila Mackeson, whom Mackie had met during his term as executive assistant to the DCC. She was a director of the consultancy which the police used to recruit civilian staff.

To his surprise, the thin man blushed to the top of his domed head. 'We're getting along,' he said, with a self-conscious smile. 'She isn't in there cooking, mind you, just helping me unpack the food shop we did on the way back.'

He held the door open, ushering Skinner into the hall. As he stepped inside, a tall blonde woman appeared in the doorway opposite. She was dressed in shorts and a cotton top, and she held a pack of four toilet rolls in her hand. 'Where do we keep these?' she asked, then saw Skinner, and turned as pink as Mackie.

The DCC smiled. 'Hello, Sheila.' He glanced at his colleague. 'Yes, Brian, I'd say you were getting along.'

'Okay, Boss. It's a fair cop. Sheila's moving in with me, as of today.' Mackie smiled, diffidently, at his new partner.

'Good for you, mate,' said Skinner. 'Good for you, too, Sheila. If I'd known I wouldn't have come empty-handed.'

'Would you have a drink with us, Mr Skinner; to celebrate?' Sheila asked.

'Thanks. I'll have a Coke, or something like that.'

The woman nodded and headed back to the kitchen, as Mackie showed the DCC into his sitting room. 'What did you want to talk to me about, Boss?' he asked quietly, as they sat on the shiny new lounge suite.

'First, I've got something to tell you. I understand that you were giving evidence the other day when Lord Archergait died.'

'That's right. The old chap took a heart attack, right before my eyes.'

'No, he didn't, Brian.' Calmly, Skinner explained the cause of the judge's death, watching the other man's face as the astonishing truth registered.

'I want you to think back,' he went on, 'and try to recall the scene. What happened in the period just before Archergait took his attack?'

Mackie closed his eyes and leaned back, searching his memory, as Sheila came into the room with a tray, loaded with two bottles of Rolling Rock beer, and an iced glass of Coca-Cola.

'Kilmarnock, the defence counsel, was being a prat,' he answered at last, taking one of the bottles from the tray. 'The old judge was getting annoyed with him, and it showed. Then Kilmarnock said something else stupid, and I thought the old boy was about to explode at him. But he wasn't. He just gasped for air and fell across his desk. I left the box and jumped up on to the Bench to try to help him, but he died in my arms.'

'Anything else?'

The Superintendent closed his eyes once more. Then he nodded. 'His water carafe. A couple of minutes before he died, I saw him pour himself a glass. I didn't see him drink from it, but when he fell, he knocked it over. There was no water on the Bench or on the floor, so I guess he must have drunk it.'

'I thought so,' said Skinner. 'Poisoning his food would have been virtually impossible in the Supreme Court Dining Room, without killing a few other people as well. Someone must have spiked that carafe with cyanide.'

'He probably wouldn't have noticed,' Mackie volunteered. 'Wee Colin, the Court Officer, told me that he liked a measure of gin and lime in his water jug.' He put the beer bottle to his lips, then froze, his eyes wide.

'Bloody hell,' he whispered. 'I was going to take a drink from that carafe, until Colin stopped me.' On the couch beside him, Sheila Mackeson gave a little cry of fright.

'He stopped you?' Skinner repeated.

'Yes. That was when he told me about the gin and lime. Christ, Boss, you don't think it could have been Colin, do you?'

'Naw, no more than you do. If wee Colin was going to poison a judge, I can think of a few that he'd have picked before Archergait. Still, we're going to have to talk to him.'

Finally, Mackie summoned the resolve to take a mouthful of beer. He grinned at Sheila. 'Tastes okay.'

She frowned. 'Is your job always like this?'

Skinner answered for him. 'It's nearly always repetitive and boring, Sheila. I can promise you that no-one has ever tried to poison, shoot, stab or otherwise mollicate the Thin Man, nor will anyone ever. I have a theory that some people attract violence. Christ, I'm one of them. People have been having a go at me since I was sixteen. So far, I've always walked away afterwards.'

Mackie chuckled. 'Or limped. Like the time you kicked that guy in the head and nearly broke your foot.'

'Ouch! I can still feel it! That was different though. That man only wanted to get away. The trouble for both of us was that I was between him and the door.

'Anyway, Sheila, don't worry about Brian. If there's something about me that invites attack, equally, there's something about him that invites co-operation. He may be the best shot in the entire force, but that's another matter.'

She smiled at him. 'I'll always worry about him. But I've worked for you lot for long enough to know that it comes with the territory.'

'You planning on getting married?'

'Eventually,' she and Mackie said, in unison.

All three laughed. 'It's the same with my daughter and Andy,' Skinner chuckled. 'One minute they're gung-ho, and the reception's almost booked, then something comes up and it goes on hold again. As I understand it, right now Alex wants to complete her training period with her firm, and take her exams for the Bar.'

Mackie looked at him in surprise. 'The Bar. So that would mean she could wind up cross-examining Andy in a murder trial?'

'Exactly: a point which has occurred so far to neither of those bright people, but one which I might have to bring up myself.'

Mackie was serious once more. 'What are you going to do about Archergait's murder, Boss? How are you going to investigate it?'

'I'm going to use McGuire and McIlhenney. Their brief will be get it sorted before we have to go public on it. They're a good combination. They can handle sensitive situations, but they can be ferocious too, when the need arises.'

'Tell them to go easy on wee Colin, eh. No way did he do it.'

'No, but it's his job to fill up that carafe. After he did, someone must have had access to it. He's going to have to explain how that happened. Better he's interviewed by two guys he doesn't know, rather than by a couple of his pals, like you and me.'

24

The little man looked round the door, then stepped into the room. 'The Principal Clerk told me to come and see you, gentlemen,' Colin Maxwell announced. He wore a light check jacket and fawn trousers, having had no time to change into his formal black Court uniform.

'Yes, that's right,' Mario McGuire nodded. 'Come in and take a seat, Mr Maxwell.' The two policemen were in an office in the Supreme Courts administration unit. It was on an upper floor and looked out on to the back of the newly built complex in Chambers Street which housed the Crown Office and Edinburgh Sheriff Court.

Maxwell's eyes narrowed as he looked at McGuire. 'Here,' he said, 'you're the guy that succeeded Brian Mackie in Special Branch. What's this about?'

'It's a very confidential matter, sir, and not to be discussed outside this room. Is that clear?'

The Court Officer nodded.

'Sergeant McIlhenney and I have been asked by the Lord President to review security within the Supreme Court building,' McGuire went on.

Unexpectedly, the little man threw back his head and laughed. 'That's a good one. This is the most insecure building in bloody Edinburgh. These fellas at the front door, they're a waste of time. Not that they're bad at their job, like. It's just that this is the High Court. We get some right bad buggers on trial here,. A lot of their friends are right bad buggers too, yet they're allowed to swan in here unchecked.

'Have you seen all those advocates' boxes down thon corridor? The idea is that solicitors leave papers in there for Counsel, but the fact is anybody could leave anything. The public ... all those hooks and crooks in for trials ... walk right by that corridor on their way to the Courts.'

'We've noted that already,' McIlhenney acknowledged. 'Maybe we can persuade the Courts Administration and the Faculty to put the boxes in a more secure part of the building.'

'What about the Courts themselves?' McGuire asked.

'They're open to the public.'

'What happens during the lunch adjournment?'

'Sometimes they're left open. If there's a lot of productions lying about then the Court'll be locked, though.'

The Irish-Italian detective leaned back in his chair and grinned. 'Let's take a theoretical example, Mr Maxwell. Poor old Archergait popped off

86

the other day. For the sake of argument, suppose someone had it in for him, how easy would it have been for them to nip into Court during lunch and put something in his water jug?'

The little man laughed, softly. 'In that case it would have been bloody difficult. I always changed old Billy's jug at lunchtime. He liked his gin and lime in the afternoon, you see. Everyone around here knew that.'

The smile left his face. 'Mind you,' he mused. 'I suppose they could always have gone into the retiring room.'

'What d'you mean?' asked McIlhenney.

'There's an ante-room for the Judge behind the Court. I robe him in there, and that's where I mixed old Billy's gin, lime and water. It's conceivable that someone could go in there.'

'Is there a tap in there?' The sergeant's enquiry was casual.

'Not for drinking water. I fill a bigger jug in the morning, and that does us through the day.'

'The ante-rooms aren't locked?'

'No. They're left open just in case the judge gets back early from lunch, to work on someone for the afternoon. There are lockable cupboards for the robes and wigs. The Court Officers have the key to them.'

'How many doors are there to each room?' McGuire fired at the man. 'Just the one leading from the Court?'

'Some of them have a second door out to the corridor behind.'

'As a matter of interest, have you ever found anyone in a judge's room?'

Maxwell looked at the policeman curiously, then shook his head. 'Never that I can recall. Not without an invitation, anyway.'

'You didn't see anyone hanging around, for example, on the day Lord Archergait died?'

'No.' He paused. 'Mind you, I wouldn't necessarily have seen anyone that day. Old Billy was late back from his lunch. I did the carafe, then I had to go and chase him up from the dining room. So I suppose . . .'

The Court Officer's eyes narrowed, almost to slits. 'Here,' he said, quietly. 'What are you guys leading up to? Are you trying to tell me . . .'

McGuire looked at him, impassively, unsmiling. 'We're not trying to tell you anything, Mr Maxwell. We're asking you. About security. Okay.'

The little man's gaze dropped. 'Aye, okay.'

'And you'll keep our enquiries to yourself?'

'Sure.'

'And if anything occurs to you . . . about any aspect of our conversation . . . ' The Inspector pushed a card across the desk. 'you'll get in touch with us?'

'Of course.' He stood up to leave, turned towards the door then stopped. 'One thing occurs to me. I've still got the rest of that bottle of gin, and the lime. I don't drink the stuff, so you'd be as well finishing it as anyone else.'

25

'D'you think I should cancel my holiday, Bob?' Sir James Proud wore a heavy frown. 'After all, you came home early from yours. When news of Archergait's murder breaks . . . as it will . . . what will people think if I'm away?'

Skinner grinned at him. 'They'll think, correctly, that you have absolute confidence in your Deputy. Listen, Jimmy, apart from your doctor, I'm the only person who knows the outcome of your last medical. You've been told to take a good holiday this summer . . . without a mobile phone.

'Your ferry is booked, and like it or not you are heading off tomorrow for four weeks at my place in Spain. If you're going to be difficult about that, I'll pick up the phone and tell Lady Chrissie. She'll sort you out.'

The Chief Constable held up his hands in surrender. 'I give up. Och, but man, you know how it is, being away when there's a crisis.'

Skinner nodded. 'I know. Tell you what, I will fax you every so often, to keep you in touch with current affairs: football results and that sort of thing. If I should happen to slip in details of the investigations . . . well just don't let Chrissie see them, that's all.'

Proud Jimmy smiled at him, mollified. 'Rugby results, rather than football, please. I never understand why they call it the beautiful game. Why there's hardly a team in Scotland has a flat pitch to play on.'

He swivelled in his chair and looked out of his window. When he turned back to face Skinner, his mood had changed. 'How long do you think you'll be able to keep the wraps on Billy Archergait's murder?' he asked.

'Long enough to clear it up, I hope. McGuire and McIlhenney are up at the Court now, beginning a very discreet investigation.'

'Are you going to check back through his case log, to see if there's someone he sent down in the past who might fit the bill?'

The DCC nodded. 'Yes, we are. The Lord President's going to help us there. The trouble is the old boy was a judge for so long, it's a needle in a haystack job. We're going to talk to Archergait's sons as well, of course.

'I'm seeing Norman King later on today.'

Proud looked at him. 'Tell me straight, Bob, are you optimistic about a speedy conclusion to this one.'

Skinner frowned and shook his head. 'Without a big slice of luck, no I'm not. There's an answer somewhere in the old boy's career, or in his past life somewhere, but we won't find it by pushing a button on a computer.

There's lot of sifting and analysis to be done, I fear.'

'What about the inquiries?'

'It's the same story there. We've established that McDonnell, the missing prison officer, the man we think set the Bennetts up, caught an Air UK flight to Amsterdam yesterday. His ticket was waiting for him at Edinburgh Airport. It was a direct booking with the airline by telephone, and he paid for it there, by cheque.

'The deaths of the Bennetts and his disappearance has closed off one line of enquiry, but there are other things we can do. It'll mean still more sifting and analysis, but I know the very boy to do it. I'm just off to see Andy about that.

'Once I've done that, I'm off down to the Borders. I'm attending the funeral of Harry Riach, the civilian victim in the Gala hold-up, with John McGrigor.'

'You'll represent me at PC Brown's service tomorrow, won't you?'

'Don't worry, Chief, I'll even wear my uniform. I'll go to Archergait's as well. I believe the family are trying to fix it for Thursday.'

'Sounds like a grim week, Bob. You make me feel all the more guilty to be going away.'

Skinner shot him a thin smile as he rose. 'Listen, I don't want to be following your coffin as well. Four weeks' rest, man. Doctor's orders. Give me a call when you get there, to confirm that everything in the house is okay for you.'

Sir James stood and walked him to the door. 'Good luck, then,' he said, 'on all fronts.'

Outside in the corridor, the DCC turned and headed for the CID suite. He found Martin in his office poring fruitlessly over interview statements by neighbours of Hannah Bennett and by the residents of the block from which her brother had been assassinated.

'Anything there?'

The Head of CID looked up from his desk. 'Not a thing. Deaf, dumb and fucking blind, the lot of them. One bloke round the corner from Hannah thinks he might have seen a red car parked outside his house late in the evening, or it might have been blue, or maybe dark green. It could have been a Vauxhall, but then again, maybe a Ford.'

'What about the woman herself? Did you learn anything new about her?'

'She was fairly pally with the lady four doors up it seems. According to her, Hannah didn't have a boy-friend, as such. There was one bloke she had dinner with from time to time. He was an elder in her church, but he got engaged to someone else a couple of years back. Since then, there's been no-one.'

'What about the brother?'

'No-one seems to know much about him. A dour bugger who ignored most people: that's how he struck the neighbours. That was how he came across in jail as well. Dan Pringle's lot spoke to all of the untried prisoners at Saughton, and that's how most of them described him, one way or another.'

He looked up at Skinner from behind his desk. 'Actually, I was thinking I might ask Brian to organise some re-interviewing up at Bonnyrigg, concentrating on Nathan this time. I mean, someone there must have got to know him. I'm going to find out where he drank, and ask me questions there.'

'Fair enough, Andy, but there's something else I think we have to do, too. We're agreed that these robberies were meticulously planned, yes?'

Martin nodded.

'Okay, in that case the planner, the organiser, the Boss, if you're right, may well have been in every one of those banks. We know that they all have video security, with recording systems. If those systems are any good, every one of those branches could have him on tape.

'It'll be a hell of a task, I know, but we should have someone reviewing all those recordings from at least three months before the first robbery, looking for the same face showing up, one, two, three, four times.'

Andy Martin flashed a twisted grin. 'Who do you have in mind for that job? How about wee Mark, given the memory that he's got?'

'You're probably right, but it wouldn't say much for the strength of our resources if we had to use a seven-year-old. Actually, I was thinking of someone a bit older.' He jerked a thumb over his shoulder, towards the outer office.

'Sammy? Good idea. He's a bright spark and he's got the patience for the job. Why don't you call him in, so we can give him the good news.'

26

For Bob Skinner, the rare occasions on which he was obliged to wear uniform were among the few unappealing aspects of Command rank. Nevertheless, awareness of his duty as Sir James Proud's deputy, and a sense of respect for the bereaved, had made him struggle into the uncomfortable blue serge trousers, and into the high-buttoned tunic, emblazoned with badges of rank.

There were ribbons too, among them that of the Queen's Police Medal, awarded in the wake of his recovery from his near-fatal stabbing. He guessed that Proud Jimmy would have worn his medals to a funeral, but he had stopped short of that.

Normally, he would have driven his own car to Galashiels, but for this occasion he had asked for a police driver, to avoid the inconvenience of parking. As he stepped out of the car a battery of TV and press cameras homed in on him. A young woman stepped forward with a microphone, but he ignored her and strode off.

John McGrigor was in uniform also as he met the DCC at the entrance to the tall-spired parish church. It might have fitted once, but now the silver buttons strained to contain the beefy Superintendent.

Skinner looked up at the red sandstone building. 'So this was Big Harry's church,' he mused.

'Very, very occasionally,' whispered McGrigor. 'But now he's a hero, the minister's welcomed him back with open arms.'

The policemen stepped inside, where they were met by an usher and shown to a pew reserved for VIPs. Skinner recognised the local MP, the Parliamentary Under Secretary of State for Home Affairs, and Councillor Marcia Topham, Chair of the Police Advisory Board. He nodded briefly to all three as he sat on the hard wooden bench seat, next to the Councillor.

She leaned her head towards him. 'How's the investigation going?' she whispered.

'Positively,' he replied, emphatically, in a tone which invited no further questions. He glanced towards the altar, where Harry Riach's massive dark wood coffin stood on trestles, with a single wreath on top and others laid before it.

'The big one in the middle's from us,' McGrigor muttered. 'The big fella would have appreciated the irony in that. It's as if we were saying goodbye to a valued customer.'

Skinner looked sideways at him and was surprised to see a tear in the corner of his eye. However at that moment the organ burst into life and the congregation rose to its feet. The family entered, led by a stocky middle-aged woman in black, leaning on the arm of a tall, solidly built man in his twenties. He was wearing an army uniform, with sergeant's stripes. Two other men, younger than the first, followed behind, each supporting an elderly relative.

'The three sons?' the DCC whispered.

'Aye. The old folk are Harry's parents.'

The service was formal and relatively short, typical of Scottish Presbyterian funerals: the twenty-third psalm, a prayer, a eulogy delivered by the minister, full of unconscious signs that he was not too well acquainted with the man he was burying, a hymn and a benediction.

It seemed no time before the congregation was filing out behind the family mourners, to form a cortège of cars behind the hearse, as it wound its way to the nearby ceremony, where, it seemed to Skinner, around half of the town of Galashiels was waiting.

The gathering parted to allow the two policemen to move to the graveside. As they approached the burial site, McGrigor touched the arm of the DCC's uniform. 'If you'll excuse me for a moment, sir.'

Slowly and deliberately, the Superintendent stepped forward, handed his uniform hat to the undertaker, and took up the position of the second mourner, at the foot of the coffin as it was lowered on to two bars across the waiting grave.

As Skinner watched the scene, his mind swept back almost twenty years, to another funeral, that of his first wife, in Dirleton Cemetery. He saw himself standing at the head of her coffin, Myra's father directly opposite him, in the position where McGrigor stood now, three of their nearest and dearest on either side. He almost felt the cord in his hands and the sudden weight as the burden was lifted first, to allow the supports to be withdrawn, then lowered reverently into the earth.

The undertaker's instructions were the same as they had been on that day, the worst of Bob Skinner's young life. 'Drop your cords, gentlemen.' Involuntarily, he lowered his eyes as the eight bearers allowed the tasselled ropes to fall into the grave, seeing again the brass name plate with its simple lettering, 'Myra Skinner, wife and mother'.

It seemed like an age to him, but barely two minutes had elapsed before McGrigor was back by his side. The two men stood as the congregation dispersed, waiting for an opportunity to express their condolences to the widow, who sat in the funeral car with Harry Riach's aged parents, being consoled by friends through the open door.

'Thank you for doing that, Uncle John. My Dad would be pleased.' Skinner looked away from the car to see the oldest of the Riach brothers standing with the Superintendent.

'*Is* pleased, Henry. He is pleased. If you believe anything that was said in that church, you'll believe that he's watching us.'

The sergeant nodded. 'I'd like to believe that, Uncle John. I'm trying; I really am.'

The Superintendent turned. 'Sir, this is Henry Riach, Harry's oldest son. Henry, DCC Skinner.'

'Pleased to meet you, sir,' said the tall young man. 'I'm pleased that you came.'

'It's an honour, believe me.'

To the policeman's surprise, the young soldier smiled. 'Aye, and appropriate too. You had him often enough in his time. It's only right that you should be here to see him off.'

For once in his life, Skinner was lost for a suitable counter. Instead he said, 'Look, could you pass something on to your mother for us. There are channels through which she can receive compensation for her loss. Inadequate, I know, but still. There's Criminal Injuries, and there's also the possibility that the bank might like to express sympathy, too.

'I had a word with their head office before I came here, and as a first step, they'd like to meet the cost of the funeral.' He took a card from his pocket. 'I won't intrude further today, but that's my number at Fettes. If I can help or advise you and your mother in any way, don't hesitate to give me a call.'

'That's very kind of you, sir,' said Henry Riach.

'Not at all, Sergeant. Your father died a hero.'

The young man's eyes misted over. 'My Dad lived as a hero too, sir. All his life, he was a hero to me. A rough diamond, for sure, but a diamond nonetheless.'

He shook Skinner's hand and walked away, towards the car.

The DCC looked at his colleague. 'Uncle John, eh. I didn't realise that you were so close to the family.'

For the second time that day, a tear showed in the eye of the big bluff Superintendent. 'Harry and I were brother in arms, sir, from the age of five, when we started school on the same day. I arrested him three times when he was raising hell and threatening to dismantle the pub, yet in all our lives, there was never an angry word passed between us.

'Young Henry, there; he's my godson.'

McGrigor replaced his peaked hat, which, like Skinner, he had been holding in his hand. 'I tell you, sir, suppose no-one else catches these bastards, I will.'

'Come on then, John,' said the DCC, nodding. 'Let's the two of us get on with it.'

27

If Skinner had returned to Fettes to change out of uniform, he would have been at least fifteen minutes late for his meeting with the Lord Advocate. So instead, sitting stiffly in the hated serge, he instructed his driver to head straight for the Crown Office in Chambers Street.

He frowned as he stepped from the car, as he recalled his last visit to the recently completed headquarters of the Scottish criminal prosecution service, as an interviewee rather than as a policeman. But putting the memory aside and concentrating on the matter in hand, he strode into the building.

The clerk at reception sat straight behind his desk as he approached. 'Good afternoon, Mr Skinner,' he said. 'Lord Archibald asks if you would just go straight in. His room's . . .'

'That's all right, thanks,' Skinner retorted; a shade tersely, the clerk thought. 'I've been there before.'

Norman King looked up in surprise as the Deputy Chief Constable entered the room. Even the Lord Advocate raised an eyebrow at the sight of the tall detective in uniform. 'Funeral,' Skinner muttered, all the explanation he needed to offer.

'Ah, I see. Was it the officer who was killed last week?'

'No, it was Harry Riach, the civilian. See what you can do about posthumous gallantry awards, Archie, will you . . . for both of them.'

'I'll mention it to the Secretary of State. Pull up a chair, Bob.' He looked across at the third man in the room.

'I've asked Bob Skinner to join us at this point, Norman. There's something that he and I have to discuss with you.' The DCC looked at the man as he took his seat alongside him. He was, he guessed, around forty years old, and wore the traditional junior advocate's clothing of dark jacket, pin-striped trousers and plain white shirt, stripes being the prerogative of Silks. Skinner knew many members of the tight-knit community that is the Scottish Bar, but his path and that of King had never crossed before.

'I've just been congratulating Norman,' Lord Archibald went on, looking now at Skinner, 'for two reasons. First, he's to be appointed Queen's Counsel, and second, he has been offered and has agreed to accept, the position of Home Advocate Depute.'

The policeman's eyebrows rose as he nodded an acknowledgement to King. The Home AD was the third person on the Crown Office totem pole, after the Lord Advocate and the Solicitor General, and was the leader of the team of full-time prosecutors in Scotland's High Court of Judiciary. Appointment to the office was recognised as an important step towards high office and a seat on the Bench.

'Well done,' offered the DCC.

'Thank you, Mr Skinner. It's come as a great surprise, I must say. I didn't think I was sufficiently senior for the job, but Archie seems to have faith in me. What a pity though that my father didn't live to see it.'

The smile vanished from the Lord Advocate's face. 'Yes indeed, Norman: and that brings me to the reason for Bob's presence.' King looked round at him in sudden surprise.

'What d'you mean?'

Lord Archibald took a deep breath. 'You're aware that the Lord President asked, as a formality, for a post-mortem to be carried out on Billy?'

The son nodded. 'Yes, he informed me. As you say, it was a formality.'

Skinner took the ensuing silence as a cue. 'I'm afraid, Mr King, that Archie was over-optimistic. The autopsy has established, beyond doubt, that your father was poisoned.'

As he looked at him, the other man's face became a caricature of shock. He shook visibly in his chair, and his mouth worked as if to form words.

'You can't be serious,' he gasped, at last.

'I'm afraid I am. Another pathologist might just have been content to make the most cursory examination of the body, but Archie engaged Joe Hutchison. You'll be aware of his reputation for thoroughness.

'As far as we can establish . . . although it's still subject to confirmation . . . someone slipped cyanide into your father's water carafe.'

Norman King buried his face in his hands and rubbed it vigorously, as if trying to wipe away his disbelief, then looked across at Skinner.

'How in God's name did they do that?' he shot at the policeman.

'That's exactly what we've set out to establish. I have two experienced men up at Parliament House today, making very discreet enquiries. My Inspector phoned me while I was on my way here. They've interviewed Colin Maxwell, Lord Archergait's attendant, and they think they know: not just how, but when.

'They are now trying to establish whether anyone was seen in the corridor which leads to the judge's ante-room . . . without success so far.'

Norman King looked at Lord Archibald. 'Who would want to kill my old man?' he asked, despairingly.

'That's really what we wanted to ask you, Norman,' the Lord Advocate replied. 'Judges make a potential enemy every time they send someone down. Did Billy ever mention anything to you about any of his decisions that might have been preying on his mind?'

'What d'you mean?'

'Well, for example, can you recall a sentence which he thought in retrospect might have been too severe?'

Unexpectedly, the advocate let out an ironic chuckle. 'Archie, my Pa only ever worried about a sentence if he thought he might have been too lenient. He used to say to me that part of a judge's duty is to support the jury. He was always concerned that if he went too easy on a convicted person that might be interpreted as undermining, or disapproval of the verdict.

'He didn't like plea-bargaining, either, although he usually went along with it, since it didn't involve a jury.' He glanced towards Skinner, then back to Lord Archibald. 'The chap Charles, that fellow you put away a few months back; Pa didn't approve of that deal at all. He'd have given the bloke eight years, if it had been down to him. As it was, he refrained, since in the final analysis he always believed in supporting the police as well.'

King paused, smiling in fond recollection. 'On top of all that, my father had a keen eye for public opinion, as expressed through the media. His firm belief was that leniency is the only thing for which a judge is ever really lambasted. He was right, too. Just look at how they turned on that chap in the States.'

The Lord Advocate leaned back in his chair and looked at Skinner across his desk. 'All that, of course, just adds to the list of potential grudge-bearers.'

The detective nodded, as if in agreement. 'In theory, but I think we can disregard those who are still in jail.'

'What about their families, though?' asked Lord Archibald.

'Those avenues will be explored, don't worry. Still . . .' He hesitated, formulating his thoughts. 'If we're looking at a get-even murder by an old client or a relative, we have to consider their backgrounds. In my experience, and I'm sure in yours too, most criminals fall into two categories. There are the domestic offenders, violent husbands, abusive parents, or fairly frequently, people who have lost control only once in their lives, but with fatal results. Then there are the hooligans, the street boys. Usually, they run with gangs, and are into extreme violence . . . but with knives, clubs, or guns occasionally.

'I don't see this killer coming from the first group. Families want to put their troubles behind them. As for the second, if Lord Archergait had been attacked on his way home from Court and stabbed, or beaten to death, that would fit the pattern. But poison, no.' He fell silent, staring at the window for a few seconds.

'Look, Mr King,' he resumed. 'It's possible that your father was killed at random, by someone with an irrational grudge against the law in general. But I don't think so. This murder was premeditated and thoroughly planned. From what I've been told so far, the killer watched and waited for his opportunity, and when it arose, he took it.

'Be in no doubt that if they have to, my people are going to look over your father's career on the Bench, case by case. To help them, I'd like you to go through his notes, his papers, his diaries, any records he may have kept of his career. Speak to your brother as well; he may recall something that's slipped your mind.'

The bereaved son nodded. 'Of course I'll do that. Don't expect anything from it though. Pa wasn't a great hoarder.'

He blinked, hard, as the enormity of what he had been told began to sink in, and, as it did, the anger began to surface. 'Good luck to you and your people, Mr Skinner. When you catch this bastard, I don't imagine that I'll be allowed to lead for the Crown.' He smiled, wickedly. 'However, thanks to Archie, and my new appointment, I'll be in a position to ensure that whoever does leaves the judge and jury in no doubt as to what's expected of them!'

28

Detective Chief Superintendent Martin opened the door of the small room opposite the CID suite. 'How's the viewing going, Sammy?' he asked.

Young Constable Pye looked up at him, bleary-eyed. 'I've got nothing so far, sir,' he answered, quickly. 'The fact is, I'm still working out how to tackle it. I'll tell you now though, unless I get lucky, this is going to be a long job.'

'I'm under no illusions about that. How will you go about it?'

Martin's assistant pointed to the television screen on the table at which he sat. 'Well, sir, as you can see from that, there are a lot of people on these tapes.'

'Which bank is this?'

'This is Dalkeith, where the first robbery took place.' He pressed the pause button on the video player, and stood up to face the Head of CID. 'I've decided to run through each bank's tapes at least twice, to familiarise myself with the faces. That's not as bad as it sounds, I can fast-forward, and I can cut out obvious non-runners . . . old people, young girls delivering shop takings or getting change, handicapped people and so on.

'My reasoning is that we're looking for a male, probably in his thirties or forties, somebody with the potential to scare a guy like Nathan Bennett into silence. On my first run-through of each tape, I'll note down all the possibles by date and time reference, then go through them again, concentrating on their appearance.

'If I see the same face at more than one bank, that'll ring an alarm bell.'

Martin nodded. 'That sounds like a pretty fair plan. But are you sure you're happy to tackle this on your own? I could give you a team of watchers if you thought it would it help.'

Pye shook his head. 'No, sir. You and Mr Skinner are right. We could fill this room with people, yet everyone would still have to look at all the tapes. I've always had a good memory for faces. I'm confident that if there is a lead in here, I'll find it.'

'Okay, Sammy,' said the Head of CID. 'I'll go with that. Have you got any feel for timescale yet? I don't have to tell you how important this is.'

'I know, Boss. Let's see.' He looked at his watch. 'It's mid-day Tuesday. If I find a suspect quickly, I'll give you a shout at once. Failing that, how would it be if I report progress at close of play on Thursday?'

'That's acceptable.' The DCS stepped towards the door. 'I'll let you get on with it.'

'I'll tell you one thing, sir,' said DC Pye just as he reached it. 'After this I won't be wanting to watch telly for a long, long time.'

29

'Want to talk about it?'

Tall even in his open-toed sandals, Bob looked down at Sarah, who grinned back at him as they made their way down the high dune. 'What do you mean?' he asked her.

'You know damn well. You've been in another world since you got home this evening. Not one word of more than two syllables has passed your lips, and when I suggested that we should take the boys for a walk before we ate, you jumped at it.

'I know you, husband, and I know when there's something chewing at your brain. What is it? The bank robberies? Lord Archergait?'

He nodded as he side-footed his way down the slope, holding Jazz steady in his front-slung carrier. 'Yes,' he admitted. 'It's both of those things.

'We have our best people on each enquiry, yet so far each one's as cold as a witch's tit.'

'Tit,' Jazz repeated, enunciating clearly.

'Yes, Jazz,' said Sarah quickly, throwing a mock-frown at Bob. 'Like the birds in our new garden. Bird, bird, okay.'

'Bid, Mummy, bid,' he shouted back at her.

They cleared the last of the dunes, and stepped out on to the path which led eastwards from Gullane's curving mile-wide beach. Mark trotted on ahead of his adoptive parents, who strode out to keep him in sight.

'It's early days in both investigations, honey.' She took his hand in hers as they walked.

'Sure, but that's the time when our hopes of success are best. With every day that passes the trails go colder, it gets tougher for the team.

'What have we achieved today?' He broke off. 'Careful, Mark! The path falls away there. Keep close to the fence.'

'Well,' asked Sarah, breaking the silence which followed. He looked down at her. 'What have you achieved?'

'Sum total? We've established that someone walked into the ante-room of Archergait's Court and slipped cyanide into the water carafe which Colin Maxwell had just refilled. We've also established that no-one saw him do it.

'As for the robberies, we've established that Malky McDonnell, our last living lead, is well gone. Not exactly what I call progress, on either front, my love.'

'What about Maxwell?' She sounded hesitant. 'Are you sure . . .'

He laughed, ironically. 'Wee Colin? I suppose you're right to ask the question. There's no argument that he filled the jug that poisoned the old boy. We've only got his word for it that he left the room empty and unlocked afterwards. He even stopped Brian Mackie from taking a drink from the carafe.

'Sure, we could lift him and question him for twenty-four hours. We could give him a really hard time. At the end we might even be able to charge him. There's only one thing wrong with that scenario.'

'What's that?'

'No way did the poor man do it!'

She stopped in her tracks, pulling him to a standstill too. 'Have you ever been wrong?' she asked him.

'Sure, as you well know. But not this time.' He tugged at her hand and they resumed their walk. 'Listen, we're not being unprofessional about this. We've done checks with every chemist in town, to see if anyone's been buying cyanide lately. Colin certainly hasn't. And we're also going round all known users of the stuff, to see if any have stock discrepancies. So far, no-one has.

'I asked Norman King, Archergait's son, about Colin. He says that he and his father were good pals, going back to the old boy's days at the Bar. They played golf together at Murrayfield. Quite often they partnered each other in the monthly medal.

'No, love, trust me on this one. Colin Maxwell is not a murderer.' He smiled at her. 'Before you suggest it, he isn't one of our bank robbers either!'

He looked down. Jazz, in his carrier, was sound asleep. 'Here,' he said. 'That's enough of the shop talk. Look what it's done to the wee man.'

They walked on, to Freshwater Haven, and the spring from which it took its name, then round to the east sands. Normally the white beach was deserted, but on this warm evening two riders were exercising big, thoroughbred horses, letting them stretch their legs along the water's edge. They caught up with Mark, who had stopped and was gazing down at them from the grey wall of a ruined cottage.

'Whose are they, Uncle Bob?' he asked.

'I have no idea, son. Quite a few people around here own horses.' He was on the point of asking whether Mark wanted a horse, but bit the words back. '*One step at a time, Skinner,*' he told himself.

Leaving the galloping horses behind, they headed up from the beach and found a narrow path which ran for over half a mile around the edge of Muirfield golf course, before leading them back to the bridle path by which they had descended to the beach. By the time they reached home twenty minutes later, Jazz was stirring, but Mark was beginning to flag.

'This is the best thing we've done as parents,' said Bob to Sarah, as they watched their older son sitting on the front doorstep, wearily shaking the sand from his trainers. 'I wish I had been brought up in a place like this.

'How was school today, Mark?' he called out.

'Great,' cried the youngster.

'See what I mean?'

Sarah smiled as she took the boys off to prepare for bed, leaving Bob to set out their supper of salmon and avocado sauce, which she had cooked that afternoon, to be eaten cold. It had become their custom to dine in the conservatory, watching the sun going down towards the horizon. When Sarah appeared to take her seat at the table, having changed out of her T-shirt into a loose-fitting blouse, she was carrying a bottle of white wine in a cooler, and two glasses.

'I know we decided we weren't going to have alcohol every night,' she said brightly, 'but tonight, I think you need this.'

Bob nodded. 'Yeah, I wouldn't mind. With the funeral, then a difficult meeting with Archergait's son, the day's been pretty stressful. I don't see it getting any better this week. I've got Annie Brown's service tomorrow, then the old judge's on Thursday.'

He accepted a glass from Sarah and held it as she filled it almost to the brim. 'Christ, there won't be many of them in the bottle.'

'There's another in the fridge if you need it.'

He nodded. 'This may turn out to be the case,' he said.

As they ate, Sarah recounted Mark's description of his first day at his new school. 'He seems to have made a couple of friends already. There's a boy who lives along in Marine Terrace, and a girl round in Nisbet Road. He mentioned both of them.'

Bob grinned. 'He won't have any bother settling in, that one. It's the teacher I feel sorry for. She'll never have been hit with so many questions.'

Sarah pushed away her empty plate. 'Speaking of questions,' she said, quietly, 'you still haven't really answered mine from earlier. There's something else troubling you, isn't there, as well as these investigations.'

He picked up his glass, only to find that it was empty. Refilling it from the chilled bottle, he leaned back in his chair.

'Aye, well,' he began, swinging round to look out at the wide waterway. 'I'm trying not to let it bother me . . . and I certainly didn't let Jimmy see it . . . but I don't know how I'm going to handle being acting Chief Constable for four weeks.'

'Hey,' she broke in, brightly. 'I'd forgotten about that. You're the big cheese while Jimmy's on holiday. Are you telling me that you don't find that a challenge?'

'Sweetheart, I'm telling you that I find it something of a chore. I'm a policeman by instinct, not an administrator. Sure, I can do Jimmy's job, but right now, when everyone else in the force is bursting their balls – or their bras – trying to clear up two of the most serious crimes we've ever faced, I'm going to find it hellish frustrating to be trotting along to meetings of the Police Board, the Chief Constables' Association and God knows what else.

'Jimmy even talked me into moving into his office for the duration, since I'll be using Gerry, his secretary.

102

'The truth is my love, I'm jealous.'

'Of whom?'

'Of Andy, of Neil McIlhenney, of Maggie Rose, of Mario McGuire, of Brian Mackie, of everyone with hands-on involvement in these two investigations. Christ, I'm even envious of young Sammy Pye, stuck in a room on his own for at least a week looking at video tapes for something that may not be there!'

She could see the frustration written on his face. 'Do you know the only criticism I ever hear of you from the people under your command?'

He chuckled. 'I'm a brutal bastard to work for?'

'No! It's more that you're not. Everybody likes working for you. But what they all say is that you're lousy at keeping your hands off.'

'And you're saying that having Jimmy's job for a month is part of the process of learning to delegate. Is that what you're leading up to?'

'Yes, I suppose it is. But what is delegation of authority but a means of ensuring that one's own time and skills are put to the best possible use? In Jimmy's case, that means running with the politics of the job, and schmoozing the councillors. In yours, it most certainly doesn't.

'So sure, delegate. You're not the only guy in the Command Corridor. Pass on the committee stuff to Jim Elder and stay in touch with the investigations. Keep yourself fully available to Andy whenever he needs to consult you, as he will.'

He smiled at her. 'You're really good for me, you know. But I doubt if Jim Elder will see it that way. If I sling most of the admin. work along to him, who's going to do his Ops job?'

'Simple,' said Sarah, rising from her chair and coming round the table to sit on his lap. 'Are you or are you not a well-resourced police force?' He nodded. 'In that case, ACC Elder can learn to delegate, too.'

30

Skinner sat behind the Chief Constable's huge desk, staring morosely at
the documents piled high in the in-tray. He swung round in Proud Jimmy's
chair, looking out of the window only to see an array of vents and aerials
rising from the roof of the rear section of the headquarters building.

Suddenly, one of the telephones on his right gave an insistent beep. He
picked it up. 'Can I come in, sir, to run through the day's appointments?'
asked Gerry, his temporary secretary, who came with his temporary office.

'Sure. If there's coffee on the hob bring us in a couple of mugs.'

'Mugs, sir?'

The acting Chief grinned. 'I'm not going to copy all of the boss's ways.
You use a cup if you like, but I'll have mine in a mug; touch of milk, no
sugar. I need a serious caffeine fix.'

Within a minute the door opened and Gerry Crossley stepped into
the room, carrying a tray with two steaming mugs and a plate of
biscuits, and with a folder tucked under his arm. The young man placed
a mug on a coaster by Skinner's right hand, and made to take a seat
across the desk.

'Pull your chair round to the side,' said the DCC. 'You're bloody miles
away sitting over there.'

Gerry nodded and did as he had been asked. Skinner looked at him
appraisingly. From the day on which he had come to work for Sir James,
he had made an impression with his neatness, his efficiency and the speed
with which he got things done. Yet even in such enlightened times, a male
secretary was still regarded as a shade peculiar, and Skinner had overheard
the odd remark calling Crossley's sexuality into question.

In fact, Gerry was married to a public relations executive, who was
expecting their first child.

He opened the folder. 'Today's business, sir. At ten o'clock, you have
two pupils from St Augustine's High School coming in to receive
Certificates of Commendation for Bravery. Their names are Hugh
McQuillan and Andrew Byrne, and they tackled a man who was trying to
snatch an old lady's bag.'

'Did they detain him?'

'Yes, sir. He pleaded guilty in Edinburgh Sheriff Court and was
imprisoned for eighteen months. The boys' head teacher proposed them
for recognition, through our community relations section.'

'Which reports to ACC Elder,' said Skinner. 'In that case it's only right that Jim makes the award in the Chief's absence, rather than me. Brief him, please, Gerry. Right, what's next?'

'At ten-forty-five, sir, you're scheduled to receive a Commonwealth visitor, Mr Kwame Ankrah, from Ghana. He's a senior police officer on a Foreign Office-sponsored tour of the UK, looking at methods in this country.'

'What am I supposed to do?'

'We've been asked to give him a briefing on the force, sir, with the emphasis on criminal investigation.'

'How long?'

'It's scheduled to include lunch, sir, in the Senior Officers' dining room.

'Who's accompanying him?'

'Mr David Seward, sir, from the Police Division in Scottish Office, and Miss Hilda Thomson, from the Information Directorate.'

The DCC frowned. 'I suppose I'd better do that one myself. Ask Andy Martin to join me, though.'

'Very good, sir. The party is scheduled to depart at two p.m. After that you're due in Galashiels at three p.m. for young PC Brown's funeral.'

'That's going to be tight.'

'Traffic say that it should be easily enough time, sir, as long as you leave at two sharp.'

Skinner sighed. 'In that case, I'll have to receive them in uniform, because it doesn't sound as if I'll have time to change after they've gone.'

Gerry nodded. 'That sounds like a good idea, sir.'

'As far as I'm concerned, son, wearing uniform is always a fucking awful idea. Any evening engagements?'

'No, sir, not tonight. There's one on Thursday, though. The City Council is launching a new Zero Tolerance campaign, and you're invited.'

Skinner shook his head emphatically. 'One thing you should know about me. I never take on any engagements on Thursday evenings. That's Lads' Night. No, pass the details of the event to DCI Rose, out in Haddington, and ask her if she'd represent the force.'

'Very good, sir.'

'Tell you what, Gerry, why don't you cut down on your quota of "sirs". I'm not really a very formal guy. I look for performance rather than deference, and you have no worries on that score.'

The acting Chief Constable was immaculate, in full uniform as his secretary announced the Ghanaian visitor, and his party, at exactly quarter to eleven. While Skinner never felt comfortable in official dress, on the occasions on which it was required, he always ensured that his trousers had knife-edge creases and that his silver buttons were sparkling. He stood straight and tall as he shook hands with the stocky African, showing him to an armchair with exactly the right mix of courtesy and authority.

Beside him, Andy Martin was edgy, trying as hard as he could not to show his impatience at the interruption to his major priorities.

'How long is your visit to Britain, Mr Ankrah?' Skinner asked, as the pleasantries drew to an end.

'This is my second week. I leave on Friday. I spent all of last week with the Met, yesterday I was in Manchester, and tomorrow and Thursday, I will spend with Strathclyde. I am very pleased. You are the first Chief Officer who has met me personally. The others have sent their press officers or executive assistants.'

Inwardly, Skinner cursed himself for not thinking of delegating his guest to Alan Royston, but he kept a welcoming smile on his face. 'What is your rank in Ghana?' he asked.

'I am Mr Martin's equivalent in Accra: Head of Criminal Investigation.'

'What sort of crime do you experience?'

'Violence, robbery, rape, drugs: much the same as you, only more of it, and with less resources to fight against it.'

'What have you seen so far on your visit?'

Ankrah smiled, showing perfect white teeth. 'I have seen many police stations, Mr Skinner, and I have seen criminals in court. But I have not seen any criminal investigations.'

The DCC chuckled. 'It's easier to lay on lunch than crime. The major investigation which we have underway at the moment, is I'm afraid, stalled. Our only witness fled the country at the weekend.' Martin glanced at him, wondering for a moment why he had only mentioned one inquiry, until he realised that he would not want to talk about Archergait's murder with the Scottish Office people in the room.

'Still, this is a very fine police office, and we will be happy to show it to you, and to let you see some of our people at work. I sympathise with your lack of resources, yet in my experience, however much you have, there will always be times when it just doesn't seem to be enough.

'On the other hand, there can be times when all those resources can be irrelevant. Take our current investigation, for example. Until we can uncover new lines of enquiry, by analysing the material which we have, most of our people are sitting on their hands.

'There's another essential resource, of course.'

'Yes,' said Ankrah. 'Instinct. Some things are international.'

Skinner laughed out loud. 'You're right, of course, but that's not what I was going to say. I was talking about criminal intelligence. The greatest gift that information technology has given investigators is the ability to source facts and figures about types of crime, and the people who specialise in them, more or less at the touch of a button.

'I thought we'd start our tour with a visit to our intelligence gathering unit.'

The five rose and were moving towards the door, when there was a light knock and it opened. 'Sorry to disturb you, sir,' said Gerry Crossley, 'but I have Superintendent Pringle on the line for DCS Martin. He says it's very important.'

Frowning, the Head of CID stepped into the outer office and picked up the phone which lay on the desk. His back was to Skinner as he spoke, but the DCC could see the change in his body language as his conversation developed. At last he replaced the phone, and stepped back into the doorway.

'They've done it again, Boss,' he said grimly. 'But this time, they've changed the target. Raglan's, the jeweller in Castle Street, was held up just over half an hour ago by three men wearing Hallowe'en masks, and carrying shotguns.'

'Casualties?' Tension gripped the room.

'Not this time, thank God, but they've ripped off just about every gemstone in the place. I'd better go down there.'

Skinner turned to his Ghanaian guest. 'You say you haven't seen any action since you've been here, Mr Ankrah. Well, now's your chance. If your escorts will allow it, Andy and I will be pleased to take you to see a genuine, fresh, Scottish crime scene.'

31

Kwame Ankrah looked across Princes Street at the Castle, silhouetted by the morning sun, as its battlements frowned down on the street to which it had given its name. Changes in the traffic plan had made it a cul-de-sac, accessible only from George Street, but now the lower half was closed off completely, from Rose Street down.

Skinner looked at the face which Raglan's showed to the street. He had noticed the shop often, of course, but had never been inside, preferring to make his jewellery purchases from a family-owned business along in Frederick Street than from a public company which boasted two Royal crests above its doors.

It was a feature of the Castle Street branch that very little stock was displayed in the double window on either side of the entrance. To the left, he saw an exquisitely fashioned suite of emerald pieces, all set in platinum, and to the right, the most expensive items from the most expensive watch brand on the market. Other than that, the shallow windows, with their wood-panelled backings, were empty, but there was no sign that they had been disturbed.

The manager was slightly over-awed to see a large man in an impressive uniform, and an immaculately tailored African, step into his shop behind Martin.

Dan Pringle was surprised also, but made no comment, save a brief nod to the DCC as he stepped across to the Head of CID. 'Morning, Andy,' he said, quietly. 'God's gift to enterprising thieves, this one was.

'I don't know how their insurers let them away with it, but there's no video surveillance, and a police-linked alarm system which they actually switch off during the day. The only half-serious precaution is a button entry door, controlled from within the shop.' The Superintendent shook his head in a gesture of disbelief. 'The manager was just talking me through the stock loss.' He turned and beckoned to the man, who stood in a doorway behind a glass-fronted counter, at the rear of the shop. Like every other display case in the big unit, it was strewn with empty trays.

'Mr Rarity, this is DCS Martin,' he began. 'The officer in uniform is Deputy Chief Constable Skinner, the other gentleman . . .'

Martin helped him out. '. . . is Mr Ankrah, an African visitor who was with Mr Skinner and I when the call came in. So, Mr Rarity, can you put an approximate value on the haul?'

The man, who was in his fifties and who stood less than five feet six inches tall, chewed at his bottom lip. 'At retail prices?' he asked in a high squeaky voice. The Head of CID nodded. 'I'll need to work it out accurately, but approximately, the current sale value of our stock is around four and a half million pounds.'

For an instant Martin felt his jaw drop and snapped it shut. Behind him he heard the sudden intake of Skinner's breath and a gasp of surprise from Kwame Ankrah.

'Four and a half-million,' he repeated, keeping his tone matter-of-fact only with an effort. 'Your customer profile may be top drawer, but nonetheless, how the hell do you come to be holding that level of stock?'

Mr Rarity smiled, and gave a tiny, slightly hysterical, little laugh. 'Oh we don't always carry that much. We just happened to be holding an exceptionally large quantity of gemstones today.'

'Why was that?'

'Two reasons, really,' the little man squeaked. 'We're a key branch in that we wholesale precious stones for other retailers and craftsmen. On top of that we have a few customers who purchase unset diamonds and other stones directly from us. One of them had warned us to expect him tomorrow, and had told us that he wanted to invest at least two and a half million sterling in quality diamonds of one carat and upwards.'

'Forgive me for asking,' said Skinner, moving closer to the man, 'but why would a buyer like that come to Edinburgh and to you, rather than going, say, to the diamond market in Antwerp?'

Rarity fidgeted from one foot to another. 'I couldn't say,' he muttered.

'I could. It is because some people do not want to be seen buying such quantities of precious stones.' The DCC looked down at Kwame Ankrah, standing beside him. 'In my country, indeed on the whole of Africa, it is usual for black money – if I may use the term – to be converted into precious metals and stones. Traditionally they are the best hedges against inflation.

'Naturally enough, the people making such investments do not want to be seen trading on the main exchanges. So they buy from private jewellers. In my experience, though, African criminals usually go to Switzerland or Australia to convert their illegal money.'

The DCC looked at the little manager. 'Where does your customer come from, Mr Rarity?' he asked.

'From St Petersburg.' The answer was barely above a whisper.

'And how does he pay you?'

'In cash. Invariably in used US dollars. He carries it in a suitcase.'

'A fucking big suitcase, I'll bet. How often does he visit you?'

Rarity hesitated. 'Usually twice a year,' he answered, at last. 'Certainly, for the last three years, it's been twice a year.'

'Spending how much?'

'From memory, the least he's ever spent was three million dollars. His biggest single purchase was of stones worth eight million.'

'So if I guessed that this man has put ten million dollars a year across your counter, for the last three years at least, I wouldn't be far off the mark?'

'I suppose not.' Something stirred within the little manager. 'But in any event, it's perfectly legal. A sale's a sale. It's not for me to ask any customer how he came by his money.'

Skinner exhaled hard, the breath whistling through his teeth. 'So are you saying to me that if the people who've been knocking over banks in this area walked in here and put one and a half million pounds on the counter, you'd sell them diamonds, no questions asked?'

Rarity looked at the floor. 'No. In that case, I suppose I'd alert you.'

'But this chap's a Russian, so it doesn't count. Jesus! Do you have to clear transactions like these at Board level within your company?'

'No. Managers have local autonomy.'

The DCC laughed, harshly. 'I'll bet. So that if there's a can to be carried ... Meanwhile, with a ten-million dollar boost to your annual turnover, you're probably the company's star performer.'

Rarity flushed.

'What's this man's name?' Skinner fired at him.

'Malenko; Ivan Malenko.'

'Do you have any proof that's his real name?'

'The first time he came here he showed us a passport.'

'How does he communicate with you?'

'By fax: always by fax, giving us about two weeks notice of his arrival, and the value and types of stones which he'd like to buy. I would put an order into our purchasing department and the gems would be delivered at least two working days in advance, to give me a chance to sort and evaluate them.'

Skinner looked at Martin and raised his eyebrows. 'Who would see that fax, Mr Rarity?' he asked.

The manager shrugged his narrow shoulders, bouncing the padding of his Chester Barrie suit. 'Whoever picks it off the machine. It's located upstairs in our general office.'

'I see, so everyone on your staff would have known that you would have a large quantity of stones on the premises today.'

'Could have known, Mr Skinner. I can't say honestly that everyone would have.'

'How large a staff do you have?'

'Seven altogether, sir. Myself, Mrs Hall, who's my deputy, two sales assistants, a craftsman, a trainee, and a book-keeper cum secretary.'

'And where are they now?'

'Upstairs in the general office.'

'All of them?'

'All apart from Nick Williams, one of the sales assistants. He called in sick this morning.'

Skinner looked at Pringle. 'Dan, have . . .'

The Superintendent nodded. 'I've asked for a car to call at his address and bring him in sir, unless he's really unfit to leave the house.'

'That's good.' The DCC turned towards Martin, stiff in his uniform. 'Andy, you can see where we're headed on this. I'd better take Kwame here back to Fettes, then I'm off to PC Brown's funeral. Check in with me around five-thirty, would you. I ought to be back by then.'

'Okay, Boss. See you then.'

'Excuse me, Mr Skinner.' The Ghanaian had a gentle smile on his face. 'Do you think it would be possible for me to remain here for a while? This is really what I am here to study, and with respect to your fine officers, it would be more worthwhile for me to observe your detectives at work than to be shown them.'

The big policeman laughed. 'You'll miss a good lunch, but that's okay by me. You hang on with Andy and Dan for as long as you like. I'll go back and entertain your escorts, and let them catch up with you later.'

Half turned towards the door, he looked at Martin. 'Once you're finished here, Superintendent, I'd like you to take Mr Ankrah back to Fettes and show him our intelligence operation. After all, he must see something of our resources. When you're there though, have them plug into Interpol and see if they can come up with anything from Russia on Mr Ivan Malenko.

'If we can do them a favour in the course of this investigation, why not. Unless he reads British newspapers, he should still arrive here tomorrow. Maybe we should give him a proper welcome.'

111

32

'How was the funeral?'

'How are they all?' Skinner replied to Martin, as he stepped from the Chief Constable's ante-room having changed, thankfully, out of his uniform. His estimate of the time of his return had been over-optimistic. It was ten minutes past six o'clock. 'Never a barrel of laughs, mate; and this one, with a young woman involved, a police officer. Well, it was as you'd expect. Just like Harry Riach's service yesterday, the whole town was there. His widow and sons turned out, too. Poor Annie's family were very touched by that.'

He settled into the Chief's well-worn chair as the Head of CID sat down opposite him. 'So what's happened since I saw you last?'

'Quite a bit. For openers, I'm satisfied that this is the same organisation that's been hitting the banks, and not a spur-of-the-moment, copy-cat affair. The description of the robbers, the way they handled themselves, the type of masks they wore; everything ties in.

'One man came up to the door, and pushed it. One of the staff took a quick look and pressed the release button, then all three came in, quickly but without a fuss. The last one in pulled down the blind covering the glass panel of the door.'

'So does that mean that finally, we've got a facial description of one of these guys?'

Martin snorted. 'When he tried the door he was wearing a Panama hat and wrap-round Oakley sunglasses, the kind cricketers use. By the time the assistant looked up from pressing the entry button, he had his mask on and he had produced a sawn-off from under his sports jacket. Sorry, the description isn't worth a toss.'

'How did they behave inside the shop?'

'Efficiently as always. They rounded up the staff and laid them on the floor. Wee Rarity was shitting himself, so they left him and made Mrs Hall, his deputy, open all the display cases, then the main safe. Finally they made her show them a hidden safe in the manager's office, built into the floor under his desk.

'That's where he kept the gems.'

'When you say they made her show it, d'you mean that they knew about it in advance?'

The Head of CID nodded emphatically. 'Absolutely. This robbery was certainly an inside job. And guess what? Mr Nick Williams, the sick sales

112

assistant, and his girl-friend, are nowhere to be seen.

'They share a flat up in Marchmont. Just after he called in sick, the girl . . . her name's Arlene Regan . . . handed in the keys to the letting agency, and demanded her deposit back. Normally the agency would have inspected the place before handing any money over, but she made a hell of a fuss, and they were well in credit with the rent, so they paid up.

'I took Ankrah up with me, and one of Pringle's DCs, to have a look at the place. Stripped clean of clothes and personal effects, just like McDonnell's. They are not on holiday, you can take that for sure, and since they've paid the rent, they haven't done a moonlight either.'

Skinner's frown was so deep that it was almost a snarl. 'What do we know about this boy Williams?'

'For a start, he's no boy. He's twenty-eight, and he's worked at Raglan's for six years. He did his training with a jeweller in Perth, where he was brought up, then moved to Edinburgh. He was in good standing with the company. In fact, Rarity told us that Mrs Hall's due to retire in six months, and that Williams was lined up to succeed her as deputy manager.'

'Do we have an address for his parents?'

'Yes, the shop had that on file. His mother's dead, but the father still lives in Perth. The Tayside CID have been asked to pay a call on him, to see if he knows anything about his son's plans.'

'Some chance of that,' said the DCC, cynically. 'He's sure to have done a runner from us and left a forwarding address! What do we know about his personal life?'

'He's keen on football, according to the staff. He's a rabid St Johnstone fan; a season ticket holder at McDermid Park. He's also a keen cyclist. He trains with a road racing club in the city somewhere.'

'Is he a drinker?'

'Not as far as his colleagues know. The staff at Raglan's aren't the sort of people who go rushing into Ma Scott's at closing time, but on the odd occasion when they have had a drink together, Williams has never had any more that a pint of shandy or a single glass of wine.'

The DCS grinned, broadly. 'The girl-friend's another matter though. Mrs Hall said that at last year's staff Christmas do she got completely arse-over-tit. "Hidden talents, my man's got!" she kept on shouting, even as Williams was hustling her out the door. Mrs Hall said that everyone's looked at him in a different light since then.'

'What does she do, then, this Arlene?'

'None of the staff were very sure. One of them said she was a secretary in a factory office somewhere, but they didn't know where.'

'What about the neighbours up in Marchmont?' asked Skinner. 'Did you get anything out of them?'

'We couldn't find any. You know what those big blocks of flats can be like. Most of them are normally occupied by students and young working people, although at this time of year a few are let out to Festival visitors. In any event, they're usually empty during the day. Dan Pringle's sending people back there this evening to recanvass them.'

'Do we have a car number to go on?'

'By now, I expect that we do. Mrs Hall says that he has a big red Volvo estate. She didn't know the number, but I ordered a check through DVLC.'

The DCC pushed himself out of the chair and walked round the desk to the window. He looked out over the playing field, where the force Rugby Club was beginning its mid-week training session.

'I don't suppose Dorward's people found anything to go on?' he asked, but with no hope sounding in his voice. Martin sat in silence. 'No, I didn't expect that.

'Do you see any pattern in this, Andy, anything at all? Because so far, I'm stuffed if I do.'

The DCS stood up to lean on the windowsill beside him. 'There are no connections, Boss, that's the problem. Who do we know about in this business? There's Nathan Bennett, now deceased, Hannah, likewise, Malky McDonnell, gone, and Nick Williams, gone. If we could find something that they had in common, that'd be a start, because it might lead us to other people. But there's nothing to be seen.'

'So what do you do when you can't find anything?'

Martin nodded. 'Aye, I know. You look again. And that's what we're going to do; again and again, if necessary. I agree with you, there has to be a link. It's up to us to keep looking until we find it.'

'That's right, and meantime, I'm stuck here in Jimmy's office. I'm spinning as much as I reasonably can on to Jim Elder, but there are some things I just have to do myself. Tomorrow afternoon, for example, I've got the Chair of the Police Board coming in for her monthly coffee and biscuits. Then I've got a series of disciplinary matters to deal with.' He shuddered for a second. 'For example, there's a PC from Broxburn who thumped his wife. She wouldn't press charges, but the Divisional Commander isn't letting him off with it.

'Then I've got a uniformed woman sergeant from your old place, Haddington, who's accused of sexual harassment.'

'You're kidding!'

'I wish I was. A probationer claims she groped him in a cupboard. How would Jimmy deal with that, d'you think?'

'Awkwardly, I imagine. Who is it, anyway?'

'Karen Neville.'

Martin's eyes widened. 'I remember her; a looker, late twenties. Legend has it she had her evil way with Sammy Pye at a social evening a year or so back . . . and a few others before him. I gave her a friendly warning when I was out there. I hope that she hasn't forgotten about it, because otherwise, she's okay.'

'Mmm,' said Skinner. 'That's useful to know.' He turned round, and stood, leaning back against the window.

'I take it you delivered our visitor back to his minders,' he said.

The Head of CID grinned, and shook his head. 'No. I wanted to talk to you about that. Kwame's asked if he can scrap the rest of his programme and stay with us for the rest of the week.'

'Is it okay with Scottish Office?'

'Yes. They're quite taken with the idea, in fact. They've even offered to under-write his expenses for an extra week, so that they can treat it as a sort of informal pilot secondment.'

'Can you be bothered?'

'Certainly. He's a good guy. This afternoon he's looking at videos with Pye, giving the lad's eyes a rest. Tomorrow, I thought I'd let him sit in with Dan Pringle. If anyone needs extra help, he does.'

'In that case,' said the acting Chief, 'if it's okay with you, it's okay with me.'

'Good. Dan was thinking that he might take him back to Raglan's tomorrow, to wait for this man Malenko.'

'Oh? Did you find out anything about him?'

'Did we ever. The Criminal Investigation people in St Petersburg reported back like a shot. Ivan Malenko . . . that's only the name on the passport he uses to come here . . . is a very bad man indeed. He is the big man in organised crime in that part of Russia, and his activities extend through the Baltic States and into Poland and Germany. Drugs, prostitution, currency rackets, counterfeiting . . . he takes profit from them all.'

'Why don't they lift him then?'

'They can't. He's too well protected. He has a sort of presidential guard with more firepower than all the police in St Petersburg and Moscow put together. When we told them about his trips over here, they started salivating. So did the Germans: they have an international warrant out for his arrest.

'So the game plan is that when he turns up at Raglan's tomorrow . . .'

'*If* he turns up,' said Skinner. 'He may read the papers and find out their stock's been cleared.'

'No, we've told the press that yesterday's call-out to the shop was a false alarm. The Russians have sent us over a photograph, and we know from Midland that he and a man, his minder, we're assuming, are on their early flight from London tomorrow. When he turns up, Dan's going to lift him, take him straight to the Sheriff Court and have him held on remand, for extradition to Germany. The minder will be put on the first plane back to Russia.'

'Where we going to keep him? Not Saughton, I hope, after what happened to Bennett.'

'I've arranged with the prison service that he'll be kept in Shotts. Security there is as good as anywhere in Britain.'

'Have you advised the Russian Embassy?'

'The St Petersburg police told us not to. Malenko has people on the payroll everywhere.'

The DCC chuckled. 'You have had a busy afternoon.' He paused. 'I'd tell Dan not to take Ankrah along tomorrow, if I were you. This man

Malenko sounds pretty heavy duty, and he and his minder may not like being arrested. I wouldn't like to chance our guest being hurt if trouble does start.'

'Fair enough. Do you think I should deploy an armed unit?'

'In the city centre? No thanks. Let's contain the action within the shop.' Martin nodded in agreement.

'Is that all you have for me?' Skinner asked him.

Martin frowned. 'Not quite. McGuire and McIlhenney called in from Parliament House. They've finished their interviews, but so far they've drawn nothing but blanks. Tomorrow, they start to review Archergait's history on the Bench.' He paused. 'I don't think we can keep this confidential much longer, Bob. They've spoken to a hell of a lot of people now. This "security review" cover's wearing thin.'

'I appreciate that. Look, let's try a bit of news management tomorrow. When we announce that we've lifted Malenko, then spill the beans about the size of the Raglan's robbery, the entire media corps will go completely fucking crazy. While they're chasing their tails, let's have Alan Royston slip out a quiet statement that we're treating the judge's death as suspicious.'

With their backs to the door, which Martin had left slightly open as he entered, neither had seen the woman, nor had they heard her faint knock.

'I don't know if you'll be able to do that, sir,' said Maggie Rose. Both men, surprised, turned to face her. 'I had a call from Detective Superintendent Mackie on my mobile ten minutes ago, while I was on my way home. He was calling from a crime scene in East Lothian, and asked me to find you and Mr Martin.

'Apparently a bird-watcher found a body this afternoon, out on Aberlady Nature Reserve.

'I'm afraid we've got another dead judge on our hands . . . and this time the press are all over the place.'

As Skinner looked at his Head of CID, a slow smile of disbelief spread across his face. 'If I believed in curses, I might think that this was all aimed at me, on my first day as acting Chief.

'Come on, you two. Let's get out there and take a look for ourselves.'

DCI Rose looked up at him. 'You may have to wait a bit for that, sir. From what Brian said, I think the tide may beat us to it.'

33

It was a clear and cloudless night. Although the midnight sun still cast its aura along the northern horizon, Aberlady Bay was bathed in moonlight as the convoy, led by the Ranger's Land Rover truck, made its way along the track which crossed Luffness golf course, towards the Nature Reserve.

The silver light glistened on the wide expanse of water, and on the wilderness upon which thousands of birds were settled for the night. With Skinner, Sarah, Martin, Brian Mackie and Maggie Rose in the passenger seats of the long wheel base vehicle, the Ranger drove slowly, for fear of scaring up the great flocks of geese to which the Reserve offered safe haven.

Occasionally, a family of rabbits would start in the headlight beam, then disappear towards the many entrances to their warren, their night world disturbed.

Another Land Rover in police livery followed, and behind that, a yellow tractor, with a battery of lights arrayed on a bar above its cab. The line of vehicles was completed by a third off-roader, a deep blue shadow in the night. It carried no markings, but it was distinguished from the rest by a revolving ventilator cap in its roof.

'It's a wonderland, isn't it,' whispered Sarah, as if even within the cab she might disturb the bird population. 'And to think it's within walking distance of our doorstep.'

'Sure,' said Bob, 'but you wouldn't come here on foot at two o'clock in the morning. The terrain's rough, and even with a torch there are plenty of ways to break an ankle.'

He looked over his shoulder, at Mackie. 'What did you do with the press, Brian?'

'I've gathered them together on the beach, sir, with three uniformed officers to keep an eye on them. The Assistant Ranger's there as well. They all wanted to hang on for the next low tide, and as it's a public place, I'd have had trouble ordering them to leave.

'We'd only been there for a couple of minutes before the first group arrived. After that they began to descend like those geese at nightfall. Fortunately, no-one's been too close yet. We'll have photos in tomorrow's papers, I'm sure, but there'll be no more detail than we saw on the late television news tonight.'

'You're sure none of them know who the body is?'

'Quite sure, sir. I took the wallet from the body myself. I haven't even told our people, other than Mags, who it is. Dead judges are getting to be a habit with me.'

'Let's hope they don't come in threes.' Even on the balmy summer night, something in Skinner's voice made the truck feel suddenly chilly.

As they drove on they could almost see the wide silver band of the sea retreating on the ebb of the tide. 'The Aberlady sandflats stretch for more than a mile, from the road out of the village to the low-water mark,' said the Ranger, breaking the silence once more. 'It wasn't always like this. Aberlady had a harbour once . . . you can still see traces of the jetty . . . but over the centuries the Bay became silted up, until it was unusable.'

He glanced at the clock on the dashboard. 'The tide should be far enough out in about fifteen minutes. After that, you'll have about five hours to do what you have to do.'

As he spoke, the rudimentary track came to an abrupt end, and scrubby flat-land stretched out before them. The Ranger drove on over the rough ground, jerking and bouncing in his seat as did his passengers, until at last the vehicle crested a small dune which opened out on to the beach. He drove on for a bit, until the rest of the convoy was in sight behind him on the hard, wet sand, then drew to a halt, three hundred yards short of the water.

Skinner looked around. A distance away to the right, on the edge of the dunes, he saw the flickering light of a driftwood fire, with figures clustered around it, some sitting, others standing, looking across at the line of vehicles.

He turned to DCI Rose. 'Mags, would you dig Alan Royston out of the vehicle behind and go along to see the press people. Tell them that there will be no statements made here, but that Mr Martin will be aiming to have a briefing at Fettes at seven o'clock this morning.'

'How close will we allow the photographers, sir?' she asked, as she opened the door beside her.

'Keep them a couple of hundred yards distant. Near enough to do their work without disturbing ours.'

'Very good, sir.' The red-haired detective jumped out on to the sand. At almost the same moment, Alan Royston, anticipating Skinner's orders, stepped out of the Land Rover behind. She spoke to him, briefly, then together they headed towards the group around the fire.

The others sat in silence, with the windows wound down and the vehicle lights switched off, listening to the distant lapping of the calm sea, and to the rustling sound of a township of sleeping birds, as gradually their eyes attuned to the conditions.

'Can you see them yet?' the Ranger asked Skinner, pointing into the shining night. 'Do you know where to look.'

'Yes. I've been out there.'

'What you're looking for is in the one that's closer to us. You can head off now, if you like.' He opened the door and stepped out on to the sand. 'You can handle one of these things, can't you?'

118

'Sure, but aren't you coming with us?'

The countryman shook his head. 'No, thank you. I've seen what's out there. It was bad enough last time. I've got no wish to see it again, after another high tide.'

'Fair enough.' Skinner slid across into the driver's seat, and switched on the headlights, then the engine. Waving his right hand, beckoning the other drivers to follow, he set the four by four in motion, leading the way towards the water's edge.

He drove very slowly, steering as smoothly as he could over the mounds and through the hollows carved by the rise and fall of the estuarial tide, but always heading towards his objective. At last, he reached it, drawing to a halt with the headlights on full beam, trained on a sculpture of wet, rusted metal.

Although it was in miniature, it was still clearly in the form of a submarine. Within its ribs, there was something else; something grey-hued, with wispy hair, sodden clothes clinging to it.

'How long has it been here?' asked Martin, of no-one in particular.

'If you mean the sub,' Skinner replied, 'for over fifty years. There are a few local legends about it . . . one is that it, and the other one a bit further along, were part of an Italian raid during the war which came to grief. As far as I know though, they were prototypes built for a raid on the German battleship *Tirpitz* in the early years of the war.

'The story is that when it became clear that they couldn't do the job, they were beached here and used for naval target practice. The one along there is smashed to bits, but this one retained its shape through it all.'

He paused. 'If you mean, how long has the thing inside it been there, that's for Sarah to tell us in due course.' He winced in anticipation. 'Come on, let's take a look.'

As the four remaining occupants of the Land Rover stepped out on to the sandflat in their rubber boots and yellow waterproof tunics, the driver of the tractor guided his vehicle into position and flooded the skeletal submarine with bright white light. They cast long shadows as they stepped up to the twisted superstructure, and as they did, a fifth joined them. Mackie looked at the man who stood by his left shoulder. 'I'll bet this is a first for you, Arthur,' he muttered, grimly.

'I suppose it is,' Inspector Dorward acknowledged. 'I've seen a few bodies on beaches, mind you, but never one at low-water mark.'

'This'll be a first for Sheila as well,' said Skinner to the Superintendent, 'having you called out in the middle of the night.'

'She better get used to it,' Sarah added, as Martin, unaware of Mackie's new domestic arrangements, looked on, puzzled. 'Even our kid gets called into the act in our household.' Alex had been summoned from Edinburgh to look after her brothers, to allow her step-mother to go to the crime scene.

'So how did the poor bugger get stuck in there?' asked Dorward, oblivious to the exchange as he stared at the figure in the bowels of the submarine.

119

'Not on his own, Arthur,' Mackie told him, in a slow, even voice. 'Not on his own. You and the doc had better go and take a look.'

Sarah nodded and stepped closer to the wreck. 'From the side, ma'am,' Dorward suggested. 'Let's go through those spars as close to the body as we can. That way we won't be getting in our own light.'

She did as he suggested, with the inspector following behind, and a video-camera operator from his unit bringing up the rear, staying as close as she could to the action.

The old man's body was pressed on its right side, against the rib-like uprights on the far side of the hulk. The arms were bent behind it, and a wide strip of heavy black adhesive tape, partly detached by the water, hung from the right cheek. The face bulged, not only, she saw, through immersion, but also because of the white handkerchief which had been stuffed in the mouth, and, of which, a corner protruded.

Experienced as she was, her stomach heaved involuntarily as she looked at the head. The eyes were gone, and great strips of flesh, including the right ear, had been torn away from the face and scalp. 'Would fish do that?' she asked herself, without realising that she was speaking out loud.

'I doubt it, ma'am,' Dorward answered her. 'The water's only a few feet deep here, even at high tide. It's the birds that have been at him.' He leaned over the body. 'Look here though,' he said.

She did as she was told. Below the sleeves of the sodden tweed jacket, and the check shirt, a set of plastic handcuffs were cutting into grey swollen wrists, tethering the man to the upright behind him. His ankles, in green woollen socks beneath his plus-twos, were bound together with more of the black tape, which now hung loose. 'Oh my God,' she whispered.

'Is he dead, then, doctor?' Skinner had walked down the westward side of the wreck, and was standing outside the cage which it formed. He spoke with an irreverent irony, and she knew at once that it was not out of any lack of respect, but that it was his policeman's way of breaking the grip in which the horror of the sight was holding her.

'The poor old man,' she said, with an unexpected tear in the corner of an eye. 'Someone forced him in here, tied him up and left him to drown. Although it's possible he'd have died of fright before the tide covered him. Time will tell about that.

'Who did you say he was?'

'Lord Barnfather. A retired Court of Session judge.'

'Was he reported missing?'

'Not to us,' Brian Mackie answered. 'He was a bachelor, and lived alone in a flat in Ainslie Place. So there was no-one to report him missing, other than his neighbours. A twitcher found the body late this afternoon. He trained his field glasses on the sub because there were birds flocking around it.'

'What's a twitcher?' she asked, puzzled.

'Slang for bird-watcher.'

'Ah.' Her professional composure recovered, she looked down at the savaged remains once more. 'For what it's worth without a full autopsy,' she pronounced, 'I'd say from the state of the body that he's been here for two days. That would make it Sunday.'

'Why wasn't the body found sooner?' asked Dorward.

'It's mid-week,' the DCC replied, 'and the schools are back. In term-time, the Reserve is fairly quiet during the week. Anyway, not too many people walk out to the subs. It's a long way off the beach, and folk are afraid of the quicksand.'

The inspector looked at him with sudden alarm. 'What, sir, are there quicksands out here?'

Amused by his reaction, Skinner smiled. 'No, but they think there are.'

He looked down at Sarah again. 'There's nothing more for you to do here?' She shook her head. 'All right. Arthur, call in your lads and take all the footage and still-shots you need, quick as you can, so we can get the poor old chap out of here and into the mortuary wagon, away from these awful fucking birds.

'I never did like seagulls much.'

Dorward nodded his agreement. 'Me neither. Noisy, nasty creatures, they are.' He stepped backwards out of the wreck, keeping his shadow out of the way of the camerawoman.

'We should give the scene the once-over as well, sir. You never know, whoever brought the old chap out here might have left us a bit of cloth, snagged on some of this metalwork.'

'See what you can find, then, Arthur: but unless it's got his name on it, it won't do much good. I reckon there have been five high tides since then.'

34

'A post-mortem examination will be carried out this morning. However, you may take it that a murder investigation is underway already.' Andy Martin fell silent and looked around the room.

'Any questions?' Alan Royston invited, then pointed, as always, to John Hunter.

'When did you first become aware of the cause of Lord Archergait's death?'

'Late on Saturday, John.'

'And you've ruled out the possibility of suicide there too?'

The DCS shook his head. 'No, we haven't, but we haven't ruled out murder either. In fact we think that's more likely. We found no trace of cyanide on Lord Archergait's clothing or at his home. Nor is there any record of his having acquired the poison prior to his death.

'Since the beginning of this week, a small team of officers have been making very discreet enquiries at Parliament House. That investigation is still proceeding.'

'Whose idea was it to keep the facts from the media?' interposed Julian Finney, sounding and looking weary.

'It was a police decision, but it was taken in consultation with the Lord President and the Lord Advocate. We hoped that it might give us an advantage.'

'When would you have told us, then?' There was an aggressive edge to the Scottish Television reporter's question.

Martin was as tired as everyone else in the room, but his back straightened as he looked him in the eye. 'In the absence of an arrest before then, we had planned to make a statement this afternoon.'

'Some might say that if you had gone public immediately, Lord Barnfather's life might have been saved.'

'If they did they'd be wrong. I understand that the Lord President advised every judge, in confidence, on Sunday of the circumstances.'

'I take it that you do believe that the two deaths are connected?' asked Alastair Hutt, the Scottish correspondent of BBC News.

'We have to. There's no proof that they are, but common sense tells you that they must be.'

'Will the other judges be given close police protection?'

'It's been offered already. At a minimum, those who decline will be kept under observation.'

'More coverage from this morning's press conference will be shown in our next bulletin,' said the Breakfast News Glasgow presenter. 'And now, today's Scottish weather.'

Skinner pressed the TV remote, switching off the kitchen set. 'I reckon it'll be top of the bill on the national news as well,' he said to Sarah and Alex, seated with him around the breakfast table. 'What a story. Two judges knocked off their perch.

'It makes life twice as bad for us, though,' he added, gloomily. 'We're in trouble as it is with these robberies. We're working hard just to stand still on that investigation. The last thing we needed was some nutter trying to work his way through the Supreme Court Bench.

'Never mind the old one about being as good as your last game. We're as good as today's arrest, and it's been a while since we gave the press anything positive to write about.

'If nothing breaks on the robberies, we're going to have to come up with a lead on Archergait and Barnfather, and damn quick.'

Alex finished her cereal, and stood up to put the plate and spoon in the dishwasher. 'If hunting judges is our new national sport, it's too bad your murderer didn't start with Lord Coalville. The way our case is heading, he'd have done us a favour.'

'Alex!' Sarah gasped, as she came back to the table to finish her coffee.

'I know. Bite my tongue, bite my tongue, that was an awful thing to say. But if you'd sat in that Court for days on end and seen him nodding towards the pursuer's case and savaging ours at every opportunity! Do you know that Jack McAlpine even offered to withdraw! He thinks Coalville has a down on him.'

Bob chuckled. 'Coalville has a down on everyone, darlin'. Jack must know that. Very much between you and me, David Murray told me on Sunday that he's trying to persuade him to retire in September next year, ahead of time. He wants to create a vacancy for Lord Archibald on the Bench.'

'Can't he appoint him in Archergait's place?'

'Bruce Anderson, the Secretary of State, won't allow it. He wants Archie to do another year as Lord Advocate, to give the Solicitor General time to prepare for the job.'

'The Lord President didn't tell you who's getting the old boy's red jacket, did he? Only I thought that it might be McAlpine, and that that might have been the real reason he offered to pull out of our case.'

Skinner smiled at his daughter's shrewdness. 'No comment,' he muttered.

'I rest my case.' She stood up, and picked up her hold-all from the floor. 'I must be going. I have to pick up my briefcase from the flat.'

Sarah nodded. 'Yeah. Thanks for coming out last night. Would you like to look in on Mark and tell him to wake up and get ready for school?'

'Sure. 'Bye.'

She watched the door as it closed. 'She's loving her legal career, isn't she.'

Bob nodded. 'Yup, and doing very well at it. Mitch Laidlaw keeps singing her praises. He told me he wants her to stay after she finishes her training period.'

'D'you think she will?'

'For a while maybe, but as far as I know she still has her heart set on the Bar. It's a good set-up for women lawyers. Being self-employed they can take time out more easily if they want to have a family.'

'Don't talk like that,' Sarah warned him. 'The idea of being even a step-grandmother makes my blood run cold.'

She picked up her coffee and looked at him. 'Do you think you will get a break on the judge investigation?'

He rolled his eyes, in a 'Who Knows?' gesture. 'We'll do our damnedest. The first thing to do is to establish a potential motive. We'll start by cross-checking Archergait's judgements with Barnfather's, and see if we can find common ground. Something may jump out at us from that.'

'I'll keep my fingers crossed for you.' She grinned. 'So how did the delegating go yesterday?'

'It went as far as I could take it. I'm trapped today, though. My afternoon's full of stuff that I can't get out of.'

'Ah well,' Sarah sighed, sympathetically. 'You'll just have to find something to brighten up your morning.'

35

Campbell Rarity could feel a line of cold sweat as it ran down the length of his backbone. He was all too aware that his deodorant was not up to the extra duty which his nervous state was imposing on it.

Fortunately, the shop was empty, save for one male customer at a small table, who was examining a suite of amethyst jewellery set out before him by a sales assistant. Rarity glanced up at the clock. It showed three minutes to ten.

He almost jumped out of his skin when the buzzer sounded to tell him that someone was pressing at the door. He was shaking as he leaned across to see who was there.

A middle-aged lady, wearing a light summer dress, looked through the glass expectantly. Rarity shook his head. She stared back at him, puzzled, then pushed the door again. The manager shook his head again, more vigorously this time, and mouthed the words, 'Sorry, we're closed.' Apparently undaunted, the woman rapped her knuckles against the glass, once, twice, three times, until with a furious, baffled expression, she turned and walked away.

Oblivious to the exchange, the customer who had managed to gain admission put down the bracelet which he had been studying and picked up the matching ring.

Rarity pressed himself against his counter trying to ignore the pounding in his chest. He watched the clock as it crept up to ten a.m., then on: one minute past, two, three. When the buzzer sounded again a chill of panic swept through him, so cold that for an instant his teeth chattered.

To master it, he took a deep breath, before looking at the glass panel once more, and before pressing the entry button.

Two men stepped into the shop. The first, his powerful build apparent even in his loosely-cut, colourful Versace jacket, was a big man, but smaller than his companion. He stood at least six feet three and seemed to fill the room with his black-clad presence. Both newcomers had broad, brutal faces, and both seemed to exude menace. Ignoring the other customer, who sat with his back to them at his table, they moved towards their waiting host.

'Good to see you again, Mr Malenko.' Rarity greeted the Russian like a cousin, back from a long journey.

'Good to see my dollars again,' the man growled in return, in a harsh, hoarse voice.

'Not at all,' said the manager, inanely.

'Whatever. Let's do business.' Malenko beckoned to his companion who stepped forward and laid a big, soft nylon bag on the counter. 'There's four million dollars. You want your lady come count it, as usual?'

Rarity nodded, vigorously. 'I'll just go and get her.'

He turned and stepped through the door behind him.

As soon as he had left, the two men began to converse. They spoke in low voices, in Russian, but from their attitude anyone listening would have known that they were doing no more than passing the time.

They snapped back to attention, though, when the door behind the counter opened once more. A burly, moustached figure stepped into the room with another tall man behind him, and stepped around the counter.

'Mr Malenko, I am Detective Superintendent Dan Pringle, Central Division CID, and this is Detective Sergeant Steele. We have a warrant for your arrest in relation to alleged offences in Germany. I must ask you and your associate to . . .'

The Russian moved with remarkable speed for such a big man. He kicked Pringle hard on the shin, then butted him as he reacted to the pain. 'I don't think so,' he snarled, as the Superintendent slumped to the floor.

The gun appeared in the giant's hand as if from nowhere, pointing at the centre of the detective sergeant's chest. Somehow, the silencer made the ugly weapon look even more menacing. The minder looked at Malenko, who said something in Russian, and nodded.

The only Russian word which Bob Skinner knew was 'Niet'. Instinctively he barked it out, as he rose from his table, abandoning the amethyst jewellery, and hurled himself at the two gangsters.

The pistol swung away from the ashen-faced Steele and round towards him, but the detective was quicker than the bulky gunman. He seized his right wrist in his left hand and swung it up, towards the ceiling, at the same time slamming all his weight into him and bearing him backwards towards the wall. Thrown off balance the Russian was unable to gather his strength, or do anything to ward off Skinner's attack.

He was wide open as the heel of the DCC's right hand flashed upwards, to hit the tip of his nose, breaking it, and driving bone and gristle upwards. He screamed as strong fingers gouged his eyes, blinding him. He sobbed as a knee smashed into his crotch, crushing his testicles and sending waves of pain, indescribable in any language, shooting through his body.

Skinner was aware of the sound of scuffling behind him as he tore the pistol from the collapsing mountain's loosened grip, but all his attention was on the gunman. His face was contorted in a snarl as he whipped the barrel and silencer of the gun across his face: three blows, backhand, forehand, backhand once more.

'You were going to shoot him, were you, you bastard,' he hissed. The man was on the floor, crumpled against the wall, as the detective laid the weapon against the side of his head and pulled the trigger. He squealed in terror at the suppressed noise of the shot in his ear, and at the crushing sound of the bullet burying itself in the panelled wall behind him.

Slipping the pistol butt-first into his pocket, Skinner pulled him up with his left hand and punched him, once, very hard, with his right fist, in the middle of the forehead. The Russian's eyes glazed as he sagged, unconscious.

In the moment that the DCC stood and turned, Malenko, with his back to him, managed to break free of the young Sergeant Steele's judo hold, and hit him with a head-butt, in the same way that he had incapacitated Pringle. He had barely straightened up before the cold metal of the silencer ground into the back of his head, just above the hairline.

'I hope your English is really good, friend, and you understand what I'm going to tell you,' said Skinner. 'If you make one move, I'm going to blow your fucking brains all over that wall.' The Russian froze.

'Search him, Dan,' the DCC ordered Pringle, as the Superintendent clambered off the floor, his face covered in blood.

He nodded. 'In a minute, sir.' With great deliberation, he hit Malenko as hard as he could, a tremendous blow to the pit of the stomach. The air hissed out of the gangster's lungs in a loud groan, as he doubled over.

'I never saw that, Dan,' said Skinner.

'Naw,' Pringle retorted. 'And I never saw what you did to that other fucker either!'

He took a pair of handcuffs from his pocket and secured Malenko's arms behind his back, then frisked him, roughly, while Skinner helped the young sergeant to his feet. 'You okay, Stevie?'

'I'll live, sir.' As he spoke, the image of the gun pointing at his heart rushed back into his mind, and he went chalk-white once more, save for the livid red mark on his cheekbone where the Russian's forehead had connected.

'Yes, son, you will. With a commendation on your record, at that. If you hadn't restrained him, I'd have had trouble handling Malenko as well as that monster there.'

Steele looked at the heap on the floor. 'Ex-monster, I'd say, Boss.' The giant was still out cold.

'Malenko's unarmed, sir,' Pringle called out.

'Thank Christ for that. As soon as I get back to Fettes, I'll be on to Her Majesty's Customs. Some bugger's going to have to explain to me how a Russian can bring a firearm through any port in this country. If I had thought for one minute that they'd have been armed . . .'

Pringle shook his head. 'It never occurred to me either, sir.'

He turned to Malenko. 'Where did you arrive in Britain?' he asked. The Russian shook his head and spat on the floor at the Superintendent's feet. The burly man, still bleeding from a cut above his right eye, balled his fists, but Skinner spun the prisoner around and unbuttoned his jacket. He reached into a pocket and found a passport.

He flicked his way through the pages, until he found what he was looking for. 'Paris,' he muttered to Pringle. 'This was stamped in Paris yesterday.

127

Let me take a guess, Ivan. You flew to Charles de Gaulle, then caught the Eurostar to London.'

The gangster glowered at him.

'What did you do with the gun?' he asked. 'Wrapped in tin-foil was it, to beat the X-ray machine, and hidden in a container in your man's suitcase?' He shrugged his shoulders, and smiled. 'Yes, I guess that was probably how you did it. It's academic now. The fact is, you probably did us a favour. If he hadn't been carrying, and you two had come along quietly, I'd have had nothing on him. I'd have had to let him go.

'That's not a problem now. He'll go before a Scottish judge, charged with attempted murder. Christ, he'll probably get longer than you.'

He turned to Sergeant Steele. 'Stevie, get on the radio and tell the uniformed team to come and pick these people up.' As he spoke, there was a moan from the man on the floor. Skinner looked down to see him beginning to stir, beginning to push himself to his feet.

Quite casually, the detective kicked him on the side of the head. 'Just stay quiet now,' he said, conversationally. The minder's eyes rolled as he slumped against the wall once more.

36

'You never told me you were going to pick up Malenko,' said Andy Martin.

Skinner smiled across the table in the senior officers' dining room. 'I had an hour free, so I thought I'd go along and lend a hand.'

'You might have told Pringle, though. He said to me that he had trouble keeping his face straight when he came out of the back shop to arrest the Russians and saw you sitting there, looking for all the world like a punter in for a present for the wife.'

'I was. Sarah's got a birthday coming up soon.'

The Head of CID frowned. 'From what Pringle told me, it was just as well you were there. Who'd have thought that a Russian would have been armed in this country?'

'We should have thought of that, mate,' Skinner growled quietly. 'You and I should have, as line commanders. We put two officers' lives in danger. Firearms Act or not, the world's changing, Andy; every bugger seems to be going armed these days. We won't make a policy announcement, but from now on, whenever we go on an operation like this morning, we're going to have armed men on the team.'

He paused as a waitress stepped up behind him to clear his soup bowl. 'As I promised Pringle,' he continued after she had gone, 'I've been on to the Customs people, at the top level. There are cages being rattled in London, and in France even as we speak. It's fucking ridiculous that two Russian hoodlums got through our security with four million dollars and a firearm.'

He grinned, unexpectedly. 'That's one advantage of Jimmy's office. Even as a DCC you only get a certain level of attention from these characters in London, but when you're announced as acting Chief Constable Skinner, and you come on the line breathing fire, that's a different matter altogether.'

'Excuse me, gentlemen. Two ham salads, was it?'

'Yes thanks, Maisie,' said Skinner. The rosy-cheeked bustling woman set large, well-filled plates before them and withdrew with a smile.

'How did Dan get on at his press conference?' he continued.

'Fine,' Martin replied. 'I didn't stay all the way through, but he and Royston were well in control when I left. The hacks lapped up the Russian story all right, especially when Dan threw in the bit about the gun.'

'He didn't mention me, did he?'

'No. He said that Malenko's bodyguard . . . He's called Fydor Ostrakov, incidentally . . . had been disarmed by police officers, that one shot had been fired, but that no-one had been injured.'

Skinner almost choked on a piece of ham. 'What? Pringle sat there with stitches in his eyebrow and said that no-one had been hurt?'

'That's right,' the Head of CID confirmed, laughing. 'The woman from Scot FM asked him about it, of course. Big Dan just puts a hand up to his embroidery, touches it and says, "That? Oh that's nothing at all, my dear." There'll be *"Hero Cop Tackles Russian Hit Man"* headlines all over tomorrow's papers.'

'Good. People need to be reminded that our job can be dangerous as well as difficult. Plus, in the middle of the most concentrated crime wave that we've ever experienced, we needed a good arrest. It gives me something to throw at Councillor Bloody Topham this afternoon too.'

'You don't like that woman, do you?'

'Don't *trust*, Andy. I don't trust her. She's got no backbone, and she doesn't have an opinion to call her own either. Jimmy gets on fine with her, because he can manipulate her. I haven't the patience for that crap.'

Martin finished his salad and leaned back from the table. 'Coffee?'

'No, I'll have some with the Lady Chair.' Skinner glanced up at the clock on the wall. 'I'd better get across, in fact, she's due in five minutes.' He stood up. 'Listen, can you get hold of Mackie and McGuire? I want a briefing on the judges at close of play today. It doesn't need to be here. I'll go wherever is easiest for them, but I want a progress report.'

The Head of CID nodded. 'I'll tell Gerry where and when.'

Skinner turned and left the dining room. To his instant annoyance, he found Councillor Marcia Topham pacing the corridor outside. 'Ah, there you are,' said the Chair of the Police Board. 'I've been waiting for ten minutes, and no sign of either you or that secretary chap. I thought you'd forgotten about me.'

'How could I, Councillor?' he replied with a forced smile. 'But you are a bit early.' As he spoke, Gerry Crossley appeared at the end of the corridor, returning from lunch. Skinner showed the woman into the Chief's office through the side entrance, signalling behind her back for coffee to be brought in.

Inside, he directed her to one of the comfortable armchairs and sat down facing her. 'I'll come straight to the point, Mr Skinner,' she burst out. 'I'm not happy.'

Instantly the DCC felt his temper beginning to strain at the leash, but he kept his smile in place. 'I'm sorry to hear that, Councillor,' he replied. 'A domestic problem?'

'No, it is not,' she snapped. 'I'm having to put up with a lot of comments from constituents, friends, and just ordinary people in the street, about these terrible robberies. When are we going to see an arrest, Mr Skinner? It's just not good enough.'

'I quite agree with you. It's not good enough that you should be subjected to such harassment. I'd be quite happy if you were to refer every one of these people to my office. I'll be happy to listen to their worries.'

He paused. 'But let me ask you? What do you say to these concerned constituents?'

'I agree with them, of course. Armed men holding up banks and the police apparently doing nothing about it. It's not right.'

Skinner held up his right hand, bunched into a fist. 'D'you see that, Councillor?'

She peered at it. 'It looks swollen to me.'

'Quite right. I injured it this morning, tackling a very large man holding a silenced pistol. If I hadn't been there, or even if I'd been a second or two slower, a young officer would be dead right now.'

As he spoke, his tone became harder. 'I saw you at a funeral yesterday; that of a young police officer. Annie Brown gave her life in the service of the public, lady. Stevie Steele almost did today.

'In the office which you hold, people like them are entitled to expect unswerving public support from you. In the office which I hold, I bloody well demand it. Unless you're prepared to relinquish the Chair to someone worthier, I suggest that you try to learn a bit about the realities and the difficulties of police work.

'For example, not all criminals wear flat caps, have low foreheads, and carry sacks labelled "swag" over their shoulders. Some . . . the successful ones . . . are highly intelligent people who go about their work in a highly professional way. These robberies have been planned better than any I've ever encountered, and have been implemented with matching efficiency. It is not easy to catch people like that . . . yet if you look at the record of this force, you'll find that almost invariably, we do.

'The Chair of the Police Board should know all that. I suggest that you go away and read up the facts and figures, so that you can do your job properly by supporting my officers, not attacking them.'

He stood up, abruptly, his anger written all over his face. 'Now, as you will appreciate, with the number of live investigations which we have running, I'm busy, so this meeting is at an end.'

Councillor Topham looked up at him, red-faced. 'But Sir James always gives me half an hour,' she protested.

'In that case,' said Skinner, 'maybe you should postpone your next visit until Jimmy gets back from holiday. I think that we both have higher priorities than vacuous chat, don't you?'

She rose, at last, with ill grace. As the side door closed on her, Gerry Crossley appeared at the other end of the room, carrying a tray. The Acting Chief grinned at him. 'Sorry, but the lady's just gone. Have the other cup yourself and brief me on these hearings.'

The secretary nodded and left the room to fetch his papers. When he returned, he sat in the armchair which Councillor Topham had just vacated.

'Let me see, sir,' he began, leafing through the folder. 'In both these cases, the officers concerned have declined formal hearings into the complaints. They've opted to come straight to the Chief Constable for disposal.

'PC Green ... he's the first before you ... has taken the position that since the circumstances which led to the Divisional Commander's complaint against him were domestic rather than professional, and since no criminal charges have been laid, there's no case to answer.'

Skinner nodded. 'I can follow that line of reasoning. Will he be represented this afternoon?'

'Yes. He's exercised his right to have his local Police Federation rep. sit in on the meeting.'

'Who's that?'

'Sergeant Ewan Cameron, from Bathgate.'

'I know who you mean. He was a DC on my Drugs Squad years ago. What's he like as a Fed. guy?'

Crossley thought for a moment. 'Conscientious but cautious, I'd say, sir. He does his job properly: by that I mean he stands up for the people he represents, but that he always manages not to upset Sir James.'

Skinner laughed. 'That sounds like Ewan all right. It sums up the reason why I recommended him for promotion to uniformed sergeant. Sometimes in CID work you have to put your arse on the line. Cameron was conscientious all right, but he'd never do that.'

He took a sip of his coffee and picked up a low-fat chocolate digestive. 'What about Sergeant Neville?'

'She simply denies the allegation. There's a statement from PC Keenan, the boy she's alleged to have assaulted, describing the incident. Then there's a note from the Divisional Commander, which says that he can't judge the facts, but that she's a bloody good officer, and that the probationer has not impressed him in his attitude to the job. Finally, there's her own statement which says simply that she bumped into Keenan in the cupboard. She says that they just happened to be in there at the same time.'

'Will she have a Fed. rep. with her?'

Gerry Crossley frowned, momentarily. 'No. Sergeant Geary, from Dalkeith, is her area rep., but when I spoke to her to arrange this hearing, she refused point-blank to have him present. She said she was going to come alone.' The secretary paused, and coughed. 'I told her that in the circumstances, sir, I thought that would be completely inappropriate, so I insisted that she bring another personal representative.'

Skinner laughed out loud. 'Were you scared she'd walk out of the meeting and accuse me of groping her as well?'

The young man flushed, and smiled, awkwardly. 'No, sir, but in this office you can't be too careful.'

'I know that, son. So just you make sure that the recording system is switched on.' Crossley looked at him in sudden, shocked surprise. The acting Chief Constable grinned. 'Gerry, there's nothing I don't know about this building. You bear that in mind, and don't ever think about phoning your stockbroker from in here.' He pointed to the desk. 'Especially not through that white telephone over there.'

By the time the buzzer sounded at three o'clock, Skinner had read his way through all of the papers relating to the cases which he was to hear. He had also changed into uniform, something which made his secretary's eyebrows raise momentarily as he showed in PC Green and Sergeant Cameron.

Both men marched into the room stiffly, and stood to attention. 'At ease, at ease, for Christ's sake, and take off those bloody hats,' the DCC burst out. 'Ewan, you don't have to come to attention in front of me.

'Sit down both of you. Take one of the comfortable seats over there.' Sergeant Cameron smiled and nodded. Green seemed, in an instant, as if a weight had been taken from him.

'That's good, that's good,' said Skinner as they settled into the plush, well-upholstered chairs.

'Okay, we all know why we're here. PC Green . . . it's Mark, isn't it . . . Mark, I've read the Divisional Commander's complaint, I've read your wife's statement and I've read yours. Is there anything you want to say to me, now you're here?'

PC Mark Green gazed across at him, confidence replacing his initial apprehension. He was twenty-eight years old, small for a policeman, but with a wiry strength exuding from him, suggesting that he was someone to be approached with caution.

'Well, sir, really only what's in my statement, sir. Wendy and me, we had a wee argument; bawling and shouting and that. She threw a plate at me and I lost my temper and hit her. The next thing I knew there were two coppers at the door, two of my mates from the station.

'There was this wee nyaff of a neighbour wi' them. He's always had a down on me. Bad family they are; his son's aye in the jail. If he hadn't been there, sir, the whole thing would have been sorted on the spot, but since he was, the lads felt that they had to lift me.'

Skinner nodded, sympathetically. 'So it's all a misunderstanding, then?'

'Aye, sir. That's how I'd put it.'

'Ewan, do you have anything to add?'

The sergeant shook his head. 'No, sir. PC Green's been given the opportunity to say his piece. That's what I'm here to ensure.'

'Fine. That's fine.' The DCC paused. 'In that event, I hope we can get this sorted quickly and easily. I hear what you say, Mark, and of course, I've read your statement. I've read your wife's too. I have to say, there's nothing in there about flying plates.'

'Well, no, sir. There wouldnae be, would there?'

'No, I suppose not. But you see, I've read some other papers too. I've read the arrest reports, for example. If the arresting officers were mates of yours . . . well, all I can say is that you should pick your pals more carefully. They seem to have been out to stuff you. They both say that when they arrived, you were in a rage, and Wendy was terrified. They also said that she was bleeding from a cut lip and that her left eye was badly swollen.' As he looked across at Green, he was still smiling, but nonetheless a palpable feeling of tension had crept into the room. Sergeant Cameron shifted in his seat.

133

'Okay,' he went on. 'We've all been in the job for a long time; we all know that arrest reports can read worse than things actually were. But you see, I've spoken to the arresting officers. They stand by every word of their account. Still, it's possible they may have had a grudge against you.'

He paused again, for longer this time. PC Green sat staring at him, his right fist clenching and unclenching. 'The trouble is,' the words burst out suddenly, startling both of the other men, 'there's Wendy's recent medical history. Let's see, Mark, you've been married for going on three years. In that time, she's been treated on four occasions for domestic accidents, on three of them by her GP and on the other in the Accident and Emergency Department, after she broke her wrist.'

'She fell off a step-ladder!' the constable protested.

'At midnight? Don't insult me, Mark.' He shook his head. 'Look, I don't know anything about your wife. She may be an annoying wee so-and-so. She may even have been unfaithful to you. I don't know, and quite frankly I don't care. The way all this comes across, it's clear to a blind man that you are a serial wife-basher.'

He held Green's gaze, almost hypnotically, until the other man gave the briefest of nods.

'Good,' he said, almost gently. 'So let's proceed on the basis of honesty. I say to my officers, and I mean it, that what happens in their domestic lives doesn't affect me, until it affects their operational efficiency.

'But this is different. What you've just admitted is criminal behaviour. Even on the basis of one incident, your Divisional Commander was right to bring his complaint. On the basis of five, it was his public duty.'

The DCC glanced across at Sergeant Cameron. 'As Ewan will have told you, my powers in this case are pretty wide-ranging. I can reprimand you and enter that on your record. I can reduce in rank . . . irrelevant in this case . . . or I can dock you seniority.

'However, I can't do any of those things here. If this was an isolated incident, I'd probably dock you three years' promotion eligibility. It isn't, though. Constable, you're supposed to be a protector of the public: in fact, you're a danger to them. Maybe if Sir James was sitting here, he'd see it differently, but I doubt it. In any event, he isn't here. I am, and there's no way I can let you continue in this job.' As Skinner looked at him, he saw Mark Green begin to shake.

'There are two ways of doing this,' he continued. 'I can suspend you and institute dismissal proceedings, right now, or I can accept your resignation. I hope you'll choose the second way. In fact, I've had my secretary prepare a letter for your signature. We'll honour your full notice period, give you accrued holiday pay, and preserve your pension rights: all that stuff. But you're out today. You don't even go back to your nick to pick up your belongings. They'll be sent on to you.

'Is that acceptable to you? I can't give you time to think about it, I'm afraid; not in the circumstances.'

Green sat for a while in silence, trying to come to terms with what

Skinner had said. There was a catch in his voice when finally he replied. 'Yes, sir. I'll sign the letter.

'About Wendy, sir. She's all right, really. I should never have got married, that's all.'

'Are you seeing anyone else?'

'Yes, sir. Someone I knew before I met Wendy. I've never stopped seeing her, in fact.'

Skinner shook his head. 'Then choose, son. For everyone's sake, choose.' He rose to his feet, and the others followed. 'One thing though. You're walking out of here with a good chance of finding a new career. I will give you a personal reference based on your performance reports. But if there is ever another call-out to a domestic at your house, you're done for.

'Understood?'

'Yes, sir. Thank you, sir.'

Skinner saw the sergeant and the soon to be ex-constable to the door. As soon as it closed behind them, he left the room by the side exit, and made his way down to the headquarters gymnasium.

He opened his locker and changed into trainers and shorts, then took out a pair of boxing gloves. Slipping them on, he walked over to the heavy punching bag and began to hit it: jabs with his left hand at first, light blows, then shorter, harder-hooking punches, thrown in combinations, rising in speed and ferocity.

He pounded the bag non-stop for almost half an hour, ignoring the ache in his swollen right fist, sweat pouring from him, his face contorted with the effort, winding up the session with a huge sweeping left hook which lifted the bag up, and rattled the chains upon which it hung.

By the time his buzzer sounded to signal the arrival of Sergeant Karen Neville, he was showered and back behind the Chief's big desk. He stood as she entered . . . followed by DCI Maggie Rose. He looked at his former assistant, a question in his eyes which she answered quickly.

'Good afternoon, sir. You'll be surprised to see me, I expect. Sergeant Neville asked me if I would come along as her personal representative. She felt she'd like a woman here.'

'Understood; take a seat, both of you, please.' He showed them to the leather chairs, as Gerry Crossley came in with more coffee. He pointed to the tray as it was set down on the low table. 'I've asked for this just to emphasise that this is an informal meeting.

'Let's blow out any notion that this is a disciplinary hearing. It's not. I've looked at PC Keenan's allegation and at your statement, sergeant. I've also made enquiries about your accuser. This is a straight situation of your word against his, and nothing I've read or been told makes me inclined to find in his favour. So relax, Karen, you're off the hook on the harassment complaint.'

The blonde officer looked at him gratefully. *'Andy was right,'* he thought. *'She is a looker. Lucky young Sammy.'*

'In that case,' the DCC went on, 'you may be wondering why I didn't just cancel the hearing, and let you know of my decision in writing.'

Sergeant Neville looked at him, but said nothing.

'Well, the fact is, I did think that I had cause to speak to you. You'll recognise the name Sammy Pye, I think. In fact, I might even say that you'll be familiar with it.' In a second, the woman's face went bright pink. 'Then there's Neil McIlhenney. I understand that . . . how do I put it? . . . you made a pass at him at another gathering.' He glanced at Maggie Rose. By now she was staring at her companion in disapproving astonishment.

'You've obviously never met Olive McIlhenney,' said Skinner, with a chuckle.

'On top of that . . . if I may use the phrase . . . am I misled that your reluctance to have Sergeant Geary act as your Fed. rep. at this meeting might have had something to do with an encounter two or three years back?

'Finally, I haven't been misinformed, have I, that your former Divisional Commander once gave you a friendly warning about . . . let's say about fraternising?'

Staring at the coffee table, Karen Neville shook her head.

'Okay. I don't want to embarrass you, sergeant, any more than I have to. I'll say to you what I've said to someone else today. Your private life is your own business, within the letter of the law. As the world knows, no-one believes that more than I do.

'My point in raising all these things is to bring home to you the fact that young Mr Keenan's allegation wouldn't have left the Divisional Commander's office had it not been for the chat on the station grapevine. I spoke to Sammy Pye, and to McIlhenney. I had to lean on both of them . . . especially Pye . . . to make them confirm anything, and I'm convinced that neither of them have done any bragging.

'Since there were only two parties to these transactions, that rather suggests that you may be to blame yourself for the subsequent gossip.

'Keenan made his allegation, Karen, because he thought it would be believed.'

The woman spoke for the first time. 'I had worked that out for myself, sir. It doesn't make me proud, believe me.'

'I know, I know.' He smiled at her. 'The world's changing, but not to the point at which a lass can behave like a lad and expect the reaction to be the same. Girl Power is no more than a marketing slogan in that respect. It might not be fair, but it's fact.

'Look, as I said, there are no adverse career consequences from this, but we'd better get you out of Haddington. There's a vacancy for a sergeant in Special Branch.'

He flashed the briefest of looks, and grins, at Maggie Rose, just as her eyebrows rose.

'I won't put you there, of course, not straight from uniform. However, Sergeant McNee, who's been filling in in DCS Martin's office, will be moving across. Mr Martin's happy for you to move into his job. You don't have any problems about working with Sammy Pye again, do you?'

'No, sir.'

Skinner smiled broadly. 'That's good. Neither does he. In fact, he seemed quite keen on the idea. Just remember, though; in future keep professional and private well separated.' The smile turned into a laugh. 'The cupboard in CID's far too small anyway.'

37

The acting Chief Constable looked around the drab meeting room in the Musselburgh Police Station. 'It's a fucking awful place this, Andy,' he said. 'All that's missing are a few bloodstains on the walls, or it would pass for a Stasi interrogation centre.

'First thing tomorrow, I'm going to take a look at our renovation programme. If this place isn't right at the top, I'm going to put it there.'

Martin laughed. 'That's right, Boss. What's the use of having all that power if you don't use it? You seem to be settling well into Proud Jimmy's chair.'

Skinner shot him a dark frown. 'Don't you believe it, mate. I've made three decisions today, and I'm almost certain of a fourth. The first was to go to Raglan's with Pringle and Steele. No way would Jimmy have done that, nor I if I was full-time in the job. Yet if I hadn't, Stevie would be dead now, and probably Pringle too. Christ, those Russian bastards might have killed everyone in the place.'

He let out a weary sigh. 'The second thing I did was to end the career of PC Mark Green. It had to be done, but I hated it, even though I did my best to let the lad go with dignity. Christ, Andy, he even thanked me at the end.

'And the business with Karen Neville, that was as embarrassing for me as it was for her.' He broke off with a smile. 'Man, but you should have seen Maggie Rose's face when she thought I was going to transfer her to Special Branch beside her Mario!'

'Aye,' Martin responded with feeling. 'But just you make sure that Alex doesn't get to hear any of this now that she's coming to work for me!'

Skinner put a hand across his mouth. 'The matter is closed. Neville's learned her lesson, and she starts with a clean slate.'

'I'll keep an eye on her and Sammy though, just in case. Anyway, what's your fourth decision?'

The DCC stared out of the dirty window. 'That's about me, Andy. I've just about made up my mind that I don't want to be Chief; here or anywhere else.'

'What! That's a bit premature, isn't it? You've only been doing the job for two days.'

'Even so.' His right index finger stabbed out, pointing towards the street. 'I belong out there. I belong alongside Dan Pringle and you, and all the other people putting their lives at risk, not stuck in a big office taking run-of-the-mill decisions, and not playing politics with bloody councillors.

'Know what I did with Topham today? I threw her out of my office. She came in whining about the bank robberies, and I just fucking lost it and showed her the door. Jimmy might have the patience to deal with people like her, but I sure as hell don't.'

'Come on, Bob,' the DCS protested. 'Jimmy would have thrown her out too if she'd tried to lecture him about operational matters.'

'No, he wouldn't. He'd have given her a biscuit and explained to her, very politely, where her role came to an end. Anyway, the woman went on about people stopping her in the street. People in the street haven't a fucking clue who she is. She was doing the bidding of our old enemy Councillor Maley, and she and I both knew it.'

He threw his arms in the air. 'Anyway, it's not for me, none of it.'

'Mmm,' said Martin. 'You say that now. Wait till the time comes: you may have no choice in the matter.'

'I'll always have choice, mate.'

'We'll see.' He looked at his watch. 'What's keeping the troops? I said six sharp.'

'It's two minutes before. They'll be here.'

As it turned out, less than a minute later, the door opened, and Mackie, McGuire and McIlhenney came into the room.

'Evening, gents,' said Skinner. 'Sorry about the surroundings, but this was the most central place we could think of. Let's try not to be here long.

'Brian, do you want to kick off?'

Mackie nodded his shiny head. 'We've got the preliminary post-mortem results, sir. Sarah's hunch was right. There was no water in the lungs. Lord Barnfather died of heart failure. The estimated time of death is around seven on Sunday evening, just as the tide was starting to come in.'

The DCC whistled softly. 'The poor terrified old man. What a way to go.'

'I can smell a culpable homicide plea here, Boss,' said McIlhenney. 'The defence could say that the guy only tied the old fella up to frighten him, and that when he came back to release him he found him dead. That's unless it's a woman, of course.'

'Oh aye, and what's he or she going to say about the cyanide in Archergait's jug?' asked Mackie, with a touch of sarcasm. 'I was just trying to give him a belly-ache?'

'Where's the proof that this is the same person?' the sergeant countered. 'Even if we make an arrest in this case, there's no saying that we'll be able to charge the suspect with Archergait's murder.'

Skinner rapped the table. 'Enough, enough. You may well be right, Neil, but let's not get ahead of ourselves. We're nowhere near catching anyone yet, for either crime. Go on, Brian.'

The Superintendent nodded. 'I've spoken to the Nature Reserve Ranger, Boss. He said that there were quite a few people around on Sunday afternoon. Okay, he did say again that not many people go out to the submarines, but still there's a fair chance that someone will have seen Lord Barnfather with his killer.'

139

'That raises another question, surely,' said McGuire. 'For the old man to walk all that way out across the sand with someone, wouldn't it mean that he knew him?'

'That's a possibility,' Mackie agreed. 'Although it's one of several. He could have been persuaded to go to look at the subs, for some reason. Or he could just have been taken by the arm and forced, if his attacker was strong enough. We'll look into it, don't worry, but the first priority has to be to get a description of the person we're after.' He looked at Skinner and Martin. 'I'm proposing to issue a statement, through Alan Royston, appealing for anyone who was in the Reserve on Sunday afternoon and evening to come forward for interview.

'Someone saw something, even if they don't know it.'

'Go ahead with that,' said the DCC, 'but don't just ask Alan to issue a release. Call a briefing and make the statement yourself. A personal request for help always gets a better response.' He hesitated, then glanced at Mackie again.

'There's one group you might have a problem with, though.'

'Who are they, sir?'

'Gay men. The beach out beyond the Reserve is pretty remote, so not many of the twitchers go that far. In recent times it's become quite well known in Gullane and Aberlady as a discreet gathering place for gays. Every so often, Charlie Radcliffe used to raid it, until the Civil Liberties people complained, and the Chief told him to leave them alone.

'They're far less likely to answer your appeal.'

Martin leaned forward. 'Mind if I make a suggestion?'

'Of course not,' said Mackie.

'How about sending Maggie and Karen Neville . . . in civvies of course . . . out there in the afternoon and evening, on Saturday and Sunday? They won't frighten anyone off, or make them feel threatened.' He looked at McGuire. 'You don't mind making your own tea for a couple of nights do you, Mario?'

The inspector grinned. 'Who do you think makes it most nights?'

'I'll do that, Andy,' the Superintendent agreed. 'I'll speak to them both tomorrow.'

'Fine.' The Head of CID turned back to McGuire. 'How are you two getting on?'

'Like a house on fire today. Now that the real reason for our investigation is out in the open, we've had people seeking us out.'

'Aye,' McIlhenney interjected, 'like the head of the security firm that looks after Parliament House. He was shitting himself that his outfit might wind up carrying the can.'

'That's right,' the inspector confirmed. 'Him for one. We let him off the hook though. His boys can't be everywhere at once. Their main task is to watch the doors and keep an eye on the busy corridors, rather than the quiet ones.

'We did pick up one piece of intelligence over a cup to tea with Colin

Maxwell. Old Archergait and his son . . . the Advocate Depute . . . hated each other's guts.'

'Did they, by God,' muttered Skinner. 'I didn't pick up any hint of that from Norman King on Monday. Full of rage, he was.'

'Apparently so, Boss. The old judge used to go on about him to Maxwell when they played golf. He used to say that even as a wee boy, he was a sneaky bastard. He thought nothing of him as a lawyer either; said that he'd never have made a bean if he hadn't been his father's son.

'We had a chat with a lady Silk I know, one who's in the same stable as King. She confirmed the hatred, but she gave us the other side of the story. She said that according to the son, the old judge was an absolute monster at home. He used to thrash everyone who upset him, including his wife, with a big leather belt. As soon as the boys were old enough, apparently, they moved out. Old Archergait never gave them a penny towards their education, according to Norman. He said that his mother had money and that she paid their way through Watson's, then university.

'According to King, when she died, she left no will, and old Archergait pocketed what was left of her wealth. The sons got nothing. Norman claimed that he knew that she had made a will, because he helped her to write it. In it, she left all her dough to the sons. He tackled the old man about it, but Archergait said that she had changed her mind and burned it. He said that if the brothers wanted anything, from her or from him, they'd have to go to Court for it.'

'Some story,' muttered Martin. 'It's just as well for him that he's got an alibi.'

McGuire shook his head. 'That's another interesting thing, sir,' he said. 'After we heard all this talk, I thought we should maybe check that out. So, rather than alert the Crown Office to what we were after, I got Neil to call a pal of his on the *Scotsman*. Apparently on the day in question, one of the jurors in the case King was prosecuting in Glasgow called in sick, so the judge adjourned for the day.'

'You mean he could have been in Edinburgh when Archergait was murdered?'

'Not *could*, sir.' McIlhenney beamed in triumph. 'He *was* in Edinburgh. He caught the ten-thirty from Queen Street, along with my journalist chum.'

'Well, well, well,' said Skinner, 'that does open up a line of investigation, doesn't it.'

He threw his head back and gazed at the ceiling, thinking as the others looked on. Finally, he looked once more at Mackie, then at McGuire. 'Let's not get too excited about this, lads; cold-blooded patricide is one of the rarest crimes in the book. But still, let's follow it through.

'We need to answer two questions. One, if Norman King's hated his old man for years, what could have happened to make him decide to do him in now? Two, what possible reason could he have had for killing Lord Barnfather as well?' He stopped as a frown spread across his face.

'There's a third question too. If there is a link between Archergait and

Barnfather, does it extend any further? Tomorrow, Mario, you and Neil have another word with your pal Maxwell. He seems to know everything that goes on in Parliament House.'

He turned to Martin. 'This meeting has cost me my dinner, Andy. I think I'd better go back to see the Lord President right now. Christ, he might be on the hit list as well.'

38

'You seem more cheerful this evening,' said Alex, forking up some of her Fisherman's Pie.

'I suppose I am, love. It's the first positive day I've had in a while. Bob and Dan Pringle nicking those two Russians, that was a great result. Top item on the Scottish telly news, and on ITN, and it'll be on the front pages tomorrow too, I'll bet.

'On top of that we've got a real suspect in the Archergait murder.'

She looked at him, her big eyes narrowed. 'What do you mean? Was my dad involved in arresting those two men?'

Andy looked at her and gulped. 'Oh. A slip of the tongue. Yes, he was there. He tackled the big guy with the gun; punched his lights out, in fact. He wouldn't allow any mention of it at the press conference, though.

'Don't breathe a word to Sarah, for God's sake, or I'll be back on the beat.'

Suddenly, Alex's face was drawn and anxious. 'What the hell was he doing getting involved in something like that?' she burst out. 'He's getting too old for all that stuff.'

'That's not what the big Russian would tell you.' He reached across the table and, smiling, took her hand. 'Don't you worry about Bob. He can still handle himself better than anyone else on the force.'

'But he shouldn't have to! He's supposed to be acting Chief. What's he doing getting into scrapes like that?'

'Getting away from being acting Chief, that's what he's doing.' He paused. 'Your old man's having a bit of a career crisis at the moment. He's trying to convince himself that he doesn't want to be a Chief Constable, and that he can stay on the street forever.'

'What's brought that on?'

Andy looked her in the eye. 'So far this week, he's represented the force at two funerals. On top of that, he had to sack someone this afternoon. He was right to do it . . . the guy had been thumping his wife . . . but he still hated the experience. He's just a bit scunnered with it all at the moment.

'I wouldn't worry about it. Bob might not admit it, but he's ambitious. He's the sort of guy who has to climb the ladder, all the way to the top. But he isn't the sort of guy who'll shy away from the shitty end of any job. He'll work it all out in time.'

He picked up his fork. 'But enough of my day. How about yours? How's the case?'

'It's not getting any better. Lord Coalville gave Jim McAlpine a real savaging this afternoon. He was cross-examining one of Grimley's experts, and ... so Mr Laidlaw and I thought ... doing a good job of undermining his estimate of loss, when the judge stepped in and accused him of badgering the man. He said that all that ground had been adequately covered, and told the witness to step down.'

'So it's still looking rough for the insurance company?'

Alex gave a gasp of exasperation. 'Ahh, we're stuffed. Grimley will be awarded well into the seven figures ... and it won't stop there. It'll be very bad news for Adrian Jones.'

'What do you mean?'

'Well, at the very least, the Law Society will act on Grimley's complaint against him as soon as the case is over. They can be tough. I'd guess that his practising certificate will be restricted. It'll probably mean that he'll have to give up his partnership and be demoted to assistant. He'll take that hard. He's only been a partner for a couple of years. He was a late entrant to private practice.'

Andy shrugged his broad shoulders. 'It seems fair to me. If a promoted police officer screws up that badly he's liable to be demoted too. Why should you lawyers be different?'

'Ah, but it's worse than that for us, though. The bigger the award, the worse the consequences for Jones' firm. The way solicitors' indemnity insurance works, its premiums will be loaded to an almost crippling level. But if Jones is no longer there ...'

'So his firm will sack him?'

'Almost certainly. No; *delete* almost.'

'That'll be sad for his family, but I still say it's fair. You have to have a means of getting rid of the bad apples, just as we do. People rely on lawyers as much as they rely on the police, so they have to be protected from the Adrian Joneses of this world just as much as from the Mark Greens.'

She leaned across the table and pointed a long finger at him.

'Yes, but maybe the Adrian Joneses need to be protected from the likes of Lord Coalville.'

'And the Mark Greens from the likes of Bob Skinner?'

'Don't twist things. Who judges the judges? That's what I'm saying.'

Andy snorted. 'Hah. There's someone doing just that at the moment, it seems. And whoever it is, they believe in capital punishment!'

144

39

'Sorry I'm late, honey. I had to go to see the Lord President again, short notice.' Bob slipped off his jacket as he came into the kitchen and hung it over the back of a chair. It was nine-fifty and the children were long since in bed.

Sarah wound her arms around his waist, pressing her long, denim-clad legs against his. 'I understand. There must be a few nervous judges around today.'

'You can say that again. We're giving close round-the-clock protection to sixteen of them, and unofficially we're keeping an eye on the others . . . including the President himself. David's being very stoical about it all though. He can't conceive of anyone wanting to bump him off.'

'I'll bet Archergait and Barnfather thought the same thing.'

'Mmm. I don't know. From what we've heard about Archergait, there may have been a queue formed behind him . . . composed largely of blood relatives. He seems to have been a right old brute at home.'

'But what about Barnfather? What's his guilty secret?'

'That's what we're trying to find out. According to David Murray, he didn't have any. Archergait's domestic tyranny, and his son's hatred for him, were fairly well known among the inner circle, but the other old boy seems to have been universally popular.'

Sarah chuckled. 'You can say that again. I helped Joe again today with the autopsy. It was something of a surprise. I mean you wouldn't normally expect a man of his age to have a sexually-linked condition.'

'What?'

'You heard me. His crotch had been shaved, and there was evidence of recent infestation. Crabs to you, my dear. He also had an anal infection. Joe's inescapable conclusion is that the old gentleman had been indulging in homosexual activities.'

'The report will be on Brian Mackie's desk tomorrow morning as instructed.'

She released her grip on his waist and led him to the table, where a plate of sandwiches sat, sealed with kitchen film.

'Does that news affect your investigation?'

'It may well do,' Bob answered, sitting down and helping himself to two of the sandwiches. 'This evening we agreed to send Maggie Rose and Karen Neville to interview the gays down on the beach at Jovey's Neuk. Now you're telling me that the old chap might have been one himself.'

He sat in silence for a while, munching his smoked salmon sandwich and considering the new development. 'Maybe the two murders could have been a coincidence after all,' he murmured, as Sarah handed him a glass of chilled Vouvray.

'Just suppose Barnfather didn't go to the Reserve for the bird life, but for something else. Suppose his death was gay persecution, taken to extremes. Suppose Norman King did kill his father. There needn't be a connection between him and the other judge.

'God dammit. Just when I thought we could see something in this morass, the fucking water's gone cloudy again.'

Sarah pushed the table back and swung around, facing him, straddling him. 'Let me try to make it a little clearer,' she whispered. 'All work and no play makes Bob an inefficient policeman.' She took the glass from his hand and laid it on the table, then kissed him, flicking her tongue against his teeth, running her long, strong fingers through his hair.

He held her a little away from him and smiled. 'I hope you've washed your hands.'

'No, I've just rubbed them with chilies. Fancy living dangerously?' She kissed him again. 'Time for bed, I think.'

'Yeah, it's been a hell of a day. I'm shagged out.'

'Not yet, lover,' she said smokily. 'Not yet.'

He stood, picking her up in the same movement with his great strength, and carried her through to their bedroom. The curtains were open, but the house stood high on the side of the hill, and they were completely private, with the panorama of the twilit sea spread out before them.

They undressed each other slowly, deliberately, as they had done so often before, enjoying the moments, prolonging them, until finally they slid, naked, under the duvet in its fawn satin cover. He bent his head down to kiss her nipples, sucking them gently, until he felt her shiver and heard her gasp. His hand moved over her belly, but she stopped him, pushing him back and rolling on top of him. Almost before he realised it he was inside her, and she was moving on top of him like a writhing snake, flexing, thrusting, squeezing him with strong hidden muscles. He raised himself up, offering all that he possessed, which she accepted, with hunger in her wild eyes.

Her hair fell over his face. She whispered in his ear, urging, entreating with ever-greater intensity and excitement in her voice. He felt the sudden, hot rush as she threw her head back and cried out, he felt the pulsing as it rushed through him, bathing every nerve-end in warm oil. His hands clamped on her clenched buttocks, holding her tight against him as she gripped, released, gripped again, until he heard himself, a voice outside his body, moaning as his orgasm mingled with hers.

When it was over, they lay there for at least ten minutes, Sarah still mounted on him, recovering their breath and their senses, smiles of contentment on their faces.

'When you come to the end of a perfect day,' he whispered in her ear, at last.

146

She raised herself up, her forearms resting on his chest and her fingers interlocked. 'That's not what I heard,' she said. 'Alex called me earlier, just before she and Andy went to the movies. She was worried about you. She thought you were getting depressed.'

Bob smiled. 'I suppose I must have sounded that way to Andy this evening. This learning to delegate isn't as easy as you seem to think it is, my darling. Nor is acquiring patience in your mid forties, when it's a virtue you haven't possessed before.

'Different people are cut out for different things. I'm not sure that I'm cut out to be a Chief Constable, that's all.'

She leaned down and kissed his forehead. 'Who'd suspect it?' she murmured. 'Skinner the insecure, Skinner the self-doubting.' She grinned, then gasped with pleasure as he traced the tip of his index finger down her backbone. 'Just do two things for me. Trust in the people . . . like me and the kids, like Andy and Alex, like Jimmy . . . who know what you are and believe in you. And remember, when the doubts do surface, that I'll always be here to drive them away.'

Slowly he smiled, then wrapped his arms around her and rolled her over, powerfully, on to her back.

'Relaxation therapy, doctor, is that it?' He pressed his lips to hers, and she felt him begin to stir once more. 'I'll come to your clinic, I promise; as often as you like.'

40

Deacon Brodie left his mark on the world in ways which not even he could have imagined: in the continuing legends of his escape from the gallows . . . of his own design . . . upon which he was publicly hanged, through Stevenson's compelling tale of Jekyll and Hyde, for which he was said to have been the model, and in the tavern on the Royal Mile which still bears his name, and upon the wall of which his story is written, to intrigue passers-by and to lure them within.

In the wake of the sensational publicity which had followed the revelation of the circumstances of the deaths of the two judges, Colin Maxwell had been less than keen on being seen in conversation in Parliament House with Mario McGuire and Neil McIlhenney, Instead, he had suggested, 'a jar across the road, lads, lunchtime, eh?'

Like many Edinburghers in their age group, both of the policemen were traditionalists. They disliked instinctively the plasticised, made-over bars, selling designer beer rather than draught, which had proliferated in the city for a time. Instead they sought out places like Deacon Brodie's, traditional pubs with a mature atmosphere, and with unfailingly good ale.

McGuire settled back into the bench seat, watching McIlhenney as he made his way from the bar, three pints of brown, white-crested heavy beer nestling securely in his big hands. He laid them on the table then took three rounds of polythene-wrapped sandwiches from the capacious pockets of his double-breasted jacket.

'Chicken Tikka?' said the Inspector. 'They're all bloody Chicken Tikka.'

'Very true,' the bulky sergeant retorted. 'I like Chicken Tikka and I'm buying. Sling them over here if you don't fancy them.'

With a muted growl, the swarthy, piratical McGuire ripped his pack open, leaning forward as he did and turning towards the little court officer, who sat quietly, tasting his beer. 'Aye,' he mused. 'The best pint in these parts, this is. Cheers, lads.'

'Cheers.' McIlhenney looked at him, over the top of his glass. 'How's the Court today then? Any judges left?'

Maxwell grunted, his eyebrows coming together. 'Mine's bloody twitchy, I can tell you. He fairly rattled through the witnesses this morning. He kept looking down at the accused too, as if he was saying "Why don't you plead guilty, you bastard, and let me out of here." The boy's getting the message, I think. I wouldn't be surprised if the trial folds this afternoon.'

'Colin,' said McGuire, pushing the crust of his first Chicken Tikka sandwich back into the plastic casing, 'we were very interested in what you had to tell us about Lord Archergait's attitude to his son. From what we can gather, Norman King didn't like his father much either.'

The little man's face clouded. 'That's true enough. I've heard those stories too, about what a bloody awful father he was, but I take as I find, and I liked the old boy.'

'What about Barnfather? Did you know much about him?'

Maxwell took a long swallow of beer. 'Old Walter? Nobody ever knew too much about him. There were stories, though.'

'What kind of stories?'

'The kind that get the Bench a bad name.'

'Can you be more specific?'

The little man leaned forward. 'Boys,' he whispered.

'You mean he was a paedophile?' asked McIlhenney.

'No, no. I don't mean children. I mean young men: above the age of consent, although I've never heard of one carrying a birth certificate.'

'What's the big deal though? There are gay advocates these days. There are gays in just about every walk of life.'

'Aye, but a gay judge is something else. The tabloids have a field day with that sort of thing. There's gays and gays, too. The rumour about old Walter was that he liked them young, and so he went with male prostitutes; the rough trade down in Leith. Know what I mean?'

'Did you ever hear of him having a special friend?'

Maxwell shifted in his seat. As the policemen watched him, he ate a sandwich in silence. 'There was a story,' he said at last, 'about him and old Archergait. But that's all it was, only a story. They were good friends, I know that . . . They came to the Bar at around the same time . . . but I'm sure there was never any of that stuff.' His face twisted into an expression of distaste.

'Do you know of any connection between them other than just friendship?' McGuire asked.

The Court officer frowned again, and launched an attack upon his second sandwich. When he was finished he crumpled up the packaging, turned for a moment as if looking for a wastebin then, finding none, laid it back on the table.

'Well,' he began, at last. 'Old Billy told me a story one day at the golf; in confidence, but they're both dead now, so what the hell. He and Barnfather were planning on leaving all their money to the Faculty of Advocates, to be used to support youngsters training for the Bar, and in their first year in practice.

'Walter didn't have any family to inherit his, and old Billy only had the two boys: one he hated, and the other earns upwards of two hundred grand a year, so he doesn't need it.'

'Surely Norman King must be a high earner too?' McIlhenney interrupted.

'No' really. He has a mainly criminal practice, and Legal Aid fees are bloody tight these days.

'Anyway,' he went on. 'Billy told me . . . this was just two or three weeks back, mind . . . that they were in discussion with the Dean, and some sort of joint trust was going to be drawn up, wills changed and so on. I don't know if it ever was though. I hope so, for it can be tough for a young advocate with no pay during training and precious little for the first year or so. On top of that, most of them that come up from now on will still be carrying debt from student loans.'

'Poor souls,' said McGuire, without a scrap of sincerity in his voice. 'Let's hope everything was signed.' He drained his glass, 'Neil, we'd better get back across the road, There's someone we have to talk to and we might just catch him before business starts again for the afternoon.'

41

'The Dean confirmed it, sir. The arrangements for the joint bequest were complete, the wills and trust documents were in preparation, and the whole thing was due to be signed and sealed next week.'

'How much money are we talking about, Mario?' asked Andy Martin, as he stood by his office window, looking at the street outside.

'The Dean said he couldn't be sure but he reckoned that Archergait was worth about seven hundred thousand, and Barnfather maybe a bit less. Under the terms of the deal they were both transferring their properties to the Faculty now, the value to be realised on their death.'

'So Norman King may have had a lot to lose next week.'

'That's right.'

The Head of CID turned to face McGuire and McIlhenney. 'If Maggie and Sergeant Neville can come up with a witness out at the Nature Reserve who'll identify Norman King . . .

'But I'm getting ahead of myself. We need to check whether King was a loser. For all we know there might be an existing will which disinherits him anyway. I don't suppose the Dean mentioned the names of the solicitors acting for the old boys, did he?'

The big sergeant smiled. 'As a matter of fact, sir, he did, in passing. You're going to love this one. Old Archergait's lawyers are Curle, Anthony and Jarvis.'

'Oh Christ,' Martin gasped. 'That's Alex's outfit. I can see her now, digging in her heels and going on about legal ethics and confidentiality and all that stuff.' He paused.

'I think I'd better get her old man in on the act . . . without delay!'

151

42

'The trouble is, Bob, although I'm the head of the firm, there's a limit to my powers of compulsion over my partners. In fact, in theory I don't have any.' Mitchell Laidlaw looked at Skinner across the desk, unblinking.

'You know Hannah Johnson, the head of our Private Client Division, don't you?'

'Thanks for your delicacy, mate,' Skinner growled. 'You're bloody well aware that I do, since you recommended her to draw up my separation agreement a while back.'

'Well in that case, it won't have escaped your notice that Hannah is a stickler for propriety. Between you and me, when she gets on her high horse it can be difficult to persuade her to dismount.

'I suggest that you speak to her and see how she reacts. Better that it's just the two of you, I think. I wouldn't want Mrs Johnson to get the idea that I was trying to lean on her in any way.' The DCC nodded agreement, and the burly lawyer picked up his telephone. He spun his chair round so that his back was to Skinner, leaving his guest to admire the view of Edinburgh Castle as he spoke to his colleague.

After a minute or two he turned again and replaced the receiver. 'Give her a couple of minutes, and she'll see you. I haven't told her what it is, only that it's official rather than personal business.'

He paused. 'Incidentally, if I may be indelicate for a change, how are you and Sarah getting along?'

The policeman smiled. 'Couldn't be better,' he replied. 'It's a funny thing, but surviving a thing like that can bring you closer together than ever as a couple. I guess some bonds are unbreakable.

'The new house was a good idea too. We're going to throw a party before the summer's over, so keep a Saturday in September free.' He stood up, and Laidlaw led him to the door and out into the panelled corridor.

'There's a meeting room available just along here, Bob.' In a few strides he reached a dark wood door which he threw open. 'Hannah will join you any minute now.

'See you tonight?' Laidlaw asked, as Skinner stepped past him into the windowless room.

'Lads' night? I never miss it if I can avoid it. And after the week I've had so far, I'm looking forward to letting off some steam.'

'That sounds ominous. See you later, then.'

He left the policeman alone in the meeting room. However, he barely had time to glance at the pictures on the grey-papered walls before the door opened once more and the slim grey-suited figure of Hannah Johnson entered.

'Good afternoon, Mr Skinner,' she began. 'It's nice to see you again . . . I think. How can I help you?'

'You act for Lord Archergait, I believe, Mrs Johnson . . . or at least for his estate.'

'That's right.'

'As you'll be aware, his death, and that of Lord Barnfather, are the subject of police investigations. It's been brought to our attention that the two of them were in the process of setting up some sort of joint trust, vesting their property in the Faculty of Advocates.'

The solicitor reached up a slim hand and touched her immaculate silver-blonde hair. 'That's correct,' she said slowly. 'The documents were being finalised when Lord Archergait died.'

'Finalised but not signed?'

'That's correct.' She flashed him a quick, mischievous smile. 'Unfortunately for the poor boys and girls up in Parliament House.'

Skinner grinned back at her. 'They'll survive, I'm sure.

'The thing is, Mrs Johnson, this is all potentially relevant to a murder investigation. So far, my officers have been told a few stories about Lord Archergait, and his family relationships. We need to sort out truth from fiction, and I was hoping that you would be able to help us, informally.'

The woman's slim features creased into a frown. 'Did Mitch Laidlaw say I would?'

'Absolutely not. He was quite emphatic that you would follow your own instincts, and that he couldn't influence you.'

'Are you asking me to breach my duty of confidentiality to my client?'

The policeman scratched his chin. 'No, I don't think I am . . . since your client is dead.' He paused. 'As far as the interests of the Estate are concerned, why don't I try you with a few specific questions. If you have a problem with any of them, tell me about it, and we'll see where we go from there.'

Hannah Johnson raised an eyebrow. 'For example, we might go to Court, to force me to co-operate?'

'God forbid,' said Skinner. 'The last thing I want to do is take legal action against my daughter's employers.'

She laughed. 'Yes, I'd forgotten about Alex. Okay, let me see how far I can help.'

'Good. So let's begin. First, can you tell me how long the firm has acted for Lord Archergait?'

'Since before my time here. This is an old-established practice, as you know. I believe that decades ago Lord Archergait completed his initial training here before going to the Bar, and that we've acted for him since then.'

'So that means that you acted throughout his marriage to Lady

Archergait and in the period leading to her death.'

'Yes we did, although at one point, Lady Archergait used her own family solicitors.'

'How do you know that?'

'Because at one point, they were involved in drawing up a will on her behalf.'

The DCC showed surprise, involuntarily but only momentarily. 'We've been told that Lady Archergait had made a will leaving all her property to her two sons,' he continued. 'According to our source, at the time of her death Lord Archergait destroyed it and denied its existence.'

'Then either your source or their source is malicious,' said the solicitor. 'Because that story just isn't true. Lord Archergait didn't tear up the will: it was superseded, about five years before Lady Archergait's death, by a joint will in which they left their property to each other, passing to the sons after them.'

'That's funny. It doesn't quite fit the picture painted for us of Lord Archergait as a domestic tyrant.'

'Don't be so sure. The joint will was Lord Archergait's idea. I was only an assistant then but I was entrusted with drawing it up. I got the impression that he had only just found out about Lady A's earlier arrangement and had made her change it, naming him as principal beneficiary. From a hint she dropped once, I formed the impression that she had only agreed on the basis that the sons were named as second beneficiaries.'

'I see,' muttered Skinner. 'So presumably that joint will remains in existence, given that Archergait never did sign the most recent one in favour of the Faculty?'

Mrs Johnson hesitated. 'This is where it starts to get difficult for me.' She stared at the ceiling for a few seconds, then back at the policeman. 'Oh, what the hell. You're a client too, so this is just between you and me.'

'Until it gets to the witness box.'

'Fair enough. The joint will is no longer in force. Lord Archergait gave me a letter a month ago, renouncing its terms.'

'Why did he bother?'

'It was part of the setting-up process for the bequest. He and Barnfather knew that it couldn't be done overnight, so to guard against either one of them dying during the setting-up process, they entered a joint minute of agreement setting out their intention and naming each one as the other's executor, in the event of death, with power to complete the transaction.'

The DCC threw his head back and sucked in a long hissing breath. 'I see.'

He looked across the table at the lawyer. 'So what's the position now?'

'There's no-one left to execute the trust deed. In theory both old men died intestate.'

'In theory?'

'Yes, because the King brothers could execute the deed, on their father's behalf at least. Alternatively, they could go to Court to have the original will reinstated. Or they could do nothing and it would have the same effect, since they're the only blood relatives.'

'For the brothers to execute the deed, would they have to be in agreement?'

'For sure. If either one objected, it couldn't be done ... unless, of course the Faculty tried to raise an action to implement the joint minute of agreement.'

'Would such an action succeed?'

Hannah Johnson smiled again. 'It might, but my guess would be that it could be appealed all the way up to the House of Lords. In that event the whole estate would go on legal fees.'

'Have you had any indication yet of what might happen?'

She nodded. 'I've had a letter from solicitors acting for Norman King, asking for information on the amount of the estate. I've spoken to them. They didn't confirm it but I'm in no doubt that he intends to claim a half share.'

'Do you think Norman King knew of his father's intention, and of the joint minute?'

'The letter from his solicitor seems to indicate that he did, which surprises me a little, since Lord Archergait and Lord Barnfather both stressed the need for confidentiality. I hope I need not tell you that nothing would leak from my office.'

'Of course you needn't,' said Skinner. 'But who could have told him about it?'

'That's the big question,' she answered. 'So far, I can only think of the person who witnessed the document.'

'And who was that?'

'Lord Archibald, the Lord Advocate.'

43

Bob Skinner stood at the window of the Chief Constable's office and gazed at the empty chair behind the desk.

'Where are you when I need you, Jimmy?' he pondered aloud. 'If ever I missed your sound political touch in an investigation, then it's now.'

Seated in the soft leather suite, Andy Martin, Mario McGuire and Neil McIlhenney looked up at him. 'Come on, Boss,' said the Head of CID, 'this idea of the Chief as a smooth operator is a figment of your imagination. On most of the occasions when he's had to deal with politicians he's done it with a great big club.

'He gets on with Councillor Topham because she's fucking hypnotised by him, that's all. And in the past he's seen off at least one Minister of the Crown that I know of.'

Skinner scowled at him from his seat in the fourth chair in the group. 'Maybe so, but I still wish he was here. I value his judgment as much as his skill as a hypnotist. Christ, what a situation we're in. The Home Advocate Depute is shaping up as the number one suspect in a double murder. Not only that, but the Lord Bloody Advocate could be involved too.'

He looked across at McGuire and McIlhenney. 'You checked with the Dean of Faculty, and with Maxwell, like I asked?'

'Yes, sir,' the Inspector confirmed. 'The Dean said that only he and the Treasurer of the Faculty knew about the bequest . . . and they didn't know about any minute of agreement. As for Colin, he swears blind that he didn't tell anyone about Archergait's plans, other than us.'

'The old man didn't tell his son himself, did he?' asked Martin.

'Not according to Clarissa Maclean, King's lady advocate friend,' said McIlhenney. 'She said they hadn't spoken in a year.'

'How close a friend is she?'

'Intimate, according to Maxwell. King was divorced a year or so back. His wife took him to the cleaners in the settlement too.'

'Aye,' McGuire broke in. 'There's another piece of motive. He's skint, and he hears that his old man's going to do him out of his inheritance. I've seen cases go to trial with less evidence than we've got here already.'

'So have I, Mario,' said Skinner, with feeling, 'but not with an Advocate fucking Depute in the dock. We'll need to eliminate every shadow of a doubt in this investigation. I want to be able to prove that he was in possession of cyanide, and I want a positive identification of him as the man who took old Barnfather across the sands to his death.

'The existence of the joint minute of agreement is the clincher. It meant that if King wanted to preserve his claim to the family money, he had to get rid not only of his father, but of Barnfather as well, since he had the power to complete the trust arrangements even after Archergait had been taken out.

'If Hannah Johnson's right and he did know about it and what it meant, then it looks as if only Lord Archibald could have told him.'

He shook his head and snorted. 'We're looking at a situation in which the Lord Advocate himself is the crucial witness in the trial of one of his own deputies. Christ, Andy, and you wonder why I wish Jimmy was here!'

'What will it mean for Lord Archibald, Boss?' asked McIlhenney.

'Resignation, probably before the trial, possibly as soon as King is charged. It's a real bastard, Neil, I tell you.

'Archie Nelson is a good friend of mine, and it looks as if I'm going to be the man who brings him down. Not a happy prospect.'

He looked round at Martin.

'Have there been any other happenings to brighten up this lovely day?' he asked.

'No more robberies, thankfully,' the Head of CID responded. 'I had a call from John McGrigor this afternoon though. Someone found a body in a wood near West Linton, tied up and shot in the head.

'The early indications are that it's a domestic. Apparently the victim was shagging someone else's wife.'

'Indeed,' said Skinner. 'I'd leave John to get on with it, if I were you. It'll do him good to have a nice ordinary murder to investigate. It might even stop him promising to catch Harry Riach's killer, even if the rest of us can't. Because knowing him, he might even do it, and I'd worry about what he'd do if he succeeded!'

44

She lay in bed, propped on an elbow and looking at him as, still towelling himself off, he emerged from the en suite bathroom, back into their bedroom. She was as familiar with his body as with her own, with every feature, and with every one of the scars he had collected in some of his rougher moments. As he turned to toss the towel into the basket of items destined for the washing machine, she saw the most recent, bluer than the rest, less conspicuous than the jagged rip at the back of his right thigh, but even more deadly at the time.

'Bob?' she murmured.

'Uh-huh?'

'Promise me something, yeah?'

'Try me?'

'This weekend. Promise me you'll spend it all with me and the kids.'

'If it's in my power, I promise.'

'It is in your power. You're in charge, for God's sake.'

'Yes, but the way things are just now . . .'

'Andy is boss man of the Criminal Investigation branch, isn't he?'

'Yes, but . . .' He grinned at her and gave up.

'Okay, I promise that come hell or high water, I will spend the whole weekend with you, Mark and Jazz . . . always provided that you don't go off to cut up a body somewhere.'

She beamed back at him in satisfaction. 'I can promise that, okay. Joe Hutchison's going away for the weekend.'

'That's good. Are you doing anything professional today?'

'Yes, as a matter of fact. I forgot to tell you last night, before we got side-tracked. The Prof.'s giving me a lot of work just now. I'm assisting again this morning.'

He nodded. 'That'll be McGrigor's stiff, I expect. A breach of the Seventh Commandment; still punishable by death in West Linton, apparently.' The casual aside was made without a thought. He glanced at her quickly, but she smiled back.

'Wow! Ain't we lucky.'

He stepped across and sat on the edge of the bed. 'Yes, my love,' he said, 'we surely are.'

His mouth still tasted of toothpaste as she kissed him. 'And we'll never forget it, will we?'

'No chance.' For a moment he almost slipped back into bed. 'No, no, no,' he muttered, standing up and opening a drawer. 'Got to go!'

He began to dress. 'You're covered for a baby-sitter today, yes?'

'Of course. And tomorrow night, for the party.'

'Oh Christ, yes. We'd better get ours organised too. Pick a date . . . first Saturday after Jimmy gets back will do . . . and ask the Mallard to do the catering. Give them an approximate number for now and we'll sort out the guest list over the weekend.'

She slid out of bed, and into her robe. She was never lovelier, he thought, than first thing in the morning, tousled, musky, still with the haze of sleep lingering upon her. 'Okay,' she said. 'I'll fit that into my day.' She hugged him as he adjusted the knot of his silk tie.

'When are you due at the Crown Office?'

'Archie said he'd see me at eight-thirty.'

'Poor guy. I hope he has a good breakfast, because I don't think he'll feel like lunch.'

'Not a word to Joe about that, remember,' he warned her. 'Don't even mention that I'm going to the Crown Office.'

'As if I would. Wherever it is, darling, our home's still as sacred as the confessional.'

They ate their cereal together in the conservatory, scanning through the newly delivered morning papers and enjoying the view, still a novelty for them, of the morning sun as it bathed the Forth estuary, until it was time for Bob to go.

He had always preferred to leave Gullane slightly early to beat the worst of the traffic, although it had grown in density over the years to the point at which a journey which once had been completed comfortably in thirty-five minutes now took fifteen minutes more. Nevertheless he reached Chambers Street with five minutes to spare for his meeting with the Lord Advocate.

The receptionist was not yet on duty as he entered the Crown Office, but the night security attendant was expecting him. 'Just go through, sir,' he said. 'The Advocate's waiting for you.'

'Good morning, Bob,' said the plump, jovial Lord Archibald, as the policeman entered his office. 'I could barely wait to get in here today, to find out what's behind your urgent request for a meeting. Sorry about having to make it so early, but I'm off to Lord Archergait's funeral this morning.'

Skinner smiled. 'I thought it was important that I keep you in touch personally with the latest developments in the Archergait and Barnfather investigations.'

'That's good of you, Bob, I appreciate the courtesy.'

'Actually, Archie, something came up yesterday. I hoped you could help me with it.'

The Lord Advocate looked puzzled. 'If I can, I will. Go on.'

'Thanks. I understand that recently a document was drawn up, on the instructions of the two gentlemen, to pave the way for a bequest they

159

intended to make to the Faculty of Advocates. I understand also that you were the witness to their signatures.'

'That's right. We signed it in Hannah Johnson's office, down in Castle Terrace.'

Skinner paused. 'In that case, I have to ask you; since then, have you mentioned the existence of this document to anyone else?'

Lord Archibald leaned back in his chair, frowning. 'No, I don't think I have.'

'Are you sure about that?' The DCC held the law officer in his gaze.

'Yes,' he began, scratching his head. He paused. 'No, hold on; I did discuss it with Norman.'

'In what context, exactly?'

'I just happened to mention that I had done a piece of business for his father. Norman said, "What piece of business was that, then?" and I told him. I assume that he knew about it.'

'Did you mention simply the existence of the minute of agreement or its content?'

'Its content.' The Lord Advocate gazed at his friend, thoughtfully. 'It's a funny old world, Bob,' he said. 'Not so long ago, I was cross-examining you in this room. Now it seems that it's the other way around.'

Skinner smiled briefly, but ignored the comment. 'Did you mention specifically the powers of executry and attorney contained in the minute?'

'Well yes, I suppose I did.'

The policeman looked out of the window for a moment. 'Shit,' he whispered.

'Archie, I'm sorry to have to tell you but in both murders there's a pretty strong chain of circumstance pointing towards a suspect.'

'Go on,' said Lord Archibald. He seemed to sag into his chair. 'Tell me . . . as if you need to.'

'Norman King.'

In an instant, the Lord Advocate's face seemed to turn as white as his hair. 'Are you sure?'

'We need two more links to complete a chain that I'd take before a jury, but the evidence is there. We know that King and the old boy hated each other's guts. We know that inheritance was a source of concern to Norman. We understand that he was tight for cash after his divorce. We know that he would have had the opportunity to spike the water jug with cyanide.

'Now, thanks to you, I'm afraid, we know for sure that he was aware of the judge's plan to leave everything to the Faculty, and of the content of the joint minute. That gives him the motive to kill Barnfather too, to prevent the trust being executed even after his father's death.'

'What about the brother? Could it have been him?'

'He's been eliminated as a suspect in both cases.'

'But how could Norman have hoped to get away with it?' asked Lord Archibald, plaintively.

'Why should he not? We'd never have known that Archergait had been

160

murdered if Lord Murray hadn't ordered a PM. As for Barnfather, given that he was homosexual, that might easily have been investigated as a one-off gay-bashing that went wrong.'

'You mentioned two more links. What more do you need to charge him?'

'I need to show that he could have had access to cyanide, and I need to place him in the Nature Reserve last Sunday.'

Scotland's senior Law Officer stared across his desk at the policeman, his small eyes almost piercing him for several long seconds. 'Then go for it,' he whispered, at last, 'with all you've got.'

'Don't worry, My Lord, we will.'

Archibald sighed. 'Fucking hell,' he said, still quietly but vehemently nonetheless. 'Imagine the indictment: "Her Majesty's Advocate versus Her Majesty's Advocate Depute." What a bloody mess!

'If you get what you're looking for, of course, I'll be a Crown witness.' He rubbed the back of his right hand across his mouth in an anxious gesture. 'I'll have to go, Bob. Resign.'

'I hope sincerely that you'll do no such thing, Archie.'

'Oh but Bob, I must. I've just appointed the man as Home AD, for goodness' sake. I'll call the Prime Minister this morning.'

'Absolutely not!' said Skinner, his right index finger stabbing the air for added emphasis. 'That could prejudice our investigation. It could tip King off that we're after him. You must not resign before he is charged. You must not breathe a word of this to anyone. Does your wife know King's ex, or his girl-friend?'

'She knows Cheryl King.'

'Then don't even tell Lady Archibald about this. It wouldn't be fair.

'Archie, this isn't your fault. I hope you won't resign, but whatever you decide, I have to ask you to behave normally towards King until this matter is resolved.

'I hate this as much as you, but if it is him, I'm going to have him.'

45

'I can't emphasise enough, Andy, how delicate this is. I've already had to restrain the Lord Advocate from chucking it on the spot. But if there's the faintest hint that Norman King is in the frame for his old man's murder, the balloon goes up for us all.

'Imagine the public reaction if it becomes known that we let a man continue to prosecute in the High Court while he was under investigation himself.'

Martin nodded in agreement. 'Couldn't the Advocate take him off Court work for a while?' he asked.

'That's his job. He'd smell a rat right away.'

'Well, why not interview him now and let Lord Archibald suspend him on that basis?'

'Come on,' said Skinner. 'You know the answer to that one.'

'Aye okay,' the Head of CID admitted. 'If we did that and it made the press, there'd be no end of nutters coming forward to identify him at the scene of Barnfather's murder.'

'Not only that, suppose he is innocent? It could damage his career, and give him a comeback against us.

'I want this sorted out as quick as possible. Get Maggie and Neville out in the Reserve first thing tomorrow, and keep them there till they get a result. But don't tell them about the King development. Better they don't know whose face might fit. Put people in the car park too. A lot of families go out there every weekend.

'Meanwhile have McGuire and big Neil check out the cyanide angle. If we can place him in proximity to the stuff, we're one step nearer.'

Martin nodded. 'How long have we got on this? Has the Lord Advocate given us any sort of a deadline?'

'No, but I have. I reckon if we're no further forward by Tuesday, you and I are going to have to interview King formally.' He pushed himself out of Proud Jimmy's well-worn chair.

'You still haven't settled into that, have you?' Martin commented.

'No, nor will I ever,' said Skinner shortly. 'Now, what's the score on the robberies?'

'No score, so far, Boss. I suppose that the good news is that we haven't had any more this week.'

'I was thinking about that,' said Skinner. 'The banks are operating at maximum security levels, we're sending armed teams in support of big

162

payroll deliveries, and every jeweller in the territory has installed press-button entry systems.

'My hunch is that they may have run their course, for now at any rate. The clever bastard behind these things is bound to have done a risk analysis. I suspect he's decided to suspend operations for a while.

'With all the cold trails we have, that's going to make it all the more difficult for us to catch him. What are we doing, currently?'

Martin sighed, wearily. 'Interviewing and re-interviewing potential witnesses: neighbours of Hannah Bennett, the residents in the block of flats from which her brother was shot, people who were in the banks at the time of the robberies.'

'How about Rarity? Did you get any more out of him?'

'Aye, a sob story. He's been sacked.'

'Now there's a surprise,' said the DCC, his voice heavy with irony. 'After a loss like that someone was bound to carry the can. I'm sorry for the poor wee bugger, but he did bring it on himself.' He paused.

'What about Officer McDonnell? Any word of him?'

'Not a cheep. Nor of Nick Williams either. We've looked into their lives so closely that I could almost tell you the sort of aftershave they use, but I can't find even a fragment of a connection between them.'

'And the girl-friend?' Skinner asked.

'Arlene Regan? She hasn't been one of our priorities.'

'Mmm. It might be worth telling Pringle to take a closer look at her. Let's see what sort of fragrance she uses.'

Martin smiled. 'I'll do that. I'll suggest that he lets Stevie Steele do some digging. I'm quite impressed by him.'

'Aye, me too.

'Speaking of bright young men, how's Sammy Pye doing with those videos?'

'The poor bugger's square-eyed by now,' the DCS replied. 'But so far he's come up with nothing in the way of a link. I let the Ghanaian stay with him for a while, until yesterday, when I sent him out to sit in with John McGrigor on the West Linton shooting.'

'Any arrest for that yet?'

'Not so far. They pulled in Martin Sturrock, the husband of the victim's paramour. At first he denied ever having heard of the bloke . . . his name was Ryan Saunders, incidentally . . . but John soon got him to admit that he knew him, and that he'd heard the stories about him and his wife.'

'What does she say? Did she confirm that she and Saunders were having it off?'

Martin laughed. 'Oh yes. Straight away. She says her husband did it, no question. According to John, he threatened to do it as well. "I'll blow his fucking brains out!" she quoted him as saying. And that was before the big fellow had told her that Saunders had been shot dead.'

'What does he do, this Sturrock?'

'He's a small farmer. According to his wife, he has a rifle. If that's

163

true . . . for he denies it . . . it's unlicensed, and well hidden. John turned his place over but couldn't find it. I think he's going to charge him anyway.'

'Okay, if the Fiscal's happy. What about Saunders? What did he do?'

'Apart from doing Patricia Sturrock, on a regular basis? He did fuck all. He was a time-served plumber, but he's been on the dole for a couple of years.'

Skinner's right eyebrow rose for a second, then he shrugged his shoulders. 'What about Kwame Ankrah? Is that him finished with us, today being Friday?'

'No, Boss, it's not. The Scottish Office has fixed it for him to stay for another month. He's well chuffed, and so am I. He's dead keen and very bright.'

'That's good,' said the acting Chief Constable. 'The way the balls have been running for us lately, we need all the help we can get. Ask him to look in on us next time he's in Edinburgh. I'd be interested to hear his thoughts on the way we work. When you're too proud to learn from the experience of fellow professionals, you're in real trouble.'

'I'll do that,' said Martin, rising from his seat. 'You going across the corridor for lunch later on?' he asked.

'Not today. I have a lunch date already; with my wife. We don't have too many opportunities to meet in town these days, so it's a bit of a treat for us both.'

46

'What made you choose here?'

'The food's good, and I like the view,' Sarah answered. 'I like the atmosphere too. Lunch doesn't always have to be an intimate occasion. It's fun to eat café-style once in a while.'

Bob laughed. 'If you'd said, you could have come to the senior officers' dining room down at Fettes.'

'No, thank you very much! I said café-, not canteen-style.'

'It's good wholesome food.'

'Exactly, and if you and Andy didn't eat so much of it, you wouldn't have to spend so much time working out. No, in the middle of the day, I prefer this.' She looked down at the brimming bowl of crab bisque and at the bread roll which lay on a plate beside it.

Bob investigated his tuna salad then paused, turning in the bench seat to look out of the window. 'You're right about the view, though, especially on a nice day like this.' In common with most Edinburgh people, Skinner detested the visual impact on the city of the grey concrete St James Centre and its vast disused office block. But inside the building, in the top floor restaurant of the John Lewis store, it was a different matter. The window seat looked out across the north of the city, offering a panorama which stretched from the lower slopes of the New Town on the left to the Fife coast and widening river mouth on the right.

He admired the prospect for a few minutes, before turning back to eat, smiling, laughing, joking with his wife, making the small talk that loving couples do.

Finally, as they both pushed away their plates and turned their attention to their coffee, Sarah asked him, quietly, 'So how was your morning, honey? What did the Lord A. have to say?'

' "Help, Mammy, Daddy", just about covers it,' Bob replied, dropping for a moment into his broadest Lanarkshire accent. 'He's deeply upset, as you'd imagine. He's an honourable man is wee Archie. I feel heartily sorry for him.'

She glanced around, making sure that the table behind her was still empty. 'Will he have to resign?'

'No, he won't have to, as such, but if we charge the man, I don't think that anything or anyone will dissuade him from handing in his seal of office. I really hope that the bloke turns out to be innocent, but the way it's going . . .'

He stopped, abruptly. 'Enough of Archie's troubles, though. What have you and Professor Joe been up to?'

Sarah replaced her coffee cup in its saucer. 'It was pretty routine stuff today,' she said, 'as murder autopsies go. You were right; the subject was a male from West Linton.'

'Ryan Saunders.'

'That was the fella. An otherwise healthy specimen, despatched from this life very neatly by a single gunshot to the back of the head.' She reached her right hand behind her and touched the base of her skull with a finger. 'There. It was fired at close range we believe. The hair was scorched around the entry wound.

'You know,' she mused, 'I often ponder on the fact that a human life can be switched off in less than the blink of an eye by just a little piece of metal. Don't you?'

He shook his head, firmly. 'Nope. I do not. Nor should anyone, if their job is likely to put a gun in their hands. If you start brooding about things like that, one day you might delay in pulling a trigger, or you might not pull it at all. In that event, an innocent person could die . . . maybe even you.

'Ask Andy, ask Brian Mackie . . . they've pulled that trigger . . . and they'll tell you the same.'

He frowned. 'I would be interested, though, to know what was in the mind of the man who sent Ryan Saunders to wherever he's gone.'

'Can't help you there,' said Sarah, with a quick, wicked smile. 'Saunders never said a word.'

'Christ, this new job's giving you a copper's gallows humour.'

Suddenly she was serious. 'Yes, it is, but you know why.'

'Sure.' A silence hung over the table for a second. 'Do you ever dream,' he asked, 'of a day when we'll be leading a life that isn't wrapped around with the aftermath of brutality?'

'Of course I do, and one day, darling, we will. Till then, someone's got to do these things; better it's people who are good at them, like we are.'

'I suppose,' he nodded. 'So Saunders was a run-of-the-mill dissection then?'

She smiled again, and at once he was intrigued. 'Almost, but not quite. There was one peculiarity.' She reached back and touched herself once more, this time just below her right shoulder-blade.

'Apart from the gunshot, there was a single knife wound, right there in the back. It was in a fleshy area just beside the spine, a surface wound, a bit less than an inch deep. Not life-threatening threatening in any way.'

'That's odd. Were there any other marks?'

'None, apart from severe bruising to the wrists. They were bound together, with considerable force.'

'Wasn't there an exit wound?'

'No. The rifle was small calibre, and a soft-nosed bullet was used. Very efficient: it didn't exit, just bounced around inside the skull and turned the brain to mush.'

'Eh?'

'Yup. Absolute soup, it was. When I removed the cranium it more or less ran out.'

Bob shuddered. 'When will we have the report?' he asked.

'By close of play today. It won't be complicated. Apart from having no brain left, Mr Saunders was in perfect health.'

47

'I'm very pleased to hear that you're staying with us for a few more weeks, Mr Ankrah,' said Skinner. They were in the main communications room at Fettes, as the DCC finally completed the tour of the headquarters building which he had scheduled for the day of the visitor's arrival.

'It's a privilege for me,' said the African. 'Already I am learning a great deal about how methodical your detective work is.'

'Boring, some would call it,' the DCC retorted with a grin, as they left the radio room and began the walk back up to his office. 'It has to be, though. We lay heavy emphasis on the rights of the accused person, as well as the victim. Our prosecution service demands meticulous attention to detail in preparing a case for court, so we have to make sure that every witness is interviewed exhaustively, and that answers exist to every possible question which the defence might ask in Court.'

Ankrah nodded. 'We aspire to such standards too in my country. But I envy you all these facilities and your many trained officers. We have to rely much more on our instincts.'

'Good for you, mate,' said Skinner, sincerely. 'A nose for the job is just as important to us as all the stuff you see here. When detectives stop following their instincts, by and large they're no good to me.'

As they reached the top of the stairs which led to the command corridor, Andy Martin was waiting for them. 'This is the pathologist's report on the West Linton murder,' he said, holding up a document.

'I know what's in it,' said Skinner, leading the way into his temporary office. 'Sarah told me. The man was tied up and shot once in the back of the head.'

'That's right,' the Head of CID confirmed, looking at Ankrah.

'If it was Sturrock he was very efficient. One shot and the man was gone. The only oddity was a small stab wound in the middle of the back. I can't figure out why he did that.'

'I think I can tell you,' said Kwame Ankrah, quietly, and for once unsmiling. The two Scots looked at him, surprised.

'Before I came here,' the Ghanaian began, 'I paid an official visit to the People's Republic of China. While I was there, my hosts were kind enough to take me to see an execution. Ten executions, to be more accurate.' He grimaced, and shuddered slightly.

'There was no ceremony about it. The condemned people . . . two of them were women . . . were forced to kneel, and shot in the back of the

168

head with a single bullet, just like this man Saunders. But in that position, the natural reaction is to pull the head down and to cringe away from the bullet.

'So, when the marksman was ready, another person would put a knife into the back of the criminal, very quickly and without warning. That made him straighten and pull his head up. As he did so, the executioner would fire.

'They used big, heavy, soft bullets,' he said. 'Very messy, but they did not waste a shot.'

The Ghanaian shivered again. 'I think perhaps, that Superintendent McGrigor should be looking for Mr Sturrock's knife, as well as his gun.'

Skinner smiled at Martin. 'I told you we could learn from this man. Kwame, welcome to the team, even if it's only for a month. It's good to have you around.'

48

'You never know what's going to happen in this job, do you?' said Detective Sergeant Karen Neville. 'One minute I was up before the Boss, thinking I might be put in charge of female traffic wardens in Newtongrange, or shoved into some other backwater, the next I'm in headquarters, working for the Head of CID.

'Is Mr Skinner always as unpredictable as that?'

Maggie Rose, not given to spontaneous laughter, chuckled nonetheless. 'The day the Big Man becomes easy to read, he'll chuck it. You've only seen unpredictable so far: wait till you come across volatile.'

'What, you mean he chucks telephones, that sort of thing?'

'Hah, that's small-time. If Big Bob was a chucker, he'd throw the switchboard, operator and all. No, but he does have a temper. Usually he blows up and that's it. But you really know there's trouble brewing when he goes quiet. There's a look comes into his eyes then, and you don't want to be on the end of it.

'I've seen him interview a really hard case, and beat the guy to a pulp just with that stare of his.'

'What about Mr Martin?' asked Neville. 'I met him when he was in uniform out in Haddington, but none of us really got to know him then.'

'The DCS is the opposite of Mr Skinner in some ways. He's very controlled, most of the time. In fact I don't think I've ever seen him lose his temper. He's the perfect foil for the Boss; they used to call them Batman and Robin, when they were both younger. He's a really nice bloke, and you'll enjoy working for him.'

'Yes, that's what Sammy Pye said . . .'

'You've told Sammy you're joining the team?'

The sergeant shook her head. 'No, not yet. He told me how good a boss he is a few months ago, one night when we were out for a meal.'

'Indeed,' said Rose, expressionless, but with her reaction in her voice.

It was Karen Neville's turn to grin. 'I am capable of discretion from time to time. Sammy's a good friend. We see each other quite a lot but so far, apart from one brief fling, that's it.'

'So the story about you and the lad was true.'

'Yes.'

'And the story about you propositioning big Neil?'

'Ah,' said the sergeant, 'but I was drunk at the time. I seem to have been risking life and limb there. From what the Boss said, his wife must be formidable.'

This time Maggie Rose did laugh. 'Neil's my husband's best pal, so I know Olive. She keeps him in line, all right, but he builds up her legend. For all that he says, he loves her madly, and their kids.'

The sergeant fell silent for a time, as the two women, wearing light shirts, shorts and sandals in the pleasant August morning sun, trudged along the path. 'Listen, ma'am,' she said at last, 'you won't say anything to Sammy about young Keenan and his complaint, will you? It's all been kept in-house up to now, but I'm afraid that if he found out . . .'

'He might think that there was fire, after all?'

'No, that's not what I meant. I'd be afraid that he might go out to Haddington and beat several colours of shit out of Keenan.'

'What, quiet young Sammy?'

Sergeant Neville glanced at her senior colleague. 'You don't know him as well as you think.'

Rose chuckled. 'I hope he keeps his temper, then, when he's interviewing the twitcher families with our guest from Ghana.'

'Sammy's here?'

'Yes. He volunteered, with Mr Ankrah. He said that after a week of staring at videos he was desperate for a day out. Bloody typical; they get to wait by the bridge, talking to the anoraks and the family outings, and we get to trudge out here, in search of the gays.' She paused, with a quick, flashing grin. 'Not that I've got anything against gays, you understand.'

'Are we nearly there yet?' asked Karen, looking ahead to a high sandy dune, overgrown with coarse marram grass.

'I think we must be. I can hear the sound of the waves.'

Laboriously they climbed to the top of the great sand bank, although the path through the grass led round the foot of it. When they reached its summit, it levelled out, offering a panoramic view of a wide golden strand, gloriously inviting, yet almost deserted. Maggie looked around and spotted an open area, a clearing within the grass, and led the way towards it. She sat down gratefully, and slipped her arms out of the straps of the knapsack which she had been carrying on her back.

'Let's have a break, and work out how we're going to tackle this,' she said, producing a flask and two plastic cups, as Karen flopped on to the sand beside her, kicking off her sandals.

'Good idea, ma'am,' she said. 'Senior officers should show initiative.' She reached into her shoulder bag. 'I took the easy option. I brought the KitKats.'

They sat on their lofty perch, sipping hot coffee and nibbling chocolate biscuits, and looked along the expanse of the golden beach below them. The tide was on the ebb, but still high, and a few people were walking along the water's edge. Neville pointed at two of them, a man and a woman, who were walking dogs. They were thirty yards apart, but approaching the two officers' vantage point. 'We should talk to them,' she said. 'Maybe they come here every week.'

'Okay,' Rose agreed. 'We'll go down once they get closer.'

She finished her coffee, wiped the inside of the cup with a tissue then replaced it, with Karen's, in the knapsack. She was fastening the plastic catches when the voice sounded from behind them.

'Good day, ladies.'

The policewomen turned simultaneously, looking over their shoulders and upwards. It was a friendly voice, a plummy voice, with a kindly ring to it. Karen was reminded at once of a bachelor uncle who had died when she was a child.

He looked to be in his early forties, slightly younger than Uncle Alfred must have been at the end, she realised. He was of medium height, as he stood amid the grass just above them, dressed in fawn cotton slacks and a rather garish checked shirt, predominantly yellow in colour. His greying hair was swept back from his forehead, and his tanned skin shone with health.

'Enjoying the morning, are we?' the man went on. 'It's shaping up to be another lovely day, is it not.'

'Looks like it,' said Maggie Rose. As she spoke a second man appeared on the crest of the dune. Unlike his companion he was out of breath, despite the fact that he was around fifteen years younger. He was very attractive, with chestnut hair which caught and reflected the sun, and wearing a T-shirt and shorts which seemed to cling tightly to the curves and muscles of his body. He was also carrying a large blue nylon bag.

The older man looked over his shoulder and grinned. 'You're out of condition, Donovan,' he pronounced, with mock-severity in his rolling tones.

'I am carrying the bloody gear, David!'

He glanced down once more at the two women. 'They don't look after themselves, these young people, do they.'

'Oh yes we do,' said Karen, grinning.

'Oh, but I didn't mean to offend,' the man responded, with a show of mock-contrition. 'What brings you here?' he went on quickly. 'Let me guess; you're sun-worshippers like us. You must be, since you've found our private place. D'you think we might join you? There should be room for us all.'

Rose nodded, smiling up at him. 'We didn't see any towels on sun-beds, so we didn't know it was private. But sure, be our guests.'

David turned to Donovan, who dropped the bag in the clearing, unzipped it and produced two rush mats and two towels. 'I have two spare mats,' he said, in a voice much less cultured than that of his companion. 'Would you like them?'

'Thanks,' said Karen, looking into his eyes and flashing him a smile. The young man produced two more rolled, red-trimmed strips and handed them across, but his gaze avoided hers.

172

'I think I'll swim now, David.'

'Of course, my boy. I shall talk to the ladies.'

Donovan peeled off his cherry-red T-shirt, picked up one of the towels and plunged off down the dune. The three sat on their mats, watching him as he ran across the beach towards the water's edge. He stopped just short of the hard, wet sand, dropped the towel, stepped out of his shorts, turned back towards them with a smile and a wave, then ran, naked, into the sea.

David made a tutting noise. 'Frightful exhibitionist, the boy. I tell him time and time again not to do that, especially at weekends when it's busy. That's the sort of behaviour that brings the police out here.'

'Only if someone complains to them,' said Karen.

David eyed her thoughtfully for a moment. 'That's right,' he agreed. 'And you ladies wouldn't, would you.'

'No,' said Rose, quietly. 'But then we are the police.'

The man's mouth fell open in surprise, but quickly his expression changed to one of anger. 'Oh really,' he burst out. 'This persecution is just too much; I thought it was over, but apparently not. We don't do any harm to anyone out here. Why can't you leave us alone?'

'David,' Neville broke in, soothingly, 'we're not here to persecute anyone . . . although –' she nodded her head towards the sea, and grinned '– if someone persists in flashing his impressive tackle in a public place we might have to prosecute him.

'We're looking for help.'

He looked at her doubtfully.

'Really,' said Maggie. 'We are. I'm Detective Chief Inspector Rose and this is Detective Sergeant Neville. We're engaged in a murder investigation. Didn't you see our colleagues at the car park?'

'No. We park in Gullane, then walk around the edge of the golf course.'

'Well, don't you read the newspapers?'

'Never!' said David vehemently. 'I can't stand newspapers: the way they assume the right to pry into everyone's lives. Television's just as bad these days. Donovan and I prefer just to run our little gallery and let the world get on with its own business.'

He looked across at Rose. 'Where did this murder of yours take place?'

'Here in the Nature Reserve, last Sunday.' She pointed westwards, across the water. 'A man was tied up in one of the old submarines out there, and left for the tide to come in.'

'Oh, how awful! The poor chap, what it must have been like. Who was he?'

'Have you ever heard of Lord Barnfather, the judge?'

David gave a gasp. 'Oh no, surely not.'

'You knew him?' the DCI asked.

'Yes. He was a customer of ours, at the gallery.'

'Did you know he was gay?'

'Of course I did, my dear. Oh, the poor old fellow!'

'Were you here last Sunday by any chance, David?' Karen Neville asked.

He nodded. 'Yes. I only open the gallery from Monday to Friday during the Festival, for my business customers. We don't go in for special exhibitions, so all the private buyers are usually elsewhere at weekends. The weather was fine last weekend, so we came down here on both days.'

'Do you recall seeing Lord Barnfather here, on either day?'

David scratched his head. 'One sees so many people here whom one knows. We saw His Lordship in the Reserve quite often.'

'Do you mean on the beach?' asked Rose.

'Oh no,' he replied, frowning. 'He never came here with chums. He may have been an old queen, my dears, but he was also a serious bird-watcher.'

'So, last weekend. Concentrate and think back. Did you see him?'

The man put his hands behind his head, fingers interlinked, and closed his eyes.

He sat there, motionless for almost a minute, until at last, his eyes opened. 'Yes,' he whispered. 'I'm certain that I did. It was last Sunday, late in the afternoon.' He turned and stretched out a hand, pointing westwards. 'Over there, almost at the point at which the beach bends into the bay.'

'Was he alone?'

'No. He was with a man. They were both wearing outdoor clothes as I recall, and they were walking close together.'

'How near to you were they?' asked Rose.

David shrugged his round shoulders. 'They were thirty, perhaps forty yards away.'

'Did Lord Barnfather see you?'

'No, I'm sure he didn't.'

'Did you call out to him?'

'No. They seemed engrossed in their conversation.'

'When you say they were close together,' asked Neville, 'how close?'

'Their arms could have been linked.'

'Or Lord Barnfather could have been held by an arm?'

David looked at her. 'I suppose he could.'

'In which direction were you walking?' the sergeant asked.

'East. I had been stretching my legs and I had just turned to come back here.'

'And them?'

'Westward.'

'Towards the submarines?'

'If they went that far, yes.'

'And the tide?'

'It was almost fully out.'

Rose paused. 'Can you describe the man with Lord Barnfather?' she asked him.

'He was in his early middle age . . . perhaps about my own age, forty-two . . . tallish, approaching six feet, with dark hair. I think he was clean-shaven.'

'Was Donovan with you when you saw him?'

174

David laughed softly. 'No, he was off waving his wand at the water for one last time, before we went home. We were having a supper party that evening.'

'Was there anyone else nearby?'

'Not that I can recall.'

The red-haired detective looked at him. 'If we showed you some photographs, could you pick this man out?'

'I won't know until I try . . . but I do have a good memory for faces.'

Rose reached into her knapsack and took out her business card. 'In that case, I'd like you to call in at our headquarters at Fettes Avenue, tomorrow, at around twelve mid-day. Ask for the Head of CID's Office, show them this and tell them I sent you. Detective Superintendent Mackie will be there will let you see some photographs. Maybe one will be the man you saw.'

49

Even in his home village Bob Skinner was aware of the need to guard his tongue at parties. During the years of his widowhood he had tended to turn down invitations, but since his marriage to Sarah he had been drawn back into the Gullane social circle, among whose number, he had discovered, the consumption of alcohol seemed to have declined with age.

Nevertheless, as he mingled among his friends and neighbours, listening to the inevitable golf chat, he kept a mental note of his own score in cans of Boddington's Draught.

In a crowd most of whom had been together for twenty years, there were no conversational no-go areas. While he was prepared to discuss his own work in general terms, he had to be careful not to slip into specifics.

Questions were asked and were answered in general terms or the conversation was politely turned into other areas. Therefore Skinner was not surprised, or disturbed, when during a lull in a discussion of the lack of success of Scottish international rugby, one of the newer arrivals in the village . . . it was only nine years since his move from Newcastle . . . leaned forward and said, 'Who's doing in the judges, then, Bob?'

He smiled, as the other three men in the kitchen coughed and shuffled uncomfortably. 'Come on, Philip, I can't tell you that before I've told the Fiscal,' he chuckled.

'Of course you can,' his stocky acquaintance persisted, as he tore the ring-pull from a bright red can of McEwan's Export. 'They're as good as the confessional, are Gullane parties.'

Bob glanced at his watch, and laughed. 'After midnight, maybe when most people are too pissed to remember anything. Until then at least, I have nothing to confess.'

'Saw some of your people today,' Philip persisted, 'down at the Reserve. One of them even stopped me; asked if I was there last weekend. Even showed me a photo of the old boy what got done in. Since when did you start employing Africans, by the way?'

The policeman ignored the question. 'And were you there?' he asked.

'As a matter of fact I was. I go there most weekends with the dog.' He chuckled, looked over his shoulder, then leaned into the circle. 'Golf in the morning, walk the dog in the afternoon. Anywhere but bloody Tesco. D'you know, lads, if I sit on my arse for one second, that bloody wife of mine's at me to be doing something. DIY, shopping, anything. Can't bloody stand seeing me enjoy myself, Mary can't.

'Think I'll get a mistress.' He smiled up at the policeman, con-spiratorially. 'You've had some experience there, old lad. D'you recommend it?'

As he spoke, Sarah appeared behind him, framed in the kitchen doorway, holding two empty glasses. The grin froze on her face. Two men on either side of Skinner stiffened involuntarily.

But Bob simply leaned against the worktop at his back, smiling. 'Not as a general rule, Phil,' he said, then paused. 'Mind you, in some cases it can come as a blessed relief to the wife involved.'

The man's bonhomie was shaken for a second, as he struggled to interpret Skinner's comment. Finally he gave a forced chuckle. 'Take that as a compliment, shall I?'

'Take it any bloody way you like, mate,' Bob answered, as he leaned over to fill his wife's two glasses, the second of which was, he guessed, for the long-suffering Mary, with whom he had seen her deep in conversation earlier.

'Yes,' the indefatigable Philip said, his voice lower now as Sarah departed, 'I suppose some of us might be too much for the wife to handle.'

He ploughed on, returning to his original subject. 'Anyway, as I was saying, it's quite a novelty, being interviewed by the Old Bill.'

'You didn't see Lord Barnfather, I take it.'

'Wouldn't know him if I found him in my soup, old son. I never see anyone I know down there. The place is full of odd bods with gaiters and field glasses . . .' He paused. 'No. I lie. I did see someone I knew last Sunday: chap I played squash with when I was a member of the Grange Club. Bumped into him . . . literally . . . on the path through the bushes. Didn't talk to him, though. He just nodded and hurried off.

'What was his name again? Christ I'm bloody awful at putting names to faces.' He shook his head.

'It's the first sign of dementia, you know, Phil,' said Bob.

'What is?'

'I forget.'

He reached for another Boddington's and turned to the man next to him. 'On the links today, Eric?' he asked, as he ripped the top off.

'Aye,' said his neighbour. 'The usual three-ball. We all played quite well for a change. Were you out?'

'Yes, Sarah and I played Witches Hill this afternoon.'

'Did you tame it again, then?'

Bob laughed. 'No such luck. It took an expensive revenge. I had two in the water.'

'Got it!' Phil's cry of triumph turned every head back towards him.

'King; that's his name. Norman King.'

50

'How are Maggie and Neville getting on at the beach, by the way?' asked Neil McIlhenney. 'Are they picking up a tan, then?'

'They are that,' McGuire replied. 'They slogged up and down the beach for a bit, then Karen worked out that if they just got the cossies on and lay on the sand, most of the punters would come up to them. She was right, apparently.'

'How are Mags and she getting on?'

'Fine. A lot better than Maggie thought they would in fact, given her reputation. I told her it'd be okay. I said to her that anyone who'd proposition you was more to be pitied than anything else.'

McIlhenney threw the Inspector a look of the deepest disdain. 'She's a very nice girl, is Karen, and she has excellent taste. She has all sorts of qualities, in fact,' he added, slyly.

Mario's dark eyes narrowed. 'Here, you didn't . . . did you?'

The big sergeant looked at him for a long time, in silence, a grin flicking around the corners of his mouth.

'You didn't . . .'

'No,' said McIlhenney, at last, beaming. 'But if I'd been as pissed as she was . . .'

'. . . You'd have regretted it till your dying day.'

'Which would have been the day that Olive found out. Aye, I know.'

'So what are these other qualities she has, then, big fella?'

'Everything that goes to make a bloody good copper; because that's what Sergeant Karen is, behind the flashing eyes and the splendid tits.'

McGuire nodded. 'That's what DCI Rose says too.'

'What? That she's a good copper or that she's got splendid tits?'

'Both, in fact. They found a witness, a gay bloke who'd seen Barnfather with a man last Sunday. Apparently Karen handled him like a natural. Later on, when they were lying on the beach in their bikinis, the other two things came into play. Like fucking magnets they were, Maggie said. She just lay there propped up on her elbows and smiling and the punters came up to them in their droves.'

'Were there a lot of gays out there, right enough?'

'A few; even they seemed to be drawn by Neville's orbs. They were all very co-operative. A couple of young chancers did try to pick them up at one point, but Maggie saw them off with only a single flash . . . of her warrant card.'

178

'So what sort of a result did they get overall?'

'Not bad. Four people thought they had seen the old boy with someone, but couldn't describe him. David, the gay bloke, though; he's another story. He's coming into Fettes today, so that Brian Mackie can show him some mug shots, including one of King.'

'Ah, I saw the Thin Man coming in. That's why he's here, is it, and not with the new bidey-in.' McIlhenney grinned. Mackie's new domestic arrangements were still the subject of much internal discussion within CID. 'How about the guys in the car park?' he went on. 'Any result there?'

McGuire shook his head. 'Nothing. I said to Maggie that maybe *they* should get their tits out today.'

'Somehow,' McIlhenney muttered, 'I don't think our Sammy would impress too many people in that way.'

He smiled. 'We do have another lead, though.'

'Oh?' McGuire looked at him, curious.

'Aye. The Boss called me this morning. He was at some local piss-up last night, when out of the blue, one of his neighbours said that he'd seen Norman King in the Reserve last Sunday afternoon. The Big Man said that he managed not to bat an eyelid at the time, but he's going round today to talk to the guy again.'

'Christ,' exclaimed McGuire, 'that makes what we're doing all the more important.' He looked across his desk in the Special Branch suite, then down at a sheet of paper which lay before him. 'That place this morning in Wallyford was the last of the metal finishers on our list, and not a lead out of any of them.

'The only two other registered keepers of cyanide, that we know about anyway, are these two farms. One's down near Peebles, and the other's out by Linlithgow. Which do you fancy visiting first?'

McIlhenny twisted his massive trunk around in his seat and looked out of the window. 'Looks like a nice day for a trip to Peebles,' he said.

'Fine, sergeant,' McGuire agreed. 'In that case, you can drive, and I'll enjoy the scenery.'

Fortunately, most of Edinburgh's Sunday drivers head for the coast. By the time they had escaped the city and slipped under the by-pass heading for Penicuik and the A703 to Peebles, the traffic was relatively light. McIlhenney drove dead on the limit, forcing his companion to view the scenic woodlands and fields as they zipped past them.

The Borders countryside south of Edinburgh is lush and very accessible. Barely any time seemed to have passed before they were bearing down on the attractive county town of Peebles. With McGuire navigating, they drove though and found the B-road leading to Traquair.

'The place is a mile or so along here,' said the Inspector. 'As far as I can see there's a right turn off this road. Look for a sign saying Craigmark Mains.'

'Okay. What's the farmer's name?'

'I'm not sure. It's listed as Maclean Farms Limited.'

179

'What do farmers need cyanide for anyway?'

'Some of them use it to poison vermin.'

'Maybe that's what the guy who spiked Archergait's carafe thought he was doing,' the big sergeant mused.

Less than a minute later, McGuire pointed ahead, at a sign which hung out on the far side of the road, beside an opening. 'That's it, look. Slow down now, don't overshoot.'

'Teach your granny.' McIlhenney braked smoothly, indicating a right turn, and pulled up short of the Craigmark Mains sign, to allow an oncoming car to pass. Yet as they watched it, the vehicle, a silver Volvo S40, slowed down and swung ahead of them, without indicating, into the farm entrance.

Something made the big sergeant look across at his colleague. McGuire's face was a picture of astonishment. 'Did you see who that was?' he gasped.

McIlhenney shook his head. 'No, I was watching the car, not the driver. Who was it, then?'

'Clarissa Maclean, that's who. Norman King's lady-friend.'

51

Brian Mackie was a conscientious officer, and the police service had always been the most important thing in his life. Therefore it was a novelty for him to feel irritated, as he parked his car in the staff spaces beneath Police Headquarters.

Having spent the previous day in conference with Dan Pringle, comparing notes on the murders of Archergait and Barnfather, and beginning the preparation of a report to the Lord Advocate, he had been looking forward to spending Sunday with Sheila, much of it horizontally.

Instead, Maggie Rose's telephone call had plucked him from their bed and sent him into Headquarters, to meet her star witness, and show him a range of photographs. He had thought of delegating the task, until he had realised that there was no-one to whom he could pass it on.

So, grumbling for almost the first time in his adult life, he had answered the call of duty. Using the duty CID man he had combed the police library for a series of photographs of present and former customers, not the classic numbered full face and profile of dour, bewildered, and occasionally savage faces taken on arrest, but a collection of half a dozen other shots from the Serious Crimes section, some formal, some snatched by surveillance units.

He had taken his rogues' album up to Andy Martin's office suite, where he had added a glossy black and white photograph of Norman King, given secretly to Skinner by the Lord Advocate himself.

Happily, David Beaton prided himself on promptness. Mackie glanced up at the clock as the call came from reception to announce his arrival. It showed twelve noon, exactly.

'Bring him up,' he said.

'There's only me on the desk, sir,' said the duty officer.

'The bloody door's locked. Bring him up,' he ordered again, testily, grinding out the words.

'Sir.' The duty officer decided to stop chancing his arm.

'Mr Beaton,' said the Detective Superintendent, as the visitor was shown in, immaculate in cream trousers, a pink shirt and a lightly checked sports jacket, 'I'm Brian Mackie. DCI Rose told me about your encounter in the Nature Reserve yesterday.

'It was very helpful to us. Let's hope this meeting will be even more so.'

He showed him through to Martin's private office, where a folder containing the seven photographs lay on the briefing table.

'Have a seat, please,' said the detective, 'and, when you're ready, open the folder and look at the photographs inside, one by one.'

Beaton sat down, glanced at the slim green cardboard covering, then looked up at him. 'I'd rather expected to be looking at some sort of book with hundreds of photographs in it. This suggests to me that you have a firm suspect, and that his face is in here.'

'I can't comment on that,' said the Superintendent, impassively. 'Just look, please, and tell me if the man you saw is there.'

The witness nodded, opened the folder, and looked down intently at the first photograph. He gazed at it for over a minute, then turned it over and concentrated on the second. The third likeness was that of Norman King. Watching him, Mackie imagined that he saw a slight tensing of the neck muscles as he turned over the second picture and looked at the shot. If there had been it was gone in an instant, for Beaton treated it in exactly the same way as the others, and as the four which followed, staring down at each one.

When he was finished, he looked up at Mackie once more. 'Might I look at them all together,' he asked, 'spread out on the table?'

'Of course.' The policeman picked up the folders and spread the seven photographs on the surface, at random rather than in the order in which Beaton had looked at them first.

The man stood up and walked along the line of faces, left to right, back again, left to right once more. At last he stopped, and stood looking down once more, holding his chin loosely with the fingers of his right hand. He stared at the table for another full minute, until he looked round at Mackie and nodded.

'Yes,' he said. 'I'm as certain as I can be, in the circumstances, and considering the distance there was between us. That's the man who was with Lord Barnfather.'

He reached down and touched the fifth photograph in the line, tapping his fingertips on the face of Norman King.

52

'So what's the set-up with King's girl-friend?' Skinner asked.

'Maclean Farms Limited turned out to be her family business, Boss,' said Mario McGuire, looking at the DCC across the conference table in Martin's office. 'She and her mother own it jointly. The father's dead, and the place is run by a manager.

'When we saw her there, we decided not to go in, in case she told King and he worked out what we were up to.

'So instead, we pulled off the road and went round the side to have a look. There was another car there, a wee MGF sports car. We checked the number and it turned out to be his.'

'That's good,' said Skinner. 'I'd have been narked if you'd tipped our hand.'

Martin, in the chair at the head of the table, leaned forward. 'How are we going to confirm that she is holding cyanide?' he asked.

'I've arranged for an Environmental Health Officer from the Council to pay a routine visit to the farm first thing this morning, sir.' McGuire glanced at his watch. 'He's probably done it by now.'

The DCC nodded his approval, then turned to Rose and Neville. Both women sported healthy sun-tans. 'So, ladies. How was the weekend on the beach?'

'Productive, sir,' the DCI answered, 'as you've probably heard.'

'Yes . . . you're both looking well on it, too,' he added, with a grin. 'Brian said that your man Beaton was meticulous in his identification, although he qualified it to an extent. How do you think he'll be in the witness box?'

'I don't think that David will be flustered at all, Boss. As Brian said, he's a careful sort of person. Now if it had been his partner, Donovan the skinny-dipper . . .'

'Eh?' Neil McIlhenney burst out.

'Ah,' said Rose, 'Mario didn't mention him?'

'He was the highlight of my weekend,' Karen Neville volunteered, then added, '. . . almost.'

'Stick to the subject please, folks,' Martin called from the head of the table.

'Yes; sorry, sir,' the DCI acknowledged. 'Fortunately Donovan isn't involved in our case, or I think we could have trouble with him in the box. David, on the other hand, will be fine. I think he'd even stand up to old Christabel, if it came to that.'

Skinner broke in. 'All he has to say on oath is what he said to Brian. When we add that to my party friend Philip's positive identification of King in the Reserve on the afternoon in question, we've got enough for the jury.'

He looked round the table. 'Ladies and gentlemen, what do we have on Mr Norman King, QC?' He raised his left hand and began to check-list items on his finger as he spoke. 'One; a threat to his inheritance: a strong motive to kill both of these old men. Two; a known and undisguised hatred of his father. Three; proximity to the scene of the first murder. Four; a positive identification at the scene of the second. Five; subject to confirmation, access to the poison used in the Archergait murder.'

The DCC gazed at Martin. 'So, Chief Superintendent, what do you think?'

'I think, sir, that as soon as we receive confirmation from Mario's Environmental Health Officer that cyanide is kept on premises to which Norman King is a known visitor, we have sufficient reason to ask Lord Archibald's permission to interview the Home Advocate Depute as the principal suspect in these murder investigations.'

'My thoughts exactly, Andy.' He glanced at his watch, which was showing 10:50 a.m.

'I think you and I had better make ourselves available at around four o'clock. King's prosecuting in a trial in Edinburgh today. I think Archie might prefer us to wait until the Court rises, rather than arrest him in the middle of proceedings.'

184

53

Having found a parking space in Market Street, Andy Martin walked up the Mound, and round the great statue of David Hume . . . the Jolly Green Giant, as it had become known as soon as it had been erected . . . before crossing Parliament Square.

Aware that he was running late, he stopped outside the entrance to the Supreme Courts, on the spot where he had arranged to meet Alex, and checked his watch. It showed 12:40 p.m., ten minutes after their date. Kwame Ankrah was with him. On a whim, he had invited the African to join them, to give him a taste of the Supreme Court atmosphere.

Curious, Andy entered the building with his companion and made his way along to the courtroom where his fiancée's case was being heard. There was no-one in the corridor outside. He peered through the glass panel in the door and saw that the Court was still sitting, with the grim-faced Lord Coalville on the Bench. Out of curiosity he slipped inside and into the public gallery.

Alex was seated in the front row, next to Adrian Jones and his wife. From her body language the detective could tell at once that things had gone to very much worse. He glanced along the row and, even from behind, recognised the man who had appeared in the doorway of Gordon's Trattoria. Bernard Grimley was grinning at Jones, triumph etched on his face.

Lord Coalville paused in his address, gathering his papers together. Martin focused his attention on him.

'To sum up,' said the red-robed judge, with a baleful glance at Jim McAlpine, 'I find the counter-arguments of the defenders entirely unconvincing and find for the pursuer in the full amount of his claim.' He nodded to his left, towards McAlpine, Elizabeth Day and Mitch Laidlaw. 'Costs are awarded against your clients.'

He stood, and the Court rose with him, some more slowly than others. As the door behind the Bench closed on Lord Coalville, the policeman glanced at the senior counsel for the defence and saw a glare of pure hatred.

The silence held for a second or two, then babble of conversation broke out in the courtroom. Advocates, solicitors and clients stood and mingled, the triumphant hugs and handshakes on the right contrasting with the gloom on the left.

As Andy stepped out of the public benches and moved towards her, Alex turned. Before she noticed him, he saw the anger and frustration written on her face, and realised, to his surprise, that she was not far from tears. 'I know the feeling, love,' he whispered as he took her hand.

'Yes,' said McAlpine, overhearing. 'Don't take it to heart, Alex. Your preparation work was immaculate. What you have to keep in mind is that when a case like this gets this far, someone is going to be disappointed.' His face hardened again. 'Mind you, I could still choke the life out of that bastard Coalville.'

'Will you appeal it?' Andy asked.

'I'll have to consult our clients on that,' said Mitch Laidlaw, from behind him, 'but I very much doubt it. The Appeal Court might reduce the amount of the award, but that would probably be offset by the extra costs. My firm has a pretty strong credit balance with the insurers in this type of action. I'm pretty sure they'll write this one off.'

Martin turned. Adrian Jones was standing beside Laidlaw, grim-faced, his eyes as hard as steel. 'That's all very well, Mitchell,' he hissed, 'but what about me? What about my career? Are you all simply going to walk away from me?' The policeman could almost feel the strength of his anger.

'Look, Adrian,' Alex's boss retorted, quietly but firmly. 'I am very sorry about the personal implications for you and your firm, but I must remind you that you are not my client. Nor has your liability been an issue. That was admitted almost two years ago. What we've been quantifying here has been the cost of a cock-up.

'If you're worried about your career, maybe you should get out of commercial law. You never know, your old employers might take you back. The same risks don't apply in that field.'

Jones glared at him. 'No thank you very much. I think I'll follow another course of action. Maybe I'll sue you for negligence.'

For a second, Martin thought that he was going to have to step between the two solicitors, but the intervention, when it came, was from another quarter.

'I've been waiting for a couple of years to say this, Mr Jones,' boomed Bernard Grimley, in rough Glaswegian tones. 'Thank you, thank you, thank you. You've transformed my life.

'I want you to know that when I'm sitting on the Costa del Sol, there won't be a day goes by when I don't raise a sundowner and say out loud, "Thank you, Adrian, for being such a fucking awful lawyer." I'll send you my address, when I get set up. Drop in any time you like.'

'I'd be a little careful, Mr Grimley,' said Laidlaw. 'The question of an appeal isn't quite decided yet.'

'That doesn't worry me, pal. This place is a fucking club, and you know it.' Grimley ran his fingers through his thick dark hair. 'I'll see you down the road if I have to.' He turned on his heel and walked away.

Jim McAlpine, QC, looked at his instructing solicitor. 'Unpleasant man, Mitch, wouldn't you say? Unfortunately, he's right. I can't see Coalville's finding being overturned at appeal. These things hinge very much on the

186

judge's view of the witnesses. That old bastard decided at an early stage that he wasn't going to like ours.

'I do wish you'd let me withdraw. Elizabeth, here, could have led perfectly well.' His junior looked up at him with a smile, but, as usual, said nothing.

'To hell with it all,' Laidlaw burst out. 'Let's get on with our lives.' He nodded curtly at Adrian Jones. 'Goodbye, and good luck. I'm sorry it didn't work out better. For what it's worth, if I'd been the judge, I'd only have given him one and a half million.'

He turned his back on Jones and looked at Martin. 'Andy, when it became clear this was going to wind up, I called my office and told them to lay on a buffet lunch for the team. Would you and your colleague care to join us?'

The detective glanced at his watch once again. 'Thanks, but I'm afraid I'm stuck for time now,' he said. 'Kwame might like it though.' He introduced the African. 'This is Mr Ankrah, a senior policeman from Ghana. He's with us on a fact-finding visit.'

'Delighted to meet you,' boomed Laidlaw, sincerely, offering a hand-shake. 'Yes, please do come with us. I'd be very interested to learn about your country. My firm has expansion plans, you know.' He glanced back at Martin. 'What's your problem, Andy?'

'I'm meeting Alex's dad at the Crown Office at two o'clock.'

'Serious business, eh?'

'Isn't it always?' Martin replied. He squeezed Alex's hand. 'You take Kwame off to your wake, love. I'll grab a sandwich in the café under St Giles.'

'Okay,' she nodded. 'When will you be in this evening?'

'I have no idea. This could turn out to be a very long day.'

54

The door of the Lord Advocate's office opened slowly. 'You wanted to see me, Archie?' said the Home Advocate Depute as he slipped into the room.

'Hello, Norman,' said Lord Archibald. 'Your case is over, I hear.'

'That's right,' said the dark-haired advocate. 'The jury was out for less than half an hour. Guilty, of course,' he added with a smile.

'That's good. Actually, it isn't me who wants to speak to you.'

King seemed to notice the other two men in the room for the first time, as they rose from their seats at the Lord Advocate's conference table.

'Good afternoon, sir,' said Bob Skinner. 'Have you met our Head of CID, DCS Martin?'

'No, I don't think I have.' He extended his hand, and the detective shook it, looking at him, curiously. 'What can I do for you?'

'We have a few questions we'd like to ask you, about things that have come up in the course of our investigation into your father's murder.'

'Fine, Mr Skinner. I'll do anything I can to help.'

The DCC nodded. 'That's good. Let's begin then.'

'What, here? Now?' King glanced round at Lord Archibald.

'That's all right, Norman. I have the time, and this is as good a place as any.'

The man's eyes narrowed very slightly as he sat but he said nothing.

'I'll begin, Mr King, by asking if you can tell us anything about your father's will?'

The advocate frowned at Skinner. 'Not really. There was a will which left his property to be divided between my brother and me.'

'Is it still in force?'

King hesitated. 'To tell you the truth,' he began, 'I'm not entirely sure. There was some talk . . . I heard it from Archie, actually. My father and I never discussed these things . . . that he might have been planning some sort of memorial bequest to the Faculty of Advocates.'

'Do you know much about that?'

'It was a joint affair, as I understand it . . . with old Barnfather, ironically. I know they had got as far as drawing up a joint minute of agreement, but I'm not certain whether the thing had been executed.'

'Have you taken any steps to find out?' Skinner asked, his voice deliberately friendly.

'I've asked my solicitors to write to Hannah Johnson, Dad's lawyer, at CAJ. So far, there's been no reply.'

188

'You have a clear interest though.'

'Naturally. My old man was worth a packet.'

'If the bequest hasn't been executed, what will you do?'

King frowned. 'I'll consult my brother, I suppose. We might decide to give some cash to the Faculty; fifty thousand, maybe.'

'But not all of it?'

'God no! We're talking serious money here.'

'Mmm.' Skinner gazed at the table thoughtfully for a few moments. 'Can I turn to the day of your father's death,' he went on. 'You were in Court in Glasgow, I think.'

The Home Advocate Depute nodded. 'That was the idea. But we had to adjourn for the day, first thing in the morning, so I came back through to Edinburgh.'

'Ahh,' said the DCC casually, 'straight back to the Crown Office?'

'Not quite. I called in at Parliament House to check my box, and spent some time working in the library.'

'Was your father a man with many enemies, Mr King?'

'He was a judge, officer.' The man's tone was sharp. 'They tend to make a few.'

Only Martin saw the muscle clench at the base of Skinner's jaw. He knew how dangerous it was to attempt to patronise his friend.

'How were your own relations with him?'

King stared at him. 'Mine? He was my father, man.'

'Once upon a time, I arrested a man who disembowelled his father.' The DCC glanced at the Lord Advocate. 'As a matter of fact, Archie was an AD at the time. He led for the Crown at the trial. So I'll ask you again. How close were you to Lord Archergait?'

'I respected him very much.'

'But you hated his guts nonetheless, isn't that right, as he hated yours?'

Slowly, the man nodded. 'Look,' he asked, in a hesitant voice. 'Where is this taking us?'

'This is an informal conversation, sir. You must appreciate that in an investigation as complicated as this we have to examine every possibility.'

'Yes, but . . .'

'What were you doing in Aberlady Nature Reserve eight days ago, sir?'

King swung round to stare at Andy Martin. 'What the . . .' He broke off and looked at the Lord Advocate. 'Archie, what is this?'

'Let's see what it is, Norman, shall we,' said Lord Archibald. 'Please answer.'

'I was walking my girl-friend's dog, if you must know.'

'Your girl-friend, sir?'

'Clarissa Maclean. She was staying at my place for the weekend. She had some work to do in the afternoon so I took her dog out to the Reserve for some exercise.'

'The person who saw you didn't mention a dog, sir.'

'I'd probably put the bitch back in the car by then. She was in heat, and

189

half the bloody hounds in the Reserve were straining at the leash to get at her.'

'Did you put her back in the car before you met Lord Barnfather, or afterwards?'

King stared at Martin, then at Skinner, who looked back at him, impassively. 'I never saw old Barnfather!' he exclaimed.

'We have a witness,' said the DCC, quietly, 'who has identified you as being with him. He says that the two of you were walking out across the sands, in the direction of the place where the old man was tied up and left to drown.'

The advocate sat speechless.

'Then there's the cyanide,' Martin went on. 'Your girl-friend keeps cyanide on her farm. The same poison that was used to kill your father.'

Norman King let out a long, gasping sigh. 'You cannot mean all of this.' he whispered.

'Let me ask you something, sir,' said Skinner. 'If you were someone else . . . let's say you were Archie . . . and I reported all these circumstances to you, what would you say?'

The man looked back at him, tight-lipped.

'Let me tell you, then,' the policeman went on. 'You'd say "Charge him. I'll prosecute the case myself."'

He straightened up in his seat. 'Now before we get round to a formal caution and interview, I'm going to ask you something, informally. If the answer is "Yes", then with the Lord Advocate's permission, we'll give you an opportunity to submit yourself for psychiatric examination before we do anything else.' He paused, and stared across the table.

'Did you kill your father, and Lord Barnfather?'

Norman King looked back at him, stunned. His mouth twitched and twisted, but eventually, he found his voice. 'No, gentlemen,' he muttered, 'I did not.'

Across the room, the Lord Advocate coughed. 'In the circumstances, Norman,' he said, heavily, and in a formal tone, 'that is something which a jury may be asked to decide.'

55

The Media Relations Manager gulped, almost theatrically, as Skinner told him what had happened.

'This is the hottest potato we've had to handle for a while, Alan,' he said. 'It has all sorts of political overtones, not the least of which is the Lord Advocate's own future.

'King's been cautioned and formally interviewed, but not charged; not yet. He denies both murders, but we can't ignore the evidence against him. For now he's at liberty, on the basis that he stays with Clarissa Maclean and makes himself available to us at all times. I expect that he's consulting his solicitors.

'I've dumped the final decision in Lord Archibald's lap. He wants to involve the Solicitor General in the decision, and advise the Prime Minister and the Secretary of State; but it's a matter of when they decide to charge King, not if.

'When that does happen, he'll be whipped in front of a Sheriff in Chambers. There'll be no plea taken at that stage but he'll be remanded in custody. I've suggested to Archie that he be kept in Shotts Prison rather than in Saughton.'

'Why's that, sir?' asked Alan Royston.

'Confidentiality. We don't propose to tell the press who it is we're holding until he appears at a pleading diet in a couple of weeks, or at the very least until Lord Archibald has resolved his own position.

'He may choose to resign when King is charged.'

The press officer frowned. 'Wouldn't there be a chance that could be seen as prejudicial to the defence?' he asked.

'Exactly,' Skinner agreed. 'On the other hand, if he waits until he's formally cited as a witness in the case, that would certainly be acceptable. There's another option, though, which I'm pressing on him. If the Prime Minister agrees, he could simply stand down from office during the course of the trial.'

The DCC frowned, and glanced across at Andy Martin. 'In any event, we want to let him reach his decision without being influenced by any hysteria in the media, hence my wish to keep King's identity secret until his appearance in open Court.

'D'you think we have a chance of getting away with it?'

Royston whistled. 'Won't King be missed from the High Court?'

'Not necessarily. He wasn't due to be prosecuting again until the week after next.'

191

'Won't there be a few people in the know when he appears before the Sheriff, for formal accusation and remand?'

Skinner shook his head. 'I don't think so. The Sheriff Court is right next door to the Crown Office, remember. King will present himself as ordered, he'll be charged and he'll be taken to Shotts by Mr Martin –' he nodded to his left '– and Sammy Pye. Once he's locked up we'll announce that a man has been charged, but give no further details.

'The only person in the know who might talk to the press is King himself, through his solicitors.'

'Do you think he might?'

'I can't say for sure, but I can't think why he'd be the first to break cover.'

The Media Manager picked up his coffee and took a sip. 'I suppose we might be able to keep it under wraps, sir. But it's a racing certainty that the press will have a source inside Shotts jail. If it leaks, that's where it'll come from. I have to tell you also that if it does, the shit will hit the fan in a very big way.'

The DCC laughed. 'Oh, I know that, Alan. I surely do!'

'Then why bother, sir? Why not just stick him in the dock in open Court, like any other prisoner?'

'Because he isn't any other prisoner. He's Her Majesty's Senior Prosecuting Counsel. Because I want to give Archie as much room to manoeuvre as I can. Because . . .'

He stopped and stared, for a few seconds, out of the long window of the Chief's office. 'Because there's this wee kernel of doubt, gnawing at the back of my mind.

'When I looked at all the evidence we've assembled against King, I was dead certain that we were right. The truth is, when Andy and I interviewed him in Archie's room, I expected him to break down.

'He didn't though. He denied the whole thing, and he still does. Remember, this is a man whose job is to assess the weight of evidence against a suspect. He knows what we've got on him, and that he has no defence against any of it. Yet he still maintains his innocence.'

'Come on, sir,' Royston protested. 'There's nothing unusual about a criminal denying everything, even when they're as guilty as sin.'

'Aye, Alan, I know. Still . . .'

He rose from the Chief's chair. 'Anyway,' he said, 'that's the background. As soon as I know when King's to be charged, I'll tell you. In the meantime you could be drafting damage limitation statements, just in case we need them.'

He walked the press officer to the door, and into the outer office, where his secretary was waiting. 'Superintendent McGrigor called five minutes ago, sir, looking for Mr Martin.'

'Did he, Gerry? You'd better call him back, then. Andy can speak to him here.'

The Head of CID switched on the hands-free telephone as it rang on the big desk. 'Hello, John,' he answered. 'What can I do for you?'

'It's this shooting, sir,' said the bluff Borderer, his voice booming metalically from the speaker. 'I'm at decision time, and I thought I'd talk to you about it.'

'Fire away.'

'I think I'm going to have to let Sturrock go.'

'You haven't been holding him all this time, have you?'

'Och, of course not . . . although I think he'd like me to lock him up to protect him from his wife. I've been hauling him in every day for questioning. There's a fair chance the bugger did it, like, but he's digging his heels in, and we still canna' find the weapon.'

'Remind me, was it a licensed gun?'

'He denies ever having owned a rifle, Andy. It's the wife who said he did.'

'Who do you believe?'

'I'm inclined to believe her. He's funny under interrogation, is this one. He denies shooting Saunders, yet he's not even trying to be convincing. There's a bravado about him, as if he likes being in the spotlight.'

'Forget him, John,' said Skinner, suddenly. 'I've seen this sort before. He didn't kill Saunders, but now it's happened, he wishes he had. You're wasting your time with him. Far better to dig as deep as you can into the victim's background. He must have had a life beyond shagging Mrs Sturrock. Find out more about it, and see what it tells you.'

'Very good, Boss,' McGrigor acknowledged. 'I'll keep Mr Martin informed, will I?'

'Please do,' said the Head of CID.

'Any leads on the robberies up there, gentlemen?' asked the Superintendent.

'No such luck, John,' Skinner replied. 'The trail's as cold as a witch's tit, but at least we haven't had any more in the last week. Don't you worry though; we haven't forgotten about it. We'll catch the bastards who killed your mate.'

56

'T. Regan.' Detective Sergeant Steven Steele muttered aloud the name on the door of the neat little terraced cottage, confirming to himself that he was at the correct address.

Years had gone by since the links between Newtongrange and mining had been severed, apart from the industrial museum which was its main attraction, and since then some of the old colliers' dwellings had been renovated and turned into modern homes. They were very attractive in their new clothes, but on occasion, as the young sergeant had discovered, there was little logic about the pattern of the addresses.

He pressed the button of the buzzer, and heard it sound loudly inside. After a few seconds he saw a figure in the obscured glass panel set in the front door, making its way slowly and laboriously towards him.

The door swung open to reveal a small, wiry figure, a grey-stubbled man who looked to be in his late fifties. He was wearing baggy trousers, a faded Viyella shirt, carpet slippers, and incongruously, a flat cap.

'Aye?'

'Mr Regan?'

'Aye, that's me, Tommy Regan.'

'I'm Detective Sergeant Steele, from Edinburgh. I'd like to ask you a few questions about your daughter.'

A look of concern swept across the little man's face. 'Oor Arlene? Whit's the matter wi' her?'

'Nothing that I know of, sir,' said Steele. 'We'd just like to trace her, that's all. I'm hoping that you can help.'

'Aye, aye. Come oan in, son.'

Tommy Regan had not been easy to find. The agency through which Nick Williams and his girl-friend had rented their flat had no note of parental addresses. Steele had been forced to pull strings with the Department of Social Security, to trace Arlene's employer, a specialised engineering company on the outskirts of the city.

There he had learned that like her boy-friend, she had left her job without giving notice. Indeed, on her last day in the office she had helped herself to money from the firm's petty cash box, leaving a note to say that it was in lieu of the wages which she was due. Her manager had been reluctant to give the detective any information, but had eventually told him that she believed Arlene had connections with Newtongrange.

Her father hirpled awkwardly along the corridor, as he led the way into his living room. He pointed to his hip. 'Industrial injury,' he said. 'I was up a gantry when it collapsed, and smashed my leg, right at the top there. Got a right few quid in compen., mind you.'

'Mmm,' said Steele. 'Are you on your own here?'

'Naw, only during the day. Betty works in the co-op. Sit doon, son, sit doon,' he muttered, lowering himself awkwardly into an armchair, its seat raised by an extra cushion.

The young policeman sat facing him, across the empty fireplace. 'When did you last see your daughter, Mr Regan?' he asked.

'The Saturday before last, she was out here, wi' thon young Nick fella.'

'Did either of them say anything to you about giving up their flat?'

Tommy Regan looked at him, his expression one of blank surprise. 'Naw. Have they?'

Steele nodded. 'Do you read the papers?' he asked.

'Sports pages, mostly,' the little man replied.

'Well, do you remember reading about a robbery in the jeweller's where Nick Williams worked?'

'Ah remember seeing something on the telly, but ah never kent that was where the laddie worked, like.'

'Yes, Nick worked in Raglan's. The funny thing is that on the day of the robbery, he called in sick. Arlene didn't go to work that day either. Instead, the pair of them left town, without trace as far as we can tell.

'So, Mr Regan, I need to ask you, have you had any communication from your daughter at all since then? A postcard, a letter, phone call . . . anything?'

The father looked bewildered. He shook his head, slowly. 'Is oor Arlene in bother, like?'

'Would it surprise you if she was?'

'Of course it wid! She's a good lassie. Aye got a good word for folk, and she's good tae her father and mother. It's that Nick, ah'll tell ye. He's a sleekit wee bastard, yon yin.' Regan's voice rose in a mixture of alarm and annoyance.

'I wouldn't jump to any conclusions, about either of them,' said Steele. 'Let's all try to find them first. Will you help me do that?'

'Aye, if ah can. Ah trust ma lassie.'

'Okay, in that case, I want you to call us as soon as she gets in touch with you or your wife. If she sends a card, let us see it. If she phones, ask her where she is, and ask her to come home.'

The little man nodded, making his cap shake on his head.

'Meanwhile,' the policeman continued, 'can you think of anyone else who might have an idea of where she could have gone?'

'No' really. She disnae hae any friends out here noo. Ye could try her part-time job, though.'

'Where was that?'

'She worked behind the bar at the Territorials' place; up Fountainbridge way. Someone there might ken something.'

195

'We'll do that,' said Steele, rising to his feet. 'Don't get up, Mr Regan, I'll see myself out.' He reached into the breast pocket of his jacket and handed over a personal card. 'Remember, as soon as Arlene gets in touch, please call me. That's my number.'

57

There was a loud rap on Andy Martin's door. The Head of CID glanced at his wristwatch, which was showing 5:55 p.m.

'Come in,' he called, 'whoever you are.'

The door swung open and detective constable Sammy Pye stepped into the room. 'I'm sorry, sir, but I'm beat. I've looked at those security tapes until I'm cross-eyed, but I can't spot anyone who appears on more than one.

'Mr Ankrah says he'll have one last go this evening, but I'm done for. Can I chuck it?'

'Yes, sure, son. It was a long shot anyway.'

Pye shook his head. 'No, Boss, the theory was right, but the resolution on most of those videos is pretty crap. My girl-friend could have been on one and I wouldn't have been able to identify her. All we've been trying to do was spot the same person on different tapes. But even if we'd been able to do that, identification would have been a problem.'

The Head of CID grinned at his young assistant. 'I didn't know you had a girl-friend on the go, Sam,' he said.

The young detective flushed. 'Figure of speech, sir,' he mumbled.

Martin raised an eyebrow. 'Karen! You still there?' he called out. A few seconds later Detective Sergeant Neville appeared in the doorway, dressed in a close-fitting grey skirt and a navy blouse which did nothing to disguise her curves.

'Well, sergeant, have you enjoyed your first day in the nerve centre?' he asked.

'Very much, sir. It makes a change from Haddington. It's nice to be out of uniform.'

The DCS chuckled. 'I felt exactly the same as you when I left that place.' He glanced at his watch again. 'Karen, as I said this morning there are no rigid start and finish times in my office. Do the job and you can keep your own hours . . . within reason.

'Take young Sammy, here, for example. Some nights he'll be behind his desk till ten o'clock. Tonight, though, he seems dead keen to get away.'

He paused. 'Anything else to tell me before you go?'

'Yes, sir. Superintendent McGrigor just called. He said that he's finding it hard to get anything on the man Saunders. There was one interesting thing though. When he questioned Mrs Sturrock again, she let slip that he gave her a very expensive diamond pendant a few days before he

197

was killed. Two and a half thousand pounds' worth.

'Mr McGrigor said he thought it was a bit generous for an unemployed plumber.'

'He was right. Did he check it against the stolen property lists?'

Karen Neville shook her head. 'He didn't need to, sir. Mrs Sturrock showed him an insurance certificate, issued by the shop where Saunders bought the piece. It was Raglan's, off Princes Street.'

Andy Martin whistled. 'Now there's a small coincidence,' he said.

'Look, before you and DC Pye disappear for the night, sergeant, I'd like you to call Mr McGrigor back and check the date of purchase with him. Then first thing tomorrow, I want you two to go and see Mrs Hall at Raglan's. Find out as much as they can tell you about Saunders and that piece of jewellery.

'Most important of all, find out if he paid cash for it. I smell something here.'

58

'You know,' said Stevie Steele, 'I often wondered why the bar in an army base is called the Mess.'

The steward looked round the panelled room and laughed. 'If you could see the state of some of the lads when they leave here, you wouldn't need to ask.'

The man, who had introduced himself as Barry Herr, nodded towards his bar. 'Can I get you a drink, sergeant?' he asked.

Steele, who had a raging thirst, looked regretfully at the brightly lit ale and lager fonts. 'I'm driving, I'm afraid.'

'Have something non-alcoholic, then.' Herr reached over the wooden bartop, picked up a pint glass and filled it almost to the top with dark cola from the soft drinks dispenser. 'That'll no' do you any harm,' he muttered, handing it to the policeman.

'Cheers,' Steele acknowledged. 'Now, about Arlene Regan . . .'

'Ah yes,' said the steward of the Territorial Army Club. 'Our Arlene. A real personality girl, if ever I saw one. She let me down, though.'

'How was that?'

'She left me in the lurch, about a week ago. She didn't appear for her evening shift. I spent all night rushed off my feet, all the time expecting her to phone me to explain where the fuck she was, but not a word did I hear from her. When she didn't turn up the evening after that, I called her, to be told by BT that her number had been disconnected.

'So I can't really say I'm surprised that you're here asking questions about her. What's she done?'

The detective shrugged his shoulders. 'Arlene hasn't necessarily done anything. It's her boy-friend that we're after. Do you know anything about him?'

'I know he existed,' said Herr, 'but I've never met him. They lived not far from here, so she usually walked home after work. She didn't talk much about him though, not when she was flirting with the Weekend Warriors. As far as I know he worked in a shop.'

'That's right. Raglan's.'

The man's eyes widened. 'What? The place that had that big robbery . . .'

'. . . on the day Arlene and her boy-friend disappeared. That's right.'

'Jesus! No wonder you want to talk to him.'

Steele sipped his cola. 'Do you know, Mr Herr,' he went on, 'whether Arlene did anything more than flirt with the customers?'

199

The steward frowned and looked at the carpeted floor. 'I doubt it,' he replied at last. 'She could be a bit loud, but behind all that she was a nice girl.'

'In what way?'

'She was a decent, friendly, honest lass. The till was never a problem with her. She never struck me as the type to have two-timed her boy-friend. Mind you, she worked here for about three years. She was only living with him for the last two. Maybe at the start there were one or two she took a shine to.

'There was a big red-haired bloke fancied her; that was his nickname, too. Big Red, his pals called him. But she never treated him as any more than one of the lads.' He paused.

'There was another guy she talked to quite a lot, though. He wasn't a member, but the Paras brought him in every so often. Hamburger, they called him . . . they all had nicknames. Arlene liked him; I could see that. If she was playing around with anyone, it'd have been him, I reckon.'

'The Paras?' exclaimed the detective, in surprise. 'Are they based here?'

Herr laughed. 'No, that's what they call themselves. Some of them were once, mind you. They're a bunch of ex-regulars who joined the TA after they were discharged. Most of them are still in. There are half a dozen of them: Big Red's one . . . although he hasn't been in for a while . . . Bakey Newton, he's another, Rocky Saunders, Big Mac, Tory Clark, and, and . . . Curly Collins.

'They were always chatting up Arlene, that lot. We have other Friday regulars, but they were the ones she talked to the most.'

'Would any of them have an idea where she might be?'

'You could ask them, next time they're in. They usually meet up on a Friday night, and sometimes on other nights during the week. I haven't seen them for a week or so, but I expect they'll be in again soon.'

'Do you have home addresses for any of them?'

'No, but they're all in . . . or they were in . . . the Lowland Territorial Infantry Division. You could try them.'

Sergeant Steele drained his glass, and reached into his pocket. 'I'll do that, Mr Herr,' he said, taking out a calling card and a pen. Scribbling on a pad he continued, 'Meantime, there are my office, mobile and home numbers. If any of them, or this Hamburger guy, come in over the next couple of days, give me a call.'

59

The rays of the sinking sun shone red on the western horizon, but a heavy blue-black cloud hung over Gullane. Bob and Sarah Skinner sat in their conservatory watching the breaking storm, listening to the heavy raindrops as they splashed on to the glass roof.

There were a few cars left in the Bents park; as they watched, their owners, most with dogs on leads, came rushing up from the beach to the shelter they offered. One by one, lights went on; one by one they drove away, until all of the green space behind the beach was empty, save for two deer which broke cover from a clump of buckthorn bushes and raced blindly towards the east, away from the direction of the storm.

'The end of summer, do you think?' Sarah asked.

'Could be,' her husband answered. 'The rain's certainly overdue. Since we've been back from Spain the golf course green-keepers have been the only people I've heard complaining about the weather.' He looked up at the roof, and at the heavy cream sun-blinds which hung from it. 'That should shut the buggers up for while,' he chuckled, as the rain began to run from the sloping glass in sheets.

He squeezed her hand. 'What sort of a day have you had then, my love?'

'Quiet, for a change. I was able to study most of the day. Joe e-mailed me the final report on the Saunders autopsy, to give me a chance to comment before he sent it to McGrigor. But apart from that . . .'

'Lucky you,' said Bob, with feeling. 'The biggest problem I have with doing Jimmy's job is not having any time to sit back and think. Maintaining a strategic overview of CID is part of my function, but it's going by the board, with the in-tray, the politics, and the bloody phone ringing. Andy's out there on his own, and it's not fair.'

'What, are you saying that Andy can't think for himself?'

'Of course not, but he deserves support. Yet in the midst of the biggest series of crises I can ever remember, I find myself just tinkering around the edges.'

'To some effect, though. You've had significant input to the judges' investigation, for a start.'

'No I haven't. All I've done is smooth things with Archie and interrogate Norman King.'

'You got a result though.'

'Andy and the team did.'

'Okay,' Sarah responded. 'You say you don't have space to think. In that case, there's no time like the present. The boys are in bed, there's nothing worth watching on television. Think, man, think.'

He laughed. 'If only it was as easy as that.'

'Why shouldn't it be? Tell me: what's worrying you right now?'

'What isn't?' He leaned back deep into the cane sofa, slipping his left arm round Sarah's shoulders. 'Well, to begin with, I had a call from the Lord Advocate just before I left the office tonight. He's decided to charge Norman King formally on Wednesday afternoon. He'll appear before the Sheriff immediately afterwards, for remand.'

'Fair enough, but why should that worry you? You've put all the evidence before Lord Archibald, but the decision's his.'

'Yes, but . . .'

'But nothing. The evidence is there. If you were on a jury would you convict on it?'

'Probably, but I'm not a jury member, I'm a copper . . . and I like things beyond even an unreasonable doubt, which this isn't.'

Sarah leaned her head forward and bit her husband lightly on the chest. 'You always want to catch your villains with a smoking gun in their hand, don't you.'

'Aye, I suppose so; but that's no bad thing, is it? I'm dead certain that I've never put away an innocent man. I'm proud of that record, and I want to keep it. I've got a niggle about King, that's all.'

'Look, the evidence against him is very strong, isn't it?'

'Yes.'

'And there aren't any other recently dead judges lying about, are there?'

In spite of himself, Bob grinned. 'No, I guess not . . .' In an instant, the smile left his lips, his eyes narrowed, and he frowned. 'Wait a minute, there is one.'

Sarah pushed herself upright. 'Are you serious?'

'Yes, I am. Remember old Lord Orlach? Had a place down in Aberlady? He died a few months ago, when you were in the States. He was buried along by, in the Kirk yard.'

'Were there any suspicious circumstances?'

'None that I knew of at the time. But maybe there are now.'

'Hold on, Bob,' she protested. 'He was an old man. And what connection could he have with the other two?'

'Just that, my love,' Bob answered at once. 'His age. Orlach, Archergait and Barnfather were the senior Supreme Court judges. Just suppose that there's something connecting the three of them that led to all their deaths.'

'But even so, how can you go about investigating Orlach's death after all this time?'

'I know where to start, at any rate.' He jumped up and paced out of the conservatory, returning a minute later with his address book and the remote telephone handset. He flicked through the book, then dialled a number.

'Miss Dawson?' his wife heard him say. 'It's Bob Skinner here. Very well, thank you. That's kind of you.

202

'Listen, I'm sorry to disturb you at home, but there's something I have to ask you. It's about Lord Orlach's death.' He paused. 'That's good. First, can you recall the certified cause?' He sat in silence for a while, nodding automatically. At one point, the watching Sarah saw his eyebrows rise.

'Indeed,' he said at last. 'There's just one other question, in that case. Who signed the death certificate?' As he listened to the reply, he made a note at the back of the address book. 'Ah, I guessed it might have been her.

'Thank you very much, Miss Dawson. There may be nothing in this, but if anything does develop, I'll let you know. You look after yourself, now.'

Sarah was looking at him intently as he finished the call. She knew of Christabel Innes Dawson, QC, and of the important part she had played in her husband's life. 'What did she have to say?' she asked.

'Heart attack. He was alone in his house in Aberlady when he died . . . that was going to have been my second question but she beat me to it. The cleaner found him dead in bed when she came in in the morning. She called in Dr Street, from the surgery three doors along, and she did the certification. There was no post-mortem.'

He smiled, up towards the roof. 'The funny thing is that Christabel was shocked that he should die so suddenly, even at his age. He had regular health checks . . . BP, heart function, lungs . . . and he was always fine. They did a lot of walking together. In fact the old boy was the patron and honorary legal adviser of the Scottish Rights of Way Association, so they were always off proving some path or other.

'The thought crossed the old lady's mind that there might have been an intruder involved . . . he was always leaving windows open apparently . . . but eventually she decided that she was being daft, and let it go. But when I called her there, she guessed what I was on about right away.'

He looked at her. 'Do you know much about this Dr Street?'

'I met her once. She's in the Aberlady practice, as you say, in her early fifties and not, I'd say, given to using too much initiative.'

Bob scratched the end of his nose. 'If you were called in to examine an old bloke, dead in his bed, what would you think?'

Sarah stood, and walked slowly to the window. It was very dark now, and solid sheets of water were pouring from the roof. She looked out, then turned to face him. 'If his lips were blue, I'd probably think heart, given his age. I'd take his medical history into account, though. From what you've said, Lord Orlach must have been quite fit.'

'Yes, he was. Now let me ask you another. If you'd certified heart failure, but you'd cocked it up, what might you have missed?'

'Any number of things. Cerebral involvement possibly, or if you're looking at murder, some form of poisoning by injection. The likeliest though would probably be simple asphyxia; suffocation with a pillow. In those circumstances, if I'd diagnosed heart failure, I'd have missed tiny petaechial haemorrhages . . . ruptured blood vessels . . . around the lips and face. Actually, it might not be too difficult to overlook them in an old person.'

Her husband's eyes were gleaming. 'Okay,' he went on. 'Let's suppose that's what happened, and that your patient's been under the ground for a few months. If we had the body exhumed, could we still determine that he'd been asphyxiated?'

'Of course you could. All you'd have to do would be to look in the chest. If there was no sign of a coronary occlusion, or other major damage to the heart, and if the lungs were distended, then suffocation it would be.'

Bob smiled up at his wife. 'See what happens when you start me thinking?' he said. 'I think I'll have a word with this Dr Street. D'you reckon her number will be in the book?'

'No,' said Sarah, 'but her husband's will. She's married to a retired naval officer, and they live in Dirleton.'

'In that case, I think I'll call her and make myself an appointment for first thing tomorrow morning.'

60

'What's put you in such a cheery mood this morning?' asked Andy Martin.

Skinner beamed at him across the coffee table. 'Let me put it this way. You know our time-honoured phrase when we're after a warrant to search someone's pad, "Let's dig up a Sheriff."?'

Puzzled and intrigued, the Head of CID nodded.

'Well tonight we're going to have a variation on that theme. We're going to dig up a judge.'

'Eh!?'

Quickly, he explained his interest in Lord Orlach's death. 'I went to see Dr Street this morning,' he went on. 'She admitted that her examination was a bit perfunctory. She said that he wasn't normally her patient, so she wasn't aware of his history, only his age, and it was on that basis, coupled with his physical appearance, that she made her decision.

'I also had a chat with the old boy's cleaning lady, She remembers that on the morning she found him dead, there was a window open at the back of the house.

'So, I've decided to take a chance. I've instructed our legal people to obtain an exhumation warrant from the Sheriff in Haddington. We'll carry it out at midnight tonight, and have the post-mortem done immediately. Unless we need to wait for lab work, my aim will be to have Orlach back underground within twenty-four hours . . . forty-eight at most.'

Martin looked doubtful. 'Bob, isn't this a hell of a big kite you're flying, on a hell of a short string.'

The big DCC laughed out loud. 'The formula for a crash, you mean? Sure it is, but what's new?' His expression grew serious once more. 'I just feel we owe it to Norman King: shit, we owe it to every defendant to turn over every stone in our investigations.'

'When you put it like that, I suppose you're right,' his friend conceded. 'Will Sarah be taking part in the autopsy?'

'Absolutely not! I feel too close personally to this one for her to be involved. Anyway, it'll be done in the middle of the night and I intend to be there, so she'll have to mind the boys.'

'Won't the grave-diggers talk about it?'

'They would if they were involved; I'm going to use police officers. Do you want to be there?'

'Digging, d'you mean?'

'If you want,' laughed Skinner.

'No. I'll give this one a miss, with or without a shovel.'

'Your choice.' The DCC picked up his coffee. 'But here,' he said, 'I'm not the only one looking perky this morning. What's put the spring in your step?'

'You're going to like this,' Martin grinned. 'I may have a lead to the robbery team. Remember McGrigor's murder? The man Saunders? It turns out that he bought his girl-friend two and a half grand's worth of sparkle at Raglan's, just before the place was done.'

'But he was . . .'

'. . . on the dole; that's right. Sammy and Karen are up there now, speaking to Mrs Hall. I reckon there's a fair chance that when he was making his purchase, he was casing the place as well.'

Suddenly, Skinner's smile was as wide as that of the DCS. 'You don't say. What's John been able to find out about him?'

'Next to fuck all so far. He didn't have any friends in West Linton, it seems, nor any family that anyone knew of. The last people to employ him, a big building firm, described him as a good worker, but said that he kept himself to himself. So did his landlord. He didn't keep a bank account, as such, only a deposit account in the Dunfermline Building Society.'

'I've told McGrigor to do better today. He can start at the Dunfermline, and go on from there.' Martin took a breath, and looked at his colleague. 'Do you have any thoughts about it, Bob?'

'He was a plumber, they said?'

'That's right.'

'So where did he learn his trade? Find someone who knew him as a kid, and you'll learn more about him.'

The Head of CID nodded. 'Good idea. I'll let McGrigor follow his own lines and put my two on to that.'

'How about the Regan girl?' asked Skinner. 'Any trace of her?'

'None so far, but Stevie Steele's made contact with the parents, and let them know that we want to speak to her. He says the father seems like an upright bloke, who'll probably co-operate with us. The old man was astonished to hear she was missing at all. He got nothing from her day job, but the manager of the TA Mess where she worked was quite helpful.

'He gave him the names of some lads she was friendly with. You never know; she might have let something slip to one of them.'

'I doubt it, since she didn't even tell her parents. But as you say, you never know. You've told Steele to get on it right away?'

'Sure. I thought I'd have trouble from Dan Pringle. He's got a sergeant off sick, and his team had a call to another suspicious death this morning, near Merchiston Castle School. He was fine about it, though, and I repaired the damage by offering him Kwame Ankrah for the rest of the week. Our friend is very sharp. He can be a real asset.'

'Into each life a little rain must fall,' said the DCC. 'Dan knows that. Not that I'm complaining about last night's lot, mind. It'll make digging a bloody sight easier.'

61

Until that moment, Detective Superintendent Dan Pringle had been remarkably cheerful for the time of day. With the onset of middle age, the detective had experienced difficulty in sleeping. Stress was something which, he believed, happened to other people, but eventually, Mrs Pringle, suffering from what she described as 'secondary insomnia', had compelled him to visit their GP.

After only two nights on the mild sedatives which the doctor had prescribed, he had enjoyed more sleep than in the whole of the previous week, and had rediscovered the pleasure of feeling fresh in the morning.

But when he leaned over the body in the copse, encased in his white crime-scene tunic, he felt all the old familiar weariness flow back, covering him like a blanket.

'Not another,' he moaned, quietly, to himself.

He looked across at Detective Chief Inspector Joseph Gibson, his second-in-command. 'What stupid fucker described this as a "suspicious death"?' he barked.

The man's curly hair was caked dark red with blood. It had flowed copiously, forming a round puddle, in the centre of which the victim lay, face-down. His wrists were bound behind his back with a strip of ratcheted black plastic, so tightly that the flesh bulged on either side of the ligature.

The dead man was wearing a light brown leather jacket, jeans and heavy boots. Gibson leaned over and pointed at the jacket, towards a mark in the middle of the back. 'Look at that,' he said. 'It's torn, and there's blood caked around it.'

'Stab wound,' grunted Pringle. 'What was the point of doing that if you're going to blow the guy's fucking brains out?'

'The same as the other one,' Kwame Ankrah interjected quietly. 'To bring up the head for the killing shot.'

The Detective Superintendent and his deputy stared simultaneously at the African. 'The other one?' asked Pringle, incredulously.

'Superintendent McGrigor is investigating a shooting in a place called West Linton. From what I have heard, the method was identical to this killing. These are executions, gentlemen.'

'We'd better touch base with Big John, quick,' said Gibson.

'With more than him, I think,' his Divisional Commander retorted. 'Let's get finished here though. Are the photographers finished for now?'

'Yes, sir.'

'Doctor too?'

'Yes.'

'Right, let's turn him over and see what he looks like . . . that's if he's got any face left.'

'He will have,' said Ankrah, bending down beside Gibson and turning the stiffened corpse over on to its back.

The man stared up at them with sightless, terrified eyes. The face was red with blood, from the pool in which it had lain, but it appeared to be unmarked. The hair which was not soaked and matted, looked thick and luxurious, and light brown in colour.

'Who found him?' asked Pringle.

'A dog-walker, sir,' the DCI replied. 'Eight-thirty this morning.'

'Why would this guy be here?'

'Depending on where he lived, he could have been taking a shortcut home, from the squash club, possibly. Or he could have been brought here.'

'Do we know who he is?'

'Not yet, sir. There's no missing person listing to fit the bill.'

'Let's have a look, then.' Pringle leaned over the body and, carefully, opened the blood-sodden jacket. He reached inside its inside pocket and took out a black leather wallet. Stepping away from the body, he opened it and looked inside. 'Thirty-five quid in readies,' he announced. 'Let's have a look at his plastic. Bank of Scotland Keycard, sort code 80-41-21; customer's name C. Collins. Sunday Times Visa Card, holder's name C. Collins. Colinton Castle Squash Club membership card . . . looks like you were right, Joseph . . . in the name of Charles Collins.' He paused. 'Territorial Army Mess membership card,' he continued, more slowly, 'in the name of Sergeant Charles Collins, Lowland Inf. Div.'

'That's who he is, then.'

He frowned slightly as an idle thought struck him. 'Here, Stevie Steele's away checking up on some TA guys for Andy Martin. Maybe we've found one for him.'

208

62

If Detective Sergeant Stevie Steele noticed the knowing look which Karen Neville threw in his direction as he entered the Head of CID's outer office, he did not react to it. Instead he walked over to Sammy Pye's desk.

'Mr Martin wants to see me,' he said.

The detective constable beamed up at him. 'I know, sergeant. He asked us to take you in as soon as you arrived.'

Steele frowned. Neville's glance had not unsettled him, but there was something in Pye's tone which did. 'Did he say what it's about?'

'He wouldn't tell us, sarge. Come on, let's not keep them waiting. You're two minutes late as it is.'

Pye stood. 'Tell you one thing though,' he whispered, mischievously. 'If you thought that Russian was tough, you should see Andy Martin on a bad day.' As Steele's jaw dropped, he led the two sergeants across the room, rapped on the Head of CID's door and stepped inside.

'DS Steele's here, Boss,' he announced.

'Bring him in, then,' said Martin, rising from behind his desk and moving over to the conference table, at which sat DCC Skinner, waiting.

The acting Chief grinned at the sergeant, registering his apprehension. 'It's all right, Stevie. Have these two been taking the piss?'

Steele glowered at Pye for a second. 'One may have, sir.'

'Sit down,' said the DCS. 'Have you got the names of those TA soldiers you told me about?'

'Yes, sir.' He took a notebook from his pocket and opened it. 'They're . . .'

Martin held up a hand. 'Let me guess at some of them. One's named Sergeant Charles Collins.'

Steele looked at him, astonished.

'Yes, Boss, Curly Collins.'

'Found shot dead in Colinton this morning.'

'Eh?'

'That's right. Let me guess another. Sergeant Ryan Saunders.'

Steele nodded slowly.

'Found near West Linton a few days ago, shot . . . executed . . . in exactly the same way as Collins. Hands tied, made to kneel, jabbed in the back with a knife, or possibly even a bayonet, to bring the head up then . . . Bang!

'A few days before that, Saunders, in uniform, paid two and a half grand in cash for a diamond pendant in Raglan's, where, shortly afterwards, a

209

major diamond robbery took place. That, of course, is the shop where Arlene Regan's boy-friend worked. The same Arlene Regan who pulled the pints for Saunders, Collins and their pals up in the TA Club.'

Skinner leaned forward. 'My turn to play now. I'll give you two more. First, Nathan Bennett.'

'Yes, sir,' said Steele, 'known as Big Red. But I had to get on to the Ministry of Defence to get his details. He was registered as an ex-serviceman, but he was never in the Territorials.'

The DCC was surprised, but he went on. 'Missing two fingers from his left hand. Shot dead in Saughton Prison while awaiting trial for the Dalkeith bank hold-up.

'My second guess. Malcolm McDonnell.'

'Yes, sir. Big Mac, a Sergeant during his service. But he was the same as Bennett. An ex-regular, but he was never a TA member either. I had to go to MoD for him too.'

'That's curious too. Anyhow, McDonnell was a prison officer, stationed at Saughton. He disappeared after Bennett was assassinated, having set him up to be killed.'

Silence prevailed for a few seconds, until Stevie Steele sent it packing. 'That's very good, sir,' he said. 'Do you and Mr martin want to try for the set?'

Skinner laughed. 'No, it's your turn now. Who are the others on your list?'

The sergeant looked down at his notebook. 'Sergeant Rory Newton, sir, still serving. Nickname Bakey, because that's his trade. Works in a supermarket as an in-store baker in Piershill. Address, 27 Feather Street, Danderhall.

'Corporal Alan Clark, still serving. Nickname Tory, though I can't think why. Works in a gents' outfitters in George Street. Address, 43a Derbyshire Street.'

Detective Chief Superintendent Martin looked along the table at the young sergeant. 'And these six were all big mates, you say.'

'Thick as thieves, sir, according to Mr Herr.'

'Literally. We've found them, Stevie. Some, maybe all of these, are our bank gang. Those robberies were carried out with military precision, we reckoned. No bloody wonder, because the team are soldiers!'

'So who's knocking them off?' Skinner pondered. 'It looks as if someone involved in this wants all the money for himself.'

'That leaves us with Newton or Clark, Boss,' Martin answered. 'Of them, it could turn out to be the one who's still alive.'

Stevie Steele raised a hand, as if he was in a classroom. 'Excuse me, sir,' he ventured, tentatively, 'but there was another man. Barry Herr mentioned him. The others called him Hamburger, nothing else. He was only there occasionally, but Arlene was keen on him.

'He wasn't a member of the Mess, though, and the nickname meant nothing to the TA people.'

'No-one knows his real name?'

'No, sir.'

'We'll have to find him, nonetheless,' said Martin. 'But first, let's pick up Newton and Clark . . . pronto. Superintendent Pringle is on his way up here. Stevie, you and he can go to the place in Piershill for your baker man. Sammy, you and I will head for George Street, to pick up this Tory chap.

'That's unless one or the other of them isn't face-down in another wood somewhere.'

63

'This is the place, sir,' said DC Pye. 'The most exclusive men's shop on George Street.'

'Do you shop here then, Sammy?' Martin grinned.

'When I'm in your job, Boss, I'll be able to afford it.' They looked at the glass-fronted edifice, behind which skeletal structures modelled the latest in designer suits. A police patrol car stood at the kerb behind them, its uniformed driver behind the wheel.

'Eh, Boss,' said the young detective, tentatively.

'Yes.'

'I think Sergeant Neville was a wee bit upset that you left her in the office.'

'Yes, I could see that. I'll have a word with her when we get back. The thing is, we don't know anything about this guy, other than that he's an ex-Para. He may not want to get into the motor and come quietly. Should that happen, I'd rather have you alongside me than Karen, for my sake, and hers.'

'I wouldn't worry about her, sir. Karen can handle herself in a bundle. She has a black belt in Tae Kwan Do.'

'Fair enough.' Martin grunted. 'But how would that help if someone grabbed her by the bra-straps and nutted her? No, Sammy; I'm all for the advancement of women in the force, but horses for courses, okay.'

He led the way into the shop, through the double doors, which swung lightly on his touch. At once, a middle-aged man approached them. The Head of CID thought that he looked a little self-conscious in his Armani jacket.

'Can I help you, gentlemen? I'm Lorimer Davidson, the manager. I saw you get out of your car.'

'And you guessed we haven't come to shop,' said the Chief Superintendent. 'You're right. We'd like to speak with a member of your staff, a Mr Clark.'

The manager sniffed, a slightly comic gesture. 'Alan? I'd like to speak to him too.'

'You mean he isn't here?'

'No, he bloody well isn't,' Davidson exclaimed. 'He had a phone call, around forty-five minutes ago . . . notwithstanding that personal calls are strictly against the rules. He took it, then, without a "please" or a "by-your-leave", just rushed out.

'I haven't seen him since. I hope he has a bloody good excuse, but with you turning up and wanting to see him, somehow, I rather doubt that he will have.'

'So do we, sir,' said Martin. 'So do we. I think you should start advertising for a new sales assistant.'

64

'Rory Newton?' the woman exclaimed. 'My bakery foreman? Of course you can see him. Come on, and I'll take you along.'

Jennifer Tate, the general manager of the Piershill superstore, was a bustling, blue-suited woman in her mid forties, who radiated charm and efficiency. Her mezzanine office, in which the two policemen sat, had a panoramic view of the shopping alleyways and the check-out counters.

Dan Pringle shopped there often with his wife, and had always been impressed by its cleanliness, its product range and its efficiency. Now he knew that it was literally under the eagle eye of such an impressive supervisor, he understood why it stood out.

She led them past the fresh fish counter, a unit which prepared pizzas with the customer's choice of topping, and a cold storage area for dairy products, up to twin doors at the back of the store, close to the bakery shelves.

'Rory,' she called out, as she pushed them open and held them for Pringle and Stevie Steele. They stepped into a spotlessly clean kitchen area, where white-uniformed staff were preparing dough for the ovens, and film-wrapping newly baked loaves, bread rolls, scones and buns.

'Mr Newton?'

A tiny woman, in a white coat and trilby hat, turned towards her, diffidently. 'Rory's no' here, Mrs Tate.'

'Is he on his break, Molly? Should we try the canteen?'

She shook her head. 'No, a dinna' think so. He's been awa' for about an hour, like.'

'Did he say where he was going?'

'Naw. It was funny, like. The radio was on like ayeways, an' the news came on. Bakey was listenin' tae something I think, and his face went a' funny. He went ower tae the phone, made a couple of calls, then he jist took aff his coat and hat and walked oot the door.'

Jennifer Tate turned and looked, astonished, at Pringle. He turned and looked, knowingly, at Steele, then reached into his pocket, took out a mobile phone and called the Fettes number.

'Alan Royston, please,' the sergeant and the general manager heard him bark, his face like thunder.

'Alan, Dan Pringle here. Did your office release the name of the Colinton murder victim?'

He waited.

'On DCI Gibson's authority, you say?' He sighed, and shook his head. 'Okay. Do you know whether it's been broadcast on radio yet?'

There was another pause.

'Aye, that's what I thought.' The superintendent's grin had a savage look to it. 'Do me a favour, Alan, will you. Call Gibson back, tell him to find the longest grass he can and hide in it, before Bob Skinner catches him.

'No. On second thoughts, tell him to take sanctuary in the nearest church. Big Bob would just set the bloody grass on fire!'

65

'Is this investigation jinxed, or what?' the Head of CID growled. 'Every time we turn up potential witnesses they either die or they go underground.'

'Look on the bright side, Andy,' said Skinner, stretching his legs as he leaned against the back wall of the squash court, deep in the bowels of the Headquarters building. His white towelling shirt and the red band around his forehead were heavy with sweat as he spun his handmade Worton racquet in his right hand. 'You've identified the gang, and they're out of business for sure.'

Like many squash players of his generation, he eschewed the modern high-tech alloy frames and synthetic strings, preferring to stick to traditional gut-strung wood. 'If you're good enough, son,' he was fond of saying to his younger friend, 'it doesn't matter what you use. So my racquet's an ounce or two heavier than yours? So your frame widens the efficiency of the striking surface? So what, if you do what you're supposed to do and hit the ball dead in the middle of the strings every time?'

If pressed, Skinner would admit that of all the ball games he played, squash was the one at which he really excelled. He was a low-handicap golfer, but he knew that his game lacked the finesse ever to allow him to make scratch. As a footballer, he was capable, but his sheer size made him less adept than smaller players, particularly in indoor sports halls. But on the squash court, he was able to blend touch, timing, power and economy of movement into an irresistible package. In middle age he played less frequently than in his twenties and thirties, when he had been the number-one player in one of the city's most prestigious clubs, but he was still good enough to be untouchable by any user of the Fettes courts.

Andy Martin had learned everything he knew about the game from his friend. However he was still a long way from having learned everything that Bob Skinner knew.

Yet, as they gulped in air during the short break between games, the older man glanced across at his opponent and smiled. Martin was playing with a ferocity born of frustration, and had taken an early lead, only to be hauled back to two-all, in the five-game match.

The Chief Superintendent slapped the side wall of the Court with the flat of his hand. 'We've identified the gang, you say. Yet the truth is, Bob, that we've stumbled over them. They might be out of business, and three of them might be dead, but the survivors are still a few million quid to the good.'

216

'I know, and that's bad luck for the insurers; but at least the public are safer than they were. You'd better postpone the rest of this conversation, though. You've got a chance of beating me here, but only if you're concentrating on nothing but the game.'

He replaced his eye protectors, tossed up the small, hollow, rubber, yellow spot ball, which he had been holding to keep it warm, fired it against the front wall once, twice, three times, at blinding speed, then caught it.

'Play.'

He had deceived his opponent. Actually, Martin had no chance of beating him. The more a squash player is in command, the more he walks about the court, rather than runs. By the time he was 2–5 down in the deciding game, the younger man was running flat out, from one corner of the Court diagonally to another. Finally, Skinner finished the match with a beautiful drop shot from the centre of the court, which kissed the front wall just above the tin and fell into the nick, running flat and unplayable back along the floor.

They were in the showers before Martin had recovered enough breath to speak. 'You conned me out there, you big bastard,' he gasped.

'I always con you, son. The one thing you've never learned about this game is how to conserve your energy. The first two games aren't important. The third, fourth and fifth; they're the ones that count, and that's when you have to have something in the tank.'

'When are we playing again?'

'Friday, if we're clear.'

'Right. I'll concede the first two games.'

Skinner grinned. 'You always do, one way or another.' He picked up his shampoo and began to knead it into his hair.

'You realise, Bob, don't you,' said Martin, his voice raised above the powerful jets from the shower heads, 'that we've got a new investigation on our hands now?'

'It's the same one we've always had, really,' the DCC countered. 'We're still looking for the man behind the robberies, only now, we're pursuing him for the murders of three of his team.'

'You don't think that either Newton or Clark could be the killer?'

'Not for a second . . . and neither do you. Those two guys have run for their lives, literally.'

'Why do you think that they bolted after Collins's murder, and not after Saunders was killed?'

'I guess when they heard that McGrigor was questioning a local man in connection with his shooting, they assumed the same thing John did, that he'd been killed by a jealous husband.'

'I suppose so. And as you say, by making a break for it, they've confirmed our suspicion that they were all part of the gang. I just wonder though. Is that all of them?'

Skinner stepped out of the shower, just as the automatic switch cut off the jet, and picked up his towel. 'Let's go through them,' he said, 'the people that Steele's bar steward pal listed. Nathan Bennett, aka Big Red; dead. PO Malky McDonnell, alias Big Mac; done a runner. Ryan "Rocky" Saunders, aka the West Linton fornicator; dead. Charles Collins . . . I think I played squash against him a couple of years back, when the force sent a team up to Colinton Castle. Beat him three-love; easy, it was . . . aka Curly; dead. Rory "Bakey" Newton; done a runner. Alan "Tory" Clark; done a runner.

'That's all six of Mr Herr's Paras accounted for. But it leaves their pal Hamburger.'

'Hold on, though,' said Martin, pausing as he rubbed himself down. 'We have absolutely no evidence that he's involved at all.'

'No, but I hope we're agreed that someone else is. Look at what happened this morning, after bloody Gibson announced over Radio Forth that Collins had joined Saunders in the mortuary. Newton heard it, called Clark, and both of them disappeared, in mid-shift . . . except that the baker went home first and gave his wife fifty grand in cash.

'Those two were the last survivors of the six, but the speed with which they left tells us that neither of them killed Bennett, Saunders or Collins. They're afraid of someone, that's for sure.'

'Hamburger?'

'Maybe yes, maybe no. In any event, we know nothing about him, and all the people who could give us a lead are either dead or missing.'

'We've still got to trace him, though,' Martin conceded, gloomily.

Skinner nodded. 'Tell you what, Andy. I'll take responsibility for that, with McIlhenney. Collins and Clark have wives; maybe the name Hamburger will mean something to them.

'There's something else; Nathan Bennett's own bank was the scene of the first robbery. Maybe the team were confident enough to hit the places where they banked themselves. We need to collect photographs of the other five, and see if we can spot any of them on Pye's video tapes. Bad news for Sammy, I'm afraid. He's in front of that screen again. But maybe Mr Ankrah will help him out.'

He paused, dropping his towel on the floor and opening the locker in which he had hung his clothes. 'Alongside that, we have to concentrate on recovering the proceeds of the robberies. McDonnell, Williams and Regan must have been paid to vanish; Newton and Clark obviously had access to money too. So it's a fair bet that Saunders and Collins had cash hidden somewhere. Let's do our best to recover it.

'As your first priority, though, I suggest that you have Royston organise a press briefing and go public on what we know. You can identify Rocky and Curly as associates of Big Red, and suspected members of the gang, then say that we're looking for Big Mac, Bakey and Tory, his other pals.

'If I were you I wouldn't even hint that there's anyone else involved. Let's regain the advantage here, if we can.'

66

Skinner had never before been in the office of the Lord President of the Court of Session, in Parliament House, the great grey building which was home to the Faculty of Advocates, the judiciary and the majority of the Supreme Courts.

Looking around him, he could not think of another senior lawyer in Edinburgh who would have been content with such a small, stuffy room, yet there he was face to face with the little man who ruled the Scottish judicial system with what a famous newspaper columnist had described as a velvet fist in an iron glove.

'Archie's been keeping me in touch with the delicate situation regarding Norman King,' said Lord Murray. 'I presume that's why you asked to see me.'

'Yes,' said the policeman. 'Directly and indirectly. I'm very worried that the Lord Advocate will rush to resignation over this business.'

'So am I,' said the judge. 'Far be it from the wearer of my robes to involve himself in politics, but I think it would be very regrettable if that were to happen. I found him determined on the matter when I spoke to him about it. However, I think I've found a way round that.' His eyes twinkled. 'I never cease to be surprised by the access which I enjoy.

'Archie came to see me again this morning, to say that he intends to have King charged tomorrow, and to resign thereafter. So I took it upon myself to have a word with the Prime Minister. Any resignation will simply not be accepted, and that's an end of that.'

Skinner smiled. 'That's good to hear. God knows what would happen to Crown Office if he did go. The Solicitor General lacks the experience for the top job, and most of the other candidates don't bear thinking about.'

'That's exactly what I told the PM.'

'Well done. There's just a chance, though, that we may get King off the hook before any of this happens.'

Lord Murray said nothing, but his expression spoke for him.

'I've had a look at the report to the Fiscal on the circumstances of Lord Orlach's death a few months back. It was treated then as a heart attack, while he was alone in his Aberlady house one night. Given what's happened recently, I think we have to be absolutely sure of that.'

'So what are you going to do?'

'We're digging him up tonight.'

The Lord President gasped, audibly, then gulped, unconsciously comic reactions which made Skinner smile.

'The Sheriff in Haddington gave us a warrant an hour ago. I've got Joe Hutchison lined up to do an immediate post-mortem. If he confirms that it was a heart attack, we'll put him quietly back below the sod straight away and with luck no-one will ever know. The grave's round behind the church in Aberlady...'

'I remember,' Lord Murray whispered. 'I held a cord when we lowered him into it.'

'... so we won't be seen from the road.'

'Let's hope so. What if it isn't a heart attack?'

'Oh, we'll still rebury him as quickly as possible. But if the autopsy shows that it wasn't a natural death, that'll be good news for King. I've already established that when Lord Orlach died King was on holiday in Portugal with his lady-friend. The chain of evidence against him in the other two murders will be weakened, if not dissolved, if we can establish even a possible connection between Orlach, Archergait and Barnfather.

'That's where you can help, David.'

'Tell me how and I will, at once,' said the judge, eagerly.

'Am I right in thinking that you have a computerised database of legal precedents which the Bench can call up?'

'Yes.'

'Could it identify judicial occasions on which the three judges were linked?'

'It could, but it wouldn't necessarily be exhaustive. But do you mean the civil or criminal court?'

Skinner shook his head. 'I suppose I mean both.'

'Then we'll have to research the Court of Criminal Appeal. That will have to be done by the old-fashioned method of looking through printed volumes, rather than by pressing a button. But don't you worry about that, Bob; I have a legal assistant attached to my office. I'll ask her to do it.'

'That's excellent,' said the DCC. 'I'll let you know Hutchison's findings tomorrow, as soon as I have them. If it does show a different diagnosis, she can get started then.'

'Oh no,' Lord Murray exclaimed. 'It's in a good cause, so I'll get her working right away, just on the off-chance. And don't worry about security,' he added, glancing around.

'This place might not look much, but it's probably the only leak-proof office in the whole of Parliament House.'

67

'Remember the "Thriller" video,' asked Bob Skinner. As he threw a sidelong glance at Neil McIlhenney, a shaft of moonlight made his face shine, eerily silver in the night. 'The Vincent Price section where the undead rise from their graves . . .'

His executive assistant looked at him and laughed, dismissively. 'Try again, if you think you're scaring me, Boss. You've never seen my Olive first thing in the morning.'

'Anything you say, sergeant,' the DCC countered, 'may be noted down and reported back to Mrs McIlhenney.'

He looked round at the man on his other side. 'Ignore him, Pat,' he said. 'I have met the lady. Not at that time of day admittedly, but she's lovely . . . the very salt of the earth.'

'Aye,' McIlhenney mused. 'I've often thought yon bloke Lot was a lucky bastard.' He leaned forward, looking round Skinner at Sheriff Patrick Boone, from the Haddington Court.

'Do you have to be present as a witness at all exhumations, sir?' he asked.

'No, not at all. I volunteered for this one though. When I was at the Bar I appeared before Orlach often enough to want to be sure that the old swine really is dead.'

The DCC grinned. His eyes having grown accustomed to the light, he glanced at his watch. It showed one minute to midnight. He led the Sheriff and McIlhenney across the grass of the graveyard towards a group of five men in overalls and rubber boots, who were standing almost in the shadow of the square tower of the old Aberlady church. Away to their left, the moonlight shone pure silver on the calm waters of the bay, a scene in stark contrast to the monsoon weather of the night before.

'We're ready to start now, lads,' said Skinner. 'Before that I'd like to thank you for volunteering for this unpleasant job, and to impress on you again that it must not be mentioned or discussed, not even at home.' He nodded towards the oldest of the five. 'You'll work under the direction of Mr Glaister here, who is the Council's burial ground superintendent. Do exactly as he tells you.'

He glanced at the Sheriff once more. 'Okay, let's begin. Mr Glaister, if you please.'

The older man stepped forward and pointed to four white pegs set in the ground, joined by string to form a rectangle eight feet long by four feet

221

wide. 'I've pegged out the area that we're going to dig around, and I've cut the top layer of turf. I've only ever been at one other exhumation, like, when I worked up in Edinburgh, but the one thing I learned then was that it's a bloody sight easier tae put a coffin in the ground than it is tae get it oot! We'll need to allow width and length to get straps under the thing, for lifting. Unless it's solid wood, and no' chipboard, the handles on the side are just for show.'

'How deep will we have to go?' asked one of the police volunteers.

'Not as deep as you think, possibly. Only aboot four feet six, maybe five feet allowing for settlement. In this lair, the wife's buried below the husband, and we've got to be careful no' tae disturb her, so ah'll stop yis every so often, so's tae check the depth.'

He looked at the four diggers. 'Everybody a'right, now?' The police volunteers nodded. 'In that case, gentlemen, take up your shovels!'

68

'Did they have much trouble getting it out of the hole?' One of the things Skinner liked most about Professor Joe Hutchison was that he was always matter-of-fact.

The policeman shook his head. 'Not a bit. The ground was soft a good way down after last night's rain, and we were lucky in that it turned out to be a solid oak box with proper brass fittings. The handles took the weight, no problem. They just tied on ropes and lifted it out. We were on our way here in only an hour and a half.'

As he looked at the coffin, lying newly washed on the floor of the examination room in the Edinburgh City Mortuary, he remembered the first occasion on which he had seen it, when he had been at the head of a queue of traffic halted in Aberlady's main street by the old man's funeral. The gleam of that day had gone from its varnish, but otherwise, its months in the ground had done it no apparent damage. The name, Orlach, etched on the brass plate on the lid, stood out clearly.

Hutchison turned to his two assistants. 'Right lads, get it open. Let's just hope they didn't bury him in his good suit, or in his robes.' He glanced heavenwards. 'An ordinary shroud, please, or we'll be here all bloody night getting it off.'

As the men began to unfasten the big brass screws on the coffin lid, he pulled his face mask into position. Skinner, McIlhenney and Sheriff Bonne did the same.

The policemen felt the Sheriff flinch between them as the oak chest was opened, and steeled themselves to ignore the smell which seemed to flood into the room. As they watched, the assistants bent, lifted the body, and placed it on the steel post-mortem table. They saw at once that Hutchison's informal prayer had been answered. The old judge had been wrapped in a linen shroud, which had once been cream in colour.

As the pathologist leaned over the table, and began to unwrap the winding sheet, Skinner pressed the mental button which switched on his professional detachment, but the sight of the old man's blackened corpse was too much for Sheriff Boone. 'Excuse me,' he murmured. 'He's dead all right . . .' He slipped from the room, his face ashen, in contrast to that of the late Lord Orlach.

Hutchison looked after him. 'No stomach, these lawyers,' he exclaimed. 'They should all be made to attend one of these, so that they really know what they're dealing with.'

He glanced at Skinner, over his mask. 'So, Bob, Sarah reckoned suffocation was favourite, did she, if Milord here didn't die of natural causes.'

'That's right.'

'In that case, that's where we'll look first.' He picked up a scalpel, then looked meaningfully once more at the policemen. 'Better prepare yourselves, lads,' he warned. 'If you thought he smelled bad before . . .'

69

The acting Chief Constable shuddered, in spite of himself. Lord Archibald threw him a shrewd and perceptive glance. 'Bad, was it?'

'I've had more entertaining nights,' Skinner replied, 'but this one's been pretty unforgettable in its own way. Christ, and that's my wife's chosen profession.'

'Never mind, Bob,' said the Lord Advocate, 'have some breakfast. That'll help dull the memory.'

'What'll it do for the smell in my nostrils?' Nevertheless, he accepted gratefully the plate of bacon, eggs and mushrooms which his friend passed across to him, and nodded thanks to Lady Archibald as she handed him a mug of coffee.

Across the table, Lord Murray poured milk into his muesli. 'Hutchison was quite certain, then?'

Skinner nodded vigorously as he spread a slice of toast. 'Beyond any shadow of a doubt. He said that he would declare under any oath you cared to specify that Lord Orlach was suffocated. Apparently his heart was in remarkably good condition for a man of his age, but his lungs were "classically distended", as Joe described them.

'He was even able to identify the facial haemmorrhaging associated with asphyxia. My Lord, your late colleague either held a pillow to his own face and put it back under his head after he was dead . . . or he was murdered.'

The Lord President looked at the Lord Advocate, their breakfast host. 'How does that affect Norman King's position, Archie?'

'At the moment, it doesn't. The fact that he is definitely placed by two witnesses as being at the scene of Barnfather's death still weighs heavily against him. Old John could have been murdered by a common or garden house-breaker.'

Skinner snorted. 'Nothing was stolen.'

'Maybe he panicked,' said Lord Archibald, lamely.

'Archie!'

'All right, all right. The discovery of a third murder raises the possibility of a connection with the other two, and we're certain that King couldn't have killed Orlach. But it still is only a possibility; it would still be very dangerous, politically, if I backed off from charging him, given the evidence I have on my desk.' He picked up his knife and fork once more.

'It would help beyond measure, David,' he ventured, 'if you could come up with a judicial connection linking the three old boys, and if you could suggest another suspect.'

Lord Murray nodded. 'I understand that. And as a matter of fact . . .'

Something in his tone made the others look up from their plates. '. . . a thought has occurred to me. I recalled it last night, in fact, at home.

'Archie, do you remember in our early years at the Bar, twenty years ago, a criminal case which became something of a *cause célèbre*, in media and other circles, HM Advocate versus Beatrice Lewis or Gates?'

The Lord Advocate's eyes narrowed. 'Yes, I do. Murder, wasn't it.'

'That's right. It happened in Dundee. Mr and Mrs Gates were a childless couple in their late thirties, affluent and living in some comfort. He was a bookmaker, and successful at it.

'They'd been married for sixteen years, until one morning Mrs Gates, according to her story, woke up in bed beside her husband. They were both covered in blood, and he had a kitchen knife right in the middle of his chest.

'She summoned the police. From the outset she denied killing Gates, and maintained that the murder must have been committed by an outsider, someone with a grudge against him; a disgruntled gambler, she suggested. It was her assertion that she had slept through the whole thing. She insisted that she was an exceptionally heavy sleeper, something which her sister, with whom she holidayed on occasion, confirmed to the police, and which was tested later by the defence and found to be true.

'Unfortunately for her, there were no signs of forced entry to the house. Even less fortunately, her fingerprints were found on the handle of the knife. Her defence to that was that she had grasped the knife on awakening, to pull it out of her husband's chest, only to find that it was stuck fast.

'Her small chances of convincing the jury of her innocence vanished altogether when the bookmaker's mistress came forward to the police. She told them that she had visited Mrs Gates, informed them of the affair, and pleaded with her to divorce her husband so that he and she could marry. Mrs Gates denied this at first, but eventually, under some fairly aggressive police questioning, she admitted that it was true.

'She stuck to her defence all the way through the trial, but the jury looked at the evidence and convicted her. She was sentenced to life imprisonment by a particularly dyspeptic judge who took it upon himself to impose a minimum recommendation of fourteen years.'

The Lord President paused in his account, pleased by the effect which it was having on his two companions, whose eggs and bacon were now as cold as his muesli.

'The fact is that Mrs Gates' defence did no particular credit to Scottish justice. The mistress was given an easy time of it in the box, and the police witness who testified to the security of the premises was not cross-examined at all. Worse than that, the defence team failed to have the woman physically examined.

'When she was given a medical on her admission to Cornton Vale, it

226

was discovered that she was in the early stages of muscular sclerosis. This accounted for her exceptionally heavy sleep pattern. It also cast serious doubts on her ability to deliver a blow as powerful as that which killed her husband. However it didn't rule it out altogether, particularly since some months had elapsed between the stabbing and the discovery of the condition.'

Skinner picked up his coffee, which was still drinkably warm. 'You seem to remember a lot about this case, David,' he said.

Lord Murray nodded. 'I should hope so, for I prosecuted it. I led for the Crown, too, when it went to the Court of Criminal Appeal. The defence tried to introduce the new medical evidence at that stage, but the appeal judges threw it out, quite rightly, as being against the rules of procedure. However they did say that the trial judge's minimum recommendation seemed excessive, and urged the Secretary of State and the Parole Board to disregard it when the sentence first fell naturally for review.

'You will have guessed by now,' said the little judge, 'that the Appeal Court Bench comprised Lords Orlach, presiding, Archergait, and Barnfather. I don't know about you, Archie, but I can't recall another occasion on which those three sat together in the Appeal Court, or even when two of them heard an appeal against the other.'

The detective replaced his mug on its coaster. 'Which begs a question,' he interjected, 'Who was the trial judge?'

'Coalville,' said Lord Murray.

'In that case, why isn't he dead? I'd have thought that the judge who sentenced her would have been first on the list.' Skinner looked across the table. 'Still, if this theory is a runner, then we must assume that Coalville is a target. Lord President, I'd like him to be taken off all duties, so that he can be placed under close protection.'

'So be it. He'll hate it, but I'll order it.'

'Good. Next, can you recall who acted for the defence?'

'Of course. Old Hammy Horne led; he died five years ago. His junior was Richard Kilmarnock.'

Lord Archibald grunted. 'That couldn't have helped the defence.'

'It did in the longer term. Kilmarnock's brother Arnold is a journalist. He was working in America at the time, but when he came home, he took up the case and ran a strong campaign over the issue. You'll both recall that for a time, it was all over the *Herald*, the *Scotsman* . . . and the *Courier* of course, given the Dundee connection. Two successive Secretaries of State looked at it, but decided that they had no powers to intervene. Eventually a third decided that he didn't care about powers, and ordered a re-trial.

'Unfortunately, Mrs Gates' MS was very bad by that time. She was declared unfit for trial and quietly released, to die in a nursing home a couple of weeks later.'

'Is Arnold Kilmarnock still around?' asked Skinner. 'I haven't heard the name lately.'

'I believe he works for *Sky News* now, in the Far East,' Lord Archibald

227

answered. 'So Richard told me.' He looked at his guests. 'This is very interesting. I'll tell you what I'll do. I'll instruct King to develop chicken-pox or some such, and to stay at home for another week. After that, we'll look at the situation again.

'Thanks, Archie,' said the policeman. 'I'll begin an investigation at once, starting with Richard Kilmarnock. Meanwhile, David, whether you like it or not, you're going to have the same level of security as Lord Coalville. Since you prosecuted this woman, if there is someone out there who's taking revenge on her behalf, you could be on his list too.'

70

The knock on the door was very light, but Skinner awoke at once. 'Come in,' he called, propping himself up on the single bed of the small, heavily curtained bedroom in the Headquarters building, and switching on the light.

The door creaked open and Ruth McConnell stepped inside. 'It's twelve mid-day, sir. Gerry asked me to come along and wake you as instructed.' She placed a mug of coffee on the bedside table, and put a newspaper alongside it. 'I thought you might like these.'

'Thanks, Ruthie,' he said, gratefully. 'Gerry's a good lad, but he hasn't mastered good coffee yet.'

'I'll tell him about the extra scoop.' She smiled over her shoulder as she left the room.

Propping himself up in bed, the DCC took a sip of his second coffee of the day and unfolded the *Scotsman* which his secretary had left. He beamed as he saw, second lead story beneath the predictable political exclusive, a full report of Martin's press briefing, headed, '*Robbery Gang Smashed As Two Are Sought*'.

'That'll take some of the heat off,' he muttered. He flicked through the rest of the paper, finding nothing of interest save the success of Heart of Midlothian in the first stage of a European competition. 'That'll please Mackie,' he grinned as he rose from the bed and stepped into the adjoining bathroom.

Half an hour later he was back in the Chief's office, showered, shaved and dressed in a fresh white shirt and in his uniform. The suit which he had worn at the exhumation and at the post-mortem had to go for dry-cleaning at once, he had decided.

'What's happening, Gerry?' he asked the young man across the desk.

'Things are reasonably quiet, sir. Mr Martin called to say that he's sent Sergeants Steele and Neville out to West Linton with a team of uniforms to search Ryan Saunders' cottage: also he's applying for warrants to search Collins', Newton and Clark's houses. Finally he said to tell you that DC Pye and Mr Ankrah have begun reviewing those tapes again.

'Oh yes,' he added, 'and Sergeant McIlhenney asked if he could have a word with you.'

Skinner looked surprised. 'I didn't think he'd be in yet. Tell him to step across.'

A minute later, his executive assistant knocked on the side door and slipped into the office, taking the seat which Gerry had just vacated. 'Hello, Neil,' said the DCC. 'I thought I told you not to come in until two o'clock.'

'Ach, I know, Boss,' the big sergeant answered, 'but it's bloody chaos in our house in the morning, with the wee one running about and everything. I managed a few hours' kip though.

'After that, I decided I'd get started on the job you gave me; going to see Curly Collins' wife, and Newton's. I caught them both in.'

'Did you get a result? Did the name Hamburger mean anything to them?'

'It meant nothing at all to Mrs Collins . . . or so she said. She started by giving me dogs' abuse for what's in the *Scotsman*. Her Curly would never get involved in robbery or anything like that, he's never been in trouble wi' the polis in his life. He goes to confession every day and twice on Sundays. The usual crap, in other words, that we get from wives who know quite well that their men are bent, and enjoy the proceeds.

'So naturally enough, she denied any knowledge of anyone called Hamburger.'

The big detective smiled. 'I got on better with Alice Newton, though, out in Danderhall. She's in a state of total and complete shock. I really believe that she didn't have a clue what her husband was up to. They've been married since they were eighteen, they've got two teenage kids and an eight-year-old, and he's always been a model husband as far as she's concerned.

'She told me that when he turned up at home yesterday morning, gave her a big bundle of cash and said that she wouldn't be seeing him for a while, it was a bolt from the blue. I believe her.'

'Why?' asked Skinner.

'Because I do, Boss. Anyway, if she was bent, she'd never have mentioned the cash, would she?'

'No; you're right there, I'll grant you.'

'I put the name Hamburger to her, and she thought she recognised it. "Just a bloke that Rory mentioned once or twice", was what she said. She'd never met him, though, and she didn't know anything about him. He was just a casual acquaintance, she thought.'

'And maybe that's all he is,' said the DCC. 'He's the only link we've got, but he's bloody tenuous. But Mrs Newton will know the rest of the team, won't she? After all, they all soldiered together.'

Neil McIlhenney shook his head. 'That's the funny thing. According to her, they didn't. She told me that Bakey took her up to the TA Club one night, a few months back. The other five were there; Collins had his wife with him, Saunders a girl-friend, who I guess could have been Mrs Sturrock, and Bennett brought his sister. The women were left at a table together, while the men went off for a blether, then they all went for a meal.

'But Alice Newton didn't know any of them before that night. She said that the men treated each other differently too. Saunders and Clark seemed to be very close, but the others were, well, pally enough, but not bosom buddies.'

'How very strange,' said Skinner, slowly. 'I wonder what, or who, brought them together?'

He sat up, abruptly. 'Neil, I'm going to do some more digging . . . figuratively, this time. Meanwhile, I want you to go back up to the TA Club. Speak to Steele's pal, Mr Herr, and find out when each of these guys joined the place, and, if he can tell you, who introduced them.'

McIlhenney nodded, rose and left by the door through which he had entered. As it closed, Skinner buzzed Gerry.

'I'd like you to make me an appointment to see an advocate, Richard Kilmarnock, QC, as soon as possible this afternoon. Once you've done that can you let ACC Elder know, since the Police Federation reps are due for a meeting, and I want to spin it on to him. First though, ask Ruthie to step in here.'

'Right away, sir.'

He sat back and waited. Seconds later, it seemed, the side door opened once more, and Ruth appeared, notebook in hand. He nodded towards it. 'You won't need that, I want you . . .'

He turned and glared angrily at the phone on his desk as it rang. 'Sorry to bother you, sir,' said Gerry, as he picked it up, 'but I have Lady Proud on the phone.'

Skinner grunted. 'She probably wants to know where we keep the detergent. Put her through.'

'Hello, Chrissie,' he said, before his caller could speak. 'How's it going out there? Are you enjoying Festa Major?'

'Not today, Bob.' As the Chief's wife answered, the anxiety in her voice transferred itself to him.

'What's the matter?'

'It's Jimmy,' she replied. 'He's not very well. We bought some fish at the market last night and cooked it for ourselves. I suppose we should have been more careful. We didn't really know what it was.

'It tasted all right at the time, but Jimmy was awful sick during the night, then he developed terrible pains in his middle. Your friend got the doctor for me, and they've taken him to hospital in Figueras. Bob, are these places all right?'

'Of course they are, Chrissie,' he said, reassuringly. 'They're as good as you'll find here. Don't worry about any language problems. I'm sure my pal will interpret for you as you need it.'

'She's already offered, thanks. Och Bob, it's probably nothing but . . .'

'I know. There's nothing worse than a crisis when you're a long way from home. How about you? Are you affected by this thing?'

'I might have been a wee bit queasy this morning, but nothing like as bad as Jimmy.'

'Well look after yourself anyway, and let me know how he's getting on.'

'I will do,' said Lady Proud. 'I feel better now I've spoken to you. Goodbye.'

He was frowning, as he turned back to Ruth. 'Something wrong?' she asked.

'It sounds as if the Chief has food poisoning. Silly old bugger,' he muttered, anxiously, 'what's the point buying fish on the market when you can go to a restaurant and have the same cooked by professionals for about the same cost.'

'Oh dear,' his secretary exclaimed. 'What a thing to happen on holiday.'

'Ahh, he'll be okay. He's as tough as old boots, is Jimmy.'

'Back to business, kid. I want you to go into my real office and get Adam Arrow's direct-line number from my safe. I thought I had it in my head, but there's so much other stuff in there right now it must have slipped out when I wasn't looking!'

She smiled and hurried from the room. As he sat waiting, Gerry buzzed through once more. 'Mr Kilmarnock will see you at the Advocates Library at four-thirty, sir. He's a pompous character, isn't he. He was quite insistent on knowing what it was about, until I told him that the acting Chief Constable simply wished to see him, and that was that. I said we could always send a car for him and bring him down here, if he wished.'

'Good for you, son. Have you told Jim Elder about the other thing?'

'Yes.' Gerry paused. 'Lady Proud told me about the Chief. What a pity; he really needed a holiday.'

'Aye,' the DCC grunted. 'And plenty of bed rest. He's getting that at least, by the sound of it.'

As he hung up, Ruth reappeared, laid a scrap of paper on the desk before him and slipped out once more. He looked at the number and dialled it.

'Hello, Bob,' said Major Adam Arrow, before Skinner had a chance to announce himself. He was probably the deadliest human being the DCC knew, yet he always found the little soldier's voice warm and reassuring.

'You do have a clever telephone, mate. I'm calling on a secure line.'

'We've got all the fookin' toys here, sunshine. 'Ow are you?'

'Personally, I've never been better. Professionally, I'm snowed under.'

'So I've been reading,' Arrow chuckled. 'I saw the story about the dead judges, and I thought to meself, "That fooking Bob's a magnet for shit-storms, so 'e is." So what can I do for you. D'you want me to sort you out a nice cushy billet down here in MoD?'

'In theory, I've got a nice cushy billet here. I'm acting Chief just now, and everyone knows that Chief Constables do fuck all . . . if only. No, Adam, I want a favour, something involving your lot that needs doing quickly, and I figured there was no-one better than the Head of Ministry of Defence security to make it happen.'

'Okay,' said the soldier. 'Flattery works. What is it?'

'I'd like to send you down half a dozen names by secure fax. They're all ex-servicemen, ex-army. Three of them have been killed, and the other three have disappeared. I want you to see if there's a common factor linking all six, and if there is, to put a name and a face to him.'

'This wouldn't be linked to your armed robberies, would it? I've been reading about them too.'

'That's how it looks.'

'And you think that your common factor might be killing them off?'

'That's exactly right. The trouble is, apart from the first, I can't figure out why.'

71

He had thought about buying a new suit before his meeting with Richard Kilmarnock, QC, but decided instead that he would go in uniform, to emphasise that his visit was official.

'Good afternoon, Mr Skinner,' said the Faculty attendant, seated at Thornton's Box, the name by which, for no clear reason, the reception desk at the entrance to the Advocates Library had become known.

'And the same to you,' said the DCC. 'Mr Richard Kilmarnock, please.'

'I'll page him for you, sir.'

Skinner had been waiting for almost ten minutes before the advocate answered the summons, but he managed to keep his irritation hidden, when finally he did appear, unsmiling and wearing an expression which suggested that he found the interruption tiresome.

Kilmarnock stood just under six feet. He was approaching fifty, but still slim and handsome, with wavy greying hair which gave him a debonair look. Like the detective, he was a member of Edinburgh's New Club, and they had seen each other there. However, apart from their single High Court confrontation, they had spoken only rarely.

'I can give you ten minutes, Mr Skinner, that's all,' he said brusquely.

The policeman noticed the attendant wince as he heard the remark, and drop his eyes to a note on his desk which had become suddenly very important. 'You'll give me all the time I require, sir,' he replied in an even tone. 'Now, where can we speak in private?'

Skinner's glare forbade anything other than a muttered, 'This way.' The Silk led him down two flights of exceptionally narrow stairs, and then turned into a corridor off which were several small consultation rooms, with tall glass panels set into their walls. The one into which he ushered the policeman was brighter than the others, and octagonal in shape.

'We won't be disturbed here,' said Kilmarnock. 'Now, if you please, what is this about?'

'HM Advocate versus Beatrice Lewis or Gates.'

The advocate blinked. 'The Gates case? But that's history . . .'

'Then I'm a historian, because I want to know about it. You acted for the defence, I believe, and your brother took the case up thereafter.'

'Correct on both counts. The case of Beattie Gates was a notorious miscarriage of justice, which was never properly corrected.'

'As I remember, there was nothing wrong with the conviction itself. I've had a word with my colleagues in Tayside, and with the officer who led the investigation. He's retired now, but he remembers it clearly. His view is that there was no reasonable doubt raised during the trial that Mrs Gates killed her husband. Obviously the jury agreed with that, because their verdict was unanimous.'

'Ah,' said Kilmarnock, raising an admonitory finger, 'but the subsequent medical evidence . . .'

'Which your team failed to uncover and introduce at the trial, I'm told.'

'Be that as it may. The subsequent evidence did establish very serious doubt. The trouble we had was that the Court of Criminal Appeal decided that it was not allowed to consider evidence that had not been put to the jury.'

Skinner frowned. 'There's no doubt that the Court was right about that, is there? That's certainly the Lord President's view.'

'It may well have been correct,' the advocate conceded. 'That's why my brother Arnold took up the case through the media.'

'Yet your brother attacked the Court of Appeal, didn't he? To a point at which Lord Orlach considered charging him with contempt, and had to be dissuaded by the Lord Advocate of the day, and, I'm told, by Christabel Dawson.'

Kilmarnock spluttered. 'That old witch!'

'She kept your brother out of jail, though. She told me so this afternoon.'

'A contempt charge would have been ridiculous, and provocative with an election coming up.'

Skinner smiled. 'You're certainly right about the latter. Orlach and Miss Dawson were well-known Tory supporters; ultimately that's why he backed off, and why your brother was able to carry on with the publication of his book.'

He paused for a moment. 'To be absolutely frank, Mr Kilmarnock, since Mrs Gates is dead, I'm not too bothered about her guilt or innocence . . . although for what it's worth, the evidence regarding the security of their property sounded significant to me. Most bookies I know protect their homes like Fort Knox.

'On the basis that this is between professionals, and therefore confidential, my concern is that there might be someone out there who does believe that she was wronged, and who is doing something about it.'

'What makes you think that?' Kilmarnock asked.

'Who were the Appeal judges?'

The Silk furrowed his brow for a few moments, then a light of understanding seemed to go on in his eyes.

'Oh!' he said.

'Exactly,' said Skinner. 'Because of that, I need to know the names of everyone to whom your brother spoke in researching his book, particularly those who were supporters of Mrs Gates.'

'I understand.'

'The couple had no children, I'm told.'

'None. Neither had a previous marriage either.'

'What about nephews?'

'Beattie had one nephew as I recall. But I can't remember his name. You won't find it in Arnold's book, either. He asked to be kept out of it.'

'Where will I find it, quickly, without going through a laborious search at Register House?'

Kilmarnock hesitated, then murmured, 'Oh I don't suppose he'll mind.' He looked up at Skinner. 'While Arnold's away, I'm holding all of his files on the case. Photographs, the lot. We kept all the scene-of-crime stuff; we also had studies of Beattie taken by a medical photographer, to illustrate the extent of her muscle wastage. That was among the material that the Court of Appeal wouldn't look at . . . or couldn't,' he added grudgingly.

'I'll give you those, if you guarantee to return them intact when you're done with them.'

'Of course,' the policeman agreed. 'When can I have them?'

The advocate glanced at his watch. 'Drive me home now, and I'll hand them over.' He threw Skinner a self-satisfied, smug glance. 'One is an Officer of the Court after all. One has an obligation to help you chaps.'

72

'Bloody hell, Boss, what's all that?' Neil McIlhenney burst out, as he stepped into Skinner's office and saw the piles of paper on his desk.

'These are the records in the case of Mrs Beattie Gates, the one that links our three dead judges together. Richard Kilmarnock handed them over. They belong to his brother, the journalist.'

'D'you want me to go through them, sir?'

Skinner smiled at his assistant's willingness. 'No, Neil. I want you to do the same as I intend: go home and spend some time with your wife and kids. Once you've told me what you've come in to tell me, that is.'

'Sit down, man, sit down.' He ushered him to one of the leather seats, where Andy Martin sat waiting. 'I thought that it would be a good idea if the three of us had a round-up of everything that's happened today. I've just briefed the DCS on the exhumation and on the post-mortem on old Orlach, also on your interviews with the Newton and Collins wives.

'What else have do you have to report?'

The big sergeant slumped wearily into a chair. 'I've been back up to the TA Club as you ordered, Boss. I spoke to the manager about the Paras gang.

'It seems that Collins and Saunders were the first to become members. They joined at the same time, a few years back. Mr Herr's recollection was that it was when they came out of the army and joined the Terriers. Clark and Newton came along after them, in the same way.'

'Together?'

'No. Individually, one after the other, about six months apart.'

'And what about Bennett and MacDonnell?'

McIlhenney shifted in his chair. 'Aye, now they were a bit different. They were both associate members. They joined at the same time, proposed and seconded by Curly Collins and Rocky Saunders.'

'When was that?' Skinner asked.

'Turn of last year, sir, early December.'

The DCC leaned forward, eyes narrowing. 'Introduced at the same time, you say. And had they known each other beforehand?'

'This is when it gets good, Boss. When I asked him whether they were old pals, Barry Herr said that he distinctly remembered Rocky Saunders introducing the two of them to each other on the first night they came to the club. "That's when the Paras became a sextet", he said to me.

'He remembered a lot about that night, did Barry. Apparently Hamburger

237

was there too. The seven of them went off into a back room and drank there, on their own. Arlene Regan waited on them. At the end of the night, they all left together, except for Hamburger.'

'Oh?'

'Aye,' said McIlhenney, with a knowing grin. 'He hung around, and left with Arlene . . . arm in arm. Herr said he'd forgotten that when he spoke to Stevie. He remembered something else too. When everyone else was gone he had a drink himself; he was just finishing clearing up, an hour and a half or two hours later, when Arlene's boy-friend phoned, asking if she was still there.'

'They only lived ten minutes away, Boss.'

Skinner smiled, nodding approval. 'What do you think of that, Andy?' he asked.

'The picture's forming, isn't it,' said the Head of CID. 'Our four ex-regulars come together first, then Bennett and McDonnell are brought in. When they all meet, it's with Hamburger in attendance. It sounds almost like a conference. I wish to hell we'd a tape of the discussion in that back room, but I'll bet that's when they began to plan the robberies.'

Skinner nodded. 'Aye, and as a bonus, our man Hamburger winds up shagging the barmaid, and finds out in the process that her boy-friend works in a jeweller's. See pillow talk, lads, and what can come of it! In this case, Nick Williams tells Arlene about the Russian diamond buyer, and she lets it slip to her bit on the side.

'Andy, you could just about write your report to the Fiscal now.'

'Except for one thing. We haven't a fucking clue who Hamburger is.'

'I don't suppose there's any chance that could be his real name could it, sir?' McIlhenney asked, tentatively.

Martin shook his head. 'We've checked that impossibility. Believe it or not, there is one man called Hamburger in the UK. He lives in Staffordshire, he's in his late sixties and he's a parish priest.'

'Ah,' said the sergeant. 'So he's unlikely to be planning armed robberies in Edinburgh, or shaggin' a bar stewardess.' He paused, and rolled his eyes. 'Mind you . . .'

Skinner let out a short sharp burst of laughter. 'We'll pull him in, if you like, Neil, and stick him in a line-up for Herr to look at.' He turned to Martin.

'Andy, do you have anything else, or can we all go home?'

'Oh yes,' said the Head of CID, with a gleam in his green eyes. 'I have something else. We've had a result out at West Linton. Neville and Steele tore Saunders' cottage apart. They found nothing there, but when they started on his van, a wee white Citroen job, they found, hidden behind the body panels in the luggage compartment, over a hundred grand in cash and a single-barrelled, short-stock, pump-action shotgun, loaded with heavy gauge, the same ammo that killed Harry Riach and Annie Brown.

'I've sent it to Ballistics for testing against the ejected cartridges that were found at the scene in Galashiels.'

'Well done your team!' said Skinner enthusiastically.

'When I get a positive match, I'm planning to issue another press statement through Royston, if the Fiscal's happy.'

'You do that.' The DCC leaned back in his chair, hands behind his head. 'I can see all this coming together now. I'd guess that all the targets were identified before the first robbery and all the team was in place. When Bennett dropped his credit card and got lifted, the rest of the operation was put on hold, to review the planning, and to make sure that he wouldn't talk.

'With O'Donnell on the payroll, the leader could keep a close eye on him while he was in the nick. Once he was happy that he was secure, the rest of the operation got underway.'

'Who's the Boss?' asked Martin, quietly.

'Hamburger. I'm sure of it. He was at the first meeting, and he's the only one who's protected his identity.'

'Who killed the Bennetts?'

'Hamburger, when McDonnell told him he thought Big Red was going to talk. Hannah obviously knew who he was, because she had to go.'

'Who killed Saunders and Collins?'

'It has to be Hamburger, doesn't it? He's wiping them out. With Newton and Clark gone, he thinks he's safe. He's got enough cash to keep him in luxury for the rest of his days, and he's probably got all the diamonds as well. He may have vanished too, for all we know.'

The Head of CID sighed. 'If that's the case, will we ever identify him?'

'The Devil alone knows,' said Skinner, '. . . but I'm in touch with him.'

His companions stared at him as he stood. 'Out of here, you two,' he shouted, suddenly. 'It's gone six o'clock. Off you go to Olive and Alex. I'm going home too.' He glanced at the pile on his desk. 'I think I'll only take half that lot with me. If I took it all, Sarah would kill me, for sure.'

73

'Where have you been?' asked Alex. 'Did you stop off for a beer with my old man?'

'Your old man went home knackered, honey. He was out all last night.'

'Oh?' she said. 'Doing what?'

'An exhumation, followed by a post-mortem on the body.'

She winced, then shuddered. 'How horrible.'

Andy nodded. 'Rather him than me. I can think of better things to do in the dark.'

'Why didn't you tell me before? Where was it? Who was it?'

'Question one: I decided not to mention it before the event. Two: it was in Aberlady churchyard. Three: it was an old judge, Lord Orlach.'

Her eyes became even bigger and more round than usual. 'Another judge? What did the autopsy show? Was it murder?'

'Joe Hutchison says that it was. Someone broke into his house and smothered him. Now we're trying to work out whether it was connected to the other two deaths, and if so, how. Bob's turned up a possible answer already.

'He's taken some paperwork home with him. Mind you, it's touch and go whether he stays awake to read it.'

'Exciting,' said Alex. She smiled at her fiancé. 'And how was your day, my love? Considering today's press, I'd have thought you'd be well chuffed with yourself.'

'I don't have any right to be,' he answered, with a frown. 'We're putting all the pieces together on the armed robberies, true, but it isn't good old-fashioned police work that's got us there. It's good old-fashioned luck.'

'This morning's papers were giving you all the credit. Don't knock it.'

'I won't . . . not in public anyway . . . for the sake of the team. But I can see the truth, and so, sweetheart, can you. We don't have anyone locked up for this. Of the gang, we have three bodies in the mortuary, and the other three have escaped, for now, at least.' He shook his head. 'Then there's the other guy.'

'What other guy?'

'The brains behind it all, the planner. Hamburger, the others called him. Our thinking is that he killed Bennett, Saunders and Collins and sent the other three into hiding. The only trouble is . . .' He sounded more exasperated than she had ever heard him. '. . . we haven't a fu . . . We haven't a clue who he is.

'With everyone taken care of, one way or another, I'd say he'll do a runner too. Wouldn't you?'

She looked at him, smiling no more. 'I suppose I would.' She put her arms around his waist, and hugged him. 'At least the city's a safe place again. So cheer up.'

He forced a grin. 'Aye, okay. So how was your day?'

'Routine for once,' she said. 'The insurers confirmed that they're not appealing the Grimley award.'

'So that case is history, is it?'

'Apart from what the Law Society do to Jones, but that won't be much. Next year's professional indemnity premium for his firm, though: that's another matter.'

She reached up and kissed him. 'Now, even though we've still to eat, can we discuss something other than work, please?'

'Okay,' he agreed, running his hands down her back and cupping them round her firm bottom. 'Such as?'

'You and me for a start. Remember earlier on this year, before other things got in the way, we were talking about getting married.'

He smiled. 'Remember? You think I'd forget? Do you want to set a date? Is that it?'

As she looked up at him, he saw her expression become a little uncertain. All of a sudden, she dropped her gaze.

'What?' he asked. 'Don't you?'

'Yes, of course I do. But there's something we have to sort out first.'

'Such as?'

'Such as babies, Andy, babies.'

He chuckled at her awkwardness. 'You're not having one, are you?'

'Don't be silly. That's just it. I don't want to, not for a long time. I've been thinking about my career. You know I've always wanted to go to the Bar? Well, Mr Laidlaw's been talking to me about that. He says I could stay with the firm, once my training period's over and I have my practising certificate, and go for Rights of Audience in the Supreme Courts as a solicitor advocate.'

'Do you want to?'

Her mouth twisted in a 'Don't know' gesture. 'It's an attractive proposition. I could have the best of both worlds; specialist practice and, eventually, a partnership in the top firm in the country.' She paused. 'But it would mean a full-time commitment for quite a few years, to establish myself with the client base, and to gain Court experience.

'It would mean not being able to start a family for a long time; until I'm around thirty, probably.'

'If that's what you want, love.' Andy kept his expression steady, but his eyes gave him away.

'But it's not what you want, is it?'

He unwound himself from her and walked over to the living-room window, staring out into the dull, damp evening. 'Alex,' he said, without

241

looking at her, 'I'm fifteen years older than you.'

'Fourteen.'

'And ten months. Don't split hairs. If that's your timetable, you're telling me that I won't be a father until I'm forty-five. That may be okay for Bob, in his second marriage, but this will be my first. Look, if I choose to retire at sixty, our first child will still be at school. I want to be able to play football with him, or go running with her. When they're at that stage I don't want to be past it.'

'Don't be daft, you won't be past it. Look at you now. You're fitter than most men in their mid twenties.'

'I'm not as fit as your dad though. He murdered me again on the squash court yesterday. Fuck me, I don't want to be stuffed by his grandson as well, not until he's left primary school at least!'

She came to him, and laid a hand on his shoulder, turning him to face her. 'Andy,' she said. 'Do you want a marriage of equals?'

'Of course,' he answered, defensively.

'Then surely we have equal career rights. Look at Maggie and Mario. She's over thirty, and she's a DCI. There are no signs of babies on the way there.'

'Forget them, this is us. Does this firm of yours not believe in maternity leave, then? I thought that was statutory.'

She shook her head violently, making her thick hair fly. 'It isn't the firm. It's the clients, and it's me too.'

'Och, Alex,' he exclaimed. 'You change with the wind. A few months ago you were all for getting married.'

'And I still am. It's what comes after that we need to agree.'

He looked at her. 'Okay then. If this is negotiation, you've given me your agenda, now I'll give you mine. I'd like to be a father within five years.'

'In that case,' she said. 'Where's the compromise?'

'That was a compromise, my darling!'

Alex flared up. 'That was an ultimatum!'

'No, it wasn't,' he replied, quietly and sadly. 'This is an ultimatum. Either we agree to start a family within five years, or this relationship will be heading for the rocks.'

74

He rolled on his back, squealing with pleasure as the strong fingers kneaded his bare stomach. He kicked his legs in the air, reaching out with his hands, grasping at nothing.

'Oooh! Yerghh!' he bellowed.

'That's enough, Bob,' called Sarah from the sofa. 'He'll never sleep if you wind him up any more.'

'Hear that, wee man,' said Skinner, tumbling over to lie on the sitting-room floor beside his younger son, and looking sideways at him, their eyes at the same level. 'Your mother has plans for you. The Sandman is coming.' He propped himself up on an elbow, looking down at Jazz, who gazed back, fascinated. 'You know, son, when you think of it, only the Americans could believe in a fairy who comes round at night and throws sand in weans' eyes.

'Us Scots, now, we simply believe in slipping a mild opiate . . . or maybe a small whisky . . . into their juice.'

In spite of the slur cast on one of her National Institutions, Sarah laughed as she bent to pick up the toddler from the floor. 'Sunshine,' she gasped, 'you are getting heavier by the day.' Jazz grinned and nuzzled his forehead against her. 'Time for bed now, your late pass has expired.'

She glanced down at her husband. 'You go and tell Mark to get ready. Honestly, the time that boy would spend on his computer . . .'

'Let him,' Bob grinned. 'It's what he likes best. He's no natural athlete is our Mark, but he may be a genius. All the time he spends exploring those CD Roms, he's learning.' He reached out and tickled Jazz once more in the ribs. 'Now this one, he's just going to be a bear when he grows up . . .'

He patted Sarah on the tail. 'Go on then, settle him down if you can and I'll spend some time with Einstein. See you back here in half an hour and you can help me go through that paper I brought home.'

In fact it was almost three quarters of an hour before he reappeared from Mark's room, having allowed him twenty minutes on the Internet, researching Scottish history. He was still shaking his head as he handed his wife an uncapped Becks. 'When Big Neil moves on, I think I'll take him on as my exec.,' he chuckled. 'He never forgets anything, and his logic circuits are bloody amazing.'

She squeezed his thigh, as he sat beside her. 'Don't forget to let him be a little boy, though.'

'As if I would. Alexis was a very clever child too, you know, and she's turned out all right.'

To his surprise, Sarah frowned slightly.

'What?' he asked.

'Nothing, nothing. You're right, she has turned out all right; very much so. But that doesn't mean you should stop being concerned about her. Alex is a volatile personality, like you . . . and like her mother. Those things you two found out about Myra, they terrify her, you know.

'Right now, I sense things going on behind those big eyes of hers, but I don't know what they are. Almost for the first time since I've known her, I can't tell what she's thinking.'

Bob looked at her. 'I'll have a word with her,' he said.

'Okay, but just you be careful.' She reached down and picked up the folder of papers which he had brought home with him. 'So what are these, then?'

'They relate to the judges' investigation. They're the papers for a book on the Beatrice Gates case.'

Sarah grinned, wickedly. 'Oh yes. I didn't like to ask you in front of the kids. How was Lord Orlach?'

'Heavily tanned. It must be very hot where he is. His deodorant doesn't work any more either. Christ, I don't think I'll ever forget that smell!'

'I can imagine. I really should have been there, you know. It would have been good experience. Even Joe enjoyed it, so he said when I phoned him.'

'You know the result then?'

'Yes. Clever you, for thinking of it.'

'Stupid me for not thinking of it earlier,' he retorted.

'Like you said once, it's a real bastard not being perfect, ain't it.' She opened the folder and recoiled involuntarily as she saw the first item. It was a photograph of a dead man, naked on an examination table with the hilt of a knife protruding from his chest.

'That's Mr Gates,' said Bob, almost conversationally. 'He woke up one morning to find himself dead. However hard she tried, Mrs Gates, who woke up alongside him, couldn't make the jury believe that she didn't do it. They were childless, so there was no-one to back up her story that he must have been killed by an intruder.'

Sarah peered at the photograph. 'She must have been pretty strong. That knife is rammed right through the sternum.'

'Yes, and although it wasn't known during the trial, they reckon she had incipient MS at the time,' Bob told her, quietly.

'The jury wasn't told that?'

He shook his head. 'Nope.'

'So what do you hope to find in here?' she asked.

'Somebody who's capable of carrying a grudge for twenty years before getting even.' He took the folder from her and laid it on his lap. Discarding the photographs, he picked up a typed document. 'This is Mrs Gates' original statement to the Tayside officers.' With his wife looking over his shoulder he read his way through it.

244

'That's just an account of what I told you. The woman claims that she was a very heavy sleeper, and that she had been unaware of the intruder or the attack.'

'It's possible, I suppose,' Sarah conceded. 'What's next?'

'Copies of all the police, medical and forensic witness statements.'

'Let's go through them, then.'

They read on together for almost an hour, studying the overwhelming evidence against Beatrice Gates, as it painted a picture of her certain guilt.

'Down the road, isn't she,' said Bob. 'No way could the jury acquit.'

'Hmmph,' his wife snorted. 'I cannot believe that the defence was so incompetent that they didn't uncover and introduce the multiple sclerosis possibility.'

'You've just read the reason. After her arrest, Mrs Gates was examined by the police surgeon. He found that she was fit, and the defence accepted that. Two psychiatrists examined her as well, and neither of them commented.'

'They were examining her mind, Bob. I suppose it's possible,' she conceded, 'that the disease only started to motor towards the end of the trial. What's next?'

He picked up the next document and looked at the heading. 'This is a transcript of an interview with Mrs Pauline Collins, Mrs Gates' sister, not by the police, but by Arnold Kilmarnock, the author of the book.'

They scanned the document, in which Mrs Collins described her surprise and concern at the depth of her sister's sleep pattern. She said also that all through her life, Beatrice had been a gentle, friendly woman and that she and her husband had enjoyed a calm tranquil marriage, which, although it had not been blessed with children, had been very happy. Pinned to the back of the report was a photograph of the interviewee, a serious, plain-featured featured middle-aged woman.

'This depth of sleep could well have had a medical cause,' said Sarah. 'Was there any professional evidence led by the defence?'

'Not that I can see.'

'Jesus! Why ever not?'

'You've never met Richard Kilmarnock, have you?' Bob remarked casually, as he picked up the next document. 'This is an interview with Mrs Collins' son, Charles.'

The transcript was brief and not entirely relevant to Mrs Gates' defence, other than as a glowing testimonial to a loving aunt and a faithful and benevolent uncle. As with the notes on Mrs Collins, there was a photograph of the subject clipped to the back. Skinner gave it the briefest glance and was about to discard the document, when suddenly his whole body stiffened.

He stared at the photograph. 'Good God,' he whispered. 'Good God Almighty.

'I've seen this man's face before. Dan Pringle's met him, too, only he was dead at the time. This is Curly Collins, one of Andy's armed robbery gang!'

245

75

'Look, Mrs Collins,' said Skinner, evenly. 'Please don't get aggressive with me. I appreciate that you've lost your husband in terrible circumstances, but that's not my fault.'

He paused. 'I think you should face the facts here. Last night, our search team found one hundred and seventy thousand pounds and a shotgun buried under your garden shed. Curly was a member of a particularly vicious gang, and he was almost certainly a murderer too.

'Our laboratory has determined that the gun in his possession killed a man called Harry Riach during the bank robbery in Galashiels. The one we found hidden in his pal Rocky Saunders' van was used to murder Police Constable Annie Brown outside the bank.'

His voice hardened. 'If your old man hadn't got himself shot, he'd have been locked away for the rest of his life, be in no doubt about that.'

'But who shot him, though?' Grace Collins shot back, running her fingers through her straggly, dyed-blonde hair, and drawing heavily on her cigarette. 'I'll bet it was your lot, with that policewoman being killed. That's why you're going on about this guy Hamburger, who probably doesn't even exist.'

'Oh, he does, lady, he does. And sooner or later we will find him, just as we'll find Newton, Clark and McDonnell. Wherever they are, it isn't far enough to be safe from us.'

He stood over her, his back to the fireplace in the compact living room of her semi-detached bungalow. 'Anyway, that's not what I want to talk to you about.'

'Why are you here, then? Are you going to offer me a job as a traffic warden or something?'

The DCC grinned at her defiance. 'I don't think so, Mrs Collins. You've got too nice a nature. No, I want to ask you about Curly's auntie. I'm taking a look at the case of Mrs Beatrice Gates, which has become relevant to another enquiry we're involved in.'

For the first time since she had opened the front door, something other than hostility showed in the woman's face. 'Auntie Beattie? I thought that was all dead and buried, like her.'

Skinner nodded. 'It was, but I've dug it up again. You speak as if you knew her. Did you?'

'Yes, I did. Curly and I were going together before . . . before that thing happened.'

'Did you like her?'

'Well enough. She was round at Curly's mum's quite a lot. She never had much to say for herself though. Quiet woman, a bit starchy, stiff-knickered. Know what I mean?'

The policeman smiled and sat down. 'I can guess. Let me ask you something. Do you think she did it?'

Grace Collins threw him a shrewd look. 'If Curly was here, I'd have to say "No way". He wouldn't hear of it but the truth is, I reckon she did. She was a bit odd, Beattie, in the way she looked at folk. It was as if her expression was painted on. As for Uncle George, her husband, he was a slippery bastard. According to Curly's mum, he couldn't have kids, and that was why he was so free and easy. Beattie just smiled her way through life while he was out with his birds.

'I reckon that the police were right. When yon girl turned up at her house and told her she was the new love of George's life, I think she just went quietly mental, waited until he was asleep and knifed the swine.'

'There's some doubt that she could have done it, physically, with her disease.'

'Hah!' she said. 'That was patchy. She'd complain about being helluva tired, sure, but other times she was okay. Curly and I went round to see his granny the week before it happened, and we found Auntie Beattie there chopping up logs for the fire.'

She pursed her lips. 'That's just my humble opinion, mind. Curly, and his mum, and his granny; they all defended her to the last. "No' our Beattie", they were always saying.'

'Did Curly talk about the case much?' Skinner asked.

'At the start of it, he could talk about nothing else. It was a real obsession with him.'

'Did it ever go away?'

'No' really. Every so often he would bring it up. Even although he was in the forces, another uniformed service, he had a real down on the police because of it. And the Courts too.'

'Look, did he ever threaten over it?'

She frowned. 'What's this leading up to?'

'Let's wait and see. Did he?'

'Not threaten as such. But every so often he'd come out with something like, "See those bloody judges. I'd like to put them away and see how they get on." Now you're telling me he shot someone. D'you think he'd have done them in too?'

'Someone has, Mrs Collins,' said the DCC quietly. 'That's the problem.'
She looked up at him in disbelief.

'Do you have children?' he asked.

'Two girls.' Grace Collins pointed to a series of photographs in a glass-fronted display cabinet near the window. 'Una and Amy. One's starts Uni next month. The other's at school.'

'Ah. It'll be hard for them, losing their dad . . . whatever he was, or did.

247

I don't want to make it harder, but I want you to be straight with me, because another man's liberty might just depend on it.

'I'm going to write down three dates and times for you. I'd like you to search your memory, wall calendars, diary, anything you have, and see if you can tell me where Curly was on each of those occasions. When you're ready, I want you to phone me at my office.

'Will you do that?'

She gazed at him, her mouth drawn in a tight line, twin red spots on her pallid cheeks. 'You're saying someone else could be in bother?'

'No. He is in bother, but he may very well be innocent. You can't harm Curly now, Mrs Collins.'

'Okay,' she said at last, 'write them down. I'll do it.'

248

76

'The pieces are coming together, Bob,' said Andy Martin, emphatically. 'We recovered a third shotgun from Tory Clark's flat, stuck in a cupboard beside his golf clubs. I don't know where Newton kept his . . . maybe it's buried in his garden . . . but he didn't make a very good job of hiding the mask he wore at the George Street robbery. We came across that in his attic, together with some cartridges.'

'How much cash have we recovered?' asked Skinner, leaning back to allow the dining-room waitress to pour his coffee.

'Just over a quarter of a million in total; from Saunders' van, under Collins' greenhouse, and from Newton's wife. We've got a slight problem with the third lot, actually. I'm sweating slightly in case Mrs Bakey goes to a lawyer. She might challenge us to prove that it came from a robbery.'

The DCC added a touch of milk to his cup. 'Don't worry about that. If it comes to the bit, hand the money over to the Fiscal and let him sort out.

'The thing I'm most pleased about,' he went on, 'is knowing Collins and Saunders shot Riach and PC Brown. And the reason I'm so chuffed is that the bastards are lying in the morgue.'

Martin hunched his shoulders. 'You don't suppose, do you, that Hamburger executed them *because* they killed by-standers?'

'What, the noble criminal? Come on, Andy, you don't really believe that. Hamburger wiped them out to protect himself, that's the way of it.'

'Why didn't he take their money, then?'

Skinner snorted. 'Because he didn't have a squad of coppers to help him look for it. He's got at least half the proceeds stashed away himself, remember, and probably all of Raglan's diamonds.

'Any trace of any of our fugitives so far?'

The DCS nodded. 'One, this morning. Arlene Regan's father called Stevie Steele to say that they had a card from her in today's mail. It was posted in Paris six days ago. The message was "All well, don't worry, love Arlene". I've alerted the French police.'

'Don't hold your breath. There are more illegals in Paris than you've had chocolate biscuits.'

Skinner picked up his cup once more, cradling it in both hands.

'How's my daughter, Andy?'

The sudden question took his friend by surprise. He looked up sharply. 'Why d'you ask?'

'Why shouldn't I? I'm her dad.' Bob smiled, a shade sheepishly. 'It was something Sarah said last night. She thought she was worried about something. Eh . . . she isn't . . .'

'No, she bloody isn't!' Martin snapped back.

'Okay, okay. I'm sorry to be so indelicate.'

'No, my apologies: I shouldn't have bitten your head off. Sarah's right, as usual.' The younger man's shoulders hunched once more. 'Alex and I have run into a problem, that's all.'

'Nothing you can't sort out, though?'

'I hope not, but . . .' He paused. 'Bob, since she and I have been together, we've made nothing of the age difference between us. But we can't kid ourselves, it's there, and it can make us look at things . . . important things . . . from different angles. If I stick to my guns, I feel like I'm being a bully, but if I capitulate, I feel like I've got a ring through my nose.'

'Hey, since this body-piercing craze started I've seen guys all over town with rings through their noses.' Skinner grinned. 'Listen, there's a big age difference between Sarah and me, but we're okay . . . now,' he added.

'Yes, but Sarah's . . . Well she's a few years older than Alex. She's done more in her life.'

All at once, the big DCC nodded. 'I think I can see where this is leading; straight into a bloody minefield.

'Son, the only advice I'll give the two of you is to ask yourselves whether right now, you're happy . . . and I know you are. Let tomorrow take care of itself, for now at least. Don't take up rigid positions about something in the future that you could regret for the rest of your days. You can tell Alex that as well. But sort it out for yourself; don't get Sarah or me involved.'

He smiled and replaced the cup in its saucer.

'I'd better go. I've got the Director of Social Work coming in to see me this afternoon, and I haven't got the heart to pass her over to Elder.'

The two rose from the table and left the dining room together, Martin heading off, still frowning, towards the CID suite, Skinner stepping back into his temporary office through the side door.

He had been working his way through his in-tray for ten minutes when the scrambled telephone rang. He picked it up, grunted an answer, and heard a reassuring voice on the line. 'Afternoon, mate, is it winter up there yet?'

'Not quite, Adam, not quite. How's it going?'

'I've been doing that digging you asked me about. Don't worry, I 'aven't told anyone what it's about.' Arrow laughed. 'What am I saying? I don't fookin' know either.

'Your mystery six, the self-styled Paras: I've tracked them down, Bob, but I can't find anything to link them all together. Two of them, Collins and Saunders, were real Paras for about ten years, all through the eighties. They saw active service in the Falklands, distinguished service too, apart from an affair after Goose Green that we don't talk about.

'McDonnell was in the South Atlantic as well. For some reason, they let

250

a Scotsman into the Welsh Guards, so 'e was on the *Galahad* when it was bombed. He sustained burns and blast injuries, but he came through all right.

'Clark was an infantryman, again all through the eighties. His unit was in Ireland in '82, so he missed the Falklands.

'Nathan Bennett was in the RAOC. He never fought anywhere. He lost two fingers in a testing accident in 1986, but stayed in for a while after that. After their injuries he and McDonnell both worked in the Advocate General's office for a while, but at different times, so they never met there.

'As for Newton, he was a cook. End of Story.'

Major Arrow took a deep breath. 'You sure these guys are linked, Bob?'

'Rock-solid certain, Adam. Someone, or something, brought them together.'

'Okay,' said the soldier. 'I 'aven't given up yet. There's another avenue I want to explore. I'll call you again in another day or so. Give my love to Sarah, now. Cheers.'

77

The change in the weather had proved to be only an interlude, and not the end of summer. With the children off to bed, Bob and Sarah sat once more in their new conservatory, watching the sea and the sunset, rather than listening to the rain.

'You were right about Alex, honey.'

'What do you mean?'

'Last night, when you said you were worried about her. She and Andy have had some sort of a falling-out. He told me today.'

'Ahh,' said Sarah. 'She's not pregnant, then. I did wonder.'

'No, she isn't. In fact, Andy bit my head right off when I sort of asked him that very thing.'

'Jesus, Bob, you didn't! You can be as subtle as an avalanche sometimes.'

'Thanks very much. The lassie is my daughter, remember.'

'Too right she is. So it's just as well you didn't ask her that question, or after she'd bitten your head off she'd have poured something nasty down the hole in your neck. Did Andy tell you what the problem was?'

'It's age-related; that's all I know.'

'That figures. Well, if it's a big deal she'll talk to me about it. She always does.'

She picked up her wine glass, and savoured her 'FAT Bastard' chardonnay. 'This is nice,' she yawned. 'It lives up to its name.'

'Yes,' said her husband. 'It's the sort of label that flies off the shelf at you.'

Sarah nodded towards the folder on the conservatory table. 'Is that the rest of the Gates case?'

'Yes. I ran into a brick wall with Curly Collins. His wife did some checking on dates. She called me back this evening to say that she didn't know where he was when Orlach was murdered, but at the time of Archergait's death he was almost certainly at his work, in an electronics factory near Bathgate, and when Barnfather was done, the pair of them were definitely visiting her parents in Arbroath.'

'Do you believe her?'

'It was the old folks' forty-fifth wedding anniversary. The whole family was there. I may check it out, but I've no real doubt that she was telling me the truth.'

She laid a hand on his thigh. 'Never mind, love. I'll help you go through the rest of the folder.' She leaned over and picked up the heavy folder. 'Where do we begin tonight?'

'With the interviews and statements relating to the defence case. I don't imagine that they'll tell us much though.'

He picked up the first interview transcript and looked at it. 'This is a precognition of a sleep specialist, would you believe.'

'Do you think he could have a word with Jazz?'

'Aye, maybe.' Leaning back on the couch, he glanced through the document. 'I suppose, having missed the MS, they were struggling for theories to throw at the jury. This guy seems to be suggesting that she might have been sleep-walking.'

'They didn't introduce that as a defence, did they?' asked Sarah, incredulously.

'No, this is a pre-trial interview, that's all. I'd guess that at this stage they were looking for something that might support a plea to a culpable homicide charge, rather than murder.'

Together they read through the succeeding documents, until they came to a series of newspaper cuttings, mostly from the *Courier*, Dundee's own daily newspaper. They were reports of the trial itself, and day by day they presented an unremitting story of gloom for Mrs Gates. Eventually, they turned to the account of the verdict and of the judge's severe minimum recommendation. Unexpectedly, it was the subject of a critical leader in the Tayside broadsheet, known for its firm views on crime and punishment.

'I guess the real story begins here,' said Bob, 'after the conviction.' He looked at the next document. 'Yes, this is a copy of the prison doctor's medical report.' He laid it aside. 'And these look as if they're specialist opinions on Beattie Gates' condition.'

'What the hell are these?' asked Sarah as he picked up the last of the reports.

'Those? Oh, they'll be the photos Richard Kilmarnock mentioned. The defence team had them taken to show how her musculature had wasted.' He glanced down at the folder, at a colour photograph, shot from directly overhead, of a naked woman, lying full length on an examination table.

'Time is all that was wasted with those,' his wife retorted, picking up the photographs as he began to read the first specialist's report.

He read carefully, noting the heavy qualifications which were made by the consultant in his assessment of Mrs Gates' condition and capabilities at the time of her husband's murder. 'A doubt,' he thought, 'but is it reasonable?'

'Bob.' Her voice came quietly, from his right.

'Mmm,' he responded, still reading.

'Beattie Gates wasn't married before, was she?'

'No.'

'And she and her husband were childless?'

'Yes. According to Grace Collins, George Gates was sterile.'

'In that case, my darling, how come his wife has a Caesarian scar?'

'You what?'

Sarah held up the photograph. 'Look here.'

He followed her pointing finger, and saw the thin blue line on Beattie Gates' white abdomen.

'It's an old wound,' she said. 'It was done many years before this photograph was taken, but there's no doubt about it. See how narrow her pelvis is, too. This woman would have had difficulty delivering a child naturally at any time, and on this occasion she had help for sure.

'George Gates may have been childless, my dear, but his wife most certainly wasn't.'

78

Grace Collins looked at Skinner as if one of them was mad.

'A baby?' she repeated. 'Auntie Beattie? Not that I ever heard of.'

'Do you think that if Curly had known, he'd have told you?'

'Yes, of course he would. Curly loved family gossip; he'd never have kept something like that to himself. But she couldn't have had a kid. George Gates couldn't . . .'

'How do you know that, Mrs Collins?' asked the policeman.

'Granny Lewis told us once. Curly's mum would never have breathed a word about anything below the waist, like, but the Auld Yin never liked Gates. I remember her laughing as she told us about it. George and Auntie Beattie had been married for over five years, when he finally said, "Enough's enough; we're going to find out what's wrong with you, woman."

'So he sent Beattie to a gynaecologist. The specialist examined her, then sent for George. She took a sample off him and found absolutely zero tadpoles.'

Grace Collins laughed, mirthlessly. 'Of course Beattie had told her mother about him sending her to the consultant, so when he got the result of his test, the old warrior made him own up to it.

'She said to Curly and me that Gates started his wandering after that. He always had regarded Beattie as a possession, as an inferior. When he found out that he was sterile, he seemed to blame it on her. It was a marriage in name only after that. He just did as he liked, all over Dundee and he never made any attempt to hide it.

'Beattie's face was rubbed in it for going on fifteen years, until the morning when she woke up and he didna'.'

'She killed him then?' The question was in the tone of Skinner's voice.

'Of course she did, and quite right too. If it'd been me I'd have cut his balls off a long time before that. It was a wonder to me that Granny Lewis never did for him herself. She was a wicked old devil, but her girls meant everything to her.'

'In that case,' Skinner asked, 'if Beattie had been pregnant once . . . before she met George, say . . . how d' you think her mother would have handled it?'

'She'd have covered it up. But she was a staunch Catholic, so she'd never have let her have an abortion.' The killer's widow paused for thought for a moment or two. 'I reckon she'd have sent her away to her auntie's, so to speak, like they did in those days . . . only in this case it would have been her uncle's. Granny Lewis was from Fraserburgh originally, and she had a brother up there: Uncle Michael, Michael Conran. I only ever met him the once, when he came to our wedding.

'Yes,' she said. 'If you're looking for Beattie's bairn, you'd be best to start with him.'

'Not quite,' said Skinner. 'I know where I'll look first.'

He thanked Mrs Collins and left. He had called in on her at 8:30 a.m. on his way into the office, but rather than heading into the city centre, and Fettes, he drove down from Craiglockhart and swung through Longstone, heading for the west of Edinburgh.

While New Register House, at the eastern end of Princes Street, is the head office of the Registrar General for Scotland, much of his department is based in an out-station in the genteel suburb of Corstorphine. Skinner found a place in the visitors' car park and strode briskly into the building. A black-suited man sat at the reception desk. 'Is Jim Glossop in?' the policeman asked.

'I'll just find out for you, sir,' the clerk replied in a sing-song voice. 'And your name is?'

'Deputy Chief Constable Skinner.'

He dialled a number. 'Hello, Mr Glossop. There's a Mr Skinner to see you, from the police. Yes, sir. Very good.'

At the receptionist's request, Skinner signed the log-in book and was given a visitor's pass. He was just clipping it on to his jacket when the man he had called to see appeared through a door behind the desk. He was in his fifties, stocky, short-necked and thick-chested, conjuring up the image of a barrel on legs.

'Hello,' he said, extending a hand. 'I've heard of you. How can I help you?' His accent reminded Skinner of Adam Arrow's Derbyshire tones, although clearly it had been subject to other influences.

'I recall that you gave some valuable assistance to a colleague of mine, Ms Rose, about a year ago.'

'That's right. Henry Wills, from the University, introduced us.'

Skinner nodded. 'I wondered if you could do us another favour, discreetly and informally.'

'Try me. Come on through 'ere.' Mr Glossop led the way through to a small but bright meeting room, just behind the reception area. 'Have a seat.'

As soon as he sat in the uncomfortable tubular chair, the policeman realised that he would rather have stood, but he began nonetheless. 'My force is investigating a serious crime. We're on the trail of a potential suspect, but the trouble is we don't know anything about him, other than his gender. We don't even know for sure that he exists.

'I need to find out about a birth. The mother was unmarried, her name was Beatrice Lewis; I believe that it may have been registered in the Fraserburgh area, around, maybe just over, forty years ago.

'I stress that it may have been. I don't know for certain.'

256

'I see. D'you want to know who the father was?'

'If possible, yes, although it may turn out to be A. N. Other. But I'm really interested in finding out about the child. My guess is that . . . assuming it was a live birth . . . the baby would have been put up for adoption. Could you trace him onwards?'

Jim Glossop clasped his hands together. 'Probably. All of us, when we're born, are given a number; a National Health Service number. It's a bit like herpes; once you've got it, you're stuck with it for life.

'What else can you tell me about Beatrice Lewis?' he asked.

'She was born in Dundee. She's dead, but had she survived she'd be sixty. The birth may have been registered by her uncle, Michael Conran, of Fraserburgh.'

As Skinner spoke, the man scribbled notes in a pad. 'That's enough to be going on with. Beatrice Lewis, Michael Conran, Fraserburgh, mid to late fifties. Leave me your number, Mr Skinner. I'll call you as soon as I have anything to tell you.

'If this woman gave birth anywhere in Scotland under the name you've given me, I'll find out about it.'

79

Alexis Skinner stared through the glass wall of her office. The thing which concerned her most was not that she and her fiancé had had a blazing row, but that they had not.

Andy was one of the calmest people she had ever known. She had never seen his temper raised to boiling point. But she knew that the way in which he had switched off, had become even calmer, and suddenly sad, during their argument over careers and babies, was a much more serious indicator of his feelings than any explosion would have been.

They had decided to drop the subject for a few days, to give each other time to reflect. The night before Andy had passed on her father's advice, to put their problem on a future agenda, and concentrate on being happy today. She knew that her dad meant well, yet also that when he and Sarah had hit their crisis, it was guidance which he had been unable to follow himself. This was something on today's agenda, and it would determine her future, and Andy's.

As her mind and her eyes came back into focus, she was aware suddenly of a figure standing in the open office area beyond the glass wall, looking at her intently. It was Mitchell Laidlaw. She gulped inwardly, and went back to the papers on her desk, yet out of a corner of her eye she still saw him move towards her, then heard the soft click of her door opening.

'Grappling with a legal poser, young lady?' the head of the firm asked.

'No,' she responded. 'I understand the issues in the Provincial Insurance matter, and I think I know the best way of approaching them. I'm sorry, Mr Laidlaw. My mind was wandering there.'

'I know,' he said, kindly. 'It's not like you to frown like that, Alex. Is it a work problem?'

She sighed, and pushed her chair back from her desk. 'Yes and no,' she confessed. 'It's partly personal, and partly professional. After our discussion the other day about my possible future with the firm, I broached the subject with Andy.

'Let's just say that he has a different vision of the future.'

'He doesn't like the idea of you aiming for a partnership here?'

'No, it isn't that, so much. Andy has his own ambitions, for the two of us. He knows what he wants, but the trouble is that his vision is likely to conflict with my career plans.'

Laidlaw frowned. 'You're not saying he's told you to choose between him and your career, are you?'

'He might as well have. What he's saying is, "Do it my way, or we may not be doing it at all", and I don't know if I can accept that.' She stopped. 'Look, I'm sorry. It's our problem and I didn't mean to bring it to the office. I promise I'll leave it at home in future and get on with my work.'

'No, no, no. This is a close-knit firm, for all its size. Tell me how I can help you? Would you like me to phone Andy?'

She looked at him in horror. 'No, please. That wouldn't help at all.'

Alex shook her head in a gesture of despair. 'I really am a silly little cow, you know. My timing always has been lousy. I shouldn't have raised this at all just now, not while he's still got this armed robbery stuff on his plate.'

Mitch Laidlaw's eyebrows rose. 'Oh? I thought that was all sorted now. At least that's the impression the press gave me.'

She glanced at him. 'Don't repeat this, but that's what the press are meant to think. Andy's still looking for someone, the man he believes planned the whole thing and then killed Bennett, Saunders and Collins.'

'Is that so? The papers are suggesting that these men Newton and Clark did that. They're talking about a feud within the gang.'

'That's just speculation that Alan Royston hasn't bothered to refute. The man Andy's searching for has been seen with the gang, and with the woman who gave them the information that set up the diamond robbery at Raglan's. He doesn't know anything about him, other than that the rest of the gang all called him by the nickname Hamburger.'

Laidlaw chuckled. 'So poor Andy and his squad are checking out every fast food bar in Edinburgh looking for suspects, are they? You did choose a bad time for a serious discussion, didn't you. A man called Hamburger, indeed.'

He looked down at her. 'To be serious once again, young lady, if you're willing, I'd like to take you and Andy for supper one night soon. I'm keen to keep you in this firm, and I'd like to talk to you about how we can best do that, and keep your relationship on an even keel as well.

'I'll ask my secretary to give you some dates to choose from.'

She smiled. 'Thanks very much, Mr Laidlaw. I'll talk Andy into coming along. There's just one thing, though. No hamburgers on the menu, please.'

The lawyer's laughter rang out as he opened the door . . . then suddenly it stopped, as he closed it again.

'Alex,' he said, 'I've just had the daftest idea. Would you like to get your fiancé on the phone, please.'

80

Sammy Pye looked out of the window of the small room near the Head of CID's suite. 'It's a nice day out there, Mr Ankrah,' he said. 'The sooner we're out of this place the better.'

'I agree. But this is a job which must be done.'

'I know. I just need to give my eyes a rest, that's all.' He stood up and leaned to one side and the other, stretching his sinews; fingers interlinked, he stretched his arms above his head until they touched the ceiling.

'What would you think of this weather in Africa, sir?' he asked.

'In Africa, Sammy, we would call this . . . winter!' The Ghanaian grinned, flashing shining teeth. 'When I go home, I plan to invite some officers from Edinburgh on a reciprocal visit. I thought you might like to be one of them.'

'Lead me to it, sir,' the young detective constable responded eagerly.

'And Sergeant Neville, of course. It would be only right to invite you both.'

'What do you mean sir?' Pye's expression was blank innocence.

'You know damn well what I mean. You may be discreet in everything you say and do, but I am a student of body language. Yours and the pretty sergeant's give you away to me.'

The DC looked at him cautiously. 'How?'

'It is in the inflection of your voice when you speak to each other; the way in which your postures relax. Your bodies are comfortable together; they know each other, and to a practised eye it shows.'

'But we're just good friends, sir.'

Ankrah nodded, and grinned again. 'Yes. But very good friends. Now come on. Let's finish viewing these tapes.' They turned back to face the monitor, and Pye pressed the play button on the video recorder.

They were watching one of the sharper, cleaner tapes. The colour was unblurred although the figures moved jerkily on the screen, a result of the slow-speed recording. The tape showed the Galashiels bank, and it had been recorded on a Monday, less than two weeks before the robbery and shooting.

The customers that morning had been few and far between; a burst of men in the first hour of business . . . Publicans, Pye guessed, depositing their weekend takings . . . but after that they had slowed to a trickle of mostly older people, interspersed by the occasional shop staff member sent out for change.

They speeded the tape, and let it run until the time recorder showed that the lunch-hour was approaching, and until the picture showed an increased flow of clients. 'Hey, just a minute,' said Ankrah, suddenly. 'Slow it down and go back a bit, Sammy. I want to check something.'

The constable did as he was instructed, rewinding the tape until his companion signalled him to stop. The two looked at the monitor as playback resumed in forward mode and at normal speed. As they did so, they saw the figure of a man come into the banking hall; tall, middle aged, fit-looking, wearing a navy blazer with gold buttons, and grey slacks.

He joined the small orderly queue at the back of the public area, waiting patiently as the staff dealt with the people before him. As he waited, he looked sideways and up, towards the wide-angle surveillance camera, once from the extreme right of its shot as it panned around the building, then from the extreme left. On the third occasion he looked directly into the lens. Then, without going up to the counter, he turned and walked, with a slight limp, out of the bank.

'I know that man,' said the Ghanaian. 'I met him quite recently.

'Have you ever seen him before, Sam?'

'No, sir. But I'm pretty sure he isn't on any of the other tapes.'

'He isn't on any others that I've seen either. I'm sure it's a pure coincidence that he's there. Still, Mr Martin asked us to report anything out of the ordinary. So, I shall do just that.'

81

'Have you heard from Lady Proud again?' The Head of CID asked the Deputy Chief Constable as together they gazed at the little man in the loud Hawaiian shirt and baggy shorts.

'No, I haven't, so I guess Jimmy must be on the mend.' Skinner grinned. 'I wonder if he dresses like that on his holidays?' The little man, his equally garish wife by his side, stood motionless. The statues were among the star attractions in the Scottish National Gallery of Modern Art, one of the jewels in the capital city's cultural crown.

The two policemen had decided to take a break from their offices, and from their telephones which had been ringing all morning, reminding each of them that the two investigations which had been dominating their lives were only a small part of their respective workloads.

'What have you got on this afternoon?' Martin asked.

'I've got to prepare for the Police Board tomorrow. Councillor Maley and her clique are bound to try to ambush me with a few awkward questions in Jimmy's absence. I'm damned if I'll give them the satisfaction of catching me out.'

'Send ACC Elder.'

Skinner laughed. 'He's a nice guy. How could I do that to him?'

They left the American tourists frozen in their little world, and moved through to the next room. 'You any further forward on Mr Hamburger?' asked the DCC.

'I'm afraid not. Kwame Ankrah and Sammy have finished the tapes. Apart from Ankrah spotting some bloke he met with me in another context, and who's got fuck all to do with this, they came up with zero. How about your source?'

'He's come up with nothing so far other than confirmation that, apart from Saunders and Collins, who fought in the Falklands, the six didn't soldier together.'

'I thought Bennett was there too.'

'No, he must have been bullshitting about that. He lost his fingers in a training accident.'

'That doesn't take us any further forward, then does it,' mused Martin. 'I did have one odd phone call this morning,' he said, 'from Mitch Laidlaw, of all people.'

'What was that about?'

'Apparently Alex had mentioned to him that the investigation had stalled.

He had her call me up, just so he could ask me if I was old enough to remember the original Perry Mason television series. That was all. I asked him what he was on about, but he just laughed, and said it was only an idea.'

Skinner stopped and looked at him. 'And are you old enough?'

'Hardly. Haven't a fucking clue what he was on about. That series was early sixties stuff, wasn't it?'

'Yes. Even I barely remember it. I don't get the joke either. It's not like Mitch to waste chargeable time kidding on the telephone. He's probably told Alex; she'll put you out of your misery.'

He paused. 'Speaking of Alex . . .'

'There's still tension in the air, Bob.'

'Knowing my lass, I didn't think it would go away overnight. One thing though, Andy. I know she's well mature beyond her years, but part of her is still a kid. You've got to let that bit continue to grow.'

'Sure,' Andy retorted. 'But what if she grows into . . .' He stopped short.

'. . . into her mother, you were going to say. I don't think there's a cat's chance of that. Looking back, I can see now that there was always something secretive, and manipulative too, about Myra. The first party we were at as teenagers, I beat the crap out of some lad because of her. I never realised at the time, but she set it up.'

'Alex isn't like that. I never knew her to keep a secret for more than half an hour. She looks like her mother, but that's it.'

His friend's laugh was heavy with irony. 'That's supposed to have cheered me up, is it? She doesn't have her mum's nature: in that case she must take after you.' He nodded. 'That figures. She's good at drawing a line in the sand then daring you to step over it.'

'D'you know what you do then?' asked Bob, quietly.

'Tell me.'

He reached out with his right foot and moved it from side to side, in an odd gesture. 'Rub out the line.'

82

Skinner had been back at his desk for an hour, studying the papers for the next day's meeting, when the memory came to him, bursting in his head like a firework.

He picked up the phone and dialled Martin's office number. 'Hey, Andy,' he said, laughing. 'I know what Mitch Laidlaw was talking about. I remember now: in the original Perry Mason stories, the District Attorney, the guy who lost every time, was called Hamilton Burger.'

'That's a big help,' the Head of CID chuckled. 'The DA done it, eh. Where does that take us?'

'Back to Norman King?'

'You mean if we can't get him for one, we'll nail him for the other? I don't think so somehow.' He laughed again. 'Wait till I see that so-and-so. Wasting police time, that's what he was doing!'

Skinner hung up and returned to his Board papers. Another hour had gone by without interruption, when Gerry's light knock sounded at the door, and he stepped into the room. 'Sorry to interrupt,' he began, 'but there's a man at the reception desk asking to see you. He says his name's Jim Glossop, and you'll know what it's about.'

The acting Chief laid down his pen. 'I do indeed, Gerry. Go and fetch him please, I'll see him right away.'

He had tucked his papers away in a deep desk drawer by the time his secretary returned with the stocky statistician.

'I'ope you don't mind me coming up to see you, Mr Skinner,' said Jim Glossop. 'To be honest with you, I'd have felt a bit uncomfortable talking about this over the telephone.'

'I understand. Have a seat . . . over here, in the comfortable area. Has Gerry offered you something to drink.'

'Yes, but I won't, thanks.'

He lowered himself into a chair, and opened his briefcase. It was black leather, with a gold crown stamped on its front. 'I've traced your birth.' Glossop laughed, self-consciously. 'Well, not yours . . . the one you were after, know what I mean.'

He drew out a sheaf of papers, in a clear plastic folder. 'There's copies here of everything you'll need.

'To sum it all up, Miss Beatrice Lewis gave birth to a son forty-three years ago, at the age of seventeen . . . I checked her birth records as well . . . in the maternity hospital in Fraserburgh. The father's name is not shown on

264

the birth certificate. As you guessed, registration was done on the mother's behalf by Michael Xavier Conran.

'The child's name is shown on the birth certificate as Bernard Xavier Lewis.'

'That's excellent, Mr Glossop. Have you been able to go on from there?'

'Yes. And we've had a stroke of luck. These days, adopted children are able, if they wish, to trace their natural parents. I thought I'd try a shortcut, so I checked to see whether that had been done in this case.' He paused, leaned forward, and said, with emphasis, 'It 'as.'

'About three years ago, a man called at New Register House. He had an adoption certificate with him, and he said that he wanted to trace his natural parents. I spoke to the officer who dealt with the case. She remembered it in particular because the chap said it was his fortieth birthday on that day, and this was how he had decided to celebrate it.

'He said that he knew that he had been born in Fraserburgh, and christened Bernard. Well it was easy, wasn't it. He asked for, and he was given, copies of his own birth certificate, of his mother's, and of his grandparents'.'

Mr Glossop looked across at Skinner. 'We were able to trace his mother on for him. That were when his birthday present turned sour on him. It turned out that she had died years before, of multiple sclerosis, and that her address at the time of her death was shown as care of Her Majesty's Prison, Cornton Vale.

'My colleague still remembers how upset the poor chap was.'

He went on. 'I've given you copies of all the certificates that he bought. Last but not least, we took a copy of his adoption certificate, for our records too; I've made another for you. Beatrice Lewis' son was adopted at the age of five months, by a couple in the second half of their thirties. They were from Shawlands, in Glasgow; by the name of Grimley. According to the adoption papers, he was a publican.'

Jim Glossop stood up from his chair. 'I hope that's helpful to you. I'll be off now, but if there's anything else you need, you know where to find me.'

Skinner escorted his visitor all the way to the front door. 'Thank you very much, Jim,' he said. 'Look, it's just possible that your colleague might be required as a witness at some point. If that looks likely, I'll tip you off. Thanks again, and goodbye for now.'

At the top of the stairs he turned right instead of left, and strode through to Martin's suite. Nodding briefly to Karen Neville, he opened the door of the inner office. 'Andy, come with me for a minute.'

Back in the Chief's room, he picked up the papers which Glossop had left. 'Remember the Court action that Alexis was involved in until a few days ago?'

'Yes?'

'You told me the name of the pursuer. Remind me: what was it?'

'Bernard Grimley.'

Skinner nodded. 'That's what I thought.' He took the adoption certificate

265

from the folder and handed it to the DCS. 'He's Beattie Gates' son.'

'Remind me again. Who was the judge at the hearing?'

'Lord Coalville.'

'Right! He was her trial judge. I've been trying to figure out, if the deaths of the three Appeal judges were linked to the Gates case, why the trial judge who gave her a fifteen-year minimum wasn't the prime target.

'It could be that with the way that compensation action was going, Coalville was too valuable to kill.'

He looked up at the astonished Martin. 'You had Mackie make some enquiries about Grimley, didn't you?'

'Yes.' The Head of CID searched his orderly memory. 'When he ran his pub through in Glasgow he was a police informant.'

'When did that stop?'

'About three years ago.'

'That coincides with the time that Grimley decided to trace his natural mother, and found that she was Beatrice Lewis, later Beatrice Gates, convicted murderess.

'Alex's case was running when Archergait was killed, wasn't it?'

'Yes.'

'So he'd have been in Court. I wonder how he could have gained access to cyanide?'

'Through his work,' said Martin, quietly. 'He's a metal finisher by trade. Alex told me he'd gone back to the tools after his business went bust.'

Skinner felt a cold fist grab his stomach. The hairs on the back of his neck began to prickle. 'We're on to something here, Andy. Have you ever seen this man?'

'Yes, twice; up at the Court.'

'What's he like?'

'He's a nasty piece of goods for a start. He was crowing over Adrian Jones after the judge announced his findings, and there was something really vicious and unpleasant about it. He struck me at the time as a real evil bastard.'

'Right, now describe him physically.'

'Well, he's early forties, as you know. Tallish, but not a giant. Medium build, clean shaven, dark hair. Not the sort of man who'd stand out in a crowd.'

'In that case, answer me this. If you didn't know either of them very well, or even at all, could you mistake Norman King for Grimley from around thirty yards away?'

Martin started at him, understanding. 'Yes, you bloody well could!'

The big DCC slammed his left fist into his right palm. 'Let's have him, then and let's stick both King and him up in a line-up before our gallery-owner friend.'

'Yes,' said Martin, 'but first, we should find out where he works. Maybe Mitch Laidlaw will know that. As soon as we pick him up, we should find out whether there's a discrepancy in the firm's cyanide stock!'

'You do that. Try to lift him tomorrow morning, Andy. Do it yourself, very quietly, early doors. Why don't you take Kwame Ankrah for back-up; give him a taste of action. Then have Neville and Pye make that check at his firm as soon as you've got him in custody.

'Meanwhile, I'm going to phone Lord Archibald, to let him know that he, and the Home Advocate Depute, may be off the hook.'

83

'Bob Skinner, you are like a cat on hot bricks tonight. Look, it was your idea to get a baby-sitter and go out for supper, so come on . . . talk to me.'

Reproved, the big policeman looked sheepishly at his wife as they sat in the window seat of the Mallard Hotel bar. At the far end of the room, the inevitable golf party discussed the triumphs and disasters of their day on the links, as they settled in for a long night.

'Sorry love. My mind was way ahead of me. I was thinking of Andy, going along to Humbie tomorrow to lift this man Bernard Grimley.'

Sarah grinned. 'You're really pleased with yourself over that, aren't you. Normally I have to coax stuff like that out of you. Not tonight though; you were hardly over the doorstep before it all came pouring out.'

He picked up his beer, glancing at her wickedly over the top of the glass as he drank. 'I think I have a right to be chuffed with myself,' he agreed contentedly, wiping foam from his top lip with the back of his hand as he spoke. 'That was a classic piece of detection. And who pulled it off? The Boss, the backroom boy, the desk jockey, while all the whiz kids were scratching their heads.'

He gave a sudden, short, explosive laugh, causing the lady behind the bar to start and look across at their table. 'My love, you should have seen the look on Andy's face when I told him who Beattie Gates' son is. Moments like that come but rarely in a career, and they are to be savoured.'

'You are sure he's the one?' she ventured.

'As sure as God made wee green apples. It's Grimley; I know it. We've put the whole jigsaw together.' His smile grew nostalgic. 'I had a second autopsy done on Lord Orlach by the prof. from Glasgow, for corroboration at the trial. They're re-burying him tonight; the old boy can rest easy now.'

A young waiter arrived to clear away their dessert plates. As he left, Sarah moved round in her seat, closer to her husband. 'What about the other jigsaw puzzle, though?' she whispered. 'Not so triumphal there, are we?'

'One at a time, please,' he answered. 'Let me have a moment longer up on my cloud.

'You're right though. We're still scratching around on the other one. I fear that our mystery man's nickname, Hamburger, can only refer to his eating habits. The only alternative theory turned out to be a spoof by Mitch Laidlaw.'

She dug him in the ribs with an elbow. 'Go on, then, desk jockey. Do it again. Let's see you stretch that big brain of yours. What's before you that you've overlooked?'

He took another swallow of William McEwan's Seventy Shilling Ale. 'Nothing that I can think of. Adam Arrow's checking out the military end for me . . . He sends his best wishes, by the way . . . but so far, that hasn't taken us any further.

'Apart from Barry Herr, the TA Club manager, who doesn't know his real name, the last people who could identify Hamburger were Tory Clark and Bakey Newton, and they did a runner as soon as they heard, courtesy of a certain detective . . . soon to be uniformed . . . chief inspector, that Curly Collins had been bumped off.'

'What, they just upped and off?'

'That's how it was reported to me. According to Dan Pringle, Bakey Newton was listening to Radio Forth at his work when the news story was broadcast. He stopped what he was doing, made a couple of calls, and disappeared . . . never to return.'

'A couple of calls?'

In an instant, Bob's brow became furrowed. 'As far as I know, that's what the witness said. If she meant it literally, one call was certainly to Tory Clark. I wonder if we know who else he phoned?'

He squeezed her hand. 'Thank you, love, for helping me pick that up. I'll have Big Neil check it out tomorrow. He could have been calling his bookie, his mistress, the organiser of his lottery syndicate. On the other hand, he could have been calling . . .' His voice tailed off for a few seconds.

'But if that's right,' he whispered. 'Why the hell would he . . .'

84

'I envy you this beautiful country, Andy,' said the Ghanaian policeman. 'I have never seen anything like this, not at this time of a summer day . . . so cool, so moist, so pleasant.'

'Summer's almost over, Kwame. Soon the wind will be lashing the rain across the fields; after that the snow could come.'

'I've heard about snow. I've never seen it, though.'

Martin laughed. 'You might get the chance. If this man winds up going to trial, it'll come up in late December, or early January. You'll be a witness to the arrest, so the Crown Office may well fly you back to Scotland to give evidence.'

Ankrah stopped, mock-horror on his face. 'In that case, I think I'll go now. I didn't actually say I *wanted* to see snow. I think Scotland might be too cold for me at that time of year.'

'Too late to back out now, friend,' said the DCS. 'You volunteered for this caper, remember.' He locked the door of his Mondeo, which was parked on the verge by the side of the A 6137 as it ran through the hamlet of Humbie. To their right a side road led away from its few cottages.

'I've checked this out. Grimley lives up there, in a farm cottage up a lane a couple of hundred yards back off the road.' He glanced at his watch. 'It's six-fifty-five just now, and he works in Wallyford, so even if he starts at eight, he should still be in.

'Let's go and interrupt his breakfast.'

He led the way down the curving side road. As he had predicted, they soon came to the opening of a rough, grassy lane, with thick scrubby woodland on either side. A silver Toyota was parked close by. A little further along, close to the first of a row of two-storey houses, stood a green Mercedes, the first in a line of half a dozen other vehicles. Martin looked down the lane. A hundred yards distant on the right he saw a single-storey, stone-built cottage. 'That's the place. Come on.'

The Scot and the African walked together down the pathway. As they approached the little house, they saw that it stood on its own, isolated behind a low privet hedge. It was freshly painted, roses grew in its small front garden, and honeysuckle hung around and over the door.

'I read The Railway Children when I was young,' said Ankrah. 'After-wards I dreamed of living in a place like this.' He laughed. 'There are not too many stone cottages like this in Ghana, though.'

They stopped for a moment at the little wooden gate, then Martin raised its latch, walked into the garden and up to the single low step at Bernard Grimley's front door. He looked around for a bell push, but found none, only a heavy brass knocker. He seized it and rapped it hard, once, twice, three times, against its keeper.

There was no answer, no sound from within the cottage. The Head of CID knocked again, three times. Still there was no sign of Grimley. 'Fuck this,' he said. He tried the handle, but the door was locked.

'Kwame, you stay here. I'll try round the back.' As Ankrah nodded acknowledgement, Martin turned and walked around the cottage, following a path which led off to the left. The door at the rear of the house was painted green also. Like the other it had two glass panels set in its upper half; but one of them was broken. He turned the handle and the door swung open.

He looked around the small kitchen. Dinner plates, a mug, and a pint glass lay in the sink, unwashed. Two lager cans, their tops punctured, lay on the table. Across the room, another door lay open.

Noiselessly Martin crept into the hall. There were four doors off; two to his left, one to his right and the front door. They were all closed save the farther on the right, which was slightly ajar. Through it he could see lace curtains, a dining chair and part of a gateleg table. At the far end of the corridor, he became aware of Kwame Ankrah's dark shadow as he leaned forward, peering through one of the glass panels of the entrance door.

He stepped across to it and turned the knob of the Yale, opening it and admitting his companion, who looked both puzzled and tense. The silence in the cottage was almost palpable. The DCS answered the question in the Ghanaian policeman's eyes with a shrug of his shoulders, then pointed towards the single open door.

Feeling suddenly very vulnerable, almost naked, he stepped through it and into the living room.

Bernard Grimley was there: on the floor. He knew that it was Grimley, even though he had no face. He knew it by his build, and by the fact that it was someone else who stood, ten feet away, in the sunlight which flooded through the uncurtained side window, a single-barrelled, pump-action, sawn-off held securely in his hands.

'What the bloody hell are you . . .' exclaimed Andy Martin, as the man raised and levelled the gun. And that was as far as he got.

271

85

Skinner sat up in bed, a feeling of unease gripping him.

'What's wrong, Bob?' asked Sarah, sensing his mood even through her drowsiness.

He swung his legs out of bed and stood, naked, running his fingers through his tousled hair. 'I don't know,' he admitted. 'Just someone walking over my grave, I guess.'

'Don't say that, it scares me. It must be more than that.'

He slipped on his bathrobe and stepped over to the big window, drawing the curtains aside to look out across the Bents, still in shadow, and at the great river, as it caught the first rays of the morning sun.

'I suppose I'm still wondering who Bakey Newton might have phoned, before he did his runner, and why.' He glanced at the bedside clock, which showed one minute before seven a.m. 'I think I'll take a quick shower, and get into the office.'

He was no more than halfway to the bathroom when the phone rang. He reached it in two strides and picked it up. 'Skinner,' he barked.

'Fookin' 'ell, I knew I shouldn't have called this early.' The tension broken, Bob laughed.

'You're dead right,' he said, sitting on the edge of the bed. 'What's the story?'

'I didn't have much choice but phone you now, I'm afraid. I'm off to the Gulf wi' the Defence Secretary in an hour, and I thought you'd want this before I got back, rather than after.'

'Go on, then.'

'Well, after I sorted out those names for you, I did a bit more checking into their service records, and something interesting came up. Two of 'em, Clark, the infantryman, and Newton, the cook, had black marks on theirs. They were both court-martialled around the same time, and for a short spell they were in detention together.

'Clark was done for insubordination, and Newton for beating the crap out of a junior NCO. They were both fined and reduced in rank. However, they both did deals. They pleaded guilty, and the prosecuting officer put forward mitigating circumstances on their behalf, so they stayed in the service.

'Another connection between them was that they were both prosecuted by the same bloke in the Advocate General's office.' As Arrow paused for breath, Skinner's right eyebrow rose, very slightly, as two thoughts converged in his brain.

272

'I'd have made nothing of that,' the major went on, 'had something not made me run a check on the prosecutor. He's long gone from the service . . . left seven years ago . . . but it were the Army that sent him to St Andrews University. They did that after he was wounded in the Falklands, as a very young officer.'

He paused. 'You keeping up with me?'

'I think so. You're going to tell me that Bennett and McDonnell worked for him in the Advocate General's office . . . not together, a couple of years apart. Then you're going to tell me . . .'

'That when he was a baby one-pipper getting his knee permanently stiffened by the Argies, seven of whom 'e killed, personally, two of the men under his command in two-Para were Lance-Corporals Ryan Saunders and Charles Collins.

'There you are, Bob, m' friend. A nice neat ribbon, tying all six of your bank gang together. What do you think?'

Skinner sat in silence. At last he said, 'Adam, you are one clever little bastard. If you ever leave the Army, I'll give you a job on the spot. All I need from you now is for you to tell me two things.

'One, that this guy is still alive, and two . . . his name!'

86

Afterwards, Andy Martin never could work out in his mind the exact sequence of events.

He never knew what had happened first; whether it was Kwame Ankrah's left shoulder slamming into his side, taking him to the floor, whether it was the shotgun blast, or whether it was the sniper's bullet shattering the window glass and tearing into Adrian Jones' head.

Whatever it was, in the immediate aftermath, he lay on the ground, his chest heaving and his heart hammering, peculiarly fascinated by Jones' twitching right leg as it did its dance of death. It had all happened too fast for him to be frightened. That would come later.

He was surprised that the sound of the motorcycle registered at all as he lay there, but it did. He scrambled to his feet, trying but failing to pull Ankrah with him, and ran out of the cottage. By the time he reached the lane, the engine noise was fading in the distance, and all he could see was a mixture of dust and exhaust.

He went back inside the house, and into the living room. Ankrah had pulled himself into a sitting position, his back against one side of the fireplace. He was wearing a dark suit, but nonetheless Martin could see that his right shoulder, and the right side of his face were bleeding.

'You're hit,' he burst out, anxiously, if unnecessarily.

The Ghanaian nodded, the movement making him wince. 'I've had worse than this at home. I caught a few pellets from the shotgun, that's all.'

He looked over at the body. 'He was a bad loser, was our Mr Jones. If Grimley had known what he was dealing with, he'd have been a bit more careful about crowing over his victory in the Court.'

Martin's features twisted in an unfamiliar snarl. 'He obviously didn't fancy his chances at appeal.' He turned and walked through to the kitchen, tearing open drawers until he found three clean dish-towels, which he used to pack against the wounded man's shoulder and to wipe his face.

'Thanks, Kwame,' he said, quietly. 'If you hadn't decked me there, I'd probably have caught most of that blast, whether or not Jones was dead when he pulled the trigger. You hold on now, I'll get help.'

He used his mobile to call Fettes and summon police and medical assistance. Next, he phoned Skinner. The DCC was in the shower, but Sarah answered. 'Morning, love,' he said. 'It's Andy. Would you ask Bob to come to Grimley's cottage up behind Humbie, asap. Tell him someone beat us to it . . . no, scratch that, tell him two people beat us to it.'

Replacing the phone in his pocket, he went back to the kitchen and made two large mugs of hot sweet tea. Handing one to Ankrah, he took his own, and sat down on Bernard Grimley's couch with his faceless body at his feet.

'You never said you had a sniper in the woods, Andy,' the African muttered, wincing again as he spoke.

'I didn't. I haven't a fucking clue who he was.' Gently, at first, he began to shake.

The violence of his rigor had passed, but he was still on the sofa, trembling slightly, when Skinner arrived, a few minutes after the emergency medical assistance. He stepped into the room without a word, and looked down at each of the bodies on the floor. 'So, Mr Jones,' he whispered. 'You couldn't let it lie, could you.'

He glanced back, over his shoulder. 'I passed an ambulance on my way in here,' said the DCC to Martin.

'That was Kwame; but he's okay. He took a few slugs from Jones in the shoulder and in the side of his face. Flesh wounds, that's all.'

'How about you?'

'Nothing a change of jockey shorts won't put right. That big Ghanaian in the ambulance saved my life though. Him and the bloke outside.'

He looked up. 'I'm confused, Bob. Confused! I'm fucking bewildered. Why should Jones kill Grimley? Okay, he was stuffed in Court, but the insurers picked up the tab.'

Skinner smiled back at him. 'He killed him because that's the kind of man he was, son. Try calling him Hamburger. He was the seventh member of the armed robbery gang . . . the Boss, the planner.'

'Eh?'

'Adam Arrow just drew the picture for me. Remember Mitchell Bloody Laidlaw's joke? He didn't know it, but he wasn't kidding. Our Ham Burger was a District Attorney right enough . . . in the Army.'

'What do you mean?'

'Jones was a captain in the Advocate General's office. Bennett and McDonnell worked for him; he prosecuted Clark and Newton at courts martial. But before he went into that line of work, he fought in the Falklands with Collins and Saunders. Natural-born killers, the three of them were, apparently.'

Martin gave a final shudder and pushed himself to his feet. 'But why the robberies?'

'Work it out with me. Jones may have been a shit-hot criminal lawyer in the Army, but in the gentle world of civvy street, and civil law, he wasn't so good. He proved this once and for all by landing his firm with a compensation claim from this fellow.' He nodded down at Grimley's body.

A cough came from behind him. 'Can I begin in here, sir?' asked Arthur Dorward, in his white tunic. The Inspector looked disapprovingly at his senior officers' clothing.

'Aye, sure Arthur. We'll be in the garden.' Skinner led the way outside through the front door. The morning sun shone on a green-painted wooden

275

bench. The two friends sat down on it, side by side.

'Jones must have seen that he was finished as a lawyer after that,' the DCC continued, 'or at least condemned to a career which was beneath his ambitions and his dignity. So he decided to look for an alternative source of income. Having seen crime first hand, he knew the best way to go about it, and the mistakes to avoid.

'He figured too that, basically, us coppers are pretty thick. If it isn't obvious to us, it's never easy.' Skinner shifted on the hard wooden bench.

'Once he had made his decision, well, he was an officer, after all, so he recruited his own platoon. Adam checked the guest list at Paras reunion dinners. They show that he kept in touch with Collins and Saunders. He must have made a point of keeping track of people, for he was able to recruit Newton and Clark, his old customers, then Bennett and McDonnell, his old assistants. Jones knew all these guys personally, though only Rocky and Curly, and Tory and Bakey, knew each other.

'But they all knew, in different ways . . . Rocky and Curly from the battlefield, Bakey and Tory from Court, Big Red and Big Mac just from being around him . . . what their pal Hamburger was capable of.

'He brought them all together, he formed the so-called Paras group up in the TA Club, and they used that as a base to plan their campaign. It really was immaculate, Andy. A group as well-trained as that, yet as disparate as that. They set about a short, sharp burst of high-value robberies, with the objective of setting each of them up for life.

'The highlight was the Raglan's jewel robbery, which fell into their lap when Jones met Arlene Regan up in the Club. They had a fling, she passed on her boy-friend's tip about the Russian and his diamond buys, and she and Nick were paid to disappear. McDonnell was too, after he reported that Bennett was looking like talking to you.

'What d'you think?'

Martin leaned against the back of the garden seat, his eyes closed in the sunshine. 'We'll need to find Clark and Newton, and Arlene, to confirm it all, but I'll go for that. I'll get a warrant this morning, and we'll search Jones' place before the day is out.'

Opening his eyes, he looked sideways at Skinner. 'Life's funny, is it not. Grimley and Jones; each chasing different rainbows and each with their hands on a pot of gold, yet they both wind up dead, in the same room.'

He paused. 'And Jones killed Rocky and Curly?'

'Looks like it, doesn't it?'

'I can't argue against any of it.' Out of the blue, Andy Martin laughed; it was a mixture of tiredness, elation and most of all, relief at still being alive to enjoy the bright morning, and to plan the uncertain future with the woman he loved.

'Which leaves us,' he said, 'with the Star Prize Question. Who rode off from here on his motorbike? Just who the fuck shot Adrian Jones?'

'That is something,' said Skinner, soberly, in contrast to his friend's borderline hysteria, 'that I don't reckon the world will ever know.'

276

87

Bob Skinner was a straight arrow, who did not approve of drinking and driving at all. Nevertheless, although his car was parked in the street outside, he nursed a pint glass as he sat in the bar of the TA Club. It was shandy, half beer and half lemonade, pressed upon him by the manager.

He had been waiting for just over twenty minutes when the man entered, immaculate in his uniform. 'A right fucking bandbox,' Skinner whispered, to no-one. 'I'll bet his dad was proud of him.' The soldier walked up to the bar, past the policeman's corner table, without noticing him.

'Pint of lager, please, Barry,' he called out.

The manager nodded and picked up a glass. 'There's someone to see you,' he said, as he slid it across the wooden top, and took the money which lay there.

Sergeant Henry Riach turned, to see the policeman sitting in the corner, smiling across at him. 'Mr Skinner,' he said, looking surprised. 'What brings you here?'

The DCC stood as he came across, extending his hand to offer a seat. 'Mr Herr mentioned to a colleague of mine that you were a regular in here on a Friday. I thought I'd drop in to let you know about our investigation into your father's death.'

'I gather it's been successful,' the sergeant replied, 'according to what I read in the papers.'

'Yes. We're still looking for three of the gang, but I'm satisfied that Curly Collins killed your father, and that Rocky Saunders shot my young police officer.'

A thin smile spread across Riach's face, and a gleam came into his eyes. 'And they're dead. Now that's what I call natural justice.'

'Not everyone would agree with that. I know a right few coppers who would call it murder.'

'You can't expect me to see it that way.'

'No, of course I can't,' Skinner agreed. 'I understand exactly how you see it. So would your Uncle John McGrigor, I'm sure . . . not that I'd ever ask him to admit it, mind you.'

He grinned at the young soldier. 'How did you find out that the Paras' friend Hamburger was Adrian Jones?' he asked. 'He never used his real name when he was in here.'

For the first time, the easy smile left Sergeant Riach's face, and his gaze dropped from the policeman. In the midst of the long silence which hung over the table, Skinner noticed that his hand was trembling slightly as he picked up his glass.

And then he looked up once more, his eyes hard and defiant. 'Rocky Saunders told me,' he said, quietly. 'Just before he died. He told me who he was, what he had done in the Army, what he did now, and where he lived.

'He'd have told me anything to stop me shooting him. Unfortunately for him, there was nothing he could have said that would have stopped me.'

'How did you happen to show up at Grimley's cottage?' Skinner asked, although, as before, he had guessed the answer.

'I followed Jones from his home. I watched him for a while, just like I watched Saunders and Collins. I found out that he never went out at night without his wife, so that gave me a problem. Finally, I decided that I'd tail him in the mornings, as he went to his work, and wait for a chance.' Riach's eyes narrowed. 'If I had to, I was even prepared to do him with a pistol through the window of his Toyota. I followed him for three days on the trot, but there were always too many people around. Then I got lucky.

'He was an early starter, so I was always there well in advance, but on that third morning I was surprised when he left so soon. He didn't take his normal route to his office. Instead he went past Queensferry, round the bypass, down the A 68, then cut off down to Humbie.

'When I saw the house, I thought that Newton or Clark . . . maybe the both of them . . . might be hiding there, so I let him go inside, and I set myself up in the woods. Mind you, when I saw him break in through the back door, and saw that he was carrying a sawn-off I said to myself, "Aye aye, something up here". Then I heard the shot.'

Riach paused. 'I hadn't a bloody clue who'd been done, and to tell you the truth, I didn't give a stuff, but I guessed it wasn't Jones. So I stayed behind my tree and waited.

'It was only a minute later when your folk arrived. The black chap threw me at first, but I recognised Martin from the telly. I just kept watching the house, and that side window. All of a sudden Jones stepped into sight. I saw him picking up his shotgun, so I let him have it.'

'What weapon did you use?' asked Skinner, quietly.

'A service carbine. It's a stumpy wee rifle, dead accurate, and it fits the pannier of my bike.'

Riach drained his glass. 'Mind if I get another?'

'Not at all,' the policeman answered, impressed by his calmness. 'You want one?'

'No thanks, Henry, I'm fine.'

He watched as the young soldier walked to the bar and returned, his glass replenished.

'Can I ask you a question now?'

'Okay.'

'How did you know it was me?'

'I just guessed, sort of.'

'But didn't your lot think that Jones killed Saunders and Collins?'

278

'Yes we did, at first.'

'Then after Jones was killed, that statement you put out said that the two of them had been rivals, and that they'd killed each other in a confrontation.'

Skinner shook his head. 'No. It said that they had *died* after a confrontation. An approximation of the truth, I'll grant you, but close enough. We'll put out a fuller statement later.'

'Still: how did you know?'

'Well,' the policeman began, 'there were a couple of things. You stabbed them before you shot them, yes?' Riach nodded. 'With a bayonet, fixed to your gun, to bring their heads up? Yes, I thought so. That was a soldier's thing, for a start.

'Something else came to me the other night. Before he disappeared, Bakey Newton made two phone calls; one was to Clark, to tell him what had happened. We checked: the other was to Jones. Now if he'd thought for one moment that his pal Hamburger was wiping out his team, he'd hardly have called him, would he?'

'Who killed Bennett, then, and his sister?' the sergeant asked.

'Oh, Jones did them all right. There's no doubt about that. We even found the sniper's rifle he used, hidden in his garage. It was a souvenir from his army days.

'That actually helped me to you. Because that's how you worked out who might have been involved in your father's murder, through the army connection.

'You knew Bennett, of course, like you knew all the so-called Paras group, for you saw them all in here, every Friday night. When you heard on the telly, or read that he and his sister had been done, and . . . the most important thing of all . . . that Big Mac had vanished: I assumed that's when you began to put the thing together.

'You knew that these hold-ups were military operations, and here were these six guys, an odd bunch of ex-regulars with this mysterious pal whose real name they never used. After Bennett's death, and McDonnell's vanishing act, I don't imagine that you had any doubt.

'Did you, Henry?'

'None at all,' Riach answered, his eyes fixed steadily on Skinner's. 'I knew Rocky and Curly were the really hard guys in the group, so I got their addresses from the Infantry Division records, and I went after them . . . Rocky first. He was easiest, living out in the country. He told me the lot.

'So,' he asked evenly, 'what are you going to do about it?'

The DCC gave a soft laugh. 'You mean how am I going to prove it?' he countered.

'Son, with no witnesses and no corroboration I know how difficult that would be, so I'm not even going to try. Anyway, I'd have shot Rocky Saunders myself, given half a chance, for killing Annie Brown. As for Curly Collins; you see the tears I shed for him.'

He finished off his warm shandy. 'It must surprise you, a copper talking like this. But I guard the public safety and the public interest. I don't see you threatening either one in the future. As for justice, it seems to me that's been served well enough.' He took a deep breath, held it for a few seconds, then let it out in a great sigh.

'There's another thing too. When you shot Adrian Jones, you saved my best friend's life.'

Bob Skinner stared back at the soldier, until the young man's eyes fell from his. 'So, Henry,' he whispered, 'this conversation's just between you and me . . . as long as no-one else turns up dead.'

88

'You don't mind me calling in like this on a Saturday, Bob, do you?' asked Lord Archibald. 'I was down at Muirfield, so I thought I'd take the chance.'

'Not at all, Archie. I was going to come and see you next week anyway.'

Sarah laid a cup of coffee and a plate of biscuits before the Lord Advocate on the conservatory table, waved a brief goodbye and returned to the kitchen.

'You're absolutely certain that Norman King's in the clear?' asked the Law Officer as she left.

'Completely. Beatrice Gates' illegitimate son, Bernard Grimley, murdered the three judges; I'm well satisfied of that. We found the remains of the cyanide, and a list of tide tables in his cottage. Most important of all we found not one, but two copies of Arnold Kilmarnock's book about the Gates case. One was clean, but the other had scribbles and annotations all over it. All of the judges' names were heavily underlined.'

Skinner picked up a biscuit from the plate.

'Just over three years ago, Bernard Grimley decided that on his fortieth birthday he would trace his natural mother. Can you imagine what it must have done to him when he found out who she was, and what she had done? Until that point, he had been a police source in Glasgow. That stopped, from that day on. Since then, he's been waiting for his moment ... or rather his moments.

'King didn't kill his father, Archie. It was this guy all right.'

Lord Archibald leaned back in his chair and let out a great sigh of relief. 'Thank Christ for that,' he exclaimed. 'Or rather, thank you and your officers, Bob.

'I'd have had to charge him you know, if you hadn't found Grimley. I'd have had no option: well, I would, but if I'd covered it up and it had ever leaked out, it could have threatened the Government.

'Yes, poor Norman would have gone to Court, with no defence beyond a denial, and he'd almost certainly have been convicted. Can you imagine what the minimum recommendation would have been? The rest of his natural life and ten years after that, probably!'

Skinner flashed a smile across the table. 'But instead, he'll be standing in the High Court next week trying to get that for some other bugger. As someone once said, it's a funny old world.'

Lord Archibald picked up his coffee from the table, admiring the view from Skinner's garden.

'What about this man Jones?' he asked.

'I'll let you have a formal report on that next week. It'll say that he took revenge on Grimley for ruining his career, that he fired on the police officers who confronted him, and that he was shot dead by a marksman.'

'That sounds very precise, Bob.'

The telephone rang, but Skinner left it for Sarah to answer. 'It will be, Archie, be sure of it. Incidentally, Kwame Ankrah's fine. They removed the shot from his shoulder and kept him in hospital overnight, but that was all.'

The Lord Advocate looked at him, quizzically. 'I take it you'll recommend that the incident be considered closed, and that no Fatal Accident Inquiry will be necessary.'

'Spot on.'

'What if the families of the dead men demand one?'

'Grimley didn't leave a family. I've spoken to Mrs Jones already; she won't do that.'

'So,' said Lord Archibald. 'A very tidy conclusion all round. That just about cleans up your crime wave, doesn't it. What about the armed robbery gang, and the Galashiels murders? What about the other two shootings?'

'Saunders and Collins, now dead, killed PC Brown and Harry Riach, respectively. We know that and we'll announce it on Monday.

'We're still "anxious to interview" . . . as Mr Plod would put it . . . Newton, Clark and McDonnell, plus the couple we suspect of setting up the Raglan's hold-up. But they all got away with a fair amount of cash, so I don't hold out any hope of an early result. We're not looking for anyone else in connection with any of the deaths.'

'Why do I get the impression you're choosing your words carefully, Bob?'

'Because I always do, Archie.'

The acting Chief Constable smiled. 'It's not all negative though. "Acting on information received", to use another piece of jargon, we've recovered the diamonds stolen from Raglan's, and more than half the proceeds of the bank robberies. That'll be in Monday's statement too.'

Lord Archibald laughed. 'How are you going to fill in your time next week?'

'Pushing pens and playing politics, no doubt, in my temporary office!'

'That's good. We all deserve a quiet life for a while.' He stood up, and turned to leave, only to see Sarah standing in the doorway of the conservatory. She held a cordless phone in her hand, and she was looking, grim-faced, at her husband.

'It's Chrissie Proud, Bob,' she said, 'calling from the hospital in Spain. I think you'd better speak to her.'